CARELESS TA…

By CO…

Volume Four …

The story continu… 1941

Also in this series.

THREADS Volume one.

YES, SERGEANT VICTOR Volume two.

THE OTHER 'ARF Volume three.

Polladras Publishers
Trew, Breage
Helston. Cornwall.
England.
TR13 9QN
writerconnieteal@mail.com

Published July 2013

A catalogue record of this book is available from the British Library.

ISBN 978-0-9562599-5-0

Printed and bound by Berforts Information Press Ltd.

Cover by Knight Design.
www.knightdesign.co.uk

CHAPTER ONE

Early May 1941

Rosie fought the heartburn that tightened her chest, now at the later stages of pregnancy seldom a day went by that she didn't develop this intense discomfort.

There had been no moment to boil the kettle and sip a measure of bicarb', young Christopher's apple had even been abandoned on the hearth rug at the first sound of the siren. The poor lad begged an apple each night as bedtime approached, nibbling at it with no more effect than a mouse, desperate to delay that time to undress and get into bed, should the air raid siren wail its urgent warning and him not be downstairs fully clad and ready at once to run with his mam. His two older brothers, Thomas and Samuel had been evacuated to Plumtree six weeks ago. Christopher had been so distressed at the notion of leaving his mam that Rosie's will had folded under the weight of his tears.

Rosie observed Maude Collins settling herself down on the opposite side of the shelter, two of her sons were serving abroad, in her pocket would be their photograph. She had shown it to Rosie so many times, holding it in the light of the candle and her hand shook no less at the last time than it had at the first.

Just then the sound of Mr.Gravely's voice took everyone's gaze to the front of the shelter.

"For God's sake missus, go back an' put somethin' more on."

Mrs.Faulds lived in a constant state of fear and confusion since the bombing of the Ransom factory at Newark, her husband had been among the dead pulled from the rubble that night in March. She reappeared within minutes, gasping for breath and still dressed only in her nightgown and slippers but with the addition of a grey felt hat.

"It's alright Mr.Gravely." Rosie called out to the warden, "I've a spare blanket, come an' sit over 'ere with us Mrs.Faulds, you'll be alright."

Christopher's eyes followed his mam's every move as she stood to wrap the blanket around the shaking woman and gently lower her to sit by them.

Maude Collins gave a loud sigh and said, "We're all like 'er if truth be told, when I went to sew up a cardigan I'd knitted for our Susan, the last sleeve I did turned out to be an inch shorter than th'other one, everythin' inside yer feels that tight you even knit tighter wi'out knowin' you're doin' it. I had to unpick the whole sleeve an' start again, me tension wer' all wrong."

The entire world's tension is all wrong, thought Rosie as she handed a toffee to Christopher and coaxed Mrs.Faulds to suck slowly on one of the small sweets.

"It'll help I promise."

The frightened woman took the toffee with her lips and let it slip onto her tongue but uttered not a single word.

While the job of undertaker was not listed as a reserved occupation the authorities nevertheless acknowledged that the city needed someone to attend its deceased, so both Tommy and Joe Spooner had volunteered for the fire service auxillary, working alongside the full time crews as much as circumstances allowed.

Rosie had been at her wits end when Tommy was absent for two whole days and nights. Birmingham had suffered unimaginable destruction at the hands of the Luftwaffe, fire crews from surrounding areas were drafted in to assist. When the back door latch had at last rattled and her husband trod wearily across the floor, the scullery had immediately grabbed the smokiness that clung to Tommy's hair and skin and cast it to all four corners of the room. As he'd sunk into his old chair Rosie had poured out her anxiety along with a natural enquiry after events. Tommy's verbal response had been no more than 'stick the kettle on love' but his sore reddened eyes had conveyed every detail and Rosie had known his thoughts. Smoothing her hand across his brow she'd not questioned further nor spoken of it since.

The nights always seemed charged with trepidation, as if the darkness hid their assailants, yet when dawn broke the realisation that day followed night regardless of war strangely produced a comfort which empowered their spirits, folk determined themselves to go about their daily tasks. Jerry couldn't beat them, sod Jerry. Harry Allsop's parrot could already say it. 'Sod Jerry, sod Jerry' it repeated over and over to anyone peering through the bars of its cage. Harry maintained his old bird had inspired more patriotic fervour than the bold, red, white and blue recruitment posters which had appeared around the city displaying the words 'Britishers enlist today'.

Nottingham over previous weeks had been comparatively quiet, whilst Birmingham and Sheffield had suffered numerous night raids but graphic reports in the newspapers, which nervous folk felt compelled to read, served to breed a sense of expectancy and every time the siren sounded Nottingham's turn seemed ever more likely.

Mr.Gravely took the names of every person present and entered them under the day's date in his little black book. Arthur Collett responded in his usual way to this bespoke register. Never actually having been told the reason for this bit of officialdom he used it to lighten the mood inside the shelter, to bring a smile to the weary faces. Tonight he was Genghis Khan, last time he'd been Emperor Nero. Mr.Gravely simply spelled aloud and very slowly, "A-r-t-h-u-r C-o-l-l-e-t-t," and moved along the line of people shaking his head and tutting.

Folk imagined some record of those present had to be kept should a bomb land directly above them, to help identify the dead and missing. It was a chilling thought and most preferred to think of sharing their gloomy surroundings with unlikely characters from history. The first time, Arthur had answered Mr.Gravely's request for his name with 'Oliver Cromwell', the confused warden had actually accepted it as genuine, now he pretended to be vexed but secretly looked forward to Arthur's latest adopted identity. The harmless fun kept Jerry at arms' length if only for a few minutes.

Just then the first thud, distant but undeniable chilled every soul and induced a whimper from Mrs.Faulds, another within seconds, an infant began to cry.

"From in 'ere yer can't tell which side o' city it's at," said Maude Collins, "but they're a way off."

Under the cover of her coat the young mother put her fractious baby to suckle and Christopher's attention became concentrated on the possible glimpse of a breast. Last Christmas his brother Thomas had returned from a visit to uncle Ernie and aunty Kathleen, having been despatched by his mother to deliver a gift for his new baby cousin, intent on whispering into Christopher's ear a revelation he deemed worthy of his younger brother's admiration. 'I saw Aunty Kathleen's titty'!

Another loud thud fixed the lad's eyes more intently on the mother and baby, if he was to die this night, then he wanted to at least see a titty before it happened.

Towards the back of the shelter a man began to play the harmonica, Mrs.Faulds' whimpering had begun to invade the senses even more than the sound of enemy advance, he played louder and faster until an explosion, less distant, dried his mouth. No tune would now come from the harmonica. All ears were compelled to listen, maintaining a silence within the shelter so intense that when Mr.Gravely was unable to suppress a sneeze everyone jumped and the soothed infant began again to cry.

Rosie pulled the blanket tighter about Mrs.Faulds and gathered Christopher closer to her side. Where would Tommy be, what inferno raged out there in the city. Please God, please, please God?

"Bloody Hell, that'll be the lads from Bulwell, 'as anybody seen Tommy, 'e wer' layin' out old Mrs.Flowers when siren went." Joe Spooner's blackened face was lit from the glow of flames rising high into the night sky over the area around County football ground. Darkness distorted directions but from the higher ground at Mapperley Park where Joe and the Shakespeare Street crew had at last begun to overcome the blaze of a direct hit, it was possible to identify with some degree of accuracy, the area which lay beneath the noise and furious fire illuminating the sky to the south of them. Mercifully there had been no casualties at Mapperley Park, occupants of the two properties, now virtually destroyed, had been in the shelter.

"Tommy could be anywhere Joe," said a voice from somewhere amongst the urgent activity, "we'll only be another 'arf hour wi' this mess then we'll get over to the others."

"Your lot can bugger off now," said a voice from behind them, "we're alright 'ere." The ARP and local defence men were satisfied no one lay buried beneath the rubble, all had been accounted for including a Jack Russell bitch called Lottie, constant companion to granddad Worbis. If Lottie couldn't go in the shelter then neither would he! Any small pockets of fire which might erupt from the embers would be beaten out by the LD men.

"Poor sods," declared Joe with real feeling as he cast a last look at what had just a few hours earlier been homes for two families and little comfort would be found in the houses on either side, the occupants must surely return to those feeling spared this time but obliged to twitch all the more now Jerry had 'marked' their street.

Another fierce explosion to the south drove the fire crews to reel in the hoses so fast one almost took the feet from under a youth who had left the shelter to survey the scene.

"Look out son."

Only just able to retain his balance the young voice cried out as he stumbled.

"I'll get the bastards, I'll bloody well get all of 'em, me dad can't do it on his own, I'm comin' dad, you an' me'll show 'em, see how they like it, bastards rotten Kraut bastards."

The emotion in the voice of the youth fell about the ears of the older men with a sickening intensity, in the shelter the lad's mam, her family spread, her home destroyed, was it any wonder that Tommy Worbis cried and that they all felt his tears sting their own faces.

In the tender, tearing through the streets, Joe and the others began to speculate on the exact location of the blaze. When it became apparent the flames and noise rose from Meadow Lane the bakery had to be the most likely victim, the early shift, the ovens baking the vital bread.

"So they want to starve us into surrender do they, take the bread from our bellies. What is it they say? An army marches on its stomach. Well I'd eat me own s........."

"Shut up Ray," said Joe, "sister works at bakery, our Joyce works at Co-op soddin' bakery, don't she, God almighty."

The noise and mayhem on reaching the scene was dire. Ambulances ferried away the injured, there were bodies laid out on the ground a distance from the fire. One of the Bulwell men shouted across.

"Take water from The Trent, there must be a fracture to the main somewhere, pressure's droppin', gas is off an' electric, don't believe anyone's left inside but tread careful."

Joe's lungs tightened from the smoke and a deepening dread.

"Has anybody seen Tommy?"

"He's 'ere somewhere, your Joyce has already gone in the ambulance, she'll be ok, broken leg they think, there's a lot worse Joe, just get the hoses goin', sooner the fire's out, sooner you an' Tommy can deal wi' the dead, the mortuary'll demand of you two long after the rest of us have finished 'ere, it's a bad en tonight, Triumph Road lads have gone to University buildin', summat gone off over there an'all, make haste Joe, make haste."

Annie breathed a sigh of relief at the sounding of the all clear. The heavy blinds that had kept Davina and herself from sight of the bombardment raging beyond the windows of the silent bedroom in which Annie sat, had served also to keep the last hours of a frail old lady's life from view of the world, Annie the only witness, the only one present to hold Davina's hand as that wonderful friend of so many years slipped quietly away whilst no one was looking.

After Sarah died Annie observed in Davina, a loss of spirit, that previously determined, robust nature which Davina displayed in the face of all tribulation, lost its charge until weakened, fainter, it eventually barely ticked over. It was not a medical condition, a doctor held no formula able to reverse the decline. Mrs.Pooley devoted her days to the care of her very elderly employer who was also her friend. Annie had sat by the bedside every night for the past week, despatching Mrs.Pooley to the shelter if the siren sounded. Now it was over, at around 3am it was to a more peaceful place that Davina Wright journeyed, Annie's heart was heavy yet she could not wish any other, freed from the troubles, from grievous news, her dear friend was safe.

Annie heard the door latch downstairs, poor Mrs.Pooley, so nervous of the air raids, fearful of death outside and within.

"It was very peaceful," said Annie, "not once did she stir or even open her eyes, about two hours ago, barely that."

Mrs.Pooley burst into tears, words unintelligible tumbling from her lips. Annie held her tightly until her distress subsided.

"They're saying it was awful out there tonight Annie, all over the city, fires, ambulances, God knows what. Do you want me to fetch Tommy Spooner?"

"No, not just yet, he's sure to be involved in the efforts of the emergency services on such a night. We can manage for now. Go down to the kitchen and put the kettle on, you should drink something hot and sweet, we both shall, then we can attend Davina."

Mrs.Pooley's tears erupted once more but she did as Annie asked and together the two women, strengthened by each other, met daylight with calm.

"I must get back to Charles but I shall find Tommy as soon as I can. Busy yourself downstairs, it will help and I'll return later." Annie kissed the tired housekeeper's cheek and squeezed her fingers fondly.

Stepping out into the street tested Annie more than she could have imagined. Davina gone from them, at not far short of her eighty ninth birthday it was difficult to despair when following last night, folk must wonder if anyone, anywhere in the world might ever again survive to such an age. Yet Annie did despair, she walked away from the house feeling utterly desolate. The smell of spent fire hung on the air but from the scene immediately about her Annie could see no evidence of the bombing. As she drew closer to the city centre however, folk moved at a hastened pace, spoke with a quickened tongue, an urgency to regain some sense of normality drove them on to their place of work, indeed to discover if they still had a place of work.

Compared to many Annie was fortunate, she would tell herself that regularly, especially when her thoughts travelled to John. Raleigh had been turned over to the production of cartridge cases for the Spitfires. The call for more men to join up resulted in several men at the factory taking the decision to enlist. George had been among the first to speak of his intention but John had displayed an unusual agitation, his customary gentle, unruffled character had been displaced, challenging his brother to think of Samuel, with no mother, George must put aside all thoughts of joining a force that might be sent to anywhere in the world. George should concentrate on turning out those vital cartridge cases and he, John, the brother without ties, without offspring must be the one to go. So insistent had he become, charging George with the duty of care for young Samuel that to restore calm to John's character George had conceded, at least for the time.

So John Eddowes had chosen to enlist in the RAF. Annie had been physically sick at the knowledge but even John was to be mastered by fate. The medical had revealed John's eyesight to be unfit for pilot training, he would join ground crew. For him it was a sense of failure, he'd wanted to take those shells made by his brother at Raleigh and with them destroy the threat to his family. To look into the eyes of the enemy before unleashing his contempt, but ground crew it must be and John was stationed at Tollerton. Some mothers endured the torment of a much greater distance from their son and more sons cruelly distanced from them.

Francis had written in her letters of Freddy's labours, constant throughout the hours of daylight. Some nights his body ached too much to allow him any sleep.

Four years ago Freddy had brought the lease of a fifty acre dairy farm at Bonthorpe. Dorothy Cropley had died on the date of Grace's first birthday. Freddy had been so upset and when Arthur passed away just eight months after his wife Freddy's grief had been plain to see. He'd come to Nottingham to attend both funerals and Annie recognised the degree of emotion that tore at his heart, all the memories of the Cropleys' kindness through the years of Freddy's progress from boy to man.

When in due course a letter had been delivered to the small cottage at Skendleby informing Freddy that he was the sole beneficiary of Arthur's estate, Francis had found no way of comforting him. She had written to Annie, 'I can do nothing but let his grief reach exhaustion, I truly hope that his dear friends, the Cropleys may feel and know the depth of his love for them'.

Annie suspected it was the realisation that Arthur hadn't touched the money paid to him by the council, on the purchase of Bobbers Mill. It was as though his very intention had been to keep it safe for Freddy. The proceeds from the sale of the small house in which Dorothy and Arthur had spent their last few years, its contents, everything was to be Freddy's. Francis remarked 'Freddy must have shed a tear for every single penny of it'.

At Michaelmas 1937 Freddy took over the lease at Bonthorpe, enabled by that very same man who had taught him as a boy, how to tend chickens in the back garden at Hood Street.

Now Freddy's labours were for his country at war but Annie knew that first and foremost, everything he did at Bonthorpe, all the tired, aching bones, the increased production, was dedicated to Arthur and Dorothy before anyone or anything else.

Hilda's husband Jack was now foreman at the pit, well liked and trusted by the men, with an intelligence that challenged Basil Stanford's determination, yet in its wisdom, allowed Stanford to believe in his own superiority. Jack had come to understand that position and status meant everything to that pompous, gesturing individual and provided Stanford could consider himself 'master' and puff out his chest accordingly then matters of actual importance could be addressed through Stafford Hinds.

Now at seventy one years of age, Stafford Hinds had reached that time of life when an easy ticket was preferable, so Jack could successfully steer a discussion to a sensible conclusion. Hinds was tired and passive, Stanford was shallow and out of touch. The country was at war, men of their disposition fell abruptly silent and retreated hastily to the shadows at the first whiff of danger. Matters of retirement and replacement seemed to be overlooked when the nation must rise up against invasion. Stafford Hinds carried the title 'manager' but in reality his task was met for him.

William, now William Annie had ever worried over, even before the outbreak of war she had lain awake nights puzzling at his remoteness. When he'd left Andrew Smithfield's employ at Brassington to work for Basil Stanford Annie had held reservations but things seemed to fit into place for William. It was not too long before he acquired a house at Wollaton, a modest property but with facilities many would envy.

Celia had given birth to a healthy baby girl who was now attending school and Mathew, their first born, proved to be a bright boy, bringing home excellent reports from his teachers with the one exception, in music he appeared to be tone deaf. It was shortly after young Emily's arrival that Annie noticed a change in William. At first she'd put it down to tiredness, new babies could deny parents vital sleep but Celia had confided her dismay at William's unaccountable mood, brooding, silent and entirely unapproachable on the subject, his quietness was favourable to angry outbursts which upset the children however, so Celia lost herself in the care of her family and soldiered on.

It was a curiosity to Annie that no one had challenged William's presence still, as Stanford's man. While he could loosely claim employment through the mine, he was not a miner. Driving the ageing Stanford here and there, running errands, at beck and call, was hardly a reserved occupation. Whether it was the men's unspoken pity of such a fate as to be Stanford's lackey that bound their contempt, or the absence of any desire to find themselves working with William Eddowes at the pit Annie could not know but surely the day must soon come that William's duty lay beyond its current level. He was neither brave nor particularly patriotic but even the self promoting William Eddowes could not fail to acknowledge the threat posed by Adolf Hitler.

Annie's love for her stepson had not ever dimmed but the pain and stress of that love had caused her many hours of heartache.

Florence had spoken of her husband's health several times in recent months, telling Annie of his 'turns'. For a few minutes Basil would be disorientated, confused, she suspected he was experiencing minor strokes but he was in total denial, refusing to seek the doctor's opinion and rounding on Florence with his alarming temper if she tried to intervene. It was a trait he and William shared, that automatic response, to lash out, ironically at those most caring of them yet to shrink from facing their true adversaries.

Charles looked up from marking the papers.

"It can't go on, Mrs.Pooley will just have to manage, sitting, waiting for the inevitable over the other side of the city every night with air raids and God only knows what. Davina had a good life, you should be here with us."

Annie realised Charles' agitation was borne of anxiety, she spoke quickly to calm his mood.

"The need is passed Charles, Davina slipped away in the early hours. There was no disturbance at The Park but the trams aren't running due to a disruption in the power supply and bombs fell about the city so buses are random. We are fortunate, the streets around here are as normal, elsewhere it is very different. The bakery at Meadow Lane took a direct hit, someone told me a number have been killed and injured, we can only imagine how awful must be the devastation. I shall find Tommy later but he is sure to be struggling with the aftermath. Has George got off to work alright?"

Charles muttered, "Yes," stuffed the bundle of papers in a bag ready for the delivery boy then continued to speak tetchily. "I suppose the Pooley woman will be off to her sister's and cousin Lawrence will come to take charge of his inheritance."

Annie resented the sarcasm in his tone, it tugged at her emotions and she fought to hold back tears.

"I'll take over the shop while you get some breakfast, at least the papers have got through." She tried to appear composed, not to let him see her weakness.

"Shop, is that what it is?"

He waved his hand vaguely towards the shelves, now bearing so much less stock, items were spread along with wide gaps between.

"They only come in here to have a moan and spread tales of woe. We hear more news of death and destruction at this counter than Tommy Spooner and the war office put together. Sometimes I think manning a gun must be better than manning this damn till, at least you could blast away at your tormentors."

Annie donned her pinafore and sighed as Charles disappeared into the back, turning the sign on the shop door to open, she took a deep breath. Annie would miss Davina greatly, everything was changing and it hurt, it hurt so very much.

CHAPTER TWO

"It was her wish Mrs.Eddowes, Davina Wright was a lady of immense character, I knew her purely through business, while you of course knew her as a very dear friend. In this situation it is entirely natural for you to feel distress at your task but to be an executor of her estate, for us to be joint executors, is to honour her wishes at the last, you as her trusted friend and myself as a trusted advisor.

The letter addressed to you that she had written and placed in her bureau and that included a copy of her Will speaks to us as clearly as if she were here in this room. You obviously meant a great deal to Mrs.Wright, you and your family. Those tangible, valuable assets which she bequeaths to your sons and daughter are only a part of her legacy, to you in particular she leaves memories, I have only to look into your face to know it is so. Folk imagine a solicitor's office to be a cold and soulless place, yet for the most part we transfer memories from one loved one to another with as much compassion as our position will allow, bound as we are be procedure," he paused, smiling, "and over stiffened collars."

Annie felt soothed by his kindly manner, she imagined that in normal circumstances it would have been Edmund Tozer with whom she spoke, but Edmund had enlisted, the RAF and unlike John no problems had arisen at his medical to prevent him undergoing pilot training. Annie felt for his wife Caroline, the young woman must live on her nerves day by day.

It was one Nigel Caffin who now dealt with 'Last Wills and Testaments' for Chaucer, Caffin and Holt. Davina would likely sigh at Annie's concerns and say, 'my dear, we mustn't despair, never despair'.

"What is it that I am required to do Mr.Caffin?" asked Annie.

He placed the palms of his hands on the edge of the desk and raised his head as though making himself more upright before answering.

"I shall need to call upon you to read and agree certain documents and to put your signature where required, but before we can begin it is necessary for us to apply to the Probate office, to be deemed fit." Again he smiled. "I feel I can say with certainty that we are both of sound mind and without criminal record."

"Yes Mr.Caffin, indeed you can." Now it was Annie's turn to smile as she observed his posture relax. "However I confess to being unworldly, my knowledge of legal matters is woefully limited but I shall endeavour to prove worthy of Davina's faith in me." Annie stood and offered her hand. As Nigel Caffin rose to his feet he said.

"I am obliged to write to all the beneficiaries, to inform them. It may be some considerable time before the Estate is finally at the stage of meeting bequests, the war affects all areas of life, the sale of Mrs.Wright's property at The Park may take longer to achieve than it would otherwise have done. We are experiencing difficult and unpredictable times, people tend to cling to the familiar when outside forces threaten." He walked from behind his desk and showed Annie to the door. "My wife has always delighted in feeding the family, indeed we have jokingly said on numerous occasions that any stray dog, cat or passing hedgehog is sure to be handed some item of food if Stella is to sleep happy in her bed. Now she spends her days with the WVS, food for the troops and so on. Our son is somewhere in the desert, in her mind Stella feeds him, the familiar you see."

As Annie walked away from the solicitor's office towards the bus stop her thoughts were mixed, it was a puzzlement, how folk perceived one another, a solicitor was surely removed from the working man, he operated at a higher level, looked out upon a greener landscape. That was the general belief of those scuttling along the streets from backyard to factory gates with no glimpse of grass at any point between. Yet Stella Caffin fed the strays and made sandwiches for other women's sons, and her husband transferred memories from one loved one to another while his own love was spread as far as the deserts of Africa.

Lawrence Hardwick had travelled from Durham to attend the funeral, his manner had been entirely gracious yet Davina had made no mention of him in her Will. A small gift of jewellery for Ivy, fifty pounds each for Harold and Molly but the proceeds from the sale of that wonderful old house and its contents, the sum of capital arrived at after bonds had been converted plus monies in two bank accounts, all was to be divided equally between William, Freddy, George, John and Hilda.

Nigel Caffin had intimated that even after legal expenses and the undertaker's fee had been discharged it would be a substantial sum due to each of them. Annie remembered from years ago Davina showing to her the envelope and placing it in the bureau, her words had been curious, 'you will see to it Annie dear, that my wishes are upheld'. Must Annie now face a confrontational Lawrence Hardwick, was that what Davina meant? She couldn't imagine what Charles' reaction might be, despite reading the contents of the envelope two days after Davina died, to discover her wishes for burial, Annie had not spoken to anyone other than Tommy Spooner. The Will had stunned her, it was almost impossible to accept its instruction and so difficult to voice the nature of it to anyone. In a strange way Annie was relieved to hear the solicitor say it could be some considerable time before Davina's Estate could be finally proved, she struggled daily with the knowledge that her friend was no longer there, at least the ongoing duty of executor bound Annie and Davina together still and kept the memories intact. For when the time actually came to convey that home, so filled with Davina's presence, to a stranger the wrench would be as much as Annie could bear.

Suddenly a familiar voice interrupted Annie's thoughts, she turned to see Susie Spooner hurrying to catch up with her.

"I'm off to fetch them home for the weekend, Joe says they must go back to Lowdham on Sunday, he'll drive them back in the evening but he's doing two funerals this afternoon so I'm going on the train to get them. Mr.Scantlebury will meet me at Burton Joyce station."

Susie threaded her arm through Annie's and if the excitement in her voice wasn't enough then the trembling of her hand confirmed Susie's eagerness at the prospect of having her two young daughters home for even a couple of days.

"I've saved two weeks ration of margarine and sugar to make Gillian a birthday cake an' mam gave me two eggs an' some jam. I do miss them so, I know one or two children have come home in the past few days. It's been quiet in the city since that dreadful night when the bakery was destroyed but Joe is firm on the subject. 'Not yet, the girls are safer where they are at Lowdham', that's what he says. I think it's because of Joe's work with the Brigade, night before last they were called to help the Leicester men. We women don't really know the half of it. Rosie says that Tommy wouldn't relent, Christopher cried all the way to Plumtree but Thomas and Samuel will look after him and the people they're staying with are very homely and kind. Besides with a new baby and Rosie still recovering from a difficult labour it must ease Tommy's mind. Rosie's mam does what she can but Audrey can't be there all day an' night and Tommy's out of the house for hours at a time, sometimes days depending on the bombing, my Joe the same."

Susie let out a deep sigh. They reached the bus stop.

"Have a lovely time with Cathy and Gillian," said Annie, "I'm sure your mam will be with you all for Gillian's birthday, tell Edna I'll see her in the week."

Susie kissed Annie's cheek and hurried away in the direction of Midland Station. The day was comfortably warm and folk moved about the streets lightly clad, the most nervous unwilling to be without their gas mask which travelled with them like some utilitarian hand bag, identical to the next.

"Hello Mrs.Eddowes, shouldn't be long now, I just missed the No13 so I'll 'ave to get on the 56. Walkin' that extra bit at t'other end plays havoc wi' me rheumatism, how's your lot then? I saw your husband when I called for me morsel o' cheese an' bacon, I did ask 'im but there's none so deaf as them that don't want to hear is there, mine's the same. I've come to think that men are like the wireless, nothin' comes out but an irritatin' whistlin' sound, the damn thing won't tune in, then when it does yer catch the tail end o' the broadcast so yer learn nowt, if yer want to know about summat ask a woman, that's what I say!"

"It's coming," said Annie feeling spared by the approach of the No56, she held out her arm and the bus pulled up at the curb. A number of people alighted, including a blind man who tapped the request stop pole with his white stick before turning to walk towards Parliament Street. Annie was the last to board the bus, her mind had turned to the children, evacuated to grandma Sarah's relatives at Ruddington. Content to let those in the queue get on ahead of her she handed her fare to the conductor and sat quietly half way along, only to be immediately joined by the talkative

Mrs.Rashleigh who had left her seat at the front and despite her troublesome rheumatism had transported herself and shopping bag further down the bus to where Annie sat.

"Them dark glasses make it hard to tell but I'm sure I know the face from somewhere, it'll haunt me 'til I remember, perhaps 'e knows." The conductor moved along the aisle checking tickets, as he drew level Mrs.Rashleigh prodded his leather satchel in a demanding fashion, "Who's that blind fella?" Such a direct enquiry seemed to baffle the conductor and without offering any reply he continued his checking of fares, whistling as he went. The frustrated Mrs.Rashleigh remarked."There what did I tell yer, just a whistlin' sound and sod all else!"

Annie had missed Samuel but George had agreed with Mavis and Maggie that to send the young ones to Ruddington was for the best. So Marie, Amy and Samuel had nervously and tearfully travelled with Annie to the farm where Uncle Moses' grandson Seth continued to run the holding in the same vein as his forbears. Old fashioned and never in haste, Seth milked a herd of Friesians, bred two sows, accommodated a motley group of chickens, saved hay each summer, attended Chapel without fail every Sunday and somehow managed to keep his wife and offspring fed and clothed amid a museum-like array of tools and machinery. Entering the farmyard was like stepping back in time and Seth's image was so perfectly in harmony with his surroundings that Annie felt she had taken the three young children into a tableau of rural history, a 'make believe' to instruct the onlooker as to a bygone age. His ruddy red cheeks flanked by mutton chop sideburns, his attire almost theatrical but for the very real evidence of 'farm yard' and the telltale odour of old milk. His smile was wide enough to span centuries and his handshake so firm as to gather up any withering doubt and restore its strength completely. Annie liked Seth Eames and found herself trusting the children to his care with a degree of confidence, if they must be evacuated from the city then to the farm and farmer at Ruddington was the best she could have hoped for. It had been deemed most sensible for Annie to accompany the children so that farewells were made at the beginning of the journey and not at the end. Waving goodbye to their mothers and in Samuels's case, his dad, was sure to be traumatic, at least some time could pass and the sobbing subside before reaching their destination. No one seemed to consider Annie's trauma, looking on those three desperate little faces, her own stomach turning somersaults. Seth's wife Doris had taken Annie to one side and whispered, 'God love 'em, don't you fret, they'll soon settle to playin' with ours an' meetin' the animals. They'll not want for food, Seth'll bolt two bits o' junk together an' somehow make his contraption work but when it comes to the children's bellies he'll not deny 'em, he puts much store by feedin' the body and nourishin' the soul. They'll enjoy Sunday school, Miss Aldis has a class of eighteen now, this war is an evil thing, yet because of it her Sunday mornin's are flourishin'. We have cuddles every night an' they can have a cuddle in the day an'all if they want one, bless their little hearts'. Then Doris had embraced Annie with such feeling, although travelling back home without them hurt terribly Doris's big heart had helped fill Samuel's empty bed that first night and shed comfort over the weeks since.

After Alice died George had remained in the house on Ainsley Road, his sister Hilda living there too, caring for Samuel. A year passed before one day George said to his mother, 'It's not fair on Hilda, she should be free to pursue her own life, to spend more time with Jack. I'm giving up the tenancy, can we come home Mam?'

Relief had swept over Annie like a cleansing wave, washing away all the anxieties that had clung to her being, causing her to feel heavy and wearied. Charles had simply shrugged his shoulders, confident in the knowledge that their return would do little to disrupt his established routine, and so Gregory Street once more became fully occupied. John had been delighted and though Hilda's love for her young nephew shone about the little boy every day, Annie nevertheless detected the joy in her daughter's eyes each time a knock at the back door confirmed Jack Haynes' arrival and noted the skip in her step when on her way through the door Hilda turned to call out, 'won't be late Mam'.

It was the events of Autumn 1934 that changed everything again. Florrie Haynes had died in her sleep. Jack and Victor were the only two dwelling still with their mother. George Haynes had followed their older brother William into the army. It had been Jack and only Jack who came home each evening to his mam and Victor, those two most vulnerable of people, Florrie frail and elderly and Victor still deserving of a child's care. In the immediate Victor had gone to stay with Billy and Edna. Despite Billy's assurance that the situation created no problems, Jack insisted it was too much to expect of Edna. It presented him with a dilemma but Hilda had felt no qualm at suggesting the solution. She and Jack must marry, over the years Victor had been in Hilda's company many times, she was familiar to him. To remain at the place he'd known as home would help Victor recover from losing his mam and besides, it had ever been the case that he and Billy Dodds spent a part of every single day, with only rare exception, in each other's company, that wouldn't change, Billy wouldn't let it change.

The wedding just before the Christmas of 1934 Annie would never forget no matter how long she lived. If ever a child needed to be evacuated from troubles then it was young Samuel that December, as Charles had ranted his opposition to the union by marriage of his daughter Hilda to Jack Haynes. At twenty one years of age, Hilda didn't need her father's permission and the tear filled misery she endured at the sight of her mother, desperately trying to reason with Charles and being lashed by his cruel tongue, his temper only just stopping short of actually striking her mother, drove Hilda ever more swiftly away from a situation that had become wretched. Yet at that place she had called home Hilda must leave at Charles' mercy, her mam, her brothers and Samuel. To have believed her father would grant his blessing now seemed nothing but a folly, a naive dream, his concession at the time of Alice's pitiable state of health had allowed them a false hope. When the marriage had become a reality that alarming defiance again reared its head but the threat was without lawful substance, Charles had no right.

Absent from the simple wedding ceremony at the registry office Charles had sat in The Standard with no company but his own festering resentment, while Annie had closed the shop for two hours, smiled on her daughter, embraced Jack and stood with George and John to witness the marriage, assuring the newly wedded couple that the trouble would pass, all would be well, then duly girded herself against whatever Charles might bring down upon her. Silence, a sullen silence that lasted for weeks was to be her trial. Throughout that period of dismay it had been Samuel, her grandson who had sustained Annie, his total trust and constant love had kept her spirit from defeat. Standing behind the counter in the shop, remembering Daniel and determining herself to raise Samuel in the strength of his father a Boucher, Harold Boucher's son, not to let Charles Eddowes ever again impose his will over any infant had carried Annie through the years since.

George's intention to enlist and John's resultant insistence that he should sign up instead of George plagued Annie's mind. Were they both so desperate to be distanced from Charles that even volunteering to fight yet another hideous war was a better prospect than living day on day with the tension that could erupt without warning in Charles. All those years ago when William had moved out of Gregory Street to live with Davina and Freddy had gone to the Cropleys Annie had harboured the same doubt, a disturbing sense of her stepsons' unhappiness. George needed to work, with Samuel still so young what other choice did he have than to place the child in Annie's care. John was a free agent, no ties, Annie had ever felt it was her youngest son's reluctance to leave her, his mam, to face without him his dad's dark moods that kept John at Gregory Street. But with John now gone and Samuel at Ruddington, how long would it be before George too chose fighting Hitler over abiding under the same roof as Charles. The thought sent a shiver down Annie's spine, although the city centre had been spared in recent weeks, bombing raids had devastated areas not so very far away, Newark especially had taken a pounding because of the airfields there.

Annie had barely time to take off her jacket and hang it over the hook before Charles left the shop to come through to the kitchen.

"I saw you walk by to the back yard, you could have come through the shop, I could count on one hand the customers we've had over the past hour, at this rate the till will seize up from lack of use. Well, what's she left you then, a pick of the furniture, a brooch, an oil painting of highland cattle?"

Annie took a deep breath.

"What Davina has left to me Charles has a value, which you could never understand. What Davina has bequeathed our children you will recognise right away as being of great value. All of her estate, with the very small exception of modest sums to Harold and Molly at Skendleby, is to be divided equally between our five children. I shall relieve you in the shop just as soon as I've changed from my best clothes."

With that Annie walked from the room and up the stairs leaving Charles to his thoughts, and to what she truly hoped might be his deep regret.

CHAPTER THREE

Edna smiled at the photograph and spoke aloud as she ran her duster over the glass and frame, "Silly beggars".

Billy and Victor looked back at her, a big grin on the face of each. Watching Billy's torment of grief when he lost Victor had pained Edna more than anything she had previously endured, the labour of childbirth, her mam's funeral, Janet's operations, none had created the rawness inside her to match the hurt Edna suffered at the sight of her Billy struggling to cope after Victor's death. It had taken months for Billy's need of spending time at the cemetery to fade, for his visits to that place to become less frequent. Even now, although he didn't always declare it Edna knew that his absence from home would likely include Billy's need of a few minutes with Victor. Edna had once voiced her own despair at the situation, describing her husband's endless pilgrimage as morbid. His response had been typical of Billy. 'I don't go to the cemetery to be miserable' he'd said, 'I go there to feel content. Me an' Victor could allus sit together wi'out uttering a single word, just the two of us on the old bench at the allotment, me feelin' happy 'cause 'e were there an' 'im feelin' happy 'cause I were there. Now I sit on the curb of 'is grave an' I feel it again, that peace, just me an' 'im. I don't 'ave to say owt, 'e knows I'm there'.

Billy had given up the allotment, 'Victor wer' me other arm, a man needs somebody to be 'is other arm if 'e's to work an allotment'.

Edna couldn't deny the truth of it and so the tenancy had passed to Ernie Searle.

Hilda and Jack had done everything they could to rally Victor's spirits after Florrie died but that bond, which had always been so strong and yet overlooked by the rest of the family as each went about their every day, following Florrie's funeral had been rent from Victor's simple world. He'd become withdrawn, timid, uninterested in his meals and at night fretful. Early in 1936 during a very cold spell, Victor had succumbed to bronchitis. Hilda had stayed by his bed, wrapped about in an eiderdown, unwilling to leave him, as she would have attended an infant so poorly but there seemed to be nothing left in Victor. Billy's presence at the bedside made little difference, Jack's coaxing, no matter how impassioned failed to reach Victor's soul and on the 16th February his lungs surrendered to the infection. It was to be a curiosity, which no one could accept as coincidence, that on the 16th February the following year Hilda gave birth to a boy, a child with the happiest nature, he was christened David Victor.

Edna placed the framed photograph back on the shelf. Joe Spooner had snapped it with a borrowed camera on the occasion of Liza's wedding the summer of 1933. Harry Ollerton had proved a good son in law and Edna felt blessed, her daughters were married to decent, hard working men who showed respect for Billy. Now Myra was courting, she'd met Archie Medlyn at a dance. He'd been more interested than Myra at the beginning, calling with a bunch of flowers, a few chocolates from Thornton's. Myra was not swept off her feet and Edna had been surprised at his perseverance, even feeling a measure of pity for the lad but his attentions seemed to win over her daughter by degrees and now they spent much of their time together outside of work. Archie was at Player's and Myra worked in the city centre, at Jessops, mainly in the underwear department, 'the knickers an' girdles counter', as Myra referred to it.

Edna ran her duster over the dresser, moving the plates from side to side and in so doing disturbed a wasp, which must have come in through the open door and settled. Now it circled about her head menacingly but retreated when threatened by the flapping duster and Edna's graphic description of what would surely be its fate if it dared to sting her. At that moment Billy walked in chuckling at the scene.

"I don't know how you'd manage to do that love, or even if a wasp 'as any for that matter."

"If the damn thing comes near me again I'll turn it inside out tryin'. Mam used to set the dog on 'em, it'd jump up an' catch the wasp in its mouth, never spat em' out, God knows how it didn't get stung. Our Ada reckoned it did but at dog's t'other end 'cause it wer forever draggin' its backside across the cobbles. Mam wer' mortified if it did it in front o' neighbours, I don't know why, Norris Pickles next door 'ad a Staffordshire an' that daft thing used to sit at mouth o' the entry airin' its 'wotsit' nearly all day long."

Billy planted a kiss on Edna's cheek. "Gertie Wainwright wer' at cemetery puttin' flowers on 'er mam's grave. I do feel sorry for the woman, Henry got 'is call up papers day before yesterday. 'Billy' she said, 'I used to pray that our two lads would stay away from the pit, after all Steve's been through I didn't want Jack or Henry to spend their days underground. Life should offer 'em more than that. Now Jack's already in the thick of it an' Henry's goin' an'all. I thought I'd never live to say it but I wish they were down the pit, I'd feel closer to 'em there than in some God forsaken foreign place bein' shot at night an' day by madmen'. I didn't know what to say to 'er so I give 'er a kiss an' told 'er you'd call an' see 'er one day next week."

So he's been with Victor again, thought Edna, but she felt fortunate, her Billy had done his bit, more than, her daughters were close by, it was little enough to do, calling on Gertie. She would go next Tuesday, Myra only worked half day on a Tuesday, they could both go. Myra had gone out with Jack Wainwright for a while but it had never been serious, the pictures a couple of times, a dance or two. Myra wasn't one to lose her heart to a young man at the first sign of his affection, in fact even now Edna wondered if Archie Medlyn might be heading for heartache. At almost twenty two years of age Myra was old enough to know her own mind and Billy had cautioned Edna, 'let 'em be, you know what you were like at Myra's age, if your mam tried to interfere you'd dig your heel's in an' be 'dickey opposite' just to be contrary'. Edna had to admit to herself at least, that it was true.

"Tea's ready, I'll dish up as soon as Myra gets in, give the pan a stir for me while I nip to the privy."

Edna stood for a moment outside the back door, there had been no siren and Billy had not spoken of any disturbance, yet in the distance she could hear ambulance bells. Newark had suffered again, bombs had fallen three nights in a row but by some miracle casualties had been few. Sheffield had taken a pounding, folk in Mansfield regularly saw the red glow of fire in the sky above Sheffield. Sometimes, just for a little while, the mind demanded release from the constant thought of war, even the simple task of dusting a room could prove sufficient to create a distraction, an ornament or picture, a photo, or a letter propped up by the clock on the mantelpiece where it awaited a reply, these everyday things engaged the mind, if only briefly and brought easement.

"Myra's late," said Billy, "did she say she wer' meetin' Archie before comin' home?"

Edna sighed. "I'll give you yours, may as well start or you'll be late leavin' for work. Edna took a bowl from the side of the range and spooned up some broth for Billy. "It caught sight of a piece of ox cheek as it wer' runnin' past for tomorrow's stew but the turnip's gettin' stringy this late in the season so if yer use your imagination yer can pretend it's a bit o' gristle." She put the bowl of broth on the table in front of Billy with a chunk of bread and a 'huff' of frustration, it was a poor meal for a working man. Billy scolded her if she voiced her feelings, 'all I do is sit on a stool an' move one arm a bit, tis the men as strain their every muscle to keep the country goin' that need feedin'. Billy's sentiment was entirely genuine and not simply for his wife's sake.

"Sod it, I'll eat wi' you, she's likely natterin' wi' one o' the shop girls, there's another fund raisin' dance at the weekend. Was a time when we give what we could to the kids' home or Sally Army, now its money for ships an' planes."

Edna was scraping the last morsel from her bowl when a knock came at the front door. The hot broth had only just coated her throat with warmth yet she shivered from chill, that irrational chill Edna felt whenever someone knocked at the front door. She had only to cast her eyes to Billy for him to recognise her fear, the dread poor Edna could do nothing to conceal.

"I'll go love, it'll be somebody collectin' likely as not, I don't mind givin' summat towards the rivets for a Spitfire." Billy gave his wife a wink to reassure her and crossed the room to the door, whistling as he went to convey his cheerfulness.

"Mr.Dodds?" The police constable spoke Billy's name as a question.

"Yes, that's me, what can I do for you officer?"

Edna on hearing an unfamiliar voice had forced herself to follow Billy and now stood behind him, a deep feeling of nausea taking hold in her stomach.

“There’s been an accident Mr.Dodds, your daughter Myra, it’s alright, the ambulance has taken her to City Hospital, she’s been run over. We don’t know the circumstances as yet, the driver has also been taken to hospital in a state of shock. I’ve a police van parked behind me and I’m authorised to drive you to the hospital if you require transport.”

Billy’s throat dried and words proved difficult to form.

“Yes, yes please officer, we’ll get our coats right away.” Edna stood transfixed. “Come on love, it’ll be alright.”

Billy took their coats from the hook and prompted Edna, it wasn’t easy for a one armed man to don his coat with any degree of haste. As if automated Edna helped Billy into his jacket, thrust her arms into her own coat and stepped out onto the pavement in a daze. Billy slammed shut the front door and helped Edna into the van. Any other time they would have seen the inquisitive folk across the street, peeping out from behind the nets, but today they saw nothing beyond the uniform clad constable driving them to their youngest daughter. Edna felt Billy’s arm about her but neither spoke, just a few minutes earlier everything had been normal, at least as normal as war would allow, now they travelled towards an unknown. Billy should have been on his way to the telephone exchange, perhaps the policeman would see that word reached Billy’s boss. It seemed a silly thing to be worrying about but it was better than imagining the worst, after all they couldn’t know how serious the accident was. Myra was a young woman, it would have been routine surely to take her to the hospital, to be checked over. Like the driver she would be suffering from shock. Billy used his thoughts to bolster his confidence and by the time they reached the hospital he was able to thank the constable in a firmer voice and by taking her arm, steer the numbed Edna to the reception desk.

“My name’s Billy Dodds an’ this is my wife Edna. We understand that our daughter Myra has been involved in an accident an’ brought ‘ere by ambulance.”

The receptionist Edna recognised from previous visits to the hospital with Annie and Janet. The latest operation on young Janet’s palate had been twelve months ago, Edna recalled the surgeon’s words as he explained the procedure and it was his reference to the tongue that had stuck in her mind. ‘We immobilise the tongue as it can have a will of its own'. Edna's mam used to often declare, 'you've got tongue enough for two our Edna'. Now someone or something had immobilised Edna's tongue, she stayed close to Billy, mute and trembling, her legs turned to jelly.

"Come with me if you will," said the receptionist, casting a smile at Edna. Fear was an emotion the woman regularly witnessed in the eyes of folk who must first approach her to seek knowledge of a loved one. She led them to a small waiting room, although it held a number of chairs there were no other occupants. "I'll tell the doctor that you're here and he will come to speak with you as soon as he can."

"But what about Myra, when can we see our daughter?" Asked Billy.

"Very soon Mr.Dodds, try not to worry." With that she left them, a faint scent of perfume lingering about the doorway where she'd stood.

Billy looked at Edna, her expression so set in trepidation, the colour completely absent from her cheeks.

"They're sure to be busy love, likely rushed off their feet what wi' the bombin', an' all that goes with it," said Billy. Edna sat staring at the door, yet not a single word of the poster affixed to it did her mind register. It asked for donations of any food that could be spared, to help nourish the most frail patients. Even hospital kitchens were obliged to work with a much reduced ration of supplies.

"If Myra 'as to stay in for a day or two we can bring 'er a bit o' dinner can't we Edna?"

At that moment the door opened and the imposing figure of Mr.Shilling appeared. He recognised Edna immediately.

"Mrs.Dodds," he said in a tone of surprise, "Janet Yeats' grandma, so Myra is your daughter." He crossed the room to shake Billy's hand firmly. "You must both take heart, Myra has sustained a serious injury to her lower right leg."

Billy had risen to his feet the moment such an important man had entered the room, Mr.Shilling smiled warmly.

"Your daughter is young and from strong stock, I am confident of that. Young flesh heals more readily than old. I shall take you to her but you will find her very drowsy. Our first action, of absolute necessity, was to sterilize the area of the wound, we gave Myra some sedation whilst we did this. We can administer pain relief, however she will be extremely sore. It looks messy but you must try not to exhibit alarm. Shock can prove as threatening to the system as blood loss, a great measure of calm strength is what Myra needs from both of you. You may weep in another place but not at her bedside."

His words carried such authority that while not actually voicing their agreement, neither Billy nor Edna would consider doing anything other than obey Mr.Shilling's command, for command it truly was. They followed him along the corridor, which seemed endless, at last they entered an area of cubicles. He paused, gave them a look which emphasised his earlier remarks, drew back a curtain and spoke directly to a nurse.

"Myra's parents Sister Foley, they are aware of their daughter's drowsiness, I think a cup of hot tea for them both might serve great purpose." Then he turned to Billy and Edna. "It is my job, to take a rent, a tear, whatever is the damage and to repair it. I cannot invisibly mend as I'm sure most ladies can," his smile was for Edna, "but you may depend I shall do my utmost and I shall indeed repair and make good. I will leave Mr.and Mrs.Dodds in your capable hands Sister, I would suggest they stay only a little while, it would be most sensible for them to go home and get some rest before returning in the morning when the situation will feel less harrowing. Myra will be awake then, the coming months will be daunting for her, in her distress she may speak out of character. I have witnessed this many times, if she does, pay it no heed, dismiss it immediately from your mind, remember nothing but calm strength is what she needs from you and of course love, love in abundance," then as if an afterthought, "don't we all, indeed don't we all."

Sister Foley took Edna's arm and led her to the head of the bed. Myra's eyes were closed. In a low voice the nurse coaxed Edna to speak.

"Let her know that you're here, she will be asleep for some time yet, tomorrow it will be different."

Edna felt Sister Foley's fingers squeeze her arm, Billy stood fighting tears, his gaze set on the area of bed where some kind of frame kept the sheet from touching Myra's right leg.

“It’s mam Myra, we’re both ‘ere your dad an’all.” Her eyes remained closed so Edna tried again. “Mr.Shillin’ is goin’ to make it alright, like ‘e is for Janet, ‘e’s the best, everybody says so, isn’t that right Billy?”

Billy couldn’t speak, instead he lowered his face to kiss Myra’s forehead. Her eyes opened, slowly, very slowly and her lips formed a word, she whispered.

“Dad.”

Her eyelids came down again and Sister Foley spoke to encourage them.

“Come and have that cup of tea, I might even find a bit of sugar. Mr.Shilling is certainly the best I’ve ever worked with and I’ve been a nurse for twenty six years.”

Edna hesitated for an instant then said. “Show me ‘er leg, I need to see it however bad.”

Billy had seen many sights in the hospital at Hemel Hempstead, surely his daughter’s leg couldn’t be anything like those horrific injuries inflicted by war.

I can uncover it for a second, but no more than a second, it is vital we prevent any infection setting in the wound, remember you must make no sound to alarm Myra, not as much as a whimper.”

Billy and Edna nodded agreement and Sister Foley eased the cover from the frame. Edna was close to collapse and Billy’s one arm seemed to lose its strength as he struggled to keep his wife upright and himself from falling to his knees as they buckled from the shock of what he had seen. Flesh rent apart, congealed blood, mutilation.

“Come with me now, come along.”

The competent nurse led them to a side room, sat them down, took the hand of each in her own and looking directly into their tear filled eyes, spoke with authority and real conviction.

“What you see now is not what you will see in twelve months time. I couldn’t do this job, day after day if I didn’t witness true miracles of healing. Every gasp you allow to escape from your lungs now will do nothing but deny you breath, breath you will need to draw on throughout the process of Myra’s treatment.”

Edna sank her head onto Billy's chest. "You, Janet, now Myra, why Billy, why is it always us?"

The lump in Billy's throat denied him any attempt at a reply. Inwardly he longed to sit on the curb in the cemetery, to find that comfort he only ever found when he was with Victor. He kissed Edna's hair and surrendered to the tear that travelled down his cheek. What was war compared to this?

It was Mrs.Glasson who delivered word of the accident, bustling into the shop just minutes before closing time to buy oats.

"Mrs.Eddowes, it's a terrible thing that's happened in town, somebody run over by a lorry, they're sayin' it's one o' Mrs.Dodds' girls, police, ambulances the lot."

Annie turned the sign on the shop door, locked up, ran through to the back where Charles sat reading the Evening Post and related Mrs.Glasson's news.

"I'm going to Winchester Street, tell George when he gets home that I shall be back as soon as I can, his meal is plated up but he'll need to hot it over a pan of boiling water."

Charles appeared genuinely shocked, the newspaper fell to his lap as he responded with.

"Surely it can't be," followed by a hefty sigh, but he raised no objection to Annie's hasty departure and for that she was thankful. Charles' careless tongue so often created a torment of mind, a sigh caused no impediment and she made her way to the bus stop with only Edna engaging her thoughts.

It was half past eight when Annie turned the corner into Winchester Street. George most nights didn't finish at Raleigh until after eight, the men worked on, turning out more cartridge cases for the war effort. It was a sad fact that demand for numerous vital parts for that great war machine, which dominated all of industry had effectively taken a labour force languishing in the doldrums and thrust it into such a hive of activity, that households were now in receipt of income enough to enable a decent living. What an irony that shops were bare of stock, that the utilities, coal, gas and electricity while still available, came with the caution, 'conserve supplies for where they are needed most'.

Annie tapped at the back door of no.24 then ventured to try the latch, half expecting to find no one home, Billy and Edna would likely be at the hospital. It was unlocked, Edna looked up from where she sat at the end of the scullery table, the skin about her eyes was red and blotchy from crying. Annie pulled out a chair and sat beside her, gathering up Edna's fingers between her own.

"Where's Billy?" She asked, surprised to think that he might be at the exchange.

Edna sniffed, "He's gone to see the others, it's best 'er sisters hear it from us rather than some garbled version that frightens them arf to death, yer know what folk are like. Do yer remember how word spread that Dolly Meakin's boy 'ad thrown a fit an' stifled. Turned out that the daft lad 'ad shoved a dried pea up each of 'is nostrils to see if it'd make 'im whistle louder." Edna paused to blow her nose. "Myra wer' on 'er way home from Jessops, the copper couldn't tell us much, the driver's in a state o' shock so 'e's been taken to hospital an'all. It's 'er leg" Edna began to tremble and Annie gripped her hands tighter. "Mr.Shillin', the doctor as sees to Janet come to speak to us in a waitin' room afore we went to see Myra. It'll be a long job, the flesh of 'er lower leg is near ripped off to the bone."

Edna could control them no longer, tears streamed down her face yet again. Annie's eyes filled too, seeing Edna in such distress pained so harshly she couldn't speak. Eventually a fragile calm returned.

"I'll make a brew," said Edna, I've got to do summat, if only make us a cuppa or I'll go off me head." The hot drink soothed their nerves.

"Would you like me to go with you to the hospital tomorrow?" Asked Annie, after quietly listening to Edna's account of circumstances. "Charles won't mind staying in the shop, it can be very quiet for the rest of the morning once the men have been in for their smokes, besides, he'll be concerned for Myra."

Edna gave a cynical look but refrained from questioning the verity of Annie's last remark. Instead she said.

"Billy'll want to go wi' me tomorrow but 'e'll 'ave to go in for 'is shift in the evenin' an' 'e'll be tired next day so perhaps you could go wi' me then. Mr.Shillin' told us it weren't unusual for people who'd suffered trauma to speak out o' character, get all worked up an' say stuff they don't mean. 'Pay it no heed', 'e said, 'it counts for nothin'. Her sisters'll want to go see her but Billy's goin' to tell 'em to wait until we've been in the mornin'."

Just then a knock came at the back door.

"I'll go Edna, you pour us another cup," said Annie, anxious that it might be a neighbour wanting to find out what had happened, so many explanations might prove too much for Edna.

"I didn't know where to go, here or hospital but me mam said I should come here first." Archie Medlyn stood at the threshold shaking from nervousness.

"Come in Archie, Edna's here, Billy's gone to see Myra's sisters to tell them what's happened." Annie smiled to reassure the young man.

Edna could do no other than relate events but the strain was evident in her voice. After a sensible time had lapsed Annie declared she must leave for home and suggested Archie walk her to the bus stop, Edna needed to get some rest.

Charles and George were both up and awaiting news when Annie finally reached home. George had a dilemma of his own, this was not the night to tell his mother that he'd given notice at work. George had made up his mind, an older man could successfully replace him at Raleigh, even single women were being called up to the land army or to work at the ordnance factory at Ranskill. George had a nine year old son who deserved a future, while others fought to defend it George could no longer accept that his days spent at Raleigh were enough. But tonight he'd kiss his mam's cheek and send her to bed with no more anxiety than she had already. For some curious reason, George held back from telling Charles of his decision, it was difficult to predict his dad's reaction to anything of late and as for William, he seemed impervious to the escalating rumble of the war machine that drove everyone else to defiance. It was as if William's mind was in denial, when they had last met George had been struck by his brother's remoteness, his vague expression and subdued approach. William's caustic tongue, as it could so often be, barely stirred itself to utter more than half a dozen words. If dear Edna had been present she would have declared 'summat's up'. The thought carried George back to the situation of Myra and the accident. Revealing his decision to enlist could wait a couple of days. One hurt at a time.

As Edna and Billy entered the hospital, so Joyce Haynes was leaving.

"Hello Mr.Dodds," she said and smiled nervously at Edna. "I heard about your Myra an' I went to the ward to see her but nurse said best leave it a day or two. If I can do anythin' to help you've only to ask. Folk wer' real kind while I wer' laid up with me broken leg. That's why I'm here today, me last check up. Fit for work again now, clean bill of health they said."

"It's good of you Joyce," said Billy, "an' we'll let you know when Myra's up to havin' visitors. How's your William, have you heard from him?"

"Not for more than a month, I thought they might have let him come home for a bit when I wer' injured but Joe said a broken leg would be considered no more than a graze out where William is."

Billy noticed the trembling of her fingers as she spoke.

"Chin up lass, 'e's a tough chap your William but what are yer going to do now bakery's destroyed?"

"Go back on the buses, but drivin' this time, so many of the men are enlistin' if more women don't take the steerin' wheel the city'll go back to horse an' cart."

The ward while filled with poorly people, nevertheless felt less forbidding than the area of cubicles where Myra had been placed the previous evening. The Sister greeted them warmly.

"Myra is awake, her spirits are very low and that is to be expected so you must prepare yourselves for her tears. Still so young, it is almost impossible for Myra to reconcile herself to months of treatment, for her to actually believe Mr.Shilling's optimistic predictions of repair and recovery. Stay strong, whatever anguish falls about you, steel yourself, be confident around your daughter, I know it's hard but you must stay strong, you really must."

Edna smoothed Myra's brow and leaned over to kiss her forehead but Myra made no response, staring up at the ceiling, lips tight shut. Billy fetched a chair and coaxed Edna to sit down by the bedside, cautioning her with his eyes not to cry. Now Billy tried.

"Our Annie's sent a picture that Janet did for you with 'er crayons, she's put kisses at the bottom, seven of 'em, one for each day o' the week she said."

Myra continued to stare blankly at the ceiling above her. Billy laid the picture on the cabinet and fought a growing despair.

Sister recognised their need of rescue and crossed the ward to where they struggled for composure. Speaking clearly, her words directed at Myra as much as they were at Billy and Edna, she explained.

"It is necessary to simply keep Myra's wound free of infection for a few days, that I'm sure she must find frustrating, after all, the sooner Mr.Shilling begins his work the sooner she will see progress. What young woman would want to be stuck in hospital a single day more than she must."

A tortured half hour then ensued before the nurse announced visiting time over. Once outside the building Edna rushed to stand over the grille of a storm drain and retched her heart up.

"Come on love, don't take on, every day things'll get a bit better. Bring a basin o' dinner for Myra when you come tomorrow wi' Annie Eddowes, they'll warm it up in hospital kitchen. I know food's scarce but our house is never wi'out the makin's of a meal."

Taking Edna's arm he propelled her home, straight home, even though he felt the need to sit on the curb at the cemetery. Billy pictured Victor's face, that contentment when he blew bubbles with his spittle and repeated whatever had been said that pleased him. Billy missed his other arm, a man needed his other arm, especially today.

Edna sat on the bus in a world of her own. The previous afternoon a policeman had come to the house. Details of the accident and how it occurred he was obliged to tell them. There had been witnesses at the scene whose accounts had been consistent when interviewed separately. The fault lay with the driver of the coal lorry.

'It was as though he had his eyes shut, just didn't stop, like he didn't see the young woman'. As sergeant Willis related the information to Billy and herself Edna felt more and more like going at once to wherever the driver then was and striking him with her own bare hands. The policeman had continued, they would bring charges of careless driving and actual bodily harm. 'Your daughter should receive compensation, the coal merchant holds insurance for just such a situation, the driver being in his employ. The driver will lose his licence, at least for a significant period and could face jail'. Edna had listened to all this with an ever growing sense of anger, then came that final assault on her nerves, the sergeant's words ringing in her head all through the night and this morning as she'd cooked for Myra a basin of stew, now wrapped in a teacloth and travelling with Edna to the hospital. 'The driver may escape a custodial sentence depending on the magistrate's view of the mitigating circumstances, either way I can't imagine he'll take the wheel of a vehicle ever again given his mental state. Apparently two days prior to the accident he'd received word of his son's death. In fact the young man had been dead for more than a month by the time his dad read the letter, killed during the Allies' continuing attempts to hold Tobruk'.

"City hospital."

The conductor's voice interrupted Edna's drifting thoughts as he called out the next stop. Making sure the basin of stew sat in the shopping bag firmly upright she made her way down the aisle of the bus. Annie had agreed to meet Edna at the hospital, whoever arrived first would wait by the main entrance. The sight of Annie waving as she approached restored Edna's spirits a little. Archie had intended visiting Myra the previous evening, perhaps he might have achieved to draw her out of her silence. Poor Susie had tried with no success and in her dismay had wept all over the ward Sister.

"I wonder how Mabel is getting on," said Annie, as they made their way along the corridor, "I've not heard from her since last Christmas, I was pleased when she wrote to say that she'd returned to nursing. She had to wait until the children were of an age but all that study, what a tragic waste it could have been if she hadn't gone back to work. May would have been so proud. I just hope they are all safe and well, at least Leicester has been spared some of the bombing, Birmingham was hit so badly, all doctors and nurses must be forever on call."

They reached the ward.

"I better ask if I can leave this basin o' dinner wi' somebody to take to the kitchen for warmin', I don't s'pose they'll want me in the kitchen pokin' about, there's not much good said about the food in 'ere at best o' times, God knows what they stick in the soup these days. They reckon that in the last war some o' the meat wer' right suspect, not so much Black Angus as Red Setter!"

Annie chuckled. "Some folk have a vivid imagination and others are gullible enough to swallow it."

"That's the trouble, we did bloody well swallow it," said Edna with real feeling.

Annie stood a little distance from the bed while Edna moved closer. Myra needed to see her mam, Annie would give them some time together before joining them. Quite suddenly Myra's voice was raised alarmingly, she shouted at her mother.

"I don't want it unless you've put poison in it, poison the dinner then I'll eat it, I'll eat it all."

Sister hurried across and spoke urgently to Myra.

"Shush, shush, you're frightening everyone," but Myra's outburst was relentless.

"Poison it, poison me dinner Mam an' tell Archie not to come here again, I don't want to see him ever again, tell him Mam, tell him."

Edna could defy the tears no longer, she collapsed into Annie's arms, her body convulsed from sobbing. With Sister's help Annie led Edna to the nearest place of sanctuary, the sluice room, and lowered her to sit on a large box containing lavatory paper. Annie too was awash with tears, Edna was in agony of torment, what could be done, this was more than any mother should be called upon to bear. Sister squeezed Edna's hands with her own then knelt in front of her to speak.

"Remember what Mr.Shilling told you, pay it no heed, Myra is lashing out at the person she knows will never stop loving her no matter what, the one she trusts above all others, you Edna, her mam. All of her words, every single one, has no meaning. We can't make Myra see beyond all this pain and disfigurement to the day when she will get her life back. You have to cast away her words, shed them from this day and from any future days, they have no significance. An infant cries to its mother for its every need, to be fed, from colic, when teething and at times a mother can feel herself weaken under the strain but somehow she always manages to endure. Think of it in that way, it will pass I promise you, next week will be better than this week and the one after that will be better again. Leave it for today. I shall see to it that the kitchen warms her dinner and however much coaxing is required I shall make sure that Myra eats sufficient of it to line her stomach against the medication which we give to ease her pain and furthermore to justify her mother's efforts in preparing it." Sister winked her eye and that simple action was curiously reassuring.

Edna found calm and a little wobbly she rose to her feet, her eyes directed at the box below.

"I wer' too much for that, it's weakened under the strain alright."

The large cardboard box now displayed a crushed area which roughly followed the contours of Edna's backside.

"It just appears that way," said Sister, "what is inside will be sound enough."

Annie and Edna together made their way back to the bus stop.

"I'll go with you to Winchester Street," said Annie.

Edna sniffed, "There's no need, I'm alright, honest I am."

"I know you are but I'm still going with you, I won't stop if Billy's at home but I don't want you to be on your own until you've had a drop of brandy to stay your strength. When we went through all that trouble around the time of Hilda's wedding I'd make myself sip a little brandy. Aunt Bella would have been despairing of me but I had to turn to something. There I've owned up, your friend is an old soak."

"Oh aye," said Edna, "an' just how many egg spoonfuls did yer 'ave, I know you Annie Eddowes, you'd never indulge in owt corruptive 'cause if yer did, your aunt Bella 'ould appear one night at the end of your bed, holdin' up a picture o' Satan."

Annie had to smile at the notion. Within minutes the bus arrived and the two women sat side by side in an easy quietness. Edna didn't speak her thoughts, it occurred to her that sitting with Annie she could be content, just like Billy was with Victor. They didn't need conversation, it had ever been that way, there for each other regardless of all else. Myra would get better, colic always passed, teeth came through, flesh healed, Edna clutched at the belief and felt encouraged. Billy would likely be at home with the kettle hot, not every woman was blessed with a good husband and a constant friend, tomorrow she'd be stronger.

Billy listened to Edna's account of their daughter's distress without saying a word, then he spoke calmly but firmly.

"Tomorrow you stay 'ere, let me go on me own love, dads 'ave thicker skins than mams, don't put yourself through the mill, you can go again the next day, 'appen our Annie'll go with yer, they might let Janet onto the ward for five minutes. Myra wouldn't upset Janet, she knows what that little lass's been through already an' she's more operations to face yet. Myra 'ould give young Janet a smile, I know she would. I'll ask the ward Sister if they'll make an exception, I know children aren't usually allowed on adult wards but Janet's used to bein' in hospital herself an' I reckon it 'ould help Myra to see her little niece."

Billy had stopped in town to buy flowers, a bunch of carnations, Myra liked carnations, particularly the white, scented ones, which she likened to the spicy aroma of cinnamon. Edna would sometimes cook apples with cinnamon and it was Myra's habit to lower her face to the dish and smell its content for several seconds before sinking her spoon into the goodness. Myra had always enjoyed her food, a bonny baby she had grown into a bonny young woman. Billy could understand why Myra might find that difficult to believe right now, at her age especially, any disfigurement must destroy all confidence, dash hope against the wall.

He stood just outside the door of the ward, looking through the glass panel, his gaze following the line of beds to where Myra lay, her leg still protected by some kind of frame beneath the bed covers. Billy lifted the flowers to his face and smelled them, let out a big sigh and forced his feet to take him along the ends of the beds, not seeing the present but imagining the past, that scene he had sent long ago to the very back of his mind, the ward at Hemel Hempstead, all the bandaging, the cries that would erupt from those who managed to find a fitful sleep and in so doing, encountered nightmares. He pictured Albert Haynes, in constant pain, worrying for his wife Florrie and for the son poor Albert never got to truly know or understand, Victor.

Myra's eyes were open but she kept them directed at the ceiling above her head. Billy laid the flowers on the cabinet and sat down as close to his daughter as he possibly could. He reached for her fingers.

"That's better," said Billy, "your old dad needs somebody to hold 'is hand. I remember the day when I needed that so much it hurt enough to make me cry. In the hospital we were all the same, flesh ripped an' burned like old rags, or summat missin' altogether, so it didn't seem so bad. When I wer' discharged at last, sent out into the streets I trembled like a leaf. On the train comin' home a dread formed in the pit o' me stomach, the closer I got to Victoria station the worse it become. When they'd last seen me I wer' normal, whole, everythin' intact. What would our Annie, Susie and Liza make o' me now. When I turned into Winchester Street I wer' more frightened o' seein' the look on their faces than I'd been in the trenches fightin' the Boche. Annie come runnin' out first, then Susie wi' them ribbons Edna used to put in her hair flyin' out behind 'er, then come Edna holdin' Liza's hand to stop her trippin' on the cobbles in her haste, all rushin' my way. They didn't even notice, it wer' dad, their old dad, 'e wer' back an' that's all that mattered. Liza caught hold of me hand an' that wer' me salvation, the feel o' them little fingers in mine stopped all the hurt, out there in Winchester Street the hurt stopped. Yet in spite of all that love I doubted meself. I knew what I looked like, I wer' lucky to be alive, but I felt awkward, less than a man. I couldn't let it show, your mam didn't need that worry, she'd 'ad more than 'er share, so I pretended I didn't care, it didn't matter that I 'ad an arm missin', no ear, a buggered up eye, it couldn't stop Billy Dodds, 'e wer' stronger than that! Then I met Victor. Never did two people on the face o' this earth need each other as much as me an' Victor. We 'ave to go on love, not so much for ourselves but for others. Don't shut us out, if your daft old dad doesn't 'ave you to catch hold of his hand 'e'll likely curl up."

Billy felt Myra's fingers tighten around his own. He stood and leaned over to kiss her forehead. Her arms raised and encircled his neck, pulling him down closer, holding on tighter and tighter 'til his heart near ruptured from emotion.

"I love you Dad."

Myra sniffled the words through her tears. Billy couldn't speak, he didn't need to speak, it was going to be alright, his daughter Myra would be alright. A voice at his side spoke softly.

"I shall put these beautiful carnations in water for you Myra." Sister lifted the flowers to her face. "Ooh, that lovely scent of cinnamon."

Annie was about to take her knitting from the drawer, she had almost completed a pullover for David. Hilda had chosen the wool, a deep blue, only a couple of inches left to knit of the sleeve then Annie could pick up the stitches for the neck. She glanced at the clock, twenty past eight. Charles had gone to The Standard, he was seldom late home these days, the black out and the ever present threat of air raids seemed to drive most folk to the comfort of home unless a duty bound them to be elsewhere. It was so quiet and empty without George, even though he left for work early and returned late Annie had nevertheless felt that sense of family, one of her children with her still to prepare a meal for, to wash and iron for, to enjoy conversation with, to love and be loved under the same roof every day.

When one night George had sat with her, explaining why, Annie had understood, of course she understood, but it had left her emotions feeling raw. 'Samuel deserves a future Mam, I can't let the responsibility pass to others, to those fighting for just that, a safe future for the children. I can't be a man if I don't stand with the rest'. George had gone to see Samuel at Ruddington and left the following day to join The Foresters.

Annie had not seen Edna for almost a week, she closed the drawer leaving the knitting inside, gathered her coat and quickly wrote a note to tell Charles where she had gone in case he arrived home before her.

It was the 10th of September, aunt Bella used to say that the air smelled different in September, autumn mellowed the senses, colours became sombre, sounds less penetrating beneath the first fogs. Annie's senses had failed to mellow, as yet everything was still sharp, too sharp. In Edna's company she would find some relief, Edna would likely be on her own too, Billy would be at the exchange.

"Hello Mrs.Eddowes, got the parish lamp to light your way tonight," said Mr.Williams the ARP warden, "you take care now."

"Thank you Mr.Williams, I promise I will."

The sky was indeed clear and the moon, although not quite full, cast its natural light over the streets. Francis in her last letter had used that same term, describing Freddy's work in the fields as being extended by the grace of the parish lamp. From the farm however, they had seen German planes fly in overland and felt such a mix of anger, frustration and sickening dread that a moonlit night once considered 'friend' had now become 'foe'. Annie reached Winchester Street without incident, she tapped at Edna's back door, it was unlocked so she entered, at once she detected tobacco smoke, a voice called out.

"Come in if you're good lookin'." Edna stood by the mantelpiece in the living room, smoking a cigarette.

"I've not ever seen you smoke before," said Annie completely taken by surprise.

"I've got to 'ave summat me nerves are in shreds, Archie got 'em for me, only a packet 'o ten an' I shall make 'em last."

Annie stood by her friend and smiled. A brown envelope was propped up against the clock, Edna's gaze seemed fixed upon it.

"Myra's call up papers would yer believe. Young, single woman wasted on knickers an' girdles, needed at Ranskill, at the ordnance factory. If it wern't so bloody tragic I'd laugh."

Annie patted Edna's arm. "How is Myra?"

"Tomorrow, that's a big day, Mr.Shillin' is doin' the first operation, 'e's takin' skin from the thigh of 'er good leg to eventually put on the bad one, it's a process 'e'll 'ave to repeat many times over the next weeks, months, however long it takes." Edna paused, "Robert, now why would any woman wi' the surname Shillin' call 'er lad Robert, it allus gets shortened to Bob, so 'is surname's Bob' an' 'is first name's Bob. Bob, bob, bobbin' along."

Annie sensed that Edna was close to tears.

"It will be alright Edna, Myra is going to recover. Just think of what Mr.Shilling is doing for Janet already. I don't imagine a man of his standing would ever have his name shortened. He would at all times be Robert Shilling, at work and at home."

"Aye, you're probably right," Edna's sigh was deep and long. "I'm goin' to keep that brown envelope up there where I can see it every day, to remind meself that Myra could 'ave been at the bloody ordnance factory jugglin' explosives instead o' stuck in city hospital wi' arf 'er leg ripped off, the buggers'll get yer one way or another." Edna sniffed her resentment.

Annie fell silent and her expression became vague. Edna noticed.

"What's up, summat's up I can tell. 'E's bein' a bloody misery again isn't 'e? How yer stick it I don't know," said Edna in a tone of dismay.

"No, it's not Charles, it's George. He's enlisted, he left the day before yesterday."

Edna took Annie in her arms and held her tight, they held one another, sharing an anguish, which through enduring friendship they understood without need of explanation, tears flowed unsuppressed.

Then in a weak, faltering voice, Edna began to sing, slowly, the words of the song trembling from her lips in a fragile procession. Annie joined in, between swallowing hard.

"When the red, red, robin comes bob, bob, bobbing along, along,

There'll be no more sobbing when he comes throbbing his old, sweet song------

CHAPTER FOUR

Charlie Jones and Bob Budgeon stood outside the door of the Masonic Hall, as yet the number of people inside was few enough, young women especially seemed slow to arrive and Charlie and Bob's appraisal of the females as they approached had so far not inspired them sufficiently to enter and join those determined to enjoy the dance about to commence within.

Charlie stubbed out his cigarette.

"It's a good job ol' Gravely didn't catch yer with a fag on," said Bob, "do yer really think Jerry can see the light from a cigarette at that distance." He looked up into the night sky. "I sometimes think me mam can see through the wall, yer know what it's like when yer fancy a bit o' self 'elp, nine times out o' ten, she'll be up them stairs shoutin', you'll go blind our Bobby. She must 'ave developed some sort o' night sight. It's only since me brother Jimmy wer' called up, me an' 'im used to share the bedroom an' 'e wer' forever at it but mam never said a word then, 'ere look up, these two aren't bad, bags I the one on the left, I spotted 'er first, just look at them tits, I could play wi' them for hours."

Charlie grinned, "Me dad reckons that any more than a handful's a waste."

"Well you would say that wouldn't yer, them missin' fingers o' yours Jones must limit you to the less well endowed o' the species."

An indignant Charlie ignored Bob's slight and instead concentrated on the two young women now entering the hall.

"Come on then Budgeon, I'll show yer how it's done."

The dance had been organised to raise funds for the war effort. All the money on the door plus the proceeds of the tombola was to be handed to the authorities. The number of people now inside had swelled considerably and the band, encouraged by various 'requests', played at a lively tempo. Due to the absence of so many men, women partnered women and young danced with old in their attempt to forget, for just a little while those troubles that dominated life. It was barely three weeks to Christmas but any festive spirit proved hard to find. Charlie and Bob decided to make their approach of the two young women, to ask for a dance. Recognising the usual soppy smile, ever present on the face of a male in pursuit, the big busted girl spoke quietly but urgently to her friend.

"I'll take the dark haired one, I can't abide a ginger top."

Not having any strong feelings one way or the other, the less curvaceous one of the two at once took Bob's arm and steered him into the centre of the throng where his bright, copper coloured hair identified his passage about the dance floor like the sight of one Rhode Island Red chicken among a feeding frenzy of Buff Orpingtons. Charlie's right arm now encircled the waist of poor Bob's chosen conquest to be.

"I should introduce meself in the proper fashion," he said, "me name is Charlie Jones, what's yours?"

"Maureen," she replied, unwilling to reveal her surname until she'd had chance to weigh him up. "So what do you do for a livin' Charlie Jones?"

It would be pointless to pretend his days were spent in any other job than the one he'd been doing for more than three years so he declared it as it was.

"I collect rubbish, that's me, a bin man. I tried to enlist but they said I weren't suitable, 'cause o' this." He held up his right hand to show the lack of digits.

"What about your friend, did he try to enlist?"

Her expression held no trace of concern at Charlie's stubby hand and he felt relief. Normally he wouldn't much care what a girl thought, he'd had that hand, minus two fingers since before he could remember, it made no difference to what he could do, he gripped a dustbin as firmly as the next man, if they'd given him the opportunity he could have gripped a rifle an'all, followed his mate Jack Wainwright. He sighed at the thought, Charlie missed Jack.

"Bob's allus had flat feet, but like me 'e didn't think it'd stop 'im fightin' but apparently it does. All the marchin' over rough ground wi' a heavy pack an' eight pounds o' bayonet an' rifle would 'ave crippled 'im, funny don't yer think, Bob can march up an' down streets over cobbles an' broken pavin's all week long wi' a bin on 'is back a damn sight heavier than eight soddin' pounds but that's not good enough for the army. So, we're both in the local defence an' what a 'rag tag' lot we are, there's more than thirty men in our troop an' arf a dozen weapons, unless you call broom handles an' shovels weapons. How they expect us to have any sense of importance I don't know. Last Wednesday night at drill, Captain Nias, God bless 'is cotton socks, decided we all had to be tested on our signal recognition, so 'e made us stand in a line an' one by one 'e come along in front of us pickin' at random some poor sod to grill. Well 'e'd quizzed nine or ten afore 'e stopped right in front o' me. 'Now Jones', 'e said, 'what does this signify'? 'E put his whistle between 'is lips an' started blowin', at the same time 'is arms wer' outstretched an' flappin' up an' down at 'is sides. I pretended to give it some serious consideration, even asked 'im to repeat it. 'Captain Nias sir', I said, 'that signifies a bloody blackbird flyin'. 'Stick with it lad 'e said, there'll be uniforms comin' soon. Uniforms! They just don't get it do they?"

Maureen recognised the frustration in Charlie's voice.

"Me dad's in the Merchant Navy," she said, "has been for years, he can be away from home for months at a time, I reckon that's why we all come along so regular in our family. Mam nearly always giv' birth nine months after he left. He'd come home and find another baby in the house. In the end she made 'im sleep in the next street at me grandma's, there wer' only two bedrooms in our house an' mam 'ad three of us in her bed as it was. Then two died, first Sammy of pneumonia an' not long after, Jenny, all of a sudden, just dropped dead. Doctor reckoned she had hole in her heart, most likely had it from birth. Poor mam, she'd had enough, I think dad must have understood 'cause he slept at home after that but no more babies come."

"My dad wer' a window cleaner for years," said Charlie, "they reckon it's down to standin' all that time wi' his feet on the rung of a ladder, muscle bound, walks like a clockwork soldier an' like me an' Bob 'e's a reject an'all, they wouldn't even 'ave 'im in the LD, wrong sort o' soldier."

Quite spontaneously Maureen planted a kiss on Charlie's cheek, smiled and said. "They'll draw the tombola at the interval, the prizes are supposed to be really good."

Eddie Wills had been on the door taking money, 3/6d for the dance and a tanner for a ticket for the tombola. Other areas were raising funds for planes and warships and the good people of Nottingham were determined to do their bit. Charlie had glanced at Bob whenever the dancing brought them closer, it was difficult to tell from his expression whether or not his partner was proving as agreeable as Maureen. Then a few bars into *'Red Sails in the Sunset'* the two couples became adjacent, looking over the girl's shoulder at Charlie, Bob gave a roguish wink, whirled his partner around with a flourish and that mop of copper coloured hair advanced at speed towards the band. Unbeknown to Charlie, earlier in the proceedings Bob had spoken with the band leader, 'My mate Charlie Jones sings like a bird, if yer play somethin' 'e knows I'll give yer the nod an' you can introduce 'im'. The band suddenly stopped playing. Folk thought it must be the interval but the band leader in his cream coloured jacket and bright red bow tie cleared his throat and declared.

"We've got a treat for you tonight Ladies an' Gentlemen, a young man is going to sing along to the music while you twirl your toes, so come up here Charlie Jones, the podium is yours."

"I'll rip that red hair right out of 'is head, it's that bugger Budgeon who's set me up," said Charlie, genuinely vexed. How embarrassing, what would Maureen think, he wouldn't do it. Charlie didn't realise how gifted he was, as a boy he'd sung Carols with his mate Jack Wainwright and never realised that it was pure soprano he delivered at every door, a sound any Church choirmaster would have taken to his charge and praised The Lord for its creation. Back then Charlie's days were about as far removed from a surplice and ruffle as they could possibly be, ripped pants and scabby knees, a quick dunk in the tin bath of a Sunday night before lessons at Bentinck Road school the next morning. 'Rough pups', that was the expression used by genteel folk to describe the likes of Charlie and Jack. When his voice broke it blessed him in manhood to be an enviable tenor, which Bob Budgeon had listened to in awe as they worked the streets tipping bins.

The band leader's own curiosity made him insistent and the assembly began to call for Charlie, it would be entertaining whatever happened, being their sentiment.

"Charlie Jones, we want Charlie Jones," they chanted over and over.

"Go on," said Maureen, "show 'em what you can do, sing for your mate Jack, for your dad, sing for me, sing one in the eye for them as don't understand."

Bolstered by Maureen's words, Charlie made his way to the podium. Instructed to play softly, the band struck up. He made for a curious spectacle, his jacket a bit on the small side, that right hand fidgeting nervously but too defiant to hide inside a pocket. Maureen was right, he'd sing this for his mate Jack Wainwright, wherever the bloody war had taken him, for you Jack, especially for you.

Charlie's tenor voice sang *'Red Sails in the Sunset'* with all the quality of a true professional, those expecting a dire rendition were amazed while others less pessimistic were rewarded for their faith in man's boundless abilities. As the last line of the song fell effortlessly from Charlie's lips the place erupted in cheers and applause even the band hurriedly laid their instruments by their feet and clapped with the rest. The band leader's hand gripped Charlie's shoulder.

"Bloody marvellous lad."

Charlie stepped down from the podium finding himself close to tears but Maureen was waiting to take his arm, to claim her 'man'.

"Good time to take a break folks," said the band leader, "Mr.Wills is going to draw the tombola."

Due to rationing the nature of the prizes was greatly changed. Instead of the usual tin of toffees, bar of chocolate, bottle of ale and other modest items of food and drink, Eddie Wills held up a fine lady's scarf donated by Smithfield's factory and a tartan blanket from the same source, two framed watercolours of 'still life' given by the school of art, ladies and gents hosiery, courtesy of Drew's, several hanks of knitting wool and bobbins of sewing thread kindly given by the haberdasher's. A quite splendid lady's hat and a gentleman's bowler from Burtons and last but not least, a squeeze box and a harmonica, both second hand but none the less desirable, proudly donated by Moffat's 'nearly new' shop.

"Oh well, better luck next time," said Charlie, when neither his ticket nor Maureen's had been drawn but an excited Bob Budgeon couldn't wait to join his friend, calling out in his eagerness.

"Bugger me Charlie, I've won the squeeze box, we'll make some bloody good music now, you an' me'll fill the Hippodrome one day."

Bob's first attempt at making music with his prize however, suggested it likely to be no time soon. The girls laughed and through the fun of it all Charlie forgave Bob for putting him on the spot

"Now 'tis only polite that we swap partners for at least one dance," said Bob, his gaze falling on Maureen.

It was after all thanks to this copper topped, flatfooted bin man that she had heard her Charlie sing. Still warm from a flush of pride and a new found happiness she was prepared to put aside her dislike of ginger hair, she would grant Bob one dance but only one, after that Sheila must resume that partnership and Maureen would reclaim her Charlie, 'her' Charlie, the thought was so engaging she found herself waltzing as the band played on with only half an ear to Bob's chatter.

The evening ended with the customary singing of the anthem and appreciation for the band. Cautioned by Eddie Wills to remain in the hall until all the lights were out, the people eventually drifted through the open door to make their way home, humming the melodies which now rang as memories in their heads. Pulling up their collars against the cold air Maureen and Sheila were about to say goodnight to Charlie and Bob but a strong arm was wrapped around each of them.

"We'll see yer safely home, our mams an' your dads 'ould expect nothin' less of us," said Bob.

"True, spoken like a true soldier," said Charlie, and winked at Maureen.

The local defence might be all that he and Bob were deemed fit for but they were as good as the next man, he began to sing, boldly, the rousing words to *'Men of Harlech'* they all joined in and Bob's squeeze box swung from his free hand, making no sound yet in perfect rhythm with the tune.

The following Sunday morning brought news of an event which produced a mixed response, shock among the men of commerce, a dignified acceptance by his immediate family and an unspoken 'long overdue', that passed from eye to eye of the miners. It was Steve Wainwright who best summed up the feelings of the men from the pit. 'If Basil Stanford's gone to meet his maker then I hope he has the decency to look him in the eye. All the years we miners have worked to fill his coffers not once has he faced us like a man. If he stares down at his feet this time then he should be sent to where his gaze takes him'.

Florence Stanford had prepared their evening meal, a simple plate of cold brisket and boiled potatoes. She had never been a big eater and over the course of the past twelve months Basil's appetite had diminished to no more than half of what it had once been. Florence had chosen her moment to voice her concern for their daughter Julia, married to Luciano who now worked in a government department in Rome and with the Fascist, ever more vocal Mussolini courting Hitler, it made for a situation over which Florence could only feel a growing unease.

Basil had put a forkful of potato into his mouth as if to dismiss any need of response, appeared to chew until swallowing then looked across the table at his wife with a vague expression and said, 'I need new glasses'. Whereupon he lurched to one side and fell from his chair to the floor. With haste Florence had tried to help him but when feeling for a pulse there was none it confirmed her instinctive belief that something catastrophic had occurred and her husband was dead.

She had called both the doctor and Tommy Spooner, she remained calm, feeling little emotion. Once in receipt of the death certificate and with the help of his brother Joe, Tommy removed Basil's body from the house, as was Florence's wish.

'Shall I fetch your daughter Caroline to sit with you?' Tommy had asked.

In reply Florence had simply said. 'No, but there is something that perhaps you might do for me, would you go to Wollaton and tell William Eddowes that I shall require his help tomorrow, you see William would not normally come here on a Sunday'.

It had been gone nine when Tommy knocked on William's front door, Celia answered. Instantly her thoughts had been for Rosie. 'Come in Tommy I do hope all is well, I told Rosie only last week that she should let me take the baby out in her pram sometimes, just so she can sit down for a little while'.

'Rosie is well thank you Celia, it's William I've come to see, if he's at home'. Tommy so hoped that William was present and that it wouldn't be necessary to speak with him in the pub. Word would get out soon enough, it was kindest to grant Florence Stanford this night at least before the news of her husband's death was on everyone's lips.

William sat by the hearth, The Evening Post folded loosely on his lap, he'd appeared deep in thought, oblivious to the caller whoever it might be. When Tommy spoke William's surprise rendered him momentarily speechless. 'It's not dad, surely not dad', had been his first anxious words. 'Basil Stanford died earlier this evening, his wife asked me to inform you and to tell you that she needs you to go to the house tomorrow morning'.

It was well over twelve months since Tommy and William were last in one another's company, Tommy observed a difference, William's face was leaner, that readiness to offer up some boast, to bluster like a cocky youth was absent from his demeanour. Tommy had wanted to say, 'What's up Will, tell your ol' mate Tommy', but years of work and changing circumstances had kept them apart, created a distance. Standing together on Bobbers Mill bridge as a train hurtled along the track below, engulfing them in that dense smoke from the engine's stack, the fun of it, which when the smoke cleared revealed a big grin on the face of each, must surely have been in a previous life.

Celia had overheard Tommy's news. 'Oh dear, poor Caroline, I shall go to see her as soon as I can. With Edmund away her nerves are already tested to the limit'.

Tommy had politely declined Celia's offer of tea, explaining his need to return home.

The doctor had confidently stated 'cause of death' as being severe haemorrhage of the brain, when Florence had described the moment just before Basil keeled over, his reference to his eyesight and told the doctor of the recurring incidents of confusion through the past months, he'd considered it entirely unnecessary to prolong Florence Stanford's ordeal by calling for a post mortem. At their last consultation Doctor Gifford had advised his patient to consider his raised blood pressure to be a warning of a very real need to study his weight and extent of tiredness. Basil Stanford had dismissed the advice as a medic's scare mongering.

Thus Tommy's work could begin without delay in the morning. Stanford had been a character strongly disliked by many folk but James Handley had instructed Tommy to deal with every corpse, regardless of any aura surrounding it, with the same application of duty. What Handley's did was not for the deceased but for those who wept from grief, or indeed those who shed tears of blesséd relief whichever might be the case. Only dignity was ever to be shown them and their corpse, human nature prescribed what lay outside of Handley's undertaking. Tommy would need to consult with Mrs.Stanford on the arrangements for the funeral. Bidding William 'goodnight' and planting a kiss on Celia's cheek as she stood at the front door to wave, Tommy drove away from the house in full knowledge of the nature of his tasks over the coming days but with little understanding of the changes in William Eddowes, his pal through those explorative years of adolescence, when an inkling of what defined manhood could only be shared with a 'best mate', just in case it proved to be an unfortunate abnormality.

Annie sat with Florence and Caroline at Moreleigh, relieved to find their conversation centred on the children. Desperately lonely after Edmund left, the young mother had gone to Plumtree to fetch her 'babies'. Not evacuated with the same family as Rosie's three boys, they had nevertheless been placed close by and had managed to see one another, especially Christopher and Jonathon, Caroline's eldest, being of a similar age and in the same class at the local school.

Now Caroline watched over them day and night and the responsibility helped keep her mind from dwelling on Edmund's role in the war. Annie supposed the distraction served also to ease the effects of her father's death. Caroline was composed, she showed no distress.

"I am sorry Annie, about William. I was very grateful when he came last Sunday morning. He drove me here to Caroline and then to Patricia's. Of course I shall see to it that he receives an amount over and above his due pay but I have no work for him to do." Florence was genuinely upset.

"You mustn't fret over William," said Annie, "the factories are working at an ever greater capacity they say, he has no experience of engineering but surely he could apply himself." She hesitated before adding. "He may decide to enlist now that your husband's need of him is no more."

"Oh dear, oh dearie me." Florence twisted the lace edging on her hanky about her fingers. "The news of Pearl Harbour is dreadful, it will propel the Americans into the conflict and some believe that can only be a good thing but the entire world will very soon be bent on destruction and I just can't find a single 'good thing' in any of it. So soon after the last madness, thousands grieve still yet pain is disregarded."

Florence fell silent at the sound of Caroline returning from the kitchen where she'd gone to make a tray of tea.

"Have you heard from George? Caroline received a letter from Edmund yesterday didn't you dear, he writes little of his actual work but detailed descriptions of his fellows and their characters, little idiosyncrasies and habits, most I imagine evolved through the process of training and fixing the mind on their task. One of his colleagues plays the spoons and with great dexterity, apparently every day at some point he sits outside their billet, takes his make shift instrument from his pocket and begins to play, singing his own version of lyrics along with the tune. I think I shall sing them often, check that I have remembered correctly the young man's name Caroline, I shall never forget his words.

Caroline took an envelope from the mantelpiece and scanned the letter.

"Bill Stribley Mother," she said.

"As I thought, I would not do the young man such a disservice as to incorrectly speak his name."

Whereupon Florence began to sing, her voice remarkably controlled.

"*Run Jerry, run Jerry, run, run, run,*

Here comes Bill Stribley with his gun, gun, gun.

You can't fly outside my beady eye,

I'll blast at your arses 'til your done, done, done."

Annie could do nothing but applaud, to hear a woman of Florence's years and background sing so robustly was inspiring, yet incongruous. In so many ways she reminded Annie of Davina. Even Caroline could not resist a smile.

"Really Mother whatever would Patricia say!"

They drank the tea and relaxed in one another's company.

"George has completed his training and by now will be en route to the Middle East. Like Edmund he writes little of his Battalion's orders, I'm sure they are forbidden to include such things in their letters home, even though by the time the letter finally reaches its destination they would likely be in an entirely different place and following another strategy. But he does describe his commanding officer as being the tallest man he has ever seen, stiff as a poker in both stature and nature, spine like a ramrod. Utterly incapable of allowing as much as a single chin whisker to grow any other way than perpendicular." Annie chuckled as she recounted the passage from George's letter. "I don't suppose you have any way of contacting your daughter in Italy, or for her to contact you," said Annie.

"I have heard from her only three times in the past seventeen months, she sent the letters via a friend in Switzerland, someone she knows from her early days at the consulate. I replied to the address in Fribourg each time but have heard nothing more since June. I'm afraid of making trouble for her so I have not written again, I've read of house arrest in such situations."

"Surely that won't happen to Julia, her husband must have some influence if he works within the government there," said Annie.

"That is what I tell myself, Luciano is a decent man, he will protect his wife from the extremes of behaviour adopted by these so called dictators, be it Mussolini or Hitler. Odious creatures dispossessed of their senses, seeking world domination. Can you imagine a more alarming prospect."

Florence spoke so vehemently it quite surprised Annie that she could then, virtually without pause, bring her eldest daughter Patricia into the conversation. Caroline sat quietly, gazing into the fire, seemingly lost in her own thoughts.

"Patricia is overseeing the funeral arrangements, Caroline and I both agreed it was as well to concede to that, whatever we might have suggested would almost certainly have been overruled anyway. Patricia has always been close to her father, they were like minded, whereas we," Florence cast her eyes towards the pensive Caroline, "we were considered by Basil to be without understanding of a man's world."

Annie looked at the mantel clock. "I should be going," she said, "Charles will need to sort The Evening Post to send with the paper boys. Please let us know when arrangements are complete and you have the date and time, I'm sure that Charles will attend and William of course."

"I shall walk with you to the corner," said Florence, "Caroline will be off in the other direction to meet the children from school in just a few minutes."

Gathering their coats from the hooks on the back door the two women shivered from the dropping temperature outside.

"Are you sure you want to come," said Annie, "you could easily catch a chill at this time of year."

"There's something I need to ask you and I don't want Caroline's head to be troubled with it. Basil naturally dealt with all matters of finance and legal affairs. I have a small income of my own from a property mother left to me, it's occupied and I receive rent, only a modest amount as the property itself is modest, a terraced two up two down, on Denman Street. I don't worry for myself but for Caroline I hold great concern. God forbid that anything should happen to Edmund but I cannot dismiss from my mind the possibility. I may be wrong, perhaps I misjudge him but I anticipate Basil's Will, when it is read, will name Patricia as the sole beneficiary. Should it be the case I must seek the advice of a lawyer. Obviously I couldn't approach the firm that Basil used, Neilson and Bradbury, they have handled all of his transactions. I believe they acted for his father too. Edmund's past position at Chaucer, Caffin and Holt, whilst the current situation keeps him from his desk, is being held for him, pray God he returns to it. However it causes me to consider them inappropriate with regard to the situation, as it might affect Caroline. I wonder who does Charles use?"

"Following the death of my dear friend Davina Wright, last May, I am joint executor of her Estate along with Nigel Caffin, Davina's solicitor of many years. Charles is with the firm his late father used. Strangely it still goes by the name of Meakin and Kirk, although Gerald Meakin died a very long time ago and no one ever seemed to know of Mr.Kirk. Their offices are on London Road, I'm sure Charles has always found them satisfactory. I had occasion to call there only once, before Mr.Meakin sadly died, but I feel confident in recommending them."

Annie felt dismayed by Florence's remarks, the poor woman's anxieties, which Annie had detected in the past despite her saying little on the subject of Basil and home life, were surely even more disturbing than she'd imagined, but it was not Annie's place to pry.

"You know my dear I dread his funeral," said Florence with a hefty sigh, "and for all the wrong reasons. Not because I shall stand there a heart broken widow overwhelmed by grief but because I must witness that ritualistic attendance by those inhabitants of his 'man's world' when there is not one among them without hypocrisy. Patricia will inspect me from head to toe should my attire not be as black as the coal that gave Basil power over all those poor men at the pit and her husband, Anthony Bradshaw will inwardly count their likely gain while pretending to sing, *'The Lord is my Shepherd'*. I would rather leave them all to their sickening performance and instead play snakes and ladders with my grandchildren. I'm sorry if I shock you Annie but I have sensed in you, above all others, a perception of the truth."

They had reached the corner. Annie kissed Florence's cheek and squeezed her hand. "Tomorrow morning and every morning thereafter I shall sing with Bill Stribley and I know that you will too. We need to muster some of his indomitable spirit, to rise to the days' challenges until the troubles are 'done, done, done."

Florence couldn't hide the wateriness of tears but she smiled bravely.

"Bless you Annie, and much love to George when you next write."

CHAPTER FIVE

William stood for a moment at the gates, walking across the yard to the factory door felt daunting, he was so exposed, that aptly described his current state of affairs, daunting and exposed.

Gerald Birkett at the bank was squeezing hard. William was three months in arrears with his mortgage. Over the course of years he'd worked for Basil Stanford, all the shining prospects dangled in front of him at the beginning, had one by one disappeared. Citing the ongoing recession as being what forced his hand, Stanford had cut William's pay each year until putting sufficient food on the table and keeping the house at Wollaton had become so acutely challenging it seemed impossible to continue.

It had been the assurances given by Stanford at that first meeting with Birkett that enabled William to acquire the house, of that he had no doubt. Without such confident recommendation no bank manager would have sanctioned a mortgage based on William's financial status, as it then was. 'I know all the right people'. So many times Stanford had made that claim and William had lapped up its sweetness like a cat with the cream.

William had come to recognise his boss as a most accomplished engineer, not of mechanical device but of human kind. When William's house was lost to him through the bank calling in the debt, Basil Stanford stood to gain financially from the process. Now not so green about the ears, William's thinking had become much more attuned to the ways of the world, he had observed the 'master' at his 'game'. He'd been close to confronting Stanford on the subject, but then Basil played his trump card and what he told William about his mother, Enid Eddowes, took the feet from under him as surely as a mighty blow at a bare fist fight. If he'd challenged Stanford over his association with Birkett then Basil's tongue would have spread the sickening evil, that was another element of the game Basil played so well. William couldn't speak to his dad, it was too awful to contemplate. So adamant had Basil been as to its truth, William preferred to cling to what he had always believed, to what he had been told, that his mother died in childbirth, the baby also. Abortion! The thought choked him, he would not allow his mother's name to be sullied, not by anyone, he didn't want to hear of such things, not even from his dad. So he'd endured those years of manipulation and servitude, helped only by the decency and understanding of Jessie Tozer. William had confided his financial dilemma to his father in law. Jessie had given William sufficient funds to enable him to keep his head above water, but only just. Ironically and indeed tragically, Jessie had died the following year, that had been four years ago. Gwendolyn, Jessie's wife had already developed a degree of dementia and her husband's death accelerated her condition. The money had not been spoken of since so William presumed Jessie had made no mention of it to either Celia or Edmund.

Gwendolyn remained at home in the care of a companion come housekeeper, recommended by Robert Cheetham's wife as being, 'thoroughly dependable and discreet'. Celia had been grateful for Mrs.Cheetham's help, fond though she was of her mother, the prospect of living with her and what that would do to William and the children, rendered the decision to engage Sybil Brewer as housekeeper a simple one to make and Edmund had been in full accord.

Florence Stanford had given William double the amount outstanding in wages but he desperately needed work. A lowly position at any of the engineering factories, which given his total lack of experience would be all he could get, wouldn't keep him afloat. When Davina Wright's Estate was finally proved he would receive more than enough to solve all his problems but that large house in The Park, as yet remained unsold.

So it was to his old boss, Andrew Smithfield, William now turned in the hope of suitable employment and salvation. It had been a long time since William last walked across the yard at Brassington. Little had changed, that same heavy door which greeted every worker, those familiar smells unique to the trade being conducted within. Before an observant foreman could notice him William made straight away to Smithfield's office and knocked at the door.

"Come in."

If he hesitated now he would surely be lost, grasping the handle, he opened the door, entered and closed it behind him, all in the space of no more than two seconds.

"William," said a startled Smithfield. He rose from his seat behind the desk and came forward, offering his hand. "It's good to see you William, all is well with the family I trust."

"Yes Sir, thank you, everyone is in good health." William took a deep breath. "For obvious reasons I am no longer in the employ of Mr.Stanford. With a wife and children to support it is crucial that I find another position. I wonder if there might be an opening for me here at Brassington, I do at least have a good knowledge of the trade, whereas engineering is outside my experience."

"Sit down William." Smithfield nodded towards the chair at the side of the desk. "The business ticks over but with clothing now rationed orders are understandably down. When the nation is at war people tend to moderate their needs. It is a fallacy that folk live for the day in case they fall before the enemy. The truth is the opposite, they put all their faith in a better tomorrow. I remember, years ago, having a conversation with Henry Wicks on this very subject. It is man's way of staying strong, convincing himself of that brighter day, refusing to allow doubts to undermine the beliefs that have sustained him so far.

"Have you asked at Players, I know that Raymond Haynes has lost a number of men through their enlisting. I take it you don't see the military as an option, army pay is not the best but it is regular."

"It wouldn't meet anywhere near what I am obliged to find each month, Celia and the children must have a home, it was different for George, he was able to move back into Gregory Street." William clutched at straws.

"Indeed your brother's situation is entirely different William, his wife died leaving him with an infant son."

Andrew detected still that side of William so ready to dismiss the troubles of others as nothing compared to his own, that self importance, which compelled William Eddowes to walk that bit above his peers. Yet he sensed a real anxiety in William, his hands fidgeted constantly in his lap, that old defiance which could barb his tongue this day seemed benign.

"If you look out there on the factory floor you will see that both foremen are too old to serve and your past instructor and colleague Robert Armistead, works diligently in the print shop still at an age when retirement must surely be but a few years away, all the others are women."

William stood up and looked beyond Smithfield's shoulder to the window.

"I should never have walked away across that yard. I've been a fool Mr.Smithfield, perhaps I deserve to be shamed but Celia has done nothing to warrant such misery and I don't know how to protect her, how to keep us from Birkett's clutches."

At the mention of that name Andrew's hackles rose.

"By how much are you in debt to Braithwaites, to Birkett?"

He asked the question so firmly, William found himself answering without reserve.

"You can start next Monday, Mr.Armistead could use some help. I have neglected the house of late, there is work you can undertake there too, nothing an intelligent, able bodied man couldn't deal with, painting mainly but some general maintenance, inside and out. Your tasks will be varied William but it is all I can offer. We approach Christmas, I shall pay you in advance for the first month. It will prevent Gerald Birkett breathing down your neck. Work hard William but be prudent, in these times through which we live nothing is guaranteed."

"You won't speak of this to anyone?" William's eyes made the appeal.

"Unlike your previous employer William, everyone here is decent and moral, therefore it is incumbent upon you to be equally so while ever you remain in my employ. It is not for me to speak ill of the dead, however, I believe we both now hold an opinion, it shall remain unspoken. It is suffice to say that we are aware."

William extended his arm to shake Andrew's hand. "Thank you Sir." His grip was strong, genuine.

It was strange how even now, after so long, a connection, any connection to Annie Eddowes stirred some inexplicable emotion within Smithfield.

"Until Monday William, 7-30 sharp."

He had cautioned this younger man to be decent, moral, yet his own thoughts lacked integrity. Another man's wife. Andrew turned to watch through the window William's progress across the yard. There were times when it proved difficult to hold faith with a better tomorrow, that brighter day. It felt unjust, that Basil Stanford should have outlived Henry Wicks. Ploughing all his capital into the project at Mapperley, Henry had brought pressure to bear on the directors, constantly calling for management decisions to create a greater prospect of employment long term, even if it meant smaller dividends for investors in the early years. Basil Stanford had been vociferous in his condemnation of the authorities' decision to grant a licence for the open cast extraction of coal at Mapperley. It allowed serious competition to his own operations but just as Henry Wicks had predicted, Stanford couldn't now afford any strike action at the pit. Production needed to be without interruption and so his tactics of the past, which had brought the miners to their knees and to capitulation, instead griped Basil's own stomach through their inertness and pressured his blood vessels through frustration. Yet Stanford outlived Henry by almost three years. Andrew had stood at his friend's funeral service that January of 1939 questioning in his mind why? Why was the good man taken while one so unscrupulous lived on. It was not until the September of that same year, declaration of war, that Andrew was able to reconcile his concerns. Henry had not lived to witness yet again that exodus of young men, that wanton waste of potential which had so preyed on his mind after the carnage of the last war.

How long might it be before William Eddowes received call up papers Andrew could not know, the textile trade was not a reserved occupation. Whatever happened the devious Birkett must not be allowed to wrap his talons around William's family. "Never." That note of his strong conviction erupted from deep inside Andrew like a stamp of endorsement, just as William strode through the gates and was gone.

"Poor kid, in hospital for Christmas an' at this rate she must wonder if she'll still be there next Christmas."

Edna studied the potato in her hand as though it were a rare diamond, before putting it back in the bucket with a sigh. Annie recognised the thought process, it was one adopted by most women, that earnest consideration given to all food, 'should I save that for tomorrow'? Edna had apparently come down in favour of holding on to her 'diamond' for another day.

"Archie must really love our Myra, there's not a day goes by that 'e don't go an' see 'er an' yet she's forever tellin' 'im to clear off. She don't mean it I s'pose. Mr.Bob Bob keeps remindin' us to disregard 'er low moments, so that's what Archie does, Myra shouts at the lad, 'e ignores 'er an' carries on, but I feel for 'im, I really do."

Edna sliced a carrot into the pan of soup, the marrowbone, which had simmered over the range most of the previous day, now sat on an enamel plate awaiting Billy's expertise. It was a marvel to Edna how, with only one hand, her Billy could achieve to pick the bone bare of 'tuffy', as folk referred to the gristly residues still adhering after cooking. 'Best of it', he'd declare, licking his fingers.

"Myra is making progress Edna," said Annie. "Given the extent of damage to her leg it's sure to take time and as Mr.Shilling explained, the procedure of skin grafting has to be carried out in stages. The physiotherapist is working on her muscles to limit the loss of strength due to her immobility but that will return when her flesh is healed."

"You sound just like Smithfield, 'e's called 'ere nearly every week since the accident an' that's what 'e tells me an'all. Myra 'ad a beautiful arrangement o' flowers delivered 'twas 'im as sent 'em. I hope William shows 'is gratitude, knowin' the way 'is mind works 'e's less likely to acknowledge Smithfield's decency than 'e is to consider the man a soft touch." Edna put the lid down on the pan forcefully creating a clatter.

"Even William must learn from his mistakes, he seems suitably humbled. I've sensed for some time that he carries a worry about with him. Mr.Stanford was far from being a straightforward character and all William's hope of advancement came to nought. I know Celia is relieved that the association is over, she had always held reservations." Inwardly Annie awarded her daughter in law much credit for having such good judgement.

Florence had confided in Annie that the content of Basil's Will was as she feared. Now Florence sought advice of one Julian Russe at the office of Meakin and Kirk. Indeed, it seemed previously routined, inconspicuous folk now held regular counsel with the legal profession. Florence through her determination to seek a fair outcome for all three of her daughters, Annie herself as an executor of Davina's Estate and now Billy and Edna. Advised to speak with a solicitor on Myra's behalf over compensation for her injuries and time spent in hospital, they had nervously placed their trust in Alex Chaucer. Edna had said to Annie, 'we'll go wi' your lot'. It had amused Annie, the remark somehow implied that she was a registered member of the firm yet at every meeting with Nigel Caffin Annie's nervousness grew no less. For Billy it had been particularly difficult, aware of the lorry driver's distress at the news of his son's death, Billy constantly reminded himself that his own daughter, while seriously injured, was alive and safe. He was fearful of what a solicitor might cost, as Billy had never had occasion to cross the threshold of this elite profession he could only imagine a grandeur to complement the wisdom of those sages within, all to be financed and maintained from hefty fees. 'It is my task Mr.Dodds, to secure from Steadman's insurers a just sum in acknowledgement of their client's liability. As hauliers of heavy goods they carry the legal requirement of cover. Also taken into account will be the costs to you, which must be met through the amount of compensation agreed in settlement. Your daughter is entirely blameless, as established by the police through the witness statements. The courts will no doubt show a measure of sympathy to the driver of the lorry, I would be surprised if a custodial sentence was imposed. However, it is by the grace of God no one was killed in the accident. His licence to drive will be taken from him for a considerable period of time and in respect of heavy goods vehicles, may well be permanently denied. Hugh Steadman I believe to be an honest man, his insurance company will respond to our claim without impediment from him'. Yet still Billy struggled with the nature of it, Edna too felt compassion, the young man killed at Tobruk, his mam, the driver's wife, what an agony of torment must be hers. But Myra would be in hospital for a very long time, her leg would be horrifically scarred, for one so young it was a devastating chapter of life that could never be erased. For her sake they must follow advice and pursue compensation, what was done could not be undone but a little money to help Myra get back on her feet was surely not too much to ask.

"What time is your bus tomorrow?" Asked Edna as she pulled the pan of soup further over the heat.

Annie was going to Ruddington, to bring the children home. Not just for Christmas but for the foreseeable future. Many families were of the same mind. It had been relatively quiet in Nottingham, the young ones were missed too much, it was time they came home.

"I'm catching the early one, I shall have to spend some time with Seth and his family, they have been kindness itself," said Annie.

"Susie's only 'ad 'em home a week an' already they're spoiled rotten, Rosie's the same, anybody'd think they'd been to Timbuktu instead of a few miles away." Edna gathered up the peelings for the compost heap, cussing the one that managed to fall to the flags at her feet. "The soddin' floor's a lot further down than it used to be." Edna put one hand at the pit of her back and stretched herself.

Annie chuckled. "I suppose grandma hasn't given any treats to Cathy and Gillian since they got back, not as much as a sherbet bonbon."

Edna huffed and changed the subject. "Any news on the sale of Davina's house?"

"No, as far as I'm aware the agents have conducted only three viewings and no offers were made. Hilda and I went to the house last Thursday, to check that all was well. It has a curious smell, not damp or musk but the smell of emptiness. Even though Davina and Mrs.Pooley barely occupied all of the space, there were always familiar scents. The beeswax on the stair rail, sandalwood from the dusting powder Davina used about her person, a faint odour of camphor when Mrs.Pooley had been checking the curtains and pelmets for moths and always in the room where Davina spent most of her time, a telltale hint of sweetness from the barley sugars and butterscotch she would suck in preference to a meal during the later months of her life. Yet when I go into the bedroom I can still smell the white hyacinths, their blooms were just beginning to fade the night she died, that night of the bombing. It was those scented flowers that kept me company, I truly believed that nothing and no one could disturb the peace within that room, the might of the Luftwaffe, the zeal of Goering, our sanctuary was impenetrable, Davina, the hyacinths and I would be perfectly safe."

"Oh bugger," said Edna, "the bloody sink's blocked again, I told Billy it needed doin'." She let out a long breath of exasperation, then reached into the pocket of her pinafore for a cigarette. "It's the first one today so don't look at me all disapprovin' Annie Eddowes, there's nowt worth mentionin' to eat an' besides it soothes me nerves, I wish I'd started smokin' a ciggy when me monthlies went haywire, it 'ould 'ave saved poor Billy a mighty load of earache. I used to feel fit to commit murder some days." Edna struck a match, lit the cigarette and drew on it. "I know what yer mean about the smell of an empty house. We 'ad to move out all o' mam's things when she died, landlord giv' us ten days to do it, 'e wanted to let the place again as soon as 'e could. She didn't 'ave much really, Ada, Vera an' meself boxed up all the small stuff an' the few bits o' furniture got spread around the family. I went back there on me own, the night afore we 'ad to give ol' man Templeton the keys. Only two weeks before it 'ad smelled o' mam, she liked Pears soap to wash 'erself with an' regularly polished 'er shoes wi' Cherry Blossom. 'Edna' she'd say, ''tis a mark o' respectability to walk out in shiny shoes'. I hated polishin' the damn things, that's why the first pair I bought meself wer' brown suede. We 'ad to leave the curtains, part o' the tenancy agreement, I put me face into the folds o' the pair at 'er bedroom window but it wer' gone, that smell o' childhood, of home, nothin' left. That night mam's little house smelled o' nowt but Templeton's greasy palms, lurkin' somewhere close by, waitin' to grab 'is bloody keys. The curtains wer' wet through when I finally walked away, I'd cried me eyes out." Edna stood by the back door sending the smoke from her cigarette out into the yard. "I'll 'ave a go at that sink in a minute, I feel like givin' summat a good clout. Mr.Bob Bob is takin' another lot o' skin from Myra's good leg tomorrow, Nellie Draper's got one o' them plungers, that soddin' sink can look out."

Maggie's eldest daughter Jennifer had completed her first twelve months of nurses training, now off duty until the week after Christmas she'd decided to travel with aunty Annie to the farm. A natural curiosity for the place to which her younger sister had been evacuated grew in Jennifer with each letter Amy wrote. Her early communications had revealed a measure of homesickness but now aged thirteen and the eldest of the three entrusted to the care of Seth and Doris Eames, Amy had found self confidence, observing the work at the farm and hurrying to help when school was finished for the day. Gradually her letters changed to lively accounts of the animals and the harvest, even describing in detail the milking and lactation. Maggie recognised the happiness behind her daughter's words, returning to the town, to that very different environment, would Amy now miss life at Ruddington. Toby had teased her, 'unless we get a sow for the back yard my love, I reckon our Amy will abandon lessons, tell a fib about her age and join the Land Army'.

Catching the early bus had proved sensible, it wasn't over full with passengers standing in the aisle as was so often the case when folk began travelling to places of work, as they would be in about an hour's time. Annie sat with a large bag on her lap containing some Christmas gifts for Seth's family. It had caused her much pondering, what best to give them, they appeared to live simply and modestly, most food items were limited by rationing, in fact the farm probably had more access to fresh vegetables, milk and eggs than did the shop at Gregory Street. Annie felt satisfied that the things she had chosen would bring pleasure and she was quite sure that the children would take delight in presenting the gifts to their new found family, for indeed Seth was family, many times Annie had heard Sarah speak of her uncle Moses and aunt Pearl and always in a most colourful narrative.

"Have you heard from George?" Jennifer's enquiry was natural enough but it sent a wave of anxiety through Annie nonetheless.

"Not since he wrote that his company was bound for the Middle East. I remember from when Charles was in Egypt the last time, his first letter took ages to arrive. John has six days leave but in the new year he's to be deployed to Castle Bromwich. His aptitude for engineering has made him a likely asset to the work force at the aerodrome factory where they make the Spitfires and Lancasters."

Annie clutched at the bag on her knees as the bus pulled up sharply to pick up a man running and holding out his arm in an attempt not to miss his ride to work. The conductor could be heard saying.

"You're cutting it fine today Mickey, asleep on your shirt tail was she?" The breathless Mickey simply grinned in reply and virtually fell onto the seat opposite Annie and Jennifer. The laces in his boots, as yet undone and his jacket fastened on the wrong button did suggest a hasty dash for the bus. After a couple of minutes catching his breath, he leaned down to tie up his loose laces, chuckled and turning to Jennifer said.

"Nine o' the little buggers, our Judy's 'ad, nine, all brown an' white, last one popped out no more than quarter hour ago."

Jennifer's expression must have shown her curiosity.

"Springer Spaniel, our Judy's a Springer, first time for 'er, the father's one o' them league o' nations, I reckon 'e's put it about a bit, that bugger's all brown an' there's a few paddin' about our way as look like 'im, must be summat in the water at West Bridgford, they say the same about a few o' the blokes an'all. Nine, just fancy that, she's only got eight nipples but I reckon she'll do alright. I've told the missus to make our Judy some porridge, if a Tommy can march on porridge then I reckon a bitch ought to make milk enough even if she is a tit short."

Jennifer turned to Annie with a smile, then back to the animated Mickey. "Congratulations to Judy and in time for Christmas too."

The young man's obvious delight was strangely encouraging and Jennifer's own eagerness at the prospect of seeing her sister again and the farming relatives set her legs swinging to and fro below the seat, just as they had done in childhood at times of simple contentment.

"A Christmas card came yesterday from Jean," said Annie, "dear Nora tries so hard to persuade her to leave London and come back to Nottingham, I'm sure Nora feels lonely at Mitchell Street, all those memories of a time when that small house was filled with family."

"Mam's had a card from aunty Jean too," said Jennifer, "I know mam worries about her, it's a pretty card but signed simply 'Jean', no other wording at all, was yours like that?"

Annie nodded and sighed. "Yes, just her name, she'd written nothing more."

Mr.Hymer had died at a great age, his wife within twelve months of her husband. Nora's services were no longer required so she had returned to No.69 Mitchell Street where perhaps fate had meant her to be. Soon afterwards Sarah became unwell, her condition deteriorated quite rapidly. Nora cared for her mother through those last months until Sarah passed away, peacefully in the familiar surroundings of home.

Randall Tennyson had died suddenly of a heart attack the previous year, so when in due course war broke out and London suffered the devastating blitz, Nora had written to her sister Jean begging her to come home, to leave the troubled Capital. Jean's letter in reply had reduced Nora to tears.

A bomb had fallen in a churchyard in East London narrowly missing the church building but leaving a large crater where once had lain the remains of four Shoreditch parishioners. Resting at the bottom of the crater, splattered by loose earth and tarnished with age, a brass breast plate from a coffin, in every other way undamaged, the name upon it easily legible. The cruel event had been reported in The Telegraph and read over and over by Jean Tennyson. Since then she had been unable to drive from her mind the notion that such an assault by Hitler's bombers could strike at the cemetery where Randall was buried. Telling Jean that if it was going to happen, then it would, whether she remained in London or moved away, at the time had been considered too insensitive by her sisters but the pleas for Jean to come home were made regularly. She had joined The Women's Voluntary Service and worked tirelessly to help those she could in whatever way she could. Nora's letters, those appeals made by the others had failed to convince Jean that she was needed in Nottingham just as much.

Annie and Jennifer were now only one stop away from their destination. Doris Eames had been insistent, 'what time does your bus get to the end of the lane, we shall come to meet you'?

The light snowfall of the previous week had melted away, replaced by wind and rain but the last two days had broken clear and bright with no more than breeze enough to put a blush on the children's cheeks. Annie was thankful, collecting the children in this weather, especially as Doris was determined to meet them, seemed less fraught. Samuel was prone to a chesty cough when harsh winter elements prevailed at length and Marie had struggled all last Christmas with tonsillitis. However, news from the farm had been reassuring, every letter conveying the children's happiness and good health. Annie so looked forward to seeing them, especially Samuel of course.

Charles had surprised her with his remark, which came out of the blue just as she was leaving to meet Jennifer. 'I'll take Mathew and Samuel into town tomorrow to choose some Meccano'. Annie had wanted to respond with, 'what about David'? But in truth, at not yet five years of age, Hilda's little boy was probably too young for a Meccano set, and Annie had no wish to shatter the fragile calm. Hilda too, for the sake of her nephew of whom she was very fond would say, 'don't upset the apple cart mam, let Samuel come home to a peaceful place'.

As the bus began to slow they could see a few yards ahead a group of people waving, jumping up and down, all calling out in their excitement. "Grandma, grandma." Annie heard Samuel's voice above the others as she stepped down from the bus, don't cry you silly old woman, she told herself, but taking the boy in her arms she held not just her grandson but his dad too, she swallowed hard on lumps of emotion.

Marie was suddenly overcome with crying, tears pouring down her face, "There, there my love, don't take on so, we're all feelin' any old how this mornin', I expect even uncle Seth'll be cryin' an'all afore the day's out."

Doris wiped Marie's face with a hanky and planted a kiss on her forehead. Amy grabbed her sister's arm and pulled her close, clinging on tight as though she'd retrieved a stray, then declared.

"Bluebell has mastitis in one quarter so we have to wrap her teat in really hot, wet cloths, like a poultice and strip that quarter every hour, uncle Seth says I have the gentle touch, that's why Bluebell stands quiet for me but fidgets when he does it."

Doris's own three children had walked the lane to meet them, a sturdy looking lad of a similar age to Amy, another boy, much leaner and bespectacled and the youngest, a girl with a mop of tight, blond curls, for all the world looking like a character from the cover of a Lucy Attwell story book.

"Come along the kettles on the side and there's a tray of lardy cake keepin' warm in the slow oven. They'll want to show you their favourite animals and believe you me they've got a whole lot of 'em," said Doris with a chuckle.

Samuel held Annie's hand, not so much to be led she sensed, but to lead.

"Olive has ten babies, four girls and six boys," he said as he skipped along beside her.

"They're not called babies, they're piglets, four gilts and six boars." Amy corrected Samuel but in a kindly, informative way. In his enthusiasm it appeared not to register as he tugged on Annie's sleeve and said.

"We must come back to the farm in February, that's when Amber will have her babies and I have to put the dab of iodine on their bellybuttons."

Annie listened to Samuel's lively chatter and wondered how far a Meccano set might go toward replacing all of the activities and discoveries Seth's farm had obviously brought to the child.

Marie now having lost her weepiness and not to be outdone declared her skills with the poultry.

"One of the White Leghorns got egg bound and I had to hold her vent over a pan of steam then massage her undercarriage until she shed it."

At last the farm came into view and by the time they reached the milk stand, Seth stood in the middle of the yard with a grin on his face from one sideburn to the other. The farm dog leapt down from the steps of the barn and raced over to greet them.

"Get down yer daft animal," said Doris, rubbing her hand vigorously over its shaggy head and ears, effectively encouraging its exuberance.

Seth looked upon Jennifer and immediately laid his strong hand on her shoulder. "My dear we're delighted to meet you, it's a grand day, come in and take some hospitality. God is good, we've food enough for all, The Lord'll provide for them as trust his word."

Inside the farmhouse was warm and welcoming, a holly bough hung over the mantel and figures of the nativity stood below. Christmas cards perched about the room, over the tops of pictures, along the heavy velveteen pelmet of indistinguishable colour, so influenced had it become by the quiet progression of age, several adorned the top of a brightly polished organ, its sheen emphasised by the winter sunshine that streamed in through the window on the opposite wall.

Doris soon had a brew of tea ready and the wonderful aroma that escaped from the slow oven, the instant she opened the door to retrieve a tray of lardy cake stirred a memory deep within Annie, how Sarah baked each day for the 'Boucher Brigade', her efforts tireless, and the rate at which it was consumed.

"When we've had a good warm and put somethin' in our bellies the young ens'll show you around. I don't believe there's a square inch o' this place they don't know like the back o' their hands," said Doris as she topped up the tea pot.

"Before all that the children have something for you, for all of you."

Annie beckoned Samuel, Marie and Amy to come to her and whispered in their ears, whereupon they delved into Annie's bag and in turn, delivered to the intended recipient each of the wrapped presents from within.

"Open them, do open them so we can see what's inside." Samuel's spontaneous reaction caused a peel of laughter.

The bubbly haired youngest pulled at the paper and danced with delight at the furry, white nightdress case, in the shape of a dog with glass eyes and embroidered nose.

"Open up the buttons Wendy and see what's inside." Annie prompted the little girl to find the pretty lilac nightgown and pair of white cotton socks with the pink ribbon threaded through the tops. The lean, bespectacled boy sat on the rug gazing at an art set, paints, crayons, paper, card and two fine sable brushes.

"Is that alright Jake?" From where Annie sat she couldn't see his expression.

"It's smashin', I shall paint the old oak tree first, if you look into the branches you can make out so many things, there's a man holdin' a gun an' a bird with a long neck, where a clump of fungus grows I can see a Billy goat's head."

"Allus had a grand imagination has our Jake," said Seth, looking amused.

Arthur, the older, sturdy youth admired a brown leather belt with a strong buckle and a cap of dark tweed.

Doris's hard working fingers slowly peeled back the wrapping from around a woven knee blanket, fringed about the edges, she drew her hand over its softness and spoke with a tremor in her voice.

"I've never had a new blanket, only the ones me mam had an' them as Seth's family left here."

Seth was the last to open his parcel, almost afraid to touch with his rough skinned fingers, whatever lay beneath the paper. A grey waistcoat and silk cravat.

"For Chapel," said Annie.

She had saved all of their coupons, neither Charles nor herself were in real need of clothing and Celia had given Annie several items for Samuel, which Mathew had outgrown. Seth crossed the room and took Annie's hand.

" 'Tis a wonderful kind thing that you've done, givin' all these blessin's but the best blessin' a man could have, you granted to me these months past. I know of folk not far from this farm who worry themselves to a shadow over their absent family, who stare at the empty places at table and weep through their prayers, an' you'll understand why better than most. Seth Eames has had no one taken away from him, but three blessin's brought in. Your young 'ens have given us joy, their learnin', their willingness to help, the way they've lived an' loved with our own fills me with gratitude, I shall miss 'em."

Poor Seth was close to tears, it was a loud clatter outside and the sudden barking of the dog that saved him. Opening the door to look for the disturbance revealed a sight for sore eyes. A large Saddleback sow stood in the middle of the yard with her snout in an upturned bucket, her litter of piglets careering about the open space like they played a game of tag. The dog stood at the open gate of the yard, barking caution whenever a piglet ventured near and the potatoes, that just a few minutes earlier had occupied the bucket, one by one surrendered to the sow's appetite.

"How the dickens did Olive get out, best go take a look."

Samuel was out through the door on the heels of Seth like he'd been launched from a catapult.

"Come on babies, come, come babies." His young voice caused the sow to raise her head and for an instant to cast her gaze over her offspring. Apparently satisfied that no danger threatened she continued her pursuit of the scattered potatoes. Amy muttered her frustration.

"Piglets, they're piglets, how hard can it be to remember something so simple."

"It'll be one o' Seth's makeshift gate fasteners you may depend," said Doris pulling on her coat. "I despair of him sometimes, he'll cobble any two bits o' junk together rather than buy new. His father wer' just the same an' by all accounts so wer' his father's father. This place hangs together with bits o' rope, lengths o' wire an' chain, any old bit o' scrap he can lay his hands on."

"Blow me down," said Seth, that crafty old sow must have stood with her front feet on the gate an' nudged the dibbler with her snout."

All eyes were on the wooden gate and post, affixed to the top of each at corresponding height, a carrying handle from an old stew pot, through which had been threaded one of Seth's various potato dibblers.

"I shall have to lower the handles so's she can't reach."

Doris lifted her eyes to Heaven. "Let's take Annie and Jennifer to see if the voles are at home while the 'adjustments' are being carried out. I've lived here all these years an' never seen the little creatures before. It wer' Jake an' Samuel found 'em." On the grass by the pig pens, lay a big sombrero pig trough. "How those boys managed to lift it up I don't know but they did."

At one side could be seen a little hollow in the sod where something small had burrowed underneath. Curious at discovering this evidence of activity Jake and Samuel had used their joint strength to raise the trough sufficiently to see that in the hollow, beneath the centre of the sombrero, a nest of dried grass and fern had been meticulously made and inhabited by Pine Voles. Mainly nocturnal, today two were curled up, fast asleep.

The ensuing hour proved to be a thoroughly delightful tour of the farm. They were introduced to the animals, so many by name, they gathered eggs from the nest boxes of the chicken houses, 'fewer this time of year,' Doris had remarked. A fallen log that conveniently came to rest over a mound, Seth had sawn at both ends to create a see-saw. 'You should see the state o' the girls' drawers after a session on that', Doris had said with a note of mischief in her voice. From a sturdy branch of sycamore tree Seth had hung two lengths of rope which held a plank of wood just the right size for a swing.

"They used to get that hot back in the summer, runnin', playin', hours at a time, that Seth found a shallow wooden tub an' put it alongside the water butt. Water from the well is too valuable for them to play with, the cows alone drink gallons that has to be kept for the animals but a bucket or two of rainwater from the butt, tipped into that tub an' they could paddle to their hearts' content." Doris chuckled at the memory.

Olive and her babies were eventually returned to their pen with the gate made snout proof. Bags and cases were packed, hugs given many times over but it could be delayed no longer, it was time to leave.

"We can manage the bags very well Seth, we shall say our goodbyes here in the privacy of the farm yard rather than wave and weep at the bus stop." Annie held him tight. "Thank you both, thank you all, so much. I promise to bring them to see you as often as I can and I'm sure I'll be given no option in February when Amber has her litter. Who else could put the iodine on the bellybuttons?" They laughed bravely through the tightening emotion.

Turning to look back every few steps, they waved until the farm was out of sight. After all the chatter, the busy tongues so eager to explain and describe, now fell silent. Even Annie felt sad at leaving but it was almost Christmas, John would be home for a few precious days and word might come from George soon.

"Lets sing," she said, "what shall we sing?"

Miss Aldis at Sunday school had not been without influence on the young lives. In their cases they carried drawings and lessons from Sunday mornings spent at Chapel. It was Marie who began to sing, her choice seemed to satisfy everyone and to suit the nature of the day, from Judy's pups to sleeping voles.

"All things bright and beautiful
All creatures great and small,
All things wise and wonderful
The Lord God made them all."

Their voices filled the narrow lane as they made their way and Annie hoped that on the breeze, the sound might carry back to Seth and Doris Eames.

Marie had been safely returned to Mavis, Jennifer and Amy had boarded their bus in the city centre and Annie with Samuel, having watched 'til the bus was too far distant to see the girls anymore, walked to their stop to catch a No.56.

Annie had detected a nervousness in Samuel the closer they drew to Gregory Street. 'Please, please let Charles be in a good mood', her silent plea drove her fingers to grip more firmly the handle of the bag and that innocent young hand that placed its trust in hers.

All was quiet. Charles came through from the shop, he stood in front of them with one hand behind his back.

"I bet they don't have these at that farm." He produced a bar of Fry's Five Boys chocolate and rubbed his hand across Samuel's hair. It was enough to make the child feel less anxious.

"Thank you Granddad." Samuel offered up a nervous smile. Annie conveyed to Charles her relief, it seemed to amuse him.

"Poor grandma, I bet she can't wait to get you installed in your room again, uncle John will be here tomorrow too, that's what grandma likes, a family to cook for and fuss over, granddad on his own isn't much good is he?"

It was a question which warranted no answer and Annie quickly suggested she serve in the shop for a little while so Samuel could tell his granddad all about Ruddington and the animals, especially the pigs.

The evening passed pleasantly enough and Samuel went to bed, tired from his busy day. When Annie peeped around his bedroom door at 8o'clock he was sound asleep. Understanding of his mixed emotions at leaving the kindly Seth and those happy activities at the farm, of his coming back to Gregory Street knowing his dad would not be there, Annie determined herself to make him happy and just as she had promised , they would visit their new found family whenever they could. If only a letter would come from George, but they would begin writing one anyway, Samuel adding a few lines each day, then as soon as they had an address they could post it. Annie tried to strengthen her resolve with positive thoughts, yet her fingers trembled on the doorknob as she gently turned it, whispering.

"Sleep tight Samuel, God bless."

Charles had cashed up and delivered his usual scornful monologue on the day's takings, but Annie's mind was not receptive of it this night, she had preparations to make, however simple, Christmas was almost upon them. Charles sat in the chair by the range, his hair now grey like the faded woollen cardigan he wore over his waistcoat, the shop could strike quite chill in the evening hours at this time of year. She'd been absent all day, her tasks could wait a little longer, she should sit with him a while, keep him company if it was not his intention to go out.

"You had a visitor today, it certainly wasn't me he came to see," said Charles.

"I wasn't expecting anyone and I didn't have any call to see Nigel Caffin." Annie made a hasty mental check in case she'd overlooked an appointment in her eagerness to fetch Samuel.

"Anthony Hemsley called, to wish us the best of the season, as he was in the vicinity, or so he said. There's something about that man that makes me feel uncomfortable."

You are not the only one, thought Annie. Anthony Hemsley had called once or twice each year since he'd become involved with the mine at Mapperley, often when Charles was not at home. Annie had been thankful for the customers in and out of the shop. His manner had been correct but she'd not offered him tea, it would have granted him time in the back room and Annie held no desire to feel again his unseemly lingering hand on hers by way of his goodbye. Annie was glad to have missed him today and hoped his business affairs would not require him to be in Nottingham again at anytime soon.

"I shall go to Wollaton to collect Mathew in the morning," said Charles. Samuel can come with me, you can manage in the shop. He's not seen his aunt Celia or Emily for a long time, William might be at home, the factory at Brassington likely shut down for Christmas yesterday. Smithfield's production isn't engaged with the war effort is it so unless he's got William cleaning out his gutters or sweeping his chimneys Samuel might see his uncle." Annie bit her tongue. "Then I shall take Samuel and Mathew into town to choose their Meccano, I know you'll have already sorted something for Emily."

Still he made no mention of their grandson David and that was much harder to ignore. Annie had posted a parcel to Francis at Bonthorpe with presents for Faith and Grace and she had some stocking fillers put away for Samuel. The previous week she had given Celia a package each for Mathew and Emily. It was weeks ago that Annie had spotted in the window at Woolworths, a small, wooden train set, she'd bought it and taken it to Hilda before going home. For it to be necessary to hide, to conceal any gift destined for David Haynes dismayed Annie. Even going to see Hilda, their own daughter, Annie was ever afraid to declare to Charles. He must surely know that she went there, that she treated David in exactly the same way she treated all their grandchildren.

The propaganda posters, which appeared affixed to prominent buildings around the town with the caution, 'Careless Talk Costs Lives', seemed so apt. At Gregory Street many times the spoken word was first cautioned and then censored to avoid misery, for every day spent in misery was a cost to life. Annie got to her feet to make a cup of tea.

"Mathew and Samuel will like that, all children love to choose a treat." She said nothing more and if Charles recognised the inference, then his recognition was swiftly screened by The Evening Post, now spread before his eyes.

Ruddington felt like another world, Annie and Samuel must brace themselves until February, when Amber might deliver relief through the urgent need of Samuel to dab the iodine on her babies' bellybuttons.

CHAPTER SIX

May 1942

"I'm afraid Mrs.Stanford our hands are tied. Whilst I can fully understand the reason for which you challenge your husband's judgement, unless we are able to prove that, at the time the Will was made his mental capacity was impaired, then the law upholds his intent and we cannot contest it. The report from his doctor clearly states that Mr.Stanford was of sound mind.

We have tried repeatedly to contact your daughter Julia in Rome through a third party but to no avail and your daughter Caroline remains adamant, she will not approach her sister Patricia regarding any share of their father's Estate.

It has been five months since you first came to see me, I cannot advocate your pursuing this further at a continuing cost to yourself.

It is to your eldest daughter that you must direct your appeal. Only by achieving to persuade Mrs.Bradshaw of a more equitable agreement will you arrive at a point of some satisfaction." Julian Russe rose to his feet. "We are living in fast changing times, industries are subject to degrees of government control, warfare leaves very little untouched and when hostilities cease and peace is won, we have learned from past experience, the world cannot find its way back to the way it was. The collieries are no exception, the mining industry is possibly the most troubled, by its very nature it takes men to an unnatural place and many above ground can be too far removed from its horrors. Mrs.Bradshaw will find her charge anything but easy to understand. Nationalisation will surely come within this decade and I understand that Stafford Hinds is to retire. Your daughter may well be feeling the strain, speak with her, you are her mother after all."

"Caroline is already a widow, with two young children, is it not enough that the evil of Hitler take the life of her husband, deny her Edmund's love, must her own father be permitted to take away her hope and destroy her future too?" Florence spoke with deep resentment. "I shall go to Patricia as the voice of reason but with a resolve to match her own. For any individual to have used their mouthpiece to speak out against Basil's domination would have required mettle and as likely as not would still have proved futile. However he is dead and gone, I am not and as you so rightly point out, I am Patricia's mother when all is said and done."

Edmund's plane had been shot down over the channel when his squadron had been scrambled to intercept a German raid. That same night bombs had fallen on Birmingham and Liverpool, John Eddowes had described Highgate, an inner city area of Birmingham as, 'trod asunder by the Devil himself, Satan's every footprint defined in brick, blood and bone'.

Florence had sat with her youngest daughter willing the tears to flow, for Caroline to release all her pent up hurt. Not until the tenth day, when Edmund's personal effects were brought to Moreleigh by none other than Bill Stribley, did she cry.

Bill had been stood down for two weeks, ordered to take a break from flying. 'It was on me way, me mother lives at Radford'. Me an' your Ed used to talk about home a lot. He went to Blackmore's, I wer' at Bentinck Road School, he played piano, I play the spoons but we sang from the same hymn sheet me an' Ed'. From now on I shall sing for the both of us, he'll hear me from where he is an' when I blast the last bloody Jerry plane to Kingdom come, when there's no more o' their bomb laden Hell raisers left in the sky, you'll hear the Hallelujahs from here an'all'.

Florence had warmed to Bill Stribley, already sharing his defiance in song she now listened each day for his Hallelujahs not doubting his word and determined to proclaim a Hallelujah of her own when she achieved to prise something for Caroline and Julia from Basil's clenched fist, that same fist he'd raised to her so many times in the past. He had condescended to grant her the right to dwell in the house on Castle Road while ever she lived, although the deed of the property was to pass to Patricia on his death.

Any happy memories attached to the house were so far back in time that they were almost impossible to reach, to even briefly touch a tender moment beyond all that had transpired since. The strains of infant laughter, the soft hum of fond words were little match for the echoes of Basil's raised voice and Florence's own cries of despair. The house held no charm for her, no real sense of home, she would gladly leave that address, hand to Patricia the vacant possession but in return she wanted the parcel of land at Colver. Florence had learned that it was mined out, it was simply a small acreage of industrial site with no value below ground.

When Basil's father Claude had bought Birchdale he had paid dear but had acquired a mine with an enviable asset. Birchdale came with its own mineral rights, few mines did, and most owners paid dues to the landlords of the coal beneath.

Patricia was to inherit all of Birchdale, the family house and whatever capital Basil had at time of death, minus legal fees. The land at Colver was little enough to ask and Florence anticipated that to have free rein at Castle Road would tempt her eldest daughter to surrender Colver in exchange.

Caroline needed her mother. The two boys, Jonathon and Gregory were too young to fully comprehend what had happened to their father and grandma's presence cushioned them against the hurt, the insecurity that would invade their innocent minds if left unguarded. Caroline was grieving, her own defences alarmingly fragile, the situation drove Florence to be guardian and protector and empowered her resolve. She spent much of her time at Moreleigh, if circumstances demanded then she could occupy the small terraced house on Denman Street at a future date. Securing the land for Caroline and Julia would give them an investment, an insurance against hard times, of that Florence was convinced.

After the last war there had been a call for new housing, the need to create employment for those men, whom despite the years of marching into Hell upon Hell, miraculously returned to the life they were barely able to recognise through images of evil, which veiled their eyes whether opened or closed. At some point, when the present age of madness was ended, again would surely come the need of work to save the sanity of those men returning. Colver site might be deemed suitable for development, it was not so very far away from the existing city sprawl, it offered hope and Florence felt bound to pursue it for the sake of her two younger daughters.

"Anthony will be home within the hour, I shall speak with him about it. I cannot imagine that Edmund Tozer did not make good provision for Caroline, he must have considered the possibility of his being killed. A solicitor of all people would have the knowledge, the information to hand. Insurance, investment, all sit within the realm of the law and his personal affairs would be in order, to spare Caroline any confusion, it's what he did for other people every working day for Heaven's sake. Caroline's pension is guaranteed as a war widow."

Patricia was so 'matter of fact' Florence wanted to respond by pointing out that heading the legal department of the council, which Patricia's husband had done for many years allowed him more information 'to hand' than most, but Florence had vowed to maintain a dignified calm, not to let circumstances drive her to speak out of turn.

Patricia continued. "As for Julia, it can only be said that her marriage to an enemy of the state, as it were, is unfortunate indeed but it is hardly father's fault."

She seemed bent on rousing her mother to retaliate with angry words, yet despite feeling her skin prickle Florence instead brought up the matter of Stafford Hinds' retirement.

"Do you have a replacement in mind Patricia? The position will prove challenging I'm sure."

Florence noticed the fidgetiness in her daughter, the hesitancy, which her remark had caused. The ageing Mr.Hinds would almost certainly have been given notice.

"I have a good head for business Mother, father knew that, I won't let him down, a new broom sweeps clean."

Florence rose to her feet feeling frustrated, annoyed yet genuinely saddened by her surroundings. The room in which they'd sat was well furnished, the decoration fresh and professionally done. The mantelpiece held ornamentation that had never seen the inside of Moffat's shop and the clock chimed the quarter hour with melodious precision. The fire screen sparkled through inlay of mother of pearl and amber coloured glass and the rug at their feet boasted a deep wool pile, which all but concealed a pink sugared almond. Florence had noticed it, by the leg of a chair halfway into their conversation, she stooped to retrieve it and handed it to her daughter.

"I have been trying to think Patricia, of what it is that's unusual about this room, then it came to me, not a single photograph, you have no pictures of family, and this mislaid sugared almond is the only evidence of life. I have a photograph of your father, it was taken at one of the Lodge dinners. He looks every part the industrialist, a significant member of that man's world. I shall give it to you for the mantel. Speak with Anthony regarding Colver. I could be out of the house very soon if he is approving of my suggestion. Julian Russe at Meakin and Kirk will act on my instruction and I'm sure Neilson and Bradbury would tie it all up quite speedily in acting for you."

Florence offered a smile, Patricia returned a mere hint of one and with marked formality kissed her mother's cheek.

As she walked away from the house Florence dared to hope that a comparatively small area of spent industrial land might be considered a reasonable exchange for vacant possession at Castle Road. Patricia was her first born child, difficult to love, yet tears threatened to weaken Florence, that maternal instinct to protect, to keep from all harm, made heavy her heart and unsteady her tread. Where was Julia, was she alive, could Caroline ever be happy again, would Patricia one day reject whatever it was that made her so unkind? Florence summoned her spirit, defied the gremlins within by singing, she sang with Bill Stribley and listened for those Hallelujahs, all the way home.

Rosie took Beryl from Susie's arms, they'd taken it in turns to carry her, to save the bother of the pram on the bus. She and Susie were on their way to Wollaton, to spend an hour with Celia. Since losing her brother Edmund, Celia had struggled to maintain cheerfulness when around Mathew and Emily, concerned for her state of mind, Rosie had visited regularly, taking little Beryl with her on the pretext of needing to deposit her baby daughter in Celia's lap so's the infant could cut her teeth on someone else's nerves for a change. It was curious how the thought of easing the weariness of her best friend Rosie Spooner, served to distract and bring relief to Celia herself. The smile she gave when Rosie's voice called out "Cooee" from the back door and the two women entered with Beryl waving a child's windmill, confirmed Celia's pleasure at seeing them.

Immediately she lifted Beryl from Rosie's arms and proceeded to count the infant's teeth, prompting her to open wide her mouth, "Like this," said Celia, doing her best to demonstrate. Susie laughed aloud.

"You're as bad as Victor used to be, mam reckoned he could smell toffees a mile off, dad had only to reach into his pocket an' Victor's mouth would open as wide as mam's new tea infuser. She's convinced it's tea leaves that keep blockin' the sink, although me an' dad tip the pot in the garden. Anyway she spotted an infuser at Moffat's. Dad says it looks like a piece of surgical equipment, the spring in the hinge is so strong that when the two perforated spoons snap shut it makes him cross his legs automatically an' pour wi' sweat."

All the women chuckled and Beryl obliged, throwing open her mouth like a baby bird at the sight of a worm.

"Lots of them, teeth enough to master a custard cream." Celia kissed the child and put her on the floor to crawl. She turned to Susie. "How is Myra? I hear news through William's mother normally but I've not seen Annie for several days, I expect you know that Samuel has been ill with chicken pox, so we've avoided mixing the children. He's almost over it now I believe."

"We all had it years ago," said Susie, "Liza's pox mark is right in the middle of her cheek so when she goes to a dance, or somewhere a bit special she applies a beauty spot to cover it up. First time dad saw it he licked his finger an' tried to rub it off, thought it was a speck of mud thrown up by a passing cyclist. Poor ol' dad doesn't understand make-up. Myra's a bit brighter now, she was very subdued when Archie left, I think she regretted all the times she'd shouted at him. After his letter came an' she knew where he was she perked up. Fancy him meetin' up wi' Jack Wainright, I don't suppose they're allowed to reveal much army stuff in their letters home but Cairo seems less alarming than some places. Charles Eddowes was there for ages during the last war an' he came home unharmed. I know that bears little relevance now but everyone has to cling to somethin'.

Harry Ollerton got his papers last week, Liza says she'll go mad if she has to stay in the house on her own so she's volunteerin' for the land army. Mam's all worried up, she's told her it won't just be growin' potatoes. Liza planted the spuds at the allotment one spring, to help dad when Victor was laid up with a throat infection. That same year dad had a bumper crop so now she's convinced herself that the land army needs her expertise. Mam just wants everyone to stay close, she'd lock us all in No.24 for the duration of the war if she had her way.

There's a lovely old chap in the hospital with Myra an' now she's allowed outside in her wheelchair he pushes her around the grounds with his belly. Barney has a fish and chip shop, one day he slipped an' fell forward, both hands went into the boiling drippin', took the skin off to the bone, his hands are completely encased in bandages. He and Myra make for an unlikely sight, Barney must be well into his sixties an' there's our Myra only twenty three. First time I saw them goin' along the path together I cried, but we've given them nick names 'Barney an' Clyde', even Myra chuckles when we call out to them if they're outside when we go to visit."

Celia made some tea and Beryl, having munched and sucked her way through two custard creams, sat on the hearth rug biting on a battle scarred teething ring, which had already served its purpose for her brothers, the item was so clearly vintage it was surely worthy of heirloom status.

"Mam bought 'er a posh new one from Burton's, but would yer believe, the little fuss pot won't use it, throws it down an' cries til I let 'er 'ave this ol' thing."

Rosie tried to prise the teething ring from Beryl's fingers but met with stiff resistance, so for the sake of peace, left the child to her chosen comforter.

"How's your mother Celia?" Asked Susie, "and William does he still have work at Brassington. Joe overheard someone talkin' about things at the factory, Smithfield hasn't managed to secure any government orders, such a lot of military uniform is produced in Leicester."

Celia moved her cup and saucer beyond Beryl's reach and sighed.

"I know William is anxious, the Celanese range and the Vyella keep them tickin' over but there's no more cotton, the government has taken over all existing supplies of cotton. A lot of the time William is doing other things, last week he was oiling the oak floors at Mr.Smithfield's house between helping Robert Armistead in the print shop. I don't ask him about his work, if he volunteers to tell me then of course I'm always interested and concerned but William doesn't like to be pressed on the subject." Another sigh erupted before she spoke again. "Mother is getting worse, Mrs.Brewer does her best but I'm sure her patience is tried to the limit some days. Last week, in the middle of the night, she heard sounds downstairs. When she crept down to look she found mother in the kitchen, spreading flour over every surface. Her mind works in such strange ways, she obviously has an awareness of the fact the country is at war, bless her, she told Mrs.Brewer that if under the cover of darkness the enemy invaded and soldiers broke into the house to steal food, then they would know because of all the tracks and disturbance in the flour.

Loosing Edmund must have affected her, yet when we told her she seemed not to take it in. I thought it best not to tell her but the doctor said as she was quite rational at times, as Edmund's mother she had a right to know. Perhaps I've just happened to see mother on her bad days as I've not found her to be rational in months."

The women chatted for a while until Beryl became sleepy.

"We best get back, there's a funeral at St.Andrew's 2o/clock, Tommy will be home for a bite to eat before that," said Rosie, gathering the teething ring from where Beryl's little fingers had let it fall, just inside the fender.

"Joe has two to collect from the hospital mortuary, I don't know when he'll be home." Susie got to her feet just as the letter box on Celia's front door clattered.

"You may as well go out of the front door," said Celia, casting her eyes at the post that lay on the mat.

"Oh no, we mustn't do that," said Rosie, "It's bad luck to leave through a different door to the one you came in by."

Celia smiled at the odd superstition and crossed the small hallway to pick up the two envelopes. The white one she recognised as being an early birthday card for Emily, the second, a manila envelope caused her to catch her breath. Addressed to William Charles Eddowes, an official franked stamp in the top right hand corner and across the top, On His Majesty's Service in bold print. Rosie held Beryl, now fast asleep in her arms and Susie stood motionless, all three women stared down at the sombre , brown envelope. There seemed to be no words appropriate to utter, not a single one.

Annie handed Samuel his clean pyjamas, pleased at the need for only a couple of dabs of calamine lotion on the last few itchy spots. Watching him read the letter from his dad with pure delight showing in his eyes at every word, made Annie feel soothed.

Charles had complained of feeling unwell, declared he must be sickening for something throughout the week that Samuel had been poorly. Annie had assured him that he couldn't catch chicken pox twice and that he had almost certainly had it as a child, the pox mark on one side of his forehead, above the right eye, was the tell-tale scar, which nature seemed inclined to leave for future reference. At last Charles' anxiety had begun to ease, Samuel had slept well the last three nights and his rash had all but disappeared.

George had written earlier in the year from Libya, typically he had mentioned nothing of his work or actual circumstances but filled the paper with descriptive passages about the indigenous people, the different food to be found there, the desert horses, or camels to be correct, how those very foreign animals were so expressive through their ambulant jaws and fluttering eyelashes. In the letter, which arrived this morning he told of his new found friend, 'Lenny', a mongrel that wandered in and out of the camp every day. The cynical among them voiced their suspicions, Lenny was a Kraut, a spy, his amiable approach and wagging tail had been drilled into him whilst confined in a secure bunker back in 'The Fatherland'. George was of a different belief, Lenny was a free agent, not answerable to any authority but ready to give his loyalty to those who scratched his ears and produced from their pocket, a tit-bit of human kindness.

George had met and spoken with William Haynes, now Sergeant Haynes. 'To find a chap from home gives such a boost to the spirits, it's hard to put into words, but if I had to liken it to anything, then it would be the first time I went to Skendleby and saw Freddy waiting at the station'. Annie seized upon that passage of the letter and by evening knew it by heart. She tucked Samuel into bed, prayers said and the precious letter tucked under his pillow.

Charles was tallying up, it seemed to take less and less time but Annie tried to remind him of the fact that they were fortunate, income may be much reduced but every day something trickled in and their outgoings were modest.

She began to prepare their meal, with meat so limited it seldom took very long. The back door opened and William stepped inside.

Over the years Annie had experienced all the changing moods of William Eddowes, she could predict with considerable accuracy whether his approach was light or heavy, he didn't need to speak, just the slope of his shoulders, the weight of his tread were indications enough for her to relax or tense. Annie strengthened herself with the thought of George and Lenny sharing an allegiance in far away Libya as she felt herself tense, William's tread was heavy and his shoulders bore the weight of the world.

"Have you had your tea? If not there's enough for you to eat with your dad and me," said Annie trying to sound cheerful.

"Is dad in the shop?" William's gaze was set at the door, he could hear the sound of coins chinking against one another, Charles had completed his tally and now let the float slip through his fingers, back into the till. "I've to present myself at Retford within a week, the papers came this morning."

Annie caught her breath, put down the bread knife and crossed the room to where he stood.

"I am sorry William, and I know your dad will be upset, he worries far more than he lets on, about John at the factory, all industrial sites are targets, and George, I'm sure he's anxious for George too. But for you to go away as well, he really will struggle with that. Celia must be distressed, I shall go to see her tomorrow, sit down, your dad's here now."

Charles stood in the doorway looking perplexed, even he could recognise the signs of trouble and with William no longer working for Basil Stanford, his eldest son's situation was sure to be less reliable, that was Charles' misguided opinion.

"What is it?" He said. "Money matters or your call up?"

Annie cast a sharp look at Charles. William raised his face from where he sat staring down at the pattern on the tablecloth, and looked directly into Annie's eyes.

"Both," he said in a voice feeble from awkwardness and fear, "both, it's both." William poured out his miseries. "Army pay won't keep us going, the bank will foreclose, I'll lose the house."

Charles remained silent, Annie was the first to respond.

"I'm sure we can work something out, can't we Charles?"

"How much money do you imagine this shop makes in wartime? It would leave us with nothing, the takings some days are hardly worth my time in counting. I thought Stanford paid you a fortune, the way you spoke while you were driving him about the place gave the impression you were minting it."

William was in despair. "I could ask Smithfield, I think he'd let me have some money to pay off the loan and then I'd owe him, but he'd wait, I could tell him about Davina's Will, that he would get his money back with interest when I receive my share, it can't be too long now surely."

"You can't let William approach Mr.Smithfield Charles, we must have some money put by, even if the loan is only reduced by half, then the monthly payments will be less accordingly and we would be able to meet them through the income from the shop." Annie pressed Charles to answer.

"You'll have to stop buying things for the young ones then, Celia would understand, and Haynes should be capable of providing for his own, do you think I don't know when you slope off to Forest Road."

Charles' tongue dripped bitterness but Annie kept her own in check for William's sake, she needed to pour oil on the water before things got worse.

I know Nigel Caffin has converted all of Davina's bonds to cash and closed her bank accounts. The monies now sit in a client account, it only remains for the house to be sold. If I speak with him he may be able to advance a sum to William. Handley's has been paid, there will be fees to the property agent when they introduce a buyer and the solicitor's fees of course will be a substantial amount but if the law permits, William might receive a part sum of his share now."

William looked at Annie as though she'd appeared on Angel's wings, a messenger of salvation sent by The Almighty.

"The others wouldn't have to be told about it would they?" He said, emotion driving his fingers to pull at the cuff of his jacket and his voice to raise to almost childlike tone.

"I don't see why Mr.Caffin would need to inform your brothers and sister, ultimately it will make no difference, you will all receive an equal share."

Charles absentmindedly chinked the salt pot against the pepper. "Do you know which regiment you're to join?" Apparently Charles had accepted the proposed solution to William's financial dilemma and now moved on to other concerns.

"I don't know any details yet," said William, "it just states military service so I presume it could be Army, Navy or Air Force. Perhaps they let me choose, draw a ticket out of a hat."

His attempt at making light of it only served to convince Annie of his state of nervousness.

"Have something to eat William," she said trying to inject a measure of normality.

"No, I best get back to Celia, she'll have plated something up, I told her I wouldn't be long." He stood but Charles remained seated.

"It won't matter which lot you go with, war begins and ends like everything else, who stands beside you makes little odds, you'll wear the same uniform, sleep the same, eat the same, swear the same. Your mam will speak to 'whotsisname' in the morning. Tell Mathew I'll take him to Wollaton Park on Saturday, Samuel can come too, he's no longer infectious, we'll look for the red squirrels by the lake."

Charles spoke as though the previous half hour had been spent in idle chatter, nothing at all out of the ordinary. Annie went with William to the back yard.

"A letter came from George this morning, I would give it you to read but Samuel has gone to bed with it under his pillow."

"Celia doesn't know about the loan business, you won't say anything when you see her tomorrow will you? Her mother's dementia gets worse by the day and she still grieves for Edmund, she's enough to worry about as it is."

William's appeal, Annie hoped might be genuine and not simply designed to spare his embarrassment. He'd obviously said nothing in the past to his wife of their situation, Celia was completely unaware .

"Not if you don't want me to, and yes, Celia does have more than enough to trouble her, but never forger William, that as your wife, as mother of your children she is entitled to be consulted on important decisions, those which affect you all as a family. I shan't speak of it but in the future, share your thoughts with her, your intentions, she's a bright young woman."

"The future!" Said William, "What will be the future? What indeed was the past?"

Annie found his words curious. "What do you mean?" She asked.

"Oh, nothing, just thinking about the last war, what a waste all that was," William lied, his remark had actually stemmed from Basil Stanford's revelation. If this war was to take him to some foreign place, there to be shot or blown to oblivion, then he would never truly know, 'what was the past'.

"Try not to worry, I shall go to Nigel Caffin first thing," said Annie. She kissed his cheek. "It will be alright, I'm sure it will."

She couldn't know just how much her words reassured William. From as long ago as childhood and throughout all the years since, whenever this woman whom he called mam had said to him, 'it will be alright', it had proved to be so, never had she told him an untruth.

"I will read George's letter when I come next time." He smiled nervously and hesitated as though he were about to say something more, then turned and walked away.

Annie sat with her fingers crossed beneath the edge of Nigel Caffin's desk. She had enquired after his son, still serving in Africa and was relieved to learn that all was well up to his last letter.

Nigel Caffin leaned back in his chair and rubbed his chin as if summoning inspiration, eventually he smiled across at Annie and sat forward in more positive mode.

“What you propose is somewhat irregular but I can think of no actual impediment in law provided the other beneficiaries are in agreement.”

“William is hoping it may not be necessary for his brothers and sister to know about his problems of finance. It could be looked upon as false pride but I’m sure you can understand his sense of failure. I don’t believe that Freddy, George, John or Hilda would for one moment, have the slightest concern over the arrangement.” Annie’s expression entered the plea on William’s behalf.

“Well, given recent developments, of which I was about to inform you, I think we can at this point grant an advance on William’s share of the Estate. In fact the letter I received yesterday from the property agent has come at just the right time. They have a buyer for the house in The Park, at the full asking price. There is no reason why the conveyance cannot begin right away, the purchase is not reliant on the prior sale of any other property, a cash buyer in other words.”

Annie’s relief was immense, sad though she would be to know finally that Davina’s house had gone to strangers, given what had transpired over the last twenty four hours she could feel no other than blesséd relief.

“That is such good news Mr.Caffin,” she said, “is it a local family?”

“Not a family at all, not even a man and wife, as I understand the buyer is a single gentleman.”

Nigel Caffin proceeded to rummage through some papers at his side on the desk, while Annie puzzled over why a man on his own would want to buy such a large property.

“Ah yes, here’s the letter, it states the gentleman’s name somewhere.” He appeared to scan the page of type until locating the information. “Yes, Hemsley, it’s one, Anthony Hemsley.”

CHAPTER SEVEN

Late June

George had three times begun to write a letter home and each time abandoned his attempt as the right words proved hard to find. A nine year old boy should receive only happy, suitably informative lines from his dad. As for his mam, George could only ever feel protective of his mam, she should look forward to his letters in the knowledge that their content would hearten her. So often the atmosphere at Gregory Street was oppressive, whether consciously or otherwise, Charles could leaden the spirit of those around him until not even the sun's rays could penetrate the grey.

Two weeks earlier George had been wounded in the left shoulder during an exchange of fire between the Allies and the Axis forces. Rommel had launched another offensive in the everlasting see-saw of battles to hold the strategically vital port of Tobruk. The bullet had buried itself in the fleshy area between his upper arm and collar bone, but on removal left no permanent damage to the muscle or nerves.

When the 'jolly them along' medic at the field hospital said, 'they'll let you have the bullet as a souvenir to carry home to your lad if you tell 'em', George had been unable to imagine anything he would want less. A souvenir of this man made horror that day on day cried out for a God, any man's God, to lay his hand upon the air and command the peace.

Now awaiting the doctor to grant his discharge from the hospital, George sat by the window, looking out at Cairo, trying to avert his thoughts from the faces, voices of those men he may never see again, the writing pad on his lap bare of words still.

It was Jack Wainwright who'd brought the news, himself shaking from a raised temperature brought on by an infected flesh wound but lucid and needing to talk. 'It wer' bedlam, bloody bedlam George. You must 'ave done same as me when yer wer' a kid, rolled a big stone just to see all the bugs an' beetles in a frenzy once they wer' uncovered. Well the poor bloody reinforcements barely had time to get under their stone afore it all kicked off. Rommel had got his own an' the Eye-ties right where he wanted 'em an' we didn't see it comin'. I found meself wi' two Gurkhas an' a Queen's Highlander, like that daft party game, when the lights go out an' everybody gets mixed up in the dark an' yer have to guess who's goin' to be sittin' next to yer when the lights go back on. I couldn't understand a bloody word the Scot spoke, I reckon his tongue had been stuck down the end of his bagpipes for too long. Could have been Hindu-bloody Stani for all I could tell. How the four of us ended up where we did I shall never know. Nearly all of 'em captured, only a mongreled up bunch o' charmed life bastards includin' me missed Rommel's grapple'.

Jack had gone on to reveal that Sergeant Haynes was not among the mongrels, nor was Roley. George had befriended Roland Cheeseman, a butcher's assistant from Derby. Married to Evie with a son and daughter his abiding fear was not of death nor wounding but of capture, of being taken prisoner by the Germans.

Roley when a young boy, had been circumcised, 'doctor told me mam that me foreskin wer' a size too small for me cock', was how he he'd described the problem to a sympathetic George, one day when the need to urinate had found them both writing in the sand, as most everyone did with nature's fountain pen, an expression first used by William Haynes, calling on them to, 'write one for Adolf lads'.

Given the stifling heat, the continuous bombardment of flies, the stench created by body odour and the cruel, relentless dysentery that rendered many raw about the buttocks, Roley's preoccupation with his slightly amended genitalia, to some seemed entirely irrelevant in this alien desert sandscape, but George understood.

To be a Jew was to be a subject of Hitler's annihilation plan, all male Jews were circumcised. Roland Cheeseman was not a Jew, as a young lad he'd sat with his mam and sisters in the Chapel at Ilkeston, singing the hymns of Wesley and listening to the preacher expounding the evils of drink and loose living, while under the cover of his trousers' pocket fingering his willy with its better fitting foreskin. He had no knowledge of Judaism, only of the Methodist creed, which taught him 'moderation in all things'. Yet his fear of being taken prisoner was not moderate, it was extreme and now as George looked down at the notepad on his lap, that same sympathy rose up the back of his throat like bile.

"Private Boucher." An urgent voice interrupted George's thoughts. "How do you feel?"

The doctor stood in front of him, white coated, smelling of carbolic and heavy about the eyes from tiredness. George could hardly respond with the truth, that he felt sick with dismay and pained by a sadness that riddled his very flesh and bone like a crippling disease, so instead he smiled, got to his feet, shook the doctor's hand and said.

"Time I was on my way Sir, I feel ready." Then saluted. That night in the barracks where he awaited his orders, George sat on his bed with his pen and notepaper and began to write.

Dear Mam, Dad and Samuel,

Sorry I've not written in a while but we are all kept on our toes and very little happens here that seems worthy of passing on in a letter to you. Events here are governed by so many different people and circumstances.

I have not seen my friend Lenny for some time, I think he will be sharing his affections among all the regiments, being as fair as a dog can be. Even we men get a bit mixed at times, I heard someone describe it as 'mongreled up'. Gurkhas with Highlanders, Sherwood Foresters with Mahratta infantry, languages, cultures, even faiths, shared over the breaking of bread.

I am in Cairo at present. I wonder how it has changed since you were here Dad, I can remember your letter, which told us of the black chickens that ran loose and layed eggs wherever they chose to. I've yet to see one, nor have I found an orchid. They do say that in the desert there are indeed orchids but not one have I come across, though it got me to thinking about flowers and in case my next letter doesn't reach you in time, when you go to the cemetery in August as I know you will, please take Alice some roses, mixed colours, she liked all colours. Her favourite frock was floral patterned, she wore it that day we went to the Well Dressing at Tissington.

I was pleased to hear that Myra Dodds is making progress, although with Edna's determination applied to the situation I don't see how Myra could fail to progress. I think Edna could bring a greater advancement to the Allies if she were to arrive here in full voice. One hefty swipe from dear Edna's tongue and Rommel would likely turn into a quivering Jerboa!

I was with Jack Wainwright yesterday, tough as ever is our Jack, although he was concerned. In her last two letters Gertie made no mention of Henry. Out in this part of the world we hear little enough news of Europe. It's difficult to comprehend that the same moon and the same sun that rise above the sands of Cyrenaica, shine down on the fields of France too, and even more difficult to believe, the cobbled streets of Sherwood and the double fronted shop on Gregory Street lay under their beam. I often think of Hood Street, when the moon was full, the roofs on the other side of the street would almost glow and No.17 had that strange cowl on the chimney pot, which cast a shadow, looking for all the world like a sinister figure in a top hat. William used to tell me it was the bogey man and I believed him until one day, when we were in town, I saw James Handley, he smiled at me and despite his black attire and top hat, I dismissed from my mind the notion of anyone at all unkind being in Hood Street, besides, I loved the moon, it was magical.

I am quite well, even spared those dire problems of stomach, must be all that Syrup of Figs you gave to us as kids Mam, it inured my gut to any threat of purge. For some among us, it is a threat that dominates every day.

Please give my best to everyone back home but save my love for you Mam, Dad and my fine son Samuel.

Take care, write soon.

George xxx Dad xxxxx

CHAPTER EIGHT

Late August

Maureen fixed her gaze on the door of the drill hall from the opposite side of the street where she stood by the brick pillar that did its best to hold up one of the fast disintegrating gates. Once the portal through which those of stout heart and even stouter arms and back entered to work their days moulding bricks, now the old iron gates, corroded with rust, awaited their fate. The yard behind them played willing host to dandelions and thistles and offered a neutral space away from home, where youths could share a cigarette, tell exaggerated stories of heroism and inveigle from one another any enlightening pearls of wisdom regarding the opposite sex. Most lads had a reasonable grasp of the female form, after all sisters were women in waiting and they'd all been put in the bath with their sisters. Breasts grew larger, certain areas developed fuzzy pubic hair, they all knew that, but it was the crucial word 'sex', which inspired debate as that coveted token of manhood, the fag, got handed around the number utilising the old brickyard on any given day.

A voice from behind Maureen began to taunt her.

"Charlie is me darlin', me darlin', me darlin', Charlie is me darlin' the young Chevalier."

"I'll tell mam, I know what you're up to, I can smell tobacco, you're not old enough to smoke our Colin, if yer start afore your pips drop it'll make yer impotent," said Maureen, recognising her young brother's mischief.

He appeared by the gate, three other lads in pursuit, silly grins on their faces, tell-tale specks of ash down the front of their singlet vests.

"What's impotent mean?" Colin asked on behalf of all four.

"It means your willy'll turn blue an' shrivel to the size of a monkey nut, not to mention your backside, that'll be bright red from mam wallopin' it wi' granddad's Exchange an' Mart."

Just then the door of the drill hall opened and the Local Defence men spilled out onto the street. Charlie Jones was third through the door, looking at once for Maureen.

Since the night of the dance, just before last Christmas, Charlie and Maureen had continued to see each other, the flicks, more dancing and a day at Skegness had found the young couple more and more drawn to one another. The first time Charlie had appeared in his new L.D. uniform Maureen's heart had skipped a beat, partly from seeing him so manly, so admirable and to the other extreme of emotion, from the inevitable connection her young mind had made to uniform and fighting. It was this moment more than any other that brought Maureen to the awareness of love, deep love, one which could make her feet barely touch the ground in her haste to be with Charlie and cause them to root stubbornly to the spot each time they must kiss goodbye or goodnight.

Maureen had come to realise that it was not until it was too late for a delivery or that the postman had brought only kindly mail did her mam begin to relax. The wireless was tuned in each teatime for the 6 o'clock news and not until the end of the broadcast, when no mention of their dad's ship had been made would her mam put her fork to her mouth. It was so much easier to understand now that Maureen's own heart had been taken over.

Charlie ran across the road, gave her a kiss and winked at her young brother Colin and his pals. Feeling the heat of the summer evening he unbuttoned his uniform jacket.

"Phew, that's better, I wer' meltin'," he said, "it's airless in that drill hall."

"Can I try it on Charlie? Go on just for a minute." Colin's chest expanded as far as he could make it go beneath the grubby singlet vest.

Charlie laughed and pulled off the jacket.

" 'Ere yer go then, let's see what yer look like."

"You shouldn't," said Maureen, "he's only a kid."

Charlie planted another kiss on her cheek then whispered to reassure her.

"And it's only a simple jacket, it won't do any harm, 'e's years away from chin whiskers yet, this bloody war'll be over an' done with afore your Colin or any o' these lads get as far as latherin' their top lip."

The jacket got handed round to each boy in turn and by the time it hung loosely about the skinny shoulders of Joey Spink even Maureen had to chuckle at the unlikely spectacle.

"Don't you be too late goin' home our Colin," said Maureen, as Joey handed back to Charlie the khaki battledress, "an' no more smokin', how many more cigarettes 'ave you got in your pockets, go on, turn 'em out?"

Bowing to the authority of their pal's elder sister, all four lads sheepishly produced a variety of items from their trouser pockets. Two acorns, several lengths of string, a rubber band, a whistle, a snail shell, a piece of old bone, six marbles, a stick of chalk, a box of matches and reluctantly declared by Sol Evans, a battered Park Drive packet containing one cigarette. Charlie began to laugh.

"If Captain Nias ordered us fellas' to turn out our pockets it would likely produce bugger-all. A few bob, some vestas an' smokes, the odd pawn shop ticket but nothin' like the enterprisin' array these lads 'ave got. The older yer get the duller yer get. I can remember goin' to school wi' all sorts o' stuff to swap at break time. I once persuaded Jack Wainwright to let me 'ave 'is roll o' caps for my big green 'alley'. When I got home I set me cap bomb off behind granddad as he crossed the yard to the privy, poor old sod wet 'isself. Mam confiscated me cap bomb an' the caps, it took me a month to save up enough picture cards from me dad's Woodbine packets to swap wi' Jack for me 'alley' back."

Maureen took Charlie's arm and steered him along the pavement, casting a cautionary look over her shoulder to Colin.

"If we hurry we can catch the ten to eight, we'll be there in time for the second showing."

There was a Bette Davis film on at the Odeon, Charlie would have preferred a Western but it was easier to let Maureen choose what they went to see at the cinema. Whatever the film it would be the newsreels that had the most impact. By the time he'd watched tanks and artillery and images of Mussolini and Hitler advancing towards him with anguished music filling the auditorium, Bette Davis might as well have been a bluebottle crawling across the screen. The last time they'd sat in the Odeon, halfway through 'Jezebel', a large hornet had landed on the screen and for the remainder of the film had crawled back and forth, up and down in all directions, at one point during the newsreel it appeared to become lost in Stalin's moustache but eventually re-emerged and continued its travels until a round of artillery fire sent it flying among those seated at the front. As one frustrated woman remarked on leaving the cinema at the end, 'that wer' a bloody disgrace, wouldn't yer think that the usherette could 'ave tried to swat the damn thing while it wer' stuck in Stalin's whiskers!'

Three people stood at the bus stop, Charlie knew them all vaguely. It was a fact that doing the bin rounds could be described as a 'social service'. It never failed to amaze him just how many folk seemed to await the sound of clattering bin lids to take the opportunity of off loading, not merely their rubbish but the contents of their troubled minds. Charlie had consoled the grieving, sympathised with the hard done by, held patience with the demented, shown tolerance of those worse for drink and one day the previous week, stood with Gertie Wainwright when she took the mail from the postman and recognised the handwriting on the envelope, it was from Jack, her eldest son, Charlie's best mate. He was safe, poor Gertie had wept all over this bin man, but Charlie had held her tight and inwardly thanked God for looking after his friend.

Not all were so fortunate, word had begun to spread of the disaster at Tobruk, a number had been informed of those taken prisoner.

"Here it comes," said Maureen.

The bus pulled in at the curb, in their hurry to get wherever they were going, the others boarded and seemed not to notice but Charlie had recognised the face of the driver, it was Joyce Haynes. Charlie sat by Maureen and felt in his pocket for their fare, in that instant he wanted his fingers to find that green 'alley', to hear Jack's voice say, 'swap yer my caps for your big marble'.

It took no more than ten minutes to reach the city centre, the Odeon looked drab, not allowed to show lights the façade displayed only posters and at this time of the evening, with natural light fading, even the scenes portrayed on those designed to attract the eye, lacked colour and failed in their purpose.

Maureen once more took Charlie's arm and steered him into the queue that had formed at the ticket office, unaware of Charlie's waning enthusiasm for the pending two hours of imagery and dialogue, so far removed from reality.

"I've saved up two toffee whirls," said Maureen, planting a kiss on Charlie's cheek as they settled into their seats. She smelled of something nice, he didn't know what it was, all perfumes had fancy names, but it lingered about his uniform jacket and in the darkness soothed his anxieties.

The beam of light that projected over the heads of the people and danced on the screen induced a sudden hush and the strained music, which ever accompanied the introduction to a film for the first few seconds, assaulted the ears. Then in large letters and amid a greater crescendo of orchestrated sound, the title appeared on the screen before them.

'IN THIS OUR LIFE'

Charlie sat back in his seat to await the hornet.

"Mr.Birkett will see you now."

The young woman smiled and held open the door for Annie to enter. His face showed age, it had been some time since they'd last had occasion to meet, his general look of well being however was undiminished, portly was possibly the kind word to apply, fat as butter, a more accurate description.

"Mrs.Eddowes, a pleasure to see you, what can I do to assist?"

Birkett rose from his chair and leaned forward over the desk to extend his hand, his corpulence denied the tips of his waistcoat any chance of avoiding a pen, which had lain on the pad in front of him and it was sent to the carpet at his feet. He appeared irritated by its fall and stooped to retrieve the item, on becoming upright his face displayed such a flush of redness that Annie felt genuine concern. Her expression apparently revealed this and through a gulp of breath he declared,

"What it is to grow old my dear," then sat back in his chair to compose himself.

"I have with me William's written authority."

Annie took an envelope from her handbag and passed it across the desk to Birkett. He read the letter, offered a lukewarm smile and said.

"Indeed, I noted the account was in receipt of a very large sum, William has found some good fortune surely."

If Gerald Birkett hoped for a full explanation of William's much increased funds then he was to be disappointed. Annie was in no doubt that as manager at Braithwaites he would have full knowledge of from where the money came, Davina herself had ever banked with Braithwaites. He spoke again.

"It is an irony that William must be absent at this time but he does his duty and I'm sure this sudden change to his finances can only be a comfort to his wife."

Annie pressed him. "As funds are now in place there can be no reason for delay, the mortgage on William's property can be redeemed, the Deeds released and the loan account closed."

She looked directly at Birkett, his mannerism told her so much of his thinking and he appeared politely vexed.

"It must have been such a blow to William, the death of Basil Stanford. Indeed a shock for many," said Birkett, "big employer, did a great deal for this city."

Annie made no response but trained her eyes on his face, she would offer no comment on the demise of Basil Stanford. Birkett's awkwardness at her reticence caused him to fidget with his watch chain and the extended silence forced him to speak again.

"I shall have the necessary paperwork prepared for you to sign on William's behalf. Is Charles not well as you are the one to whom William has given the charge?"

"Charles is in good health but busy at the shop, I can at least do this to relieve him and William simply acknowledges the sense of the arrangement. Tell me Mr.Birkett, how is your brother in law, Mr.Sneddon? I often wonder what he thinks of the shop now. I understand that he resides at one of his properties, not too far from

William at Wollaton. It's hard to believe that more than twenty years have passed since you introduced Charles to the opportunity of buying Mr.Sneddon's shop," she paused, "I trust that the necessary document will be ready for me to sign within the next working week."

Birkett got to his feet, coughed awkwardly and as he crossed the room to open the door for Annie said, "Yes within the week."

Just as Annie had chosen to make no comment over the death of Basil Stanford so Gerald Birkett remained tight lipped on the subject of George Sneddon, in both instances their silence spoke volumes.

Late September

Edna had walked along the corridors so many times, smiling nervously at nurses and porters, observing that preoccupied look on the faces of those, who like herself, made their way to loved ones. Some displayed a lighter tread as the need for their visits became ever closer to the one which allowed them to take home their son, daughter, mother, father, whoever it was propelling them tirelessly to this place of healing. Others wearing an expression which told the onlooker to acknowledge their need of peace, these people travelled the corridors in a state of abeyance, their emotions suspended between a fragile here and now.

Mr Shilling was to speak with them, 'You've to come late morning mam, when he finishes in surgery', Myra had declared urgently the previous afternoon.

"Hello Mrs.Dodds," the ward sister gave a mischievous wink, "I've told your Myra that if she doesn't contain her excitement I shall send her to the sluice room to wash the bedpans."

Edna hardly dare believe the day had finally come. It had been intimated that Mr.Shilling was to authorise Myra's discharge from the hospital, thirteen months since her admission. The longest year of Edna's life and for Myra, an ordeal that had changed forever so many things. As Billy had sensitively remarked just the week before, 'Our Myra's leg'll allus 'ave a bandage round it but if she wears them slacks like the doctor said it won't show, neither will the bandage round my heart but it'll be there just the same'.

“Mam.” Myra stood by the bed holding up her bag like a prize she’d scooped in a tombola. “I’ve packed, I told sister she may as well change the bedclothes, I’m goin’ home, Mr.Shilling is lettin’ me go, I just know he is.”

Edna couldn’t bring herself to utter a single word that might dampen her daughter’s spirits, she still felt afraid, not until Mr.Bob Bob actually stood before her and declared it to be so could Edna believe. ‘Myra is recovered, she may leave this hospital and return to her family’. Edna must here these words from the lips of officialdom, only then would she travel the corridors with that lighter tread.

“They look alright don’t they Mam?”

Myra turned slowly on the spot to show front and back of the tan coloured slacks Edna had bought for her at Jessops. Because the damage to Myra’s leg had affected her ankle, that joint was now virtually rigid and a specially reinforced shoe was necessary for that foot. Two pairs had been made at a subsidised cost and outside the bounds of the clothing ration. Not perhaps as stylish as Myra would have wished but given the circumstances, some kindly shoemaker had taken account of her age and done their best to provide her with shoes that met the hospital’s prescription yet enabled Myra to feel ‘normal’, in as much as a young woman could bearing such physical damage.

“A lot of women wear trousers now, sister says they’re attractive if gracing a nice shapely bum, mine is just right, according to Frank, one of the porters.”

Myra giggled and was about to explain the reliability of Frank’s judgement on the matter when Mr.Shilling entered the ward. Despite all the months of Myra’s treatment and the many times Edna had met this important man, who smiled his reassurance and spoke as comfortably with her as he did with his eminent colleagues, she nevertheless shrank in his presence, feeling inadequate, having little learning and no skill beyond woman’s work with needle and thread.

“Good morning ladies.” His voice brought an immediate hush to the ward, rather like the start of morning lessons at the school when teacher called the register. Myra was the first to speak.

“Mam’s here Mr.Shilling.”

He crossed to where they stood, sister Lovatt at his side.

"Yes, young lady the time has come, but before you leave us it is important that I explain the necessity of your continuing treatment as an outpatient."

He looked directly at Edna. "Sit down Mrs.Dodds, your weariness I imagine, for the most part, to be sadly ignored by us all. Within this place we concentrate our efforts on restoring the injured and curing the sick, this we do with the greatest hope of achievement, perhaps we take for granted the strength of relatives, overlook their tiredness from strain and stress. We don't mean to, believe me, you are equally important to us." His smile soothed, calmed, like a mild sedative. "Myra has done well, she is a particularly strong and healthy young woman, were it not so then the healing process would have failed to overcome such traumatic injury and in the worst situation we would have had no option but to have amputated the leg below the knee." He quickly cast his gaze to Myra and now spoke directly to her. "However, you stand and walk well. Because so much flesh was torn away in the accident your lower leg is covered by only a fine tissue which cannot be submerged in water, so just as you have been doing here at the hospital, so too must you do at home. Drape your lower leg over the side of the bath. A nurse will come to the house every day to dress your leg as the nurses have done here, bathing it in fine oil as the surface must not be allowed to dry out and crack, this would result in ulcers. Once a week you must attend the skin clinic at the general hospital, we shall send a letter home with you to present at your first appointment. You must not stand for extended periods or walk great distances without sitting to rest at intervals. The heavy bandage is vital, it provides support which you could not manage without. Now the good news." He placed his hand under Myra's chin to raise her face from where it had gradually lowered as he'd spoken, he administered his all soothing smile. "I can think of nothing you cannot do, except swim. I envy you Myra, you leave us to reclaim freedom. I am committed to my work, it gives me tremendous satisfaction but there are days when I look through a window, between the tapes applied for the air-raids and despite war and threat of invasion I feel a degree of resentment, a sense of being confined. Beyond these sterile walls, out there, in the city, life is going on and I catch but brief glimpses of it. Live it to the full Myra, live your life to the full."

Edna heard Mr.Shilling repeat the words just as Victor would say something twice and in that instant emotion defied all her attempts at holding back tears, she wept from relief, from regret, from exhaustion.

"Don't cry mam, I'm comin' home." Myra wrapped her arms about her mother's shoulders.

Mr.Shilling nodded to sister Lovatt and walked quietly away.

Edna took their coats and hung them behind the door. Myra stood in the middle of the scullery, her eyes scanning the room as though she were checking that everything was as it should be.

"You've a new tea caddy," she said.

Edna sighed. "A present last Christmas from your aunty Ada, there's a new caddy spoon in it anall, she got it from Arnold market, a bomb fell on Arnold the very next night, killed a dog and injured an old couple."

Edna filled the kettle, in over twelve months since Myra had gone in the ambulance, the only addition to No.24 Winchester Street had been a tea caddy and spoon with Nottingham coat of arms on the spoon handle. She'd not given it a thought until now, upstairs the bedrooms were just the same as they'd always been, the living room too. When the solicitor had said, 'The insurers have agreed a sum of two hundred pounds in compensation, with costs', Edna had been rendered speechless. Whatever must such an amount of money look like. She'd not ever caught sight of such wealth, even a five pound note had passed before Edna's eyes but once, perhaps twice and when Alex Chaucer had gone on to say, 'It is little enough, I will argue that it should be more if you wish', Billy had been struck dumb. Chaucer's explanation of events they both understood, Myra had been in hospital, undergoing painful and distressing operations and difficult treatment, a young woman who prior to the accident had been in full time work and entirely free of disability. Yet each visit to the solicitor's office took Billy and Edna beyond familiar ground and sapped their strength. No one would compensate the driver of the lorry for the loss of his son at Tobruk.

They yet had to tell Myra that deposited at Barclays Bank were two hundred pounds in her name. When they'd discussed what best to do, it had ultimately been Edna's wish that Billy break the news to Myra when she finally came home.

"Where's dad," Myra now stood at the back door, looking into the yard. "In the hospital the air smells funny, the first time Barney pushed me outside in the wheelchair it felt wonderful. I'd never taken any notice of it before but do you know Mam, in spite of the factory chimneys and pitheads, the old tannery and the knacker yard, Nottingham smells wonderful, it really does."

"Your dad couldn't 'ave sat there waitin', yer know what 'e's like, an ill sittin' hen, besides I didn't want 'im to come wi' me to the hospital just in case they didn't say yer could go. 'E's at Susie's paintin' 'er pantry, 'e'll be back by three, so you can look out for more waterworks. Come an' sit down, we'll drink a cuppa, I've made a sawdust cake, that's what your dad calls it, rationin's produced a whole lot o' new recipes, all taste the same, like babies' rusks. Susie reckons she's cut wisdom teeth since rationin' started."

They sat at the scullery table, Edna took Myra's hand.

"I've prayed for today, every night I've prayed that Mr.Bob Bob 'ould make you better an' you'd come home. You'll 'ave to write to Archie, let 'im know, any letters 'e sends to hospital could get lost else, a busy place like that."

"Give me chance Mam, I've only just got home, I want to go see our Annie and Susie an' the girls at Jessops."

Edna smiled but inwardly worried for Archie Medlyn, whether the lad would ever come home only God could know and if he did what heartache awaited him. Edna sank her teeth into a slice of sawdust cake and allowed her anxieties to fade as she looked at her youngest daughter. Love welled inside her, Billy would be home soon, for now nothing else mattered.

Annie topped up the water in the vase of chrysanthemums, Celia had arrived with them the previous day. The shop lacked colour, many items were unavailable and those that were failed to compensate, it was as though the shop bore sympathy with families constantly missing members serving abroad, leaving space at home bleak and colourless. The chrysanthemums in bright yellow and rich bronze Annie had placed on the counter. Folk clad themselves in sombre attire, news from the Fronts did nothing to lift the spirits, preoccupied with war only the very young appeared in clothes of cheerful shades, it was difficult to countenance any hint of indifference, loyalty, standing firm with the men governed 'the home front'. But flowers were the exception, they signified hope through a brightness that could not be denied, almost every customer to the shop had pressed their face to the blooms, some remarking on the scent of autumn, while others kept their thoughts deep within. Joyce Haynes, on her way home from work, had called for bread, she'd stroked the petals of a deep bronze flower head and said, 'Do yer think I could get wool this colour, I thought I'd knit a pullover for William'.

Since June, when word of Rommel's surprise attack had filtered back along with news of so many taken prisoner, poor Joyce had heard nothing from her husband, Sergeant Haynes. Today, in her drab, dark grey uniform jacket and with her driver's number pinned to her breast pocket, Joyce too seemed imprisoned, unable to free herself of fear and loneliness.

Annie hoped every day for a letter from George, Celia had brought with her, for Annie to read a letter she'd received from William two days ago. Unlike George, he saw fit to apprise Celia of all his torments, the heat and flies, stomach ache, lack of sleep and apparently beyond his endurance, an insect bite in his groin which drove an itchiness equal only to chicken pox and induced a swelling, so large, that it chafed mercilessly against the rough army issue underwear so beneath William's dignity! Annie worried herself endlessly over the absence of all her sons but William created anxieties in addition, that extra challenge to the day, which even as a youth he'd presented so consistently. Celia was now fretting and intent on mailing at once to Egypt a tube of antihistamine cream.

The shop door clanged and Annie looked up from where she'd been dusting a shelf before stocking up the cigarettes. Edna had said she would call for her rations this afternoon, Annie hoped it might be Edna and that perhaps Myra would come with her. In her surprise she almost knocked over the vase of chrysanthemums.

"John! We didn't know you were coming, your dad's not hear."

John chuckled at her fluster.

"I've only got an hour Mam, I couldn't let you know because I didn't know myself until yesterday evening. It's all a bit rushed. I've to go abroad with No.6 Squadron, anti tank, they need mechanics and engineers on the ground. Momentum's gathering for a big push in the western desert."

Annie's face showed her dismay.

"Where will you be based," she asked. Trying desperately to remain composed.

"They keep everything close to their chests but reading between the lines I reckon we shall be somewhere near Alexandria. I'll be alright Mam, don't go getting yourself all worried up, I'm not at the front line, just fixing up damaged aircraft back at the base, getting them repaired and into action again, to help all the lads out there driving back Rommel an' his lot. Anyway, I've something more important to tell you, I've met a young lady, Laura, that's her name, Laura Innes, she lives with her grandma next door to where I've been lodging. She's a teacher, her mam and dad run a post office on the other side of Birmingham, a distance away from the school where she works so when her granddad died last year her gran' needed company, it made sense for Laura to move to Castle Bromwich."

John didn't tell Annie that the post office and Laura's parents narrowly missed the bombing that destroyed a large area of population in April of the previous year. Fred and Moira Innes came out of the air raid shelter to look upon a scene of desolation. Laura had been visiting her grandparents and returned to find the post office propping up the end wall of the doctor's surgery, Dr.Keating himself had been attending casualties three streets away, the surgery premises, thankfully had been unoccupied but medical records and the pharmacy all lay buried beneath a mound of rubble. That night he was called upon to issue four death certificates, contained in his bag were two only, any more lay buried with the rest of his surgery, even that document to dignify death was denied by Hitler's bombers.

John leaned forward to smell the flowers.

"My Laura's lovely Mam, I've told her to come and see you while I'm away," he hesitated, "get to know her Mam."

He kissed Annie on the cheek. She sensed John had stopped short of saying, 'Just in case I don't come back'.

The shop door bell clanged again, Annie would rather it hadn't, so little time to spend with John, she wished she dare lock the door and turn the sign to closed but Charles might be annoyed and the last thing she wanted was an atmosphere, surely he would be back at any moment.

The irony was cruel, Annie's heart sank to her boots at the sight of Anthony Hemsley, now of all times. Since the Deed of Davina's house had been conveyed to him last June, the property had remained unoccupied, Annie presumed it was not his intention to reside there himself, more an investment and most likely it would be let.

"Hello Annie, at last I am installed although the pantry is empty as you would expect. I have my ration book and a modest list but please do serve your customer."

Anthony Hemsley smiled at John, not having met before neither felt any awkwardness but for Annie, Hemsley's arrival was an intrusion, it robbed her of precious minutes with John. Nevertheless, good manners came automatically to her.

"This is my youngest son John," she stifled a sigh, "he leaves for Egypt tomorrow. John I must introduce you to Mr.Hemsley, this is the gentleman who bought Davina's house."

John right away offered his hand.

"Pleased to meet you Sir, not the ideal time to be moving house I'm sure, but if anywhere can offer contentment amid the troubles of war then it must be that place where many hours of happiness were enjoyed by our family in the wonderful company of Mrs.Wright, isn't that true Mam?"

Before Annie could reply, Hemsley spoke.

"Surely Annie I am not merely the purchaser of Davina's house. You see John, your mother and I go back a long, long way, my sister and I were taught our lessons by your great aunt Bella. Circumstances dictated that our family move away from Nottingham to Sheffield so years passed without us seeing each other. Not until I became associated with the mining operations at Mapperley did we meet again. But such history is important, friendship is important. Travel safely John. I can imagine how unwelcome I must be at this moment when every minute you can spend with your mother is beyond value. I shall call back later for my items Annie, there is no hurry whatever. I promise to look out for your mother John, indeed for your father too, it will not prove in the least difficult now that I live close by."

His eyes fell on Annie, she quickly scanned his shopping list.

"Could you leave it until around five o'clock?" She asked, confident in her mind that Charles would be serving in the shop at that time whilst she prepared their meal.

"Of course," he said and lowered his face to the chrysanthemums, "what lovely flowers, you know John it is always a pleasure to call at this shop."

Charles had returned soon after Anthony Hemsley left and between a handful of customers John enjoyed catching up with family news as his mam and dad took turns behind the counter. John stayed long enough to see his nephew Samuel, when he came home from school, presented the boy with a cap badge, 'RAF', and whispered 'That's special, just for you, keep it safe'.

Even Charles struggled to keep his emotions in check as they waved goodbye and the arrival of Mabel Rashleigh, intent on telling Annie all about the blind man who got off the bus that day in town, when she'd tried to remember who he was, how his blindness was all sham, how he'd been seen shaking salt an' vinegar on his chips and picking the crispiest ones to eat first in Bellett's chip shop at Beeston, adding, 'It's Marlene Cutlers lad, went to school wi' our Cedric, drop a tanner on the pavement an' 'e'd spot the bugger afore anybody else had chance. Well 'e's been rumbled now, 'e'll be shakin' vinegar on army rations next week', swamped Charles completely. John disappeared amid Mabel's revelation which had been rendered no less tiresome when at the end she'd declared, 'I don't need owt, just thought you'd want to know' and left with an almighty clang of the door bell.

Charles was now sending off the paper boys with The Evening Post. Annie was cooking macaroni for their tea. Samuel sat at the scullery table with his crayons and drawing book, the cap badge he'd carefully put in a trinket jar on his dressing table for safe keeping. Annie had not noticed before how similar in features were Samuel and John, any likeness had to come through herself as Charles was but stepfather to George. She'd remarked on it to Edna when she came for her shopping.

'Uncles an' nephews, aunts an' nieces, yer see it often. Your George has the look of his uncle Frank, our Susie gets to look more like me sister Vera every week an' me mam, bless 'er, wer' allus sayin' I 'ad the look of me aunt Win, 'ad 'er gab an'all, mam wer' forever tellin' me you've tongue enough for two our Edna'.

Annie smiled to herself and poured the macaroni into an enamel pie dish. Edna had delivered other news, or gossip, as Annie was inclined to consider it, although it did seem too serious a matter to be idle speculation. Unable to resist lowering her face to the chrysanthemums and pressing her nose into the petals, Edna had then sniffed and said. 'There'll be a stink at council if what they're sayin' is true. It'd seem Anthony Bradshaw, the bigwig at legal department 'as been carryin' on wi' one o' the secretaries, been goin' on for a long time they reckon. I wouldn't want to be in 'is shoes, 'is missus is s'posed to be a right tartar. She's already stirin' up trouble at pit, I dare say your Hilda's Jack 'as 'ad a run in wi' 'er by now, some o' the men 'ave started referrin' to 'er as Boadicea. If things don't change by Christmas they're goin' to weld 'er a helmet an' a set o' wheels for her chariot'.

Annie closed the oven door wondering if it was a particular weakness of men named Anthony. At that moment, Samuel's voice called out eagerly.

"I've finished the picture to send to dad." He held it up proudly. A vase of chrysanthemums, bright yellow and orange, the nearest to a bronze coloured crayon he could find. "I was going to draw an animal but Miss Sampson at school said there aren't many flowers in the desert so I changed my mind, I think dad will like these, can we post it tomorrow?"

Annie nodded. Writing a letter to George to put in the envelope with Samuel's picture caused her no hardship, finding words that would overcome the lump in her throat proved too much.

Laura Innes, she would enter the name and address in her notebook, for John, kindly, gentle John.

CHAPTER NINE

Western Desert

Early November

"Me dad wer' what you'd call a practical man, he could look at two bits o' wood or two bits o' metal an' right away, in his head he'd have a plan, there behind his eyes'd be the finished article. Our house wer' like the soddin' house that Jack built, anybody who had a mind to study the furniture would have thought it had been made by hobgoblins an' blind ones at that. Poor mam used to sit on a chair that had four different legs, the chest o' drawers in our bedroom had china knobs, brass knobs an' wooden knobs an' the table we sat at to eat wer' made up of two that he'd screwed together, one wer' about quarter inch higher than t'other so if yer forgot an' put your cup down on the ridge then your brew went everywhere an' if you happened to be the poor sod sittin' at the middle, by the extra legs, then your own legs were so far apart by the time you'd finished eatin' it felt like you'd been astride the rag an' bone man's horse, 'cause his efforts at re-upholsterin' left much to be desired an'all. Nothin' matched nor stood level, if it bothered me mam then she didn't show it, except for the times he'd have a go at me, it wer' only then that she ever said owt. I wer' no good wi' hammer an' nails, it wer' figures that fascinated me. 'You're as useful as a bloody lighthouse in the desert our Alf', he'd say an' mam'd shake her head an' tell him, 'things have to tally an' somebody has to add 'em up, while you're makin' summat out o' nowt our Alf has to make nowt out o' summat'. I'm not sure what mam thought I actually did at the insurance office but I reckon her notion must have been coloured by me uncle Charlie's experience. He'd paid his premiums for years but when the end wall of his house started to move the assessor put it down to subsidence, his policy didn't cover subsidence an' the poor sod got not so much as a shillin'. Now here I am, in the desert an' if ever a place could do wi' a bloody lighthouse it's this bugger. At least we'd be able to tell which way we wer' headin', it all looks the bloody same, we think we've reached where we're supposed to be then discover we're miles short. Captain should spit it out, lay it on the line."

Noakes put on a very correct, cultured voice to say.

"Listen up men, when you smell Jerry's breath and hear his heart thumping over the sound of your own, then you are in position." He laughed half heartedly. "We've been out here for months an' so far we've made a pile o' nowt out a sight too much o' summat."

George smiled, any distraction was welcome and Noakes' chatter took his senses to another place, here was where no one wanted to be. Morale was low, the Allies had suffered big losses of both men and armaments but Rommel's losses had been greater. Word travelled down the line, desperate for fuel and supplies the enemy was weakened. Montgomery had nailed his colours to every tank, to every piece of artillery and every lorry. He'd committed his every man to the ultimate, the breaking of Rommel's defences, encirclement, advance, to the securing of the ports, to this, the final thrust that would send the enemy back and now a sense of that 'ultimate' being nigh held them in a state of tension. Some driven to talk incessantly, while others withdrew into a world of their own. Whichever their mood, all knew that life or death would be decided in this cauldron of heat, stench and blood sucking flies, fortunes shifting as the sands all about them.

Alf Noakes winced as he moved, bones ached constantly but seemed to complain with a vengeance if settled in one position for longer than two minutes at a time and soreness from dysentery flattened a man's strength 'til under the full sun his simmering brain could convince him that whilst he slept, his adversary had fed him through the rollers of a mighty mangle, now commandeered, adapted for the purpose of squeezing out every last drop of blood and sweat from humankind.

"You've got a lad haven't yer Boucher?" He asked.

George nodded, "Yes, Samuel, he's ten. How about you, do you have a family Noakes?"

Noakes rubbed a persistent fly from the corner of his mouth and spat in the sand. "Over the years I've pumped enough into my Elsie to float The Queen Mary, but nothin', not so much as a bloody 'might be'. Perhaps it's as well." He gave George a resigned look. "You must wonder, how things'd be for your lad if......., you know what I mean."

"Samuel's mother died when he was six months old, he's with his grandma," said George.

"Bloody hell, sorry mate, sorry."

Noakes sniffled, tears welled in his eyes. It was yet another symptom of desert malady, the inability to defy constant tides of emotion, they could engulf a man, laying such pressure across his chest as to crush him then as they receded, suck at his strength, undermine him 'til his steps faltered and he struggled to keep his balance. Here a man could cry as an infant cries, his torment coming from within and with no means of expressing himself other than to weep. It was never questioned, for every man present had known it for himself, it couldn't be erased by any inquiry, at most, a hand on the shoulder or the simple act of sitting together in a shared, intuitive silence.

George raised his hand. "Listen," he said, "aircraft."

Noakes rubbed his eyes free of wateriness and looked up. "They're ours," his voice suddenly lifted from the doldrums, "it's our lads, no mistakin' 'em, Jerry's engines sound like they're runnin' on scummy bath water, ours purr, like they're suppin' on Bristol Cream." He got to his feet, the palm of his hand desperately trying to soothe the soreness of his backside, then excitedly he punched George's shoulder. "It's our buggers alright, God bless yer lads." Noakes scanned the horizon and began to count, "one, two, three, four, they're still comin', I'll be dammed Boucher, there's a whole glorious sky full of 'em. Drop your load steady an' sure lads, find them bloody Panzers, turn 'em into tin tacks, blow 'em to Kingdom come."

The Captain's whistle sounded, now every man was on his feet. The previous day they had trained almost continually. Monty's orders to his officers had been specific, no days of inactivity but a maintained readiness, however weary from heat, however weakened from diarrhoea, all those capable of standing must eat, drink, swallow their salt tablet and carry on. His theory being that when the body stopped, so too did the mind and Rommel would be beaten not by guns but by the minds of men who fired their resolve, their unwavering determination down every single barrel, be it tank, artillery or rifle, the enemy would be beaten by minds which remained intent.

"Lay the flag."

Captain Seagrove's voice summoned urgently. A group of men staked out on the sand a union flag. It was the only way of identifying themselves to the pilots. From above, sand was sand and men were men but the flag enabled instant recognition, regardless of military intelligence, which could take days to catch up with the present.

In the last letter he'd received from home, Annie had told George of John's deployment, while the news did little to cheer him, the thought of his younger brother, working skilfully to ensure the airforce kept as much capability as possible, nevertheless heartened him. They were both a far cry from the production line at Raleigh but in his head George could hear John whistling as he tightened brakes and bicycle chains and picture Percy Pollard's bulbous nose protruding from the middle of his spectacles. Now the tears welled in George's eyes.

William too was out here somewhere. It was difficult to imagine, even at home with Celia and the children Will' could be grumpy and dissatisfied, in this environment George feared for his brother's sanity. Since Charles had poured out his torment over William's mother, George had at times wondered if Will' had understood more than Charles realised. Yet how could he, when his mother died he was but an infant, too young to have any recall. George had locked away the knowledge in his head, Charles was right. William and Freddy must never know.

Captain Seagrove and Lieutenant Carlisle observed the quiet gathering. Orders had come through, they were to move out, northward to roll up the Axis units still in the forward line. The sustained airborne attack of the previous day had done its best to pave the way for advancement on the ground. Now Montgomery mobilised the Allies, deploying all the might at his disposal.

It was early dawn, their Chaplain had prepared the Sacrament, using the shelter provided by a lorry to shield them from the sand rising in the wind. He led the men in a simple prayer, then speaking slowly, he read to them Psalm one hundred and twenty one in a way he believed they needed to hear.

"We will lift up our eyes unto the hills from were cometh our help.

Our help comes from our Lord who made heaven and earth.

He will keep us in his ways, ever watchful over us.

The sun shall be kind by day, as the moon by night.

He will preserve us from evil and keep safe our souls.

Our Lord will preserve our going out and our coming in,

this day and all our days.

He will hold us in his care, even for evermore.

Amen.

Nervousness travelled the lines, their eyes held fear of the day ahead, aware that by nightfall, their number would be less. Men of all denominations assembled together, the short services he held made no distinction. He called the first row forward to receive communion. Each mouth took a wafer, like a trusting infant taking a spoon of nourishment.

"This is my body, given for you." They could do nothing to conceal their trembling as he held the chalice for them to drink. "This is my blood, shed for you."

The rows came forward in turn until at the last, two men who would normally turn away before communion, stood hesitantly. Captain Seagrove and Lieutenant Carlisle now moved toward the Chaplain, they paused by the two men. It was as though without any exchange of words each understood the other's need, all four knelt before the makeshift altar, he ministered the Sacrament.

"Have no concern, but know only his peace in your heart and keep it with you."

These words he spoke for the comfort of the two hesitant men who were of Jewish faith, today they needed to be as one with the rest. All, including their Chaplain sensed the ultimate battle for El Alamein was to begin this hour. Love for his Lord, love for his men, caused to tremble even this man of the cloth, 'body and blood'.

He wiped the chalice and placed it back in the case, trying with all his tested strength to know peace within his own heart.

Their progress had been hampered, paths through the minefields were congested with burned out tanks and lorries, the tracks were broken up and strewn with debris. Their attention had been drawn every which way in the attempt to get their convoy past the obstacles and proceed northward. It was soon after 10am that they hit a wall of resistance, an Italian unit, well dug in.

"Bloody Hell, who said the wops blink first and then fire wi' their eyes shut, these buggers 'ave got their sights fixed on us an' no mistake."

Jack Wainwright drew his arm across his face to clear the dust from his own eyes. A barrage of machine gun fire had rained down on them, one truck had suffered badly, the cries of the injured men within drove the frantic efforts of the rest to erect their guns and return fire. The noise was deafening, explosions lifting dust and sand high into the air, now their Chaplain and stretcher bearers grappled their way inside the truck to bring out the wounded.

Captain Seagrove ordered there be no gaps in their fire, with no chance to dig themselves in it was vital to maintain a tight defence of their position. Sweat poured from the men loading shell after shell. Jack defied his dry mouth, a total lack of spittle, to cry 'bastard' with every shell released.

The Chaplain, or Captain Wells, as he ever seemed to become on the battlefield, defied the incoming fire to reach the casualties, trying to keep alive those ferrying any dead and wounded back of the line to their only medic'. Sweat dripped from this man's forehead onto the blood stained bodies put before him as he desperately tried to prioritise injuries. The second to reach him was beyond help and only minutes from death, his stomach rent, his eyes fixed open, one hand briefly touched the medic's arm before he died without uttering a single word. The world before Captain Childs' eyes had turned from grey brown to vivid red within no more time than it would take a man to shave. When a newly qualified doctor, he'd mastered the sight of blood by taking deep breaths, here there was no moment, not even a second granted to him. Revulsion and nausea created their own bombardment, pounding behind his brow, stripping his stomach of its lining but he carried on, just as those manning the guns carried on. Inching forward for more than two hours the fire from the Italian lines at last began to subside. Captain Seagrove ordered a pause, moving binoculars across the open ground ahead of him he hoped for a sign of surrender but there was none. They had taken losses but so too must the Italians be at much reduced strength. He called for a single volley of artillery fire to test the enemy's response, it remained intensely still.

On command they were to move in, at first on their bellies.

"Corporal Boucher, keep what men you have low to the ground on the left flank behind Lieutenant Carlisle's lead troop. Corporal Noakes will take his men likewise on the right."

A voice came from somewhere behind him.

"Noakes is dead sir."

"Then Sergeant Nicholls will take the right flank."

Chaplain Wells now stood before him.

"I should go Captain, Sergeant Nicholls will be vital to you and the remaining men if things turn out badly. I can serve most purpose by taking Corporal Noakes' place, a man can pray on his stomach as well as on his knees."

"I cannot allow it," said Seagrove, "you don't carry a rifle Padre, every man advancing on the enemy must have with him his rifle, you could die unarmed."

Wells smiled. "With respect Captain, it is at times such as this that a man needs more than a rifle and don't you think I would be better placed to meet my maker as an unarmed man, whether it be today, tomorrow or next week and next battle?"

Seagrove breathed deep and sighed long.

"Gather them up and proceed. Sergeant Nicholls, keep the guns at the ready."

Their advance was disturbed only by vultures circling overhead, now the guns stood quiet and the air had cleared of smoke, this other army, devoid of loyalty, which shadowed either side in stealthy silence, awaited its chance.

A small number of Italians stood in a line, they had laid their rifles on the ground but not one raised his arms from his side, stubbornly resisting that last humiliating gesture of submission.

Carlisle led the men forward 'til no more than a yard's length separated them and the Italians. It was a curious fact of war, that a universal language, a collaboration between speech and deed enabled an understanding to pass from one man to another in the situation that surrounded the taking of prisoners. It was by the grace of God that they were alive, perhaps it was to God they surrendered their trust when they were rounded up by their captors.

George surveyed the scene about him, the evidence of earlier battles littered the area, the Italians had fought hard to hold their position. But it was the bodies, so many bodies, blood already congealing in the heat, the stench of guts laid bare, of faeces. No matter how many times a man came upon such a scene his soul trembled within him, when God and Heaven felt to be a belief to which he could not be entitled.

"Best do somethin' with 'em before the bloody shite-hawks take their fill Corporal, the rearguard is movin' up, Captain Seagrove'll take receipt o' the Eye-ties, them as can still breathe anyroad."

George sighed, "Yes Private, tell the men to carry the dead to cover, some will prove too difficult to move, keep identification with ever corpse unless there is none remaining, and with respect for the dead Private, they held no more desire to be here than ourselves."

George walked across to where the Chaplain stood.

"Are you alright Sir?"

"My father wanted me to become a horticulturist, his great delight was to grow plants, edible or otherwise, 'good prospects son, the gentry will always pay handsomely to grace their surroundings'. He would often speak those same words as he tended his modest back garden. Have you ever seen a place so crying out to be graced Corporal? If I could achieve to plant just one lily or a humble cabbage I would feel accomplished. It disappointed my father when I chose divinity, here is death, on the ground, in the ground and I am without the ability to grant this place one shred of grace.

I fear the list will sicken us all Corporal, by now Captain Seagrove will have the names and numbers of our dead, those seriously injured and the walking wounded, yet I imagine it will be the reduction in tank and artillery numbers that is first considered in drawing up the next battle plan."

George was saved from having to reply by the arrival of Seagrove. The truck pulled up sharply sending a cloud of dust into the air, which momentarily hid the Captain from view until he appeared from within like a ghostly apparition.

"We are ordered to proceed west toward Galal. Corporal, you will oversee the necessary work here as swiftly as possible. I am sending Sergeant Nicholls to the field hospital with the seriously wounded," he hesitated, "and with the dead. I have no option but to hold the prisoners here under guard, I can spare neither the truck nor the fuel to transport them to base."

"How many," asked the Chaplain? Seagrove understood the question, albeit vague.

"Six dead, nine serious, eleven walking." Aware of his Chaplain's need to know more he continued. "Collett, Noakes, Goodman, Sallis, Baxendale and Hodge."

George spoke quickly. "Would you know if Private Wainwright is among the injured Sir?"

"Of course, young Wainwright's a relative of yours isn't he Boucher. Serious I'm afraid. As swiftly as possible Corporal, when I have any news I shall inform you directly."

He turned and jumped into the truck which travelled at speed to where Carlisle had corralled the prisoners. Chaplain Wells sighed through the fresh rising of dust left behind by the Captain's vehicle and placed his hand on George's shoulder reassuringly.

"Swiftly it is then Corporal, no time to plant the lily, Galal awaits!"

Heavy rain had rendered the ground conditions poor, fuel convoys had become bogged down, some divisions had no other course than to remain still through lack of fuel. 10th Armoured had advanced along the coastal road, with adequate supplies they pushed their tanks on towards Mersa Matruh. The enemy was on the run, pockets of resistance, mostly Italian units, had been left behind by Rommel, now desperately short of fuel, he had no vehicles to transport them from the front line, the 10th infantry had the task of effectively 'mopping up'.

"You're quiet Eddowes, it rattles me when you go quiet, have yer run out o' schemes or is it the wet gettin' to yer?"

"Shut up Banks, when this war's over you'll be sitting somewhere, scratching your arse, waiting for the labour exchange to open, but not me, I'm sick of taking orders, I shall be my own boss. The house is bought and paid for, it's a business next. War destroys but it also creates, where the bombing has left streets of rubble, houses will need to be built, factories restored, and with a modern outlook. A lot of places were that old they were due for demolition anyway, if a man puts on his thinking cap and applies his capital and his ambition then he'll make money but some are simply content to muddle through, to stare into a pint pot and bemoan the price of meat. While you're scratching your backside Banks, William Eddowes will be industrious, making his mark."

William's moods grew more antagonistic by the day, it did little to endear him to his comrades, in his mind he voiced, sensible, laudable notions, to those obliged to listen it was tiresome bragging, which amidst this relentless struggle to maintain a vestige of decency and hope grated on the nerves like a whining dog.

Suddenly an explosion several yards ahead brought their lorries to a halt. Within seconds the men had scrambled down and taken shelter behind the vehicles, the mud oozed around their boots and lapped their backsides where they squatted.

"I need a piss, I can't think straight wi' a full bladder." Banks opened his flies and urinated against the wheel.

"Bloody hell, you dirty bugger," said William, hastily wiping a splash from the side of his face.

Another explosion fell short of the track. Lieutenant Whately's instinct told him there were few behind the guns on the other side, their fire would come with far more speed and intensity if it were a unit of any size. He gave the order to position the Bazookas, feverish activity saw them in place in minutes. An exchange of fire briefly filled the divide between them and the enemy.

"Let 'em go again, fire twice more." Whately hoped a beleaguered number might surrender, the alternative would likely be a wipe-out, militarily the latter would be favourable, prisoners posed a big problem, taking them forward was not possible, neither was transporting them back, leaving them unarmed and with little ration was the only course open to him.

The air fell silent, no fire was returned. A white flag appeared in the distance, on this day clearer to see with a sky behind it heavy with rain cloud.

"Now what are we supposed to do with the buggers," said William, "it makes no sense, a minute ago we could have mown the damn lot down and moved on but once they wave a bit of white rag everything changes, bloody madness."

"I bet yer beat your missus an'all don't yer Eddowes." Banks checked his rifle, 'tis only polite, we shall 'ave to go an' introduce ourselves, wi' manners like yours Eddowes I reckon you'd best stay 'ere wi' the guns, I wouldn't subject the poor devils to a man wi' ambition an' capital intent on makin' his mark! One bloody Hitler's enough."

Their Corporal hurried over. "Italians, we're movin' forward in two rows, four abreast, our machine guns'll be trained on 'em should they try any monkey business." He called for seven men, while Sergeant Langford ordered the Bren guns in place at either side. "They'll let 'em have the lot if they open fire on us."

William would have preferred to remain and man the guns but Corporal Lewis had named those he was taking with him and Eddowes was one of them.

Slowly the eight men walked towards the white flag. In his nervousness William spoke.

"We're sittin' ducks, they say the Eye-ties fight dirty."

The Corporal made no change to his stride. "For a start Eddowes, we're not sittin' we're upright, on our own fuckin' feet an' all fights are dirty, 'aven't yer looked at yourself, look at me, look at any one of us, walkin' columns o' mud an' shite, even yer own mother'd call yer dirty."

Then his pace slowed, within his sight were just two men, one waving the flag with his right arm while supporting the other man with his left.

"Two of 'em, just two poor sods."

With their rifles at the ready, Lewis and the others closed the gap. The scene that met them was sickening, how long this remnant of enemy strength had held the spot was impossible to calculate. Vehicles riddled with holes and empty of fuel, shallow burial sites where those still alive had strived to keep their fallen mates from the vultures until weakness denied them even that act of decency. The stench of decaying flesh and faeces engulfed Lewis and his troop as they walked the remaining half dozen yards to where the Italians waited.

"Water, please water."

Their attempts at catching rain water had obviously been futile, any likely receptacle lay amongst the tangled destruction scattered across the ground.

"Good God," said Banks, as he looked at the weakest man whose head hung barely above his knees, only the arm of his comrade prevented him from falling. Corporal Lewis spoke.

"Search 'em for weapons Eddowes." William hesitated, "Now for God's sake man."

William felt up and down the upright man and as best he could along the body of the other. The clothing on both was rank from sweat and excrement.

"Nothing Corporal."

"You speak English," said Lewis.

"Some," replied the Italian. His lips were parched, cracked along their surface and banded with dried blood, flies clustered at the corners of his mouth. "No water, for three days, no water. We collect rain, just some, in shell cases," he appeared to writhe in a spasm of pain, "guts, bad guts."

"God Almighty," said Banks, "they've been drinking cordite."

"Eddowes, you an' Banks will carry the unconscious man, Cooper, you escort the prisoner back to Lieutenant Whately, the rest of us will search the area. Are you the only two, is there anyone else still breathin'?"

Corporal Lewis directed the question urgently at the Italian who shook his head and in the faintest of voices replied, 'non', by now not enough spittle was about his tongue to enable any more response, than a vaguely Italian spoken 'non'.

A strange silence prevailed the scene as the feeble prisoners were brought back to the rest of the unit, standing by the lorries in a state of disbelief, was this it, were there no more than two. Lieutenant Whately rubbed the palm of his hand up over his brow and let out a long, frustrated breath.

"Put them in the truck under cover, give them water, only slowly, sips at first, then gradually more."

The guns were stood down and Sergeant Langford watched for the return of Corporal Lewis.

Whately stood alone, pondering wrestling with his quandary. Private Banks emerged from the truck that held the two prisoners, he made his way to Whately.

"The one didn't make it Sir, to be honest I'm not sure that he wer' breathin' when we carried him across, at least, by the time we got here."

"One man Private, one solitary man to set going into this wilderness, a man barely able to speak and capable of no more than to stagger his way along, it would be kinder to shoot the poor devil."

"Well he could prove a help Sir, this wop speaks English, and he might know a useful bit o' Krautischer an'all. The state he's in he couldn't cause much trouble, I've seen more flesh on a bloody greyhound Lieutenant, beggin' your pardon Sir."

"Tell Sergeant Langford I need to speak with him, and Private, I know the conditions are dire but nevertheless remove any identification from the deceased and bring it to me, then take another man with you to bury the cadaver."

Banks considered Eddowes to be due a bit of digging. "Why me?" Protested a resentful William, "why not one of the others who did nothing but watch?"

"Do yer know Eddowes, my lad had more nous when he wer ten years old than you've bloody well got. The poor sod died when we carried him across, you an' me. I had his shoulders an' you had his feet, that's how I know. He snuffed it between that God forsaken patch o' blood stained stinkin' desert an' this Godless spot, it's only right as we should be the buggers to bury him."

The deed done, Banks smoothed the lonely mound with the back of his shovel.

"Now I lay me down to sleep,
I pray The Lord my soul to keep.
If I should die before I wake,
I pray The Lord my soul to take.

When we wer' kids, mam'd stand by our beds while we said it, every night the same. We'd chant it out, never really thinkin' about the words or what they meant. When grandma wer' took bad she had to come an' live at our house, I can remember the day she died like it wer' only yesterday. Mam gathered us all together, seven lads, an' took us in the room to see grandma. The curtains were pulled across all bar an inch, it just let a sliver o' light in the room. Funny how folk right away keep the dead in the dark, you'd think that finally puttin' 'em six foot under'd be time enough to deny 'em daylight. There she was, layin' in bed, she could have been just sleepin' for all we could tell except for one thing that made her look different. We'd never before seen her without her hairnet on, never knew that her hair wer' long, it fell on the pillow either side of her face, it didn't seem possible for it to have been contained within that flimsy bit o' net. Anyroad, we each had to give her a kiss, that wer' different though, her face wer' cold an' it smelled all clean, like the clinic smelled where we were took to be checked for rickets. Soon after, our Billy went missin', he wer' only five. Searched high an' low, couldn't find him anywhere. It must have been two hours later that Mrs.Tippet brought him home, he'd been hidin' in their coal shed. Billy looked frightened to death, 'has he been an' gone yet', them wer' his first words. 'Has who been an' gone'? Said mam. 'The Lord, has he gone now'? poor little bugger, I reckon he must have thought the lord wer' some sort o' bogey man who wer' comin' for grandma's soul."

William snorted and blew away a fly from his nostril.

"There was a house on the opposite side of Hood Street where we lived, it had a peculiar cowl on the chimney and when the moon was full, it cast a shadow across the cobbles. I used to tell my younger step brother that it was the bogey man, coming to get him."

"You've allus been the milk o' human kindness haven't yer Eddowes, bloody hell, but it makes yer wonder. 'Only good children go to heaven', that wer' another o' me mam's attempts at savin' our souls, after this lot do yer' suppose the Lord'll bother comin' for any of us?"

William scraped the mud from his boot with his shovel. "Just so long as I go to wherever my mother went."

Banks gave him a curious look, it seemed a strange remark for a man to make about his mother. But his curiosity was not to be answered as at that moment Corporal Lewis called to them.

"Aye up, sounds like we're ready to roll, yer know what they say Eddowes, whether yer go up or down you're sure to meet somebody familiar, might even bump into our Eye-tie mate." Banks cast one last look at the pathetic mound of grubby earth and sand before turning to walk away. "God bless yer lad, an' your poor mam an'all."

William followed Banks, his thoughts with his brother George, wondering where he might be. The desert was a big place, bare of humankind for miles at a time yet surely one day soon they would find themselves at the same spot, unlike the bogey man who determined himself to sit on William's shoulder wherever he went, whispering in his ear, 'only good children go to heaven'.

England, same month.

"One bugger got the mains pipe, link up to the bowser, an' watch your backs, what's still standin' could go at any minute, last lot come down wi' no warnin', missed two o' mine by inches, bloody hell, 'ere it goes."

The corner of a three story building, standing perilously, like a giant last skittle, teetered on its foundations before crashing to the street below, filling the air with terrifying sound as masonry and mortar exploded into rubble and dust on impact and cables, torn from peaceful privacy seemed to franticly reach out for any possible anchorage before thrashing the ground in their agitation.

"All electricity's supposed to be off."

The leader of the Leicester crew had himself arrived at the scene with his men only minutes before, an old hand, Bob Sewell was experienced and ever cautious. He'd barely finished shouting across his warning to the Nottingham crew when sparks raced across the surface of the street, dancing around the base of a lamppost like fiends, taunting, daring the bulbless mantle to break out from its imposed, dark silence and join in their rampage.

"Bloody hell, no hoses or we'll be cinders, find the A.R.P., tell them this lot's still live."

At that moment, a tower of flame lit up the sky to the south of them and silhouetted against the light, parachutes descending, the explosions appeared to travel in a line across the city.

"Gas works, they've hit the bloody gas works." Sewell's voice rose in volume with the heightening sound all around him.

At last the sparks ceased and the cables lay on the ground as lifeless as the hoses at the men's feet. Steps, booted, heavy, approaching with great haste and strained, irregular breathing, revealed a man too senior in years to be so stressed but mindless of his age and limitation, between gasps he confirmed, 'all power's off, hospital's on generator. They're droppin' parachute mines, Sparkenhoe Street's copped it, me sister Eunice lives there."

"Catch your breath man," said Sewell, "are any o' the others at Sparkenhoe?"

The poor man nodded, "Aye, an' Highfields is bad, incendiaries, fires everywhere, all the crews are spread out. Loughborough lads are at the shoe factory, Rutland Street's burnin' an'all."

"Nottingham's 'ere." Sewell turned to Joe Spooner. "Get the hoses goin' on this lot, once the fires out we can leave it to the L.D. an' go on to the next, looks like Aylestone Street's an inferno, God almighty it's a bad en tonight."

Ambulance bells pierced the blanket sound of explosions, for an instant close by, then growing less as the vehicles tore through the streets. A cocktail of noxious fumes hovered over the entire city, sent into the air by voracious flames that consumed rubber, linoleum, roofing felt and all manner of substances, which undisturbed, existed alongside man in convivial harmony but once assaulted and denied their rightful purpose, vent their anger by gripping man's nose and throat so tightly as to choke him.

Now the Shakespeare Street crew from Nottingham reeled in their hoses and on Sewell's orders made for Highfields. Negotiating obstacles on almost every street they sped past struggling local defence men and ambulance crews towards the densely populated area west of the city.

"What's up Ray? Asked Joe, observing his friends pained expression each time the fire engine found a pit in the road's surface.

Often finding themselves working together as auxiliaries, the two men had picked up the old friendship they'd shared when both were employed at the hospital years ago, Joe in the mortuary and Ray at the incinerator, but for some years they'd seen little of one another.

Ray had become disenchanted with the nature of his days at the hospital, added to which the pay was poor, so on marrying Monica Salmon he'd jumped at the chance of working for his uncle in north Wales at a slate quarry, a fresh start with prospects, ideal for a newly wedded couple. The first few years had proved successful, their first child arrived, a boy, but following the birth of the second, another boy, Monica sank into a deep depression and craved only the comfort of her mam. Given the family's troubled past and Monica's delicate nerves Ray had no option but to return to Nottingham where for more than twelve months he'd failed to secure any regular work, times were hard, they lived with Monica's mother. His wife's health eventually improved, whatever drove her spirits to be so low passed as mysteriously as it arrived, but a few weeks here and there with the road gangs, a bit of heavy lifting and carrying for Abel at the scrap yard had been just about all the paid work Ray could find, nothing that guaranteed food on the table. Then one day at the bus stop he'd bumped into Cuth, a porter at the hospital whom Ray knew from his earlier days at the incinerator. Their conversation led to Cuth telling him, 'get yourself along there quick, the maintenance man has just quit, had a big fallin' out wi' the management, you're up to that job'. Ray had been at the hospital ever since, maintenance and some shifts as a porter. They lived still with Mrs.Salmon but being once again the provider, not needing to be subsidised by his mother in law, had improved the atmosphere no end. She was a good woman and Ray had much regard for her but the two young lads, lively, a handful at times, tired their grandma and unable to speak out at Monica for fear of upsetting her, it was to Ray she directed her frustrations. He kept his ear to the ground for any likely house to rent within the vicinity, he felt there would be little sense in moving Monica any distance this time.

It was whilst shifting a heavy cast range one day at the scrap yard that he'd felt sudden excruciating pain in his lower back, it troubled him a lot but he couldn't let it interfere with his job or with his work as a fire brigade auxiliary, he needed to earn at the hospital and the need of, 'doing his bit for the war' was no less vital to him. Ray sighed and looking across the inside of the tender in which they travelled, to his mate Joe he said.

"It's me back, some days it can be a bugger an' others not so bad. I could do wi' a good massage, I told Monica but all she said wer', 'yes an' I could do wi' a week at Cleethorpes'. Argh," Ray grimaced and his fingers clenched as the vehicle hit a pothole.

"Jesus Ray, get somebody at the hospital to have a look," said Joe. Another member of the crew, overhearing the conversation called out.

"What yer need is a corset, my ol' man wears one an' it works a treat, strengthens your spine, Drew's sell 'em, they measure yer up an' fit it all proper like."

The engine pulled up sharply causing Ray yet another spasm of pain but the scene outside sent everyone's thoughts immediately to the misery and despair of this place.

'Armageddon, the end of the world is nigh', Joe spoke the words quietly to himself as his eyes took in the magnitude of their task. The buildings on the right of the street were burning fiercely, on the left, brightly lit by the intensity of the flames, houses, people's homes, cowering under the threat, some already yielding, slates tumbling to the ground, windows cracking from the heat, all shaken at their foundations by the heavy German bombs that found their targets with alarming accuracy, set ablaze by the incendiaries.

Another Leicester crew had arrived on the scene no more than ten minutes earlier having first had to deal with a hit at the railway station.

"Get your hoses goin' on that lot, winds gettin' up, fannin' the flames faster than we can douse 'em, watch your backs, the houses behind yer are unstable, the road's cracked right across, sewers run beneath, this one's all shite!"

The Nottingham men worked fast, at least the hydrant here supplied all vital water. Ray trained a hose at the flames which leapt into the air defiantly.

"Look out."

A frantic warning was yelled by somebody. In the turmoil identities were vague, only the white helmet, denoting leader of the crew, in this case Bob Ellis, enabled an immediate recognition. Joe and Ray worked alongside each other wherever possible, it was a fact, the presence of a mate empowered any man. The intense heat caused a bow window at the first floor of a house on the left hand side of the street to explode, propelling into the air vicious shards of glass, like a viper spitting venom, they fell to the ground, peppering it with malice.

"Bloody hell, look at this." Ray pointed to the hose, a piece of glass so sharp that it had penetrated the coarse canvas, clung to the hose by its tip, the light from the flames turning it to a vivid gold, the movement of air causing it to flex like the wing of some exotic moth. His hands heavily gloved Joe grabbed at it and wrenched it out, at first nothing happened, then pressure of water inside the hose forced a fine jet through the small tear.

"Shit, this bugger's no good, I'll tell Ellis while you fetch the spare."

Their tread over the glass fragments strewn about them was akin to walking over brittle ice, yet their faces felt intense heat.

"It happens lad," said Ellis, "just be bloody thankful it wer' the hose."

At that moment another tender pulled up, the crew piled out and made straight for Ellis.

"Sparkenhoe Street's under control, we've been sent to assist you lot, the rest are at the gasworks."

"Any bloody help's welcome, watch yourselves the row at the back of us is volatile, got to put more water on the flames, cool things down, glass is overheatin'."

Ray coupled up the replacement hose, sometimes when at the fires in Nottingham, he'd marvelled at the way water kept flowing, gallon after gallon, and for that matter, where it all went to, in the clear light of day the scene was as much as a man's eyes and mind could take in. Here it was Ray's nose that took in, a smell familiar to him, a sickening, nauseous smell, like no other, burning flesh. With so many fire crews all out working at once, water pressure was low and every drop vital. His back ache ignored Ray fixed his mind on a greater torment, willing the jet of water to defeat, to conquer this rampant aggressor. Few words passed between the men, each had command of their own task, trying to make themselves heard above the level of noise wasted too much effort, concentration was locked onto the perils surrounding them and strength was kept for the need of endurance as arms fought the strain of holding up the powerful hoses and knees threatened to buckle under exhaustion.

It was after four in the morning when apart from small eruptions of feeble flame, the battered mounds of rubble and contorted metal stood amidst ghostly smoke and vapour, like a heavily wounded battalion, slowly emerging from a battleground, through the murky residues of prolonged gunfire, the enemy finally overcome. But at such cost, where were the dead, for there would surely be dead, mutilated, charred, after every battle, always there were dead.

A sound, sudden, unexpected, revealed an elderly woman it was as if she appeared from nowhere. She was entirely calm, almost oblivious to the images about her, ironically, it was to Joe Spooner she spoke.

"He's gone, Bert's gone, arf hour ago." She pointed to a house at the very far end of the street on the left hand side. "He didn't know what wer' happenin', bless him, since he had the stroke he could hardly tell day from night, couldn't talk neither, but he could sing, all his old army songs. Belgium, that's where he wer' in the last lot, got a bullet in his thigh, fleshy thighs, Bert allus had fleshy thighs, same thing happened to Wally Freeman but it went in one side an' straight out t'other, not my Bert, the medic had to ferret around for his."

In a frail voice she began to sing, staring across the street to where only hours before had stood accommodation blocks, it was the tune of a hymn, 'Trust and obey', but the words had been changed, very likely by a long gone 'Tommy' trying to keep his spirit strong as he moved ever closer to destruction and further away from home and those he loved.

"As we march with a will,
to defeat Kaiser Bill,
what a story we'll tell on our way,
of the battles we've won,
with our bayonet and gun
and our sarge' who we trust and obey."

She was surely confused and vulnerable. Joe took her arm, it felt tiny, after gripping the hose for so long this elderly woman seemed almost too fragile to touch, yet here she was, amidst the devastation, calm, showing no panic, apparently having sat with her husband 'til life left him while all around them turned to a hell on earth. Joe dealt with grieving relatives almost every day through the course of his work at Handley's, some so distressed that finding the right words proved to be by far the most difficult element of the job, if indeed it could be called simply 'a job'.

"Mind the glass," said Joe, her feet were clad only in light shoes. "Where's your family?" He asked, concerned for her safety.

She looked at him and smiled. "There is no one dear, just me an' Bert, I'd make you all a cup o' tea but the gas is off, an' there's no electric neither. Good job I filled his hot water bottle when I did, he couldn't stand his feet bein' cold, it wer' the trenches you know, standin' in ice cold water for days at a time, even in summer Bert allus wore thick socks." She pointed across the street. "There wer' people in them buildings, army folk, billeted here since last year. My Bert wer' with The Staffordshire's, he wants the Co-op to bury him, divvy yer see."

Joe called to Bob Ellis, leader of the Leicester crew, wearied beyond measure the man was less sympathetic, short and impatient.

"Why aren't you in the shelter missus, it's no place for a woman o' your age." Some local defence men were by now busy at the scene, he called out, "Over here, there's a woman needs escortin' away from this lot."

She looked anxiously at Joe. "I can't leave Bert on his own, I'm alright, I just need to tell 'em at Co-op. Will you tell 'em for me, they'll need to know, it's Mr.Albert Grimes, number 57, Trenchard Street. I've got money to pay."

Joe's heart went out to her. "I can't go meself to the Co-op Mrs.Grimes, an' it's barely daylight, there'll be nobody at Co-op 'til mornin'. If you go with the warden I'll see that Bert's alright."

As she was led away, the city seemed at last to have found an eerie interlude, while voices could be heard both close by and distant, rumbles too, regular, ominous, as the emergency services pulled at rubble in the search for casualties and bodies, nevertheless the fires were all but extinguished.

Now an overwhelming tiredness, along with a dismay, which deepened with the realisation that this night had brought war to Leicester with a ferocity not previously experienced, achieved to subdue the spirits of all those present. They worked with stoic determination but their inner fight was spent, their efforts now would yield only misery. At least Bert Grimes died naturally, his wife at his bedside, after surviving the Great War he deserved that.

Ray stretched himself, rubbing the pit of his back with a hand sore from ripping at bricks and masonry, Joe alongside him, willing the rubble to declare no sign of human remains. He was used to handling the deceased, but the memory of that night at the burning bakery on Meadow Lane in Nottingham haunted his dreams. Burning turned the body from a peaceful shell of a human being, now this world departed, into something that bore little resemblance. Victims crushed under falling masonry, while lifeless, looked up still with eyes that had glimpsed Heaven, but a body blackened from fire and flame troubled Joe's mind. How could God recognise them? Had God recognised his own dad, blown up, burned, somewhere on the battlefields of France all those years ago.

"Over here." One of the Leicester men called out urgently. It was the first of many but it was not until a shaft of daylight broke through the retreating night clouds that Joe's heart missed a beat and his stomach turned. He'd lifted a lintel that prevented his progress through the rubble, as he'd struggled to pull it away an arm fell through a gap in the random bricks and crumpled plastering, the fist clenched, the fingers seared, fused into one agonised stump of flesh and bone. Ray observed his friend's sudden inertia, Joe's shocked expression and clambered across to where Joe stood, transfixed.

"What's up Joe?"

"Do yer remember how I used to scare them poor lads in the churchyard. You'd tell me, 'one day Joe Spooner, a hand'll come out o' that bloody urn an' frighten the shit out o' you'," Joe was physically shaking.

Ray put his hand on his friend's arm. "Come on, let's get the poor sod out o' there. St.Andrew's churchyard wer years ago Joe, we wern't much more than lads ourselves."

Joe took a deep breath. "Jack Wainwright's out wi' Monty's lot yer know, 'e'd stand at that grave 'til the very last second, once or twice I thought 'e wer' goin' to stick it out, wait for the arm, show me up as a fraud. Tough little bugger, not much more than lads ourselves yer say, well Jack'd be same age now as I wer' then an' 'e's fightin' in the Western Desert."

"We're fightin' too Joe," said Ray, "if we weren't here dealin' wi' this gruesome mess, if we hadn't grabbed the hoses an' stood 'til the skin on our faces singed, who would have done it? We'll beat bloody Adolf one way or another, you, me, Jack, all of us. Happen, watchin' at the curb o' that grave in churchyard toughened us all, waitin' for the unknown, never really sure. By the time you'd counted to eleven, behind that big headstone where I used to hide meself, my heart wer' beatin' faster than a two stroke engine, adrenalin, pure adrenalin. Sounds daft now but I couldn't help meself, what if it did, what if that soddin' arm wi' its gnarled hand come up through that bloody urn just to spite us. Yet it never did, there wer' no tormented souls in St.Andrew's Joe, but perhaps that place made us what we are, tough buggers, Jerry don't know the arf of it."

Ray winced from pain as he reached down to the rubble at their feet and began moving the broken bricks away from the body, Joe worked alongside him.

"Bloody hell Ray, if Monica won't massage your back then your ol' mate Joe'll do it."

Just then Bob Ellis called out. "W.V.S. are here wi' an urn o' tea, God bless 'em."

Ray and Joe looked at each other and smiled, each with the same thought, there was nothing in the urn but tea!

CHAPTER TEN

January 1943

"What's wrong with him Mam, why can't Jack see sense?"

Hilda rubbed a carrot over the grater with such force, it cracked and the tip flew across the table top and on to the floor. "Damn the thing." She retrieved the piece of carrot, wiped it on her apron and continued to virtually pulverise the remainder in her frustration.

Most women had come to realise that grated carrot, in the absence of dried fruit, added to a very basic cake mix, not only made bulk but also kept the cake moist.

Miners were granted a slightly increased ration, the authorities acknowledged that such physically demanding work could not be sustained on the amount of nourishment prescribed by a general ration. The difference was minimal and despite this allowance, men came up from their shift ever more lean.

With some deciding to enlist and through the urgent conscription of young men, work at the coal face was left more and more to the older ones and took from their tired bodies, far more than nature had designed men to give. At Birchdale there had been four deaths in as many months, Tommy Spooner had said of the most recent. 'I made myself hope that when I washed away the black dust that blocked his nose an' mouth, an' I lifted the weight o' the war off his chest, somehow his lungs'd rise to defy it all, to breathe, an' that there'd be nothin' wrong with his heart, he'd just needed the right to draw breath!'

The new manager at Birchdale, Hugh Porter, constantly juggled the workforce and the foremen, quite literally caught between a rock and a hard place, recognising his situation, drove every man's aching joints and straining lungs, including their own, to produce that filthy black commodity so vital to the nation. Yet seeing the exhaustion in workmates, trying to reconcile that with their strong sense of loyalty to the troops, tormented the foremen's minds by day and by night.

Hilda now had money, Davina's legacy, it sat in a bank account doing nothing, that was Hilda's torment. Why not a bigger house, not grand but offering at least a bathroom, and their own, not rented, but hers and Jack's, a family home. Hilda was expecting again, some folk maintained it was irresponsible to bring a child into the world during war but David was almost six, how could anyone know just how long the war would last. The baby was due in May, a new home with facilities to make life a little easier surely made sense, but each time she broached the subject Jack refused to discuss it, retreating behind a wall of silence, which Hilda deemed selfish and unreasonable. It created a friction, an atmosphere and Hilda had poured out to her mam, all of her frustration and resentment.

Annie felt concern for her son in law, Hilda's desire was natural and pursued through love of her husband and son, but age brought with it experience and understanding. Annie remembered Florrie, Jack's mam, the family's struggles over the years, and all that they lived through in this small house on Forest Road. She remembered Victor, innocent Victor, sheltered from the harshness of an intolerant world by the sanctuary of this simple home.

Jack's work too influenced his thinking and bound his conscience. Annie could imagine the conflict of mind if Jack walked away from the pit gates to return home, to seek his comfortable, well appointed house when his long suffering workmates must wend their weary way to those humble terraced abodes, which offered little to warm the soul yet demanded much in dues to the landlord.

Hilda spooned the mix into a cake tin, placed it in the oven and shut the door on it as though committing it to serve time in lock up as punishment for challenging her nerves.

"The country's at war, who knows, we could all be blown to bits, why shouldn't we grasp a little happiness whenever we can, moving from here to a place of our own would be no sin. You talk to him Mam, he'll likely listen to you. Stubborn, why do men have to be so damn stubborn?"

The cook pots were now thrust noisily into the sink causing Annie to caution Hilda. "If you're not careful you'll chip the enamel."

That's Jack's trouble, he's coated with enamel and try as I may I cannot penetrate it, I could scream when he goes all silent on me, I'd rather he shout, throw something, anything rather than no response at all."

Annie sighed, "You have David to consider, Jack is quite right not to create a scene in front of a child. If you think it might serve a purpose then I will talk with him but on my own, your likely outbursts and interruptions would be far from helpful. Take David to Celia's next Sunday afternoon, he'll be company for Emily. Mathew and Samuel are going train spotting for an hour with their granddad, but don't say anything to your dad about it if you see him while you are there."

Hilda paused in the midst of wiping clean the table top.

"As if I would, he'd probably have the wrath of The Almighty brought down on Jack if I did."

Annie let the remark pass, Hilda's mood was prickly, instead she said, "I promised to go to Edna's on Sunday, so I'll call in on Jack on the way home, just for a little while. You have to be aware that Jack is under great strain, what with new management at Birchdale and the Bradshaws finding their way around the complexities of the industry. By all accounts Patricia Bradshaw is her father's daughter, not known for her gentleness. But even she must be feeling out of her depth at times."

Annie proceeded to wash up the contents of the sink while Hilda moved her attentions to spreading clothes on the airer.

"You'd think after the scandal he created she would have given him his marching orders," said Hilda, "but there they are, living supposedly in wedded bliss off the fat of the land in that fancy house. Poor Mrs.Stanford they couldn't wait to get her out."

Annie knew that Hilda's assessment of the situation was not altogether correct, she had sat with Florence Stanford while the troubled woman had confided the true nature of things, but a confidence was to be held in trust and even to her own daughter Annie would divulge nothing of Florence's endeavours to secure, for Julia and Caroline, the land at Colver. Instead she responded to Hilda's comments simply by saying, "I'm sure Anthony Bradshaw regrets his behaviour and I can't imagine 'bliss' is an apt word to apply."

Just then a knock came at the back door, Hilda tutted. "Who can that be, I shall have to meet David from school at a quarter past." She glanced at the clock, just after half past two. "Don't let me forget the cake Mam," she said as she untied her apron and cast it randomly over the back of a chair.

Annie could hear a woman's voice, Hilda said, "Come in Mrs.Flowers, mam's here, she'll know what to do, don't worry I'm sure it will be alright."

The woman stepped inside the scullery, physically shaking beneath the loose, wrap-around pinafore, which her slight frame failed to fill.

"It's Mrs.Flowers from next door, she's a bit upset Mam." Hilda looked at Annie with eyes that pleaded for help.

"Sit down for a minute Mrs.Flowers," said Annie, the nervous woman didn't appear to be holding a telegram or letter. It was strange how the recipient of bad news seemed always to present the cause of their despair, that dreaded piece of paper informing them of tragedy, Annie dared to hope that Mrs.Flowers had not suffered such misery as her trembling fingers did not pass to her any letter, its content needing to be confirmed by friend or neighbour.

"It's Brian, me youngest," the poor woman sat on the chair as though she were about to be sentenced to hang, "he's done a bunk from camp, they'll come lookin' for him, sure to, they come down hard on deserters don't they? Oh dear." She put a hand to her chest and took a deep breath, "He's only been gone three weeks, what should I do? He's sittin' in kitchen eatin' a rasher o' bacon, it's all he's had since yesterday."

Annie laid her hand on Mrs.Flowers' arm. "Would you like me to talk to him?"

She nodded her head and wiped tears from her eyes with the hem of her pinafore. "He's a good lad, never skipped his lessons, not even when Goose Fair wer' in town, Phyllis Dale's lad would be out arf the night, then in bed all next day, come Monday when fair wer' packed up an' gone there'd be no sign o' Reggie at school, took him 'til the Tuesday to wake up, not that he wer' the brightest when he wer' awake."

"How old is Brian Mrs.Flowers?" Asked Annie.

She sniffled, "Eighteen last September, he wanted to be a train driver but you have to start somewhere don't yer. So he got a job as a porter at Midland Station."

"Come along then, let's see if he's finished that bacon." Annie coaxed the anxious woman through the back door and followed her to No.65.

A young man sat at the table wiping every last drop of bacon fat from his plate with a piece of bread, he went to stand up.

"It's alright Brian, I'm Hilda's mother, you know Hilda don't you?"

He nodded but didn't speak. Annie sat down beside him, so young, too young for war, it was an instinctive thing, the urge to wrap her arms around him, to tell him everything would be alright, but Annie felt she had not the authority, so she spoke of John, of his work, how she missed him, of George and William, how she looked forward to their letters. There was a measure of defiance in his voice when he spoke, not directed at Annie but for his initiation into army life.

"I wanted to see me mam," he said, "I know I've got to go back, I wouldn't get her into trouble for anythin' but that Sergeant Maitland is nothin' but a loud mouthed, uniform lovin' big head wi' not enough brains to fill the gap between his ears. He told us when we first got there that from then on he wer' goin' to be our mam, he'd be the one as tucked us up at night, give us medicine if we got sick an' checked we'd scrubbed our neck, well he wasn't goin' to be my mam, the ugly bugger. He pushed his face right into mine yesterday an' said, 'Do yer love your mam Flowers'? I know what he meant, we're supposed to treat him like some sort o' God. I had to get away from his ugly mug an' see me proper mam, so first chance I got I done a runner. I got a train, nobody bothered me, it arrived bang on time, it's a good driver that gets the train into station neither late nor early. I'll go back tonight, the worst they can do to me is make me scrub the latrines, if they didn't need me to fight Jerry they wouldn't have called me up in the first place would they? I'll fight wi' the best o' them but I'll never let that ugly bugger Maitland compare 'isself to my mam." Mrs.Flowers burst into tears, Annie held the distraught woman in her arms until her crying eased, smiled into her troubled eyes then quietly slipped away, leaving mother and son to make the most of what little time they had before Brian must make his way back to camp.

As Annie stepped inside the scullery of No.67, Hilda was taking the cake out of the oven, it filled the room with a curious smell of wartime baking, a mixture of wholesome and make do, Hilda prodded the middle with her finger.

"It's ready, just hard enough!" She said with a note of sarcasm.

It was true that creating any confection from such limited ingredients proved challenging and producing a light spongy cake now happened only in dreams.

"I'll have to go for David, will everything be alright next door?"

"I'll walk with you," said Annie, "Brian is going back, when he's had an hour with his mam. Whether or not it will be alright none of us can know, but please God let the lad come home in one piece."

Annie's voice tapered to a whisper and Hilda sensed that it was not now Brian Flowers occupying her mother's thoughts but her brothers.

"I'm sorry Mam, I didn't mean to be selfish, rattling on about a house. It is for Jack that I want better, he deserves so much more than this endless struggle at the pit with nothing different to look forward to, I want to make things better for him, for us all as a family." She threaded her arm through Annie's. "I love you Mam, the house isn't that important, I wonder if it will be a little sister for David."

Annie squeezed on Hilda's arm. "Whichever it is has already been decided and growing accordingly, a longsuffering little woman, or a stubborn little man." She looked at her daughter with a mischievous grin and both burst into laughter. "I'll spend some time with Jack on Sunday afternoon but I won't be an interfering mother in law, Jack's lost his own mam and I could never come close to being what Florrie was to Jack. Tonight, after you've tucked David up in bed, perhaps you could pop next door to check on Mrs.Flowers, sit with her for a bit, keep her company."

As they approached the school gates David came running towards them, "Mam," he shouted, simply that one word, yet the emotion it stirred within Annie was profound.

You can't have it both ways Patricia, your father, for whatever reason, favoured you over your sisters, it's just a shame that he didn't see fit to bring you to a better understanding of the Industry." Anthony drank the last mouthful of tea and put the cup down on the saucer with a sigh. "I don't imagine he gave much thought to the actual moment of his demise, in his mind he had ample time in which to familiarise you with the workings and dealings at Birchdale, besides, taking you under his wing prematurely would surely have removed that element of shock he wished to save for Florence, Caroline and Julia. They're not fools, they would have deduced from his attentions that his scheme, his plan was to leave the golden goose to you." He gazed down at the cup and saucer, they were odd, ill fitting, not from a matching set, just as he and Patricia were unmatched. For years they had lived as the respectable couple, professional, correct, entirely suited, no one could have held the slightest inkling of anything to the contrary. Patricia Stanford had turned his head all those years ago when they'd met, quite by chance, on the concourse at Victoria Station and had been obliged to share a hackney carriage. In the beginning the union was good, at least he'd considered it so, having little awareness of the constitution of marriage to enable him a comparison. But over the years his feeling of loneliness, his abiding sense of being ever subordinate to his wife, drove him to seek comfort, to find the saucer which fitted exactly his cup and held it stable, safe and secure.

"Your father put in his claim to the Commission before he died, in due course the relevant value will be paid to his Estate and then it will be yours, but the government now owns the coal and as the country is at war they dictate what happens to it, at least the Ministry of Fuel does. The masters are now the mastered Patricia, war demands compromise, for many it demands sacrifice, perhaps you should think of it as a duty."

Four years ago the Coal Act had nationalised the ownership of coal, prior to, royalties had been paid by the mine owners to the landlords of the coal beneath, the owners of the mineral rights. As Birchdale, unusually, held its own mineral rights, up to 1938 Basil had effectively paid the royalties to himself. The collieries remained in private hands and those obliged to sell their, as yet unmined coal stock, had submitted claims for compensation to the Regional Valuation Boards.

Patricia's temper flared. "Duty you say, you sit here in the comfort of my house, the adulterer, the wrong doer and you preach to me of duty. I let you live here under this roof to save face, to still the wagging tongues, what's that if it isn't compromise? I could have cast you loose, sent you to live in shame with your hussy."

Anthony rose to his feet. "I am enlisting, not too old to become a soldier, but way beyond meeting the demands of being a husband, of being Patricia Stanford's husband. I wish you well my dear, this war may solve all our problems, who knows?"

"You can't just go," her voice was shrill with bitterness, "not now."

"Hugh Porter is a capable man, trust his experience Patricia, be guided by him," he paused, "I have packed my bag, whether or not we see each other again I believe only God can decide." He walked from the room, she made no attempt to follow him and within a few seconds she heard the front door open and close. From the window she watched as he made his way, she allowed herself no emotion, 'let the hussy weep', she didn't need him. She was her father's daughter. Patricia gave an unladylike sniff at the vision of her husband disappearing into the distance of Castle Road.

Gathering up the cup and saucer she took it to the kitchen, about to lay them in the sink, she hesitated, taking the cup in one hand, with the other she smoothed her finger along the rim from where Anthony had drunk, a sudden sense of loneliness gave the odd cup a powerful significance, he was gone! Hurrying into the hall, she took her coat from the peg, opened the door and felt the rush of cold air restore her resolve, she would go to the pit, where else, her first duty was to her father's memory, yet somewhere, beneath the surface, and threatening to escape were tears, even now, as yet contained, they stung her eyes. She got into the car, 'so be it, there was much to do'.

As she drew closer to the mine, only then did the tears fall and in her turmoil Patricia could not tell for whom it was they fell, with such intent.

Sorting the Sunday papers, indeed sorting the newspapers most days, proved a trial. No matter how hard Annie tried to avert her eyes away from headlines, still she was compelled to read. The Allies were pushing hard, driving back the Axis forces through Algeria and Morocco. On the Eastern Front the Soviets battled for Stalingrad. War correspondents sent back their reports in greater depth than Annie could stand to read, yet that element of human nature which drove the individual to know, to be aware, ordered her eyes to follow the words, lines that revealed horror, the relentless desperate fight.

It was a week before Christmas when a letter came from George, as ever his narrative was cheerful, interesting, bare of anything likely to disturb.

When news of Jack Wainwright's injury reached the family Gertie had felt sure that Annie would have heard of the situation through George, but typically, he'd made no mention. Jack had been transported back to England once his condition had become stable. In hospital at Southampton the doctors had been impressed at the skill of the surgeon in Cairo. His left leg had been shattered beyond repair and the wound infected. They'd amputated just above the knee and the healing process had been without problems, at Southampton the physios had bowed to Jack's stubborn insistence that a false leg was all he needed to send him on his way and if they couldn't make him one, then he'd get his mam to knit him one! Such spirit was undeniable, Jack had come home to Nottingham on the nineteenth of January, walking a little stiffly but as cocky as ever.

Henry had leave too, now a fully fledged member of the Parachute Regiment and with more abilities that he saw fit to tell his mam. The two brothers fell back easily into one another's company for a few precious days before Henry had return to camp. Jack couldn't let it show but waving off his young brother tied his insides in knots.

Annie was on her way to Edna's, a long letter had arrived from Liza. Her work on the farm at Halam filled the sheets of notepaper with detailed accounts of rural endeavour, Edna wanted Annie to read the letter, she was so proud of her daughters, having no sons to be serving in the forces caused her to thank God in her prayers every day, she felt for those mothers living on their nerves, dreading the worst news but Edna's girls were doing their bit as best they could.

Annie and Susie were both active with the WVS and Myra had insisted on helping out by sitting with her young nieces after school and seldom were Edna and Myra's spare moments not taken up in knitting squares for blankets. Billy had remarked one afternoon when their industry was in full swing, that the sound of knitting needles going clickety clack was still ringing in his head when he lifted his earpiece at the Exchange.

Winchester Street appeared quiet apart from two children playing with skipping ropes and a dog that sat on its haunches, observing a third, who nibbled on a raw carrot, no doubt the lad having been told it would help him see in the dark.

The warmth coming from Edna's living room was comforting, outside the air was chill, even the children in the street, active though they were, displayed a blue tinge to their noses and the mittens, made from old socks helped their fingers grip the handle of their skipping rope. Annie crossed the scullery, relieved to reach the cosiness of Edna's fireplace.

"Hello aunty Annie, blow me if I 'aven't managed to kill two birds wi' one stone today, I wer' comin' to see you later."

Annie's face revealed her surprise and delight at finding Jack Wainwright present. Before she had chance to respond he was on his feet, across the room and planting a kiss on her cheek.

"I heard how Myra had been in the wars an'all, fine pair we are, but yer can't keep a Wainwright down nor a Dodds neither." In an instant he struck the fender at the hearth with his foot, a metallic clatter launched him into laughter. "No more bother wi' that soddin' corn on me little toe now aunty Annie an' cutting' me nails only takes half the time. Like I told me mam, she only needs to wash the one sock but there's no pleasin' you women, she still cried her eyes out."

Myra looked genuinely happy and Edna glanced from Jack to Annie before saying. "Madness must run in the family, Jack reminds me o' your Harold.

Billy sat quietly, not an anxious quietness Annie sensed but a pensive one, Billy's experiences in the last war must surely have come back to him. He'd not ever spoken of the trenches, since leaving the hospital at Hemel Hempstead, his family, their future, had occupied his mind fully, leaving no space for debilitating thoughts to take up lodging.

Annie rested her hand on his shoulder, he turned his head to look up and smiled, she felt he needed a distraction, in a soft voice she said. "I need to speak with Jack Haynes, I promised Hilda that I would, it's Davina's money, Hilda wants them to buy a house, somewhere a bit bigger, with the baby due in May she can't understand why Jack is so reluctant. I think I understand, I think you do too, but how do I persuade him to see that he's entitled to grasp opportunity without being disloyal to the men. Florrie I'm sure would tell him so."

"Jack Haynes is a good 'en, decent through and through," said Billy, " 'e could be wilful when 'e wer' younger but that's the way of a lad, I wer' the same, thought I knew it all, when in truth I wer' too wet behind the ears to know what life wer' like beyond the end of our street. Wi' out mam I'd 'ave been lost, kept me on the straight did mam. Jack allus did right by Florrie, looked after his mam, an' Victor, woe betide anybody as said owt to belittle Victor, mind, all them boys stood up for 'im, not one of 'em would have let as much as a fly light on 'im." Billy laughed at the notion. "Perhaps now isn't the best time, emotions run high among the men, war challenges their thinkin', unsettles 'em, an' I've heard the Stanford lass, or Mrs.Bradshaw I s'pose I should rightly call 'er, can be antagonistic an'all. Now that's a big word for Billy Dodds don't yer reckon Annie Eddowes, must be them appointments at solicitors', extended me vocabulary, don't ask me to spell the bugger though." Billy gave Annie a wide grin. "I shouldn't worry your head, things 'ave a way of sortin' the'selves out. Besides, if anybody can find the way around a problem you can. God rest 'er soul, I mean to speak no ill o' the dead but Charles' first wife Enid could put two sticks to fight. I've heard Edna say that it wer' you that went to their house an' brought calm more often than not. Hilda's a bright young woman, this war won't last forever, eventually the the politicians an' the generals'll get tired o' pushin' men around the game board. I reckon if she could just wait a year or two, 'til one of 'em's won or they call it quits, then her Jack'll feel like celebratin', a new place wi' a bit o' garden an' a shed for his own space, aye, that could tempt a man sure enough."

At that moment Edna came through from the scullery carrying a tray of tea.

"Put that draughts board away now you two, gamblin' on a Sunday indeed, whatever would the vicar say?" She went "tut-tut" with pretence of vexation.

Jack laughed and quickly counted Myra's halfpennies. "She's won, beat me by tuppence."

Edna handed Liza's letter to Annie. "Have you heard from Ruddington lately?"

“Doris wrote a couple of weeks ago,” said Annie, “she wants me to take Samuel to visit when I can. Seth has cleared an area of scrubland on the western edge of the farm, she says he’s working every hour of daylight. Freddy’s the same, at Bonthorpe they were expecting two Land Girls at New Year, I’ve not heard since.” Annie opened the envelope and unfolded Liza’s letter. Jack got to his feet.

“Ta very much for the tea an’ hospitality Mrs.D, cheers Mr.D,” he raised his cup as if to toast Billy and Edna, swallowing the last drop of beverage, “best be off now, I told me old mate Charlie Jones that I’d drop by. Met his young lady last Thursday, smitten is Jones I can tell, mind you, she’s a good lookin’ lass that Maureen. Good luck to ‘em that’s what I say.” Turning his gaze back to Myra, he teased her. “You needn’t think that you’re one up on Jacko Miss Dodds, I’ll win back me tuppence next time.”

Myra smiled openly, Edna noticed and recognised the pleasure in her daughter’s eyes, Myra was happy to know that there was to be a, ‘next time’.

There had been no news of Archie Medlyn for at least two months, possibly longer. Jack Wainwright was easy company, it was probably the connection to Annie Eddowes that made it so, yet Edna suspected Jack had long held a fondness for Myra. Two young people, both maimed and apparently bound to each other if only by tuppence!

It was Billy who interrupted his wife’s thoughts.

“I forgot to tell yer, I’m bein’ made Manager at the Exchange, startin’ March. I’ve been there, apparently, longer than almost everybody else. It can’t be down to sense can it, more to do wi’ familiarity, Arthur Chubb reckons I’ve pinched the job from ‘im, ‘e started at the Exchange two days afore I did. It’s only banter on his part, good mate is Arthur, ‘You’re a bandit Billy Dodds’, ‘e said, ‘an’ a one armed bloody bandit at that’.

As Annie approached No.67 Forest Road she clung to the happy atmosphere, which she’d just left at Edna’s, she sympathised with Hilda’s frustration but given the absence of George, William and John, of Jack’s own brothers, especially William Haynes, now a prisoner of the Germans, with hand on heart Annie would have to admit her allegiance on the subject of a new home lay with Jack. Billy was right, when the war was ended, then life could begin again, but now everyone seemed to be in a state of inertia, afraid to plan, loath to recall recent history, held up in the present, like a reel of film stuck in the projector. In her mind she had gone over and over what she would say to Jack, her son in law. It touched Annie, the way he ever referred to Florrie as 'mam' and to herself as mother. It was respectful and she let herself believe that Jack held a fondness for her too, but in Annie's book it was only correct that Jack's love as a son belonged to his mam, to her memory, to all that Florrie Haynes was. She tapped at the back door, within no more than a few seconds it opened.

"Hello Mother," he said, "Hilda hinted you might call in," he laughed, "your daughter is far too open, I can read her like the pages of a book. Let's have your coat, I've just stoked the fire. Hilda won't be back from Celia's until she's confident that you an' me 'ave had a good ol' confab."

Annie rubbed her hands together in front of the blaze. "Billy sends his best. Jack Wainwright was at Edna's, I think he was there to see Myra really. They've fitted him with an artificial leg, you wouldn't know it to look at him, in fact I can't believe that anything of Gertie's Jack could ever be false. Edna said he reminds her of George's dad, Harold, I know what she means, there was an innate cheerfulness in Harold, he always saw the bright side, travelled in hope, like the old adage, 'travel in hope or die in despair'. He was twenty six when he was killed in the accident at the slaughter yard but I know Harold didn't die in despair."

Jack sat in the chair opposite Annie, they found comfort either side of the fireplace, the flames warming Annie's toes.

"I don't think me mam an' dad ever had more than a few shillin' put by, there wer' allus food on table but I reckon all us lads walked the streets wi' patches on our breeches, darned socks an' the collars turned on our shirts, but we were decent, honest folk. Respect, first an' foremost we 'ad self respect. Dad used to say that at the end o' the day a man should answer first to his own conscience, even before answering to the Almighty.

Down that pit it's a different world, every man trusts an' respects his mates. We're all black faced, filthy wi' sweat an' layers o' coal dust. When we come up to the top it's easy to be overcome wi' a sense of inferiority, scratchin' away in the bowels o' the earth, down tunnels that travel like rat runs, black rats, filthy black rats. My job is to get as much product from each man as I can wi'out actually killin' him through his efforts, but I make sure that not one of 'em leaves pit gates, to go wherever landlord condescends to let 'em lay their head, wi'out the self respect that even the Almighty takes second place to.

I know what Hilda wants, an' I don't deny the sense of it, but yer see Mother, it's Stanford money. Mrs.Wright, God rest her soul, wer' a good woman but that money, it's not just Stanford money, tainted by all his miserable dealin's, it's blood money an'all, got from widows wi' kids to rear, from men spittin' up their lungs, valued little more than rats. You tell me Mother, how could I live in any place that wer' paid for wi' miners blood money. How could I lay my head in a place where Stanford looked down on me from the walls, that man could haunt yer, dead or alive, you mentioned Jack Wainwright, well ask his dad Steve, 'e'll tell yer how Stanford could haunt a man's brain, drive him to despair."

Annie sighed. "I've never had much money Jack, I can't imagine many women of my age and background had more than the contents of their purse and with no expectation of anything other. Sometimes an event, quite unforeseen, brings with it a measure of encouragement, a kindly fate, which seems to be sent for a purpose. When I was first married to George's dad I was a seamstress, working for Saul Eddowes. That's where I met Edna, I'd begun work when I was ten, Edna was already competent, she'd been at the workshop on Winchester Street a couple of years before I started there. For some reason, which I never understood, my aunt Bella, who raised me, resented Saul, she appeared to have no regard for him, I was placed there to earn a simple living, a convenient arrangement as we lived further along Winchester Street, but Eddowes was a name, which on hearing it, caused aunt Bella to be ill humoured. In the end I tried not to mention Saul Eddowes, to speak little of my days' work so as not to provoke her.

Yet when Saul died, I learned he had left to me ten guineas in his Will. I was shocked and felt strangely guilty because I dare not tell aunt Bella for fear of her reaction, I am convinced she would have said, 'It's Eddowes' money' and how could

I accept Eddowes benevolence! Saul always treated me well, I worked hard but I learned too, my skills at the machine improved month on month and I felt secure, his manner toward me was ever pleasant, as indeed it was with Edna and May Watkinson. Ten guineas felt like a fortune then, Harold said we should put it by, to use for something special. Not until after Harold had died did I touch any of it. Our lives had changed, George's and mine, aunt Bella fell ill and died the following year. For me, that ten guineas became hope money, there was nothing sinister about it, George deserved at the very least to be given hope.

Yes, Claude Stanford did buy Birchdale from Davina when Nathan, her husband died but I've heard that Claude was a man very different to his son Basil.

Davina Wright was one of the kindest, truly decent individuals I have ever known. Nathan died so long ago that for years and years she lived a lonely widow, why she looked on my children as family I don't know, but she did and while the money and the house at The Park were in her hands, in her care, no one could claim the right to call any part of it 'blood money'. It's the means of hope, hope for you and Hilda, for David and the family you are yet to have. When this war is over, live Jack, live for all those whose lives have been taken from them, carry on striving for the miners, for that respect your dad gave to you, for the hope they deserve, it's the only way the likes of Basil Stanford will ever be beat.

I think of Saul Eddowes still, just as I shall forever keep Davina in my thoughts. It is those events, so unexpected, kindly fate that enables us Jack." Annie stood, leaned over him and kissed his forehead. "Hilda can easily wait until after the war, just cast her a little hope, that's all."

At that moment a noise outside alerted them to Hilda's return. David was first through the door, calling out in his excitement.

"Aunty Celia's got a puppy dog, it's called Tilly and it's brown and white, aunty Celia says if we come again next week we can take Tilly for a walk and I can hold the lead for a bit."

Jack's expression became vague, he spoke, but more to himself than to the others.

"Tilly, mam's cat wer' called Tilly, every time it had kittens Victor used to try an' hide 'em, so's Brian couldn't do the necessary, 'e had to do it, we'd 'ave been overrun else, poor little sods. But there wer' this one time an' I don't know why, mam told Victor that 'e could pick one, to keep. You should 'ave seen his face, first thing 'e did wer' run off to tell Billy Dodds. Travelled in hope did our Victor." Jack's eyes found Annie's and he smiled.

The two best mates sat in the back yard on an old upturned tin bath, close together, at the least corroded end.

"Let's 'ave a look at it then," said Charlie, "couldn't very well ask yer last week, not wi' Maureen there, yer know what women are like, show 'em a splinter an' they turn the colour o' lavatory pan."

Jack rolled up the leg of his trousers, clapped the palm of his hand against the side of his new, metallic shin and declared.

"Masterpiece of engineerin', custom built and tailor made, you'll not find one o' these buggers in Burtons."

Charlie couldn't resist tapping it with his fingers, he stared at it, deep in thought.

"What's up?" Said Jack, "Are yer lookin' for the registration of its birth?"

"Bit o' good stuff that," said Charlie, "how much steel's in it, will yer 'ave to stay indoors when we get thunder an' lightnin'? Me mam puts all the knives away in a drawer if we get lightnin'. One of her cousins wer' struck dead in a storm, 'e wer' walkin' on Kinder Scout wi' a saucepan strapped to his rucksack, they reckon that it wer' the steel pan as done it. Dropped down dead as a stone."

Jack looked at Charlie in despair. "I've been nearly blown to bits in the desert by Rommel's lot an' his Eye-tie sidekicks, survived the bloody heat an' flies, the bites an' stings, fever, delirium an' the soddin' shits only to come home an' listen to you tell me I'm likely to be struck by lightnin', bloody hell Charlie! Down there, on me feet, me boots, they earth me don't they?" Jack pointed to his work boots. "Trouble wi' you Jones is you've no nous."

Approaching footsteps in the entry caused Charlie to turn from his fascination with Jack's leg.

"Aye up, it's young Colin, Maureen's kid brother, can't wait to grow up, keeps pesterin' me to ask Captain Nias if he can join the LD, or Home Guard as we've now become. I suppose the word 'guard' is meant to make us feel more important," said Charlie, somewhat disparagingly, "anyroad, I've told him time an' time again, not 'til you're eighteen. Determined little sod, 'e wer' peerin' in through drill hall windo' last Wednesday night, kids, don't 'ave fear of owt, but neither did we at his age," Charlie chuckled, "the things me an' you got up to Jack, it's a miracle we've lived so long."

Jack chuckled too, but the memory of recent months brought a hollow ring to his laughter. Colin sat down at the other end of the bath, kicking idly at a raised cobble.

"I've come out the way for a bit, Maureen's friend Sheila's round at our place an' Mrs.Roper from two doors down 'as come for our mam to give 'er a perm, just the smell o' that stuff's enough for me. I thought best make meself scarce, when the women are havin' a gatherin' it's no place for a bloke is it?"

Charlie cast an amused glance at Jack before makin the introduction. "This is my best mate Jack Wainwright."

Colin looked puzzled. "How do, nice to meet yer an' all that," he hesitated, "how come, if you're Charlie's best mate, I've not met you before?"

Jack's been overseas, in the desert wi' the army, now 'e's back," said Charlie.

Colin's eyes immediately doubled in size as the word 'army' drove his imagination, the raised cobble was left in peace now the youth's attentions had been diverted.

"Fightin', was yer fightin' Jack?" What's a big battle really like, did yer drive a tank, did yer kill the enemy?"

The release of Colin's stored up curiosity fired the questions thick and fast 'til Charlie spoke sharply.

"Give it a rest lad, afore your tongue dies of exhaustion."

Jack rubbed his hand over the top of Colin's head. "I met your sister the other day, she told me your dad's in the Merchant Navy, tough lot o' blokes the merchant seamen, I reckon that's why I went for the army, I like to feel the ground beneath me feet, rollin' around on the deck of a ship 'ould likely turn me stupid. Went in a paddle boat wi' me uncle Samuel once, on canal, there wer' hardly enough wind to put a ripple on water but I though me innards wer' goin' to swamp me tonsils, yet on troop ship I wer' alright, size o' the thing I s'pose, hundreds of us aboard, all talkin' rubbish, tryin' to sound big an' feelin' small. But the desert, now that's a funny place, like nowhere else on earth I reckon. Hot, nowt but sand, plays tricks wi' your eyes, yer think yer can see summat, movin', in front of yer, yet it's not really there, must ave' all been in your head. Battle's a bit like that an'all, when it's over yer begin' to think it never happened, couldn't 'ave been real, not summat that bad, must be the heat addlin' your brain.

When I wer' a kid, too young to understand it, there wer' an accident at pit, me dad's a miner. A section 'o the tunnel caved in. Years later 'e told me about it, one man died, several were injured, but me dad come up safe an' sound. He said, 'Jack, it's the strangest thing, at the time, you face the hell that it is an' do whatever you have to do, but when it's all over, you wonder if you dreamt it, surely nothin' real could be that hideous'. I thought of me dad's words a lot, out there in the desert. Kick a ball about wi' your pals Colin, go down Trent side wi' a fishin' rod an' some stale bread, chase the lasses an' give 'em a kiss, if your dad wer' sittin' here on this old tin bath, 'e'd tell yer same, they're real things. Battles, pitfalls, only happen when a man's brain is addled, when 'e can't think straight.

I dreamt the other night that I only 'ad one leg, now does it look to you like I'm missin' one?" Jack tapped the cobbles with both boots an' winked at Charlie.

It was Mrs.Jones calling from inside the house, 'your tea's ready Charlie' that spared the two older men any further inquisition.

"Are you comin' round to ours after tea Charlie?" Asked Colin, Charlie nodded.

"Yes, after me tea."

"I'll see yer around then Jack."

"Yes lad, you'll see me around."

Colin ran off down the entry.

"'E'll find out," said Charlie, you should 'ave shown him."

Jack got to his feet and stretched himself. "Don't know what you're on about Jones." A big grin spread across his face. "How many fingers 'ave you got?"

Charlie sniffed. "Enough to stick two up at you." He made the gesture and laughed wickedly. "See you in the week then Jack." Charlie watched his friend disappear into the entry, "Daft bugger," he whispered.

"Are you comin' our Charlie?" Mrs.Jones voice rang out with greater urgency.

"Yes Mam." The bath creaked as he took his weight off the end and in his pre-occupation with the conversation he'd just exchanged he forgot the raised cobble and stumbled forward, his hand managed to find the top of the dividing wall.

Charlie's grip held firm, saved from falling by his three fingers.

CHAPTER ELEVEN

Annie's eyes travelled down the short list of items and she arrived quickly at the total.

"That will be 17/4d please, Anthony."

Still she found it difficult to use his Christian name, to be so familiar. As she picked his change from the till the sound of the air raid siren made her jump, there had been no activity in the skies over Nottingham for several weeks. The advancing 'wail' now carried her thoughts to Samuel and Charles, Celia had sent Mathew to ask if granddad could come, it had rained hard most of the day and the drain outside the back door at Wollaton had become blocked. Celia had tried to clear it but to no avail and water was now gathering. Samuel had gone along happily, excitedly almost, to a boy of his age the possibility of averting a flood was unmissable.

"Botheration," declared Anthony, "never mind, I shall make a dash for the nearest shelter, I'm surprised Jerry has braved the weather, outside it's sheeting down, I nearly didn't attempt the shopping but the pantry would starve a mouse."

Annie could do no other than offer him their own facility in such times, the cellar, it was the best chance of safety and hopefully the all clear might not be too long. Neighbours to Celia had a shelter at the bottom of their garden and it was to the Batemans that Celia, with the children, hurried when the siren sounded. Annie convinced herself that Charles and Samuel would have been waiting for the rain to ease before setting out for home and that they too would be able to squeeze up inside the Batemans' Anderson Shelter. Celia had one day told Annie of the number gathered within, when folk from either side, in their panic, had descended upon that small place of sanctuary as distant explosions drove fear beyond all else. One occupant had developed persistent hiccups and this normally mild irritant nearly caused the individual a seizure, they became so distraught. Confined, confused and in the dark, what at any other time would be ignored as not meriting concern, suddenly grew out of all proportion. An elderly woman had picked at a mole on her face until when finally emerging into the light, the blood stains on her coat and all over her hand were so severe her poor daughter fainted at the sight.

Annie turned the sign on the shop door to 'closed' and locked it, the back door was not bolted should Charles be close by.

"We best stay in the cellar Anthony, I'm sure it won't last long, it's this way." She led him to the top of the cellar steps.

"It's kind of you Annie, be careful." He cautioned her as she made her way.

"I am well used to these steps Anthony, going down is little challenge, but I confess that climbing back up with stock, some days slows the pace and brings to mind the closeness of old age. Davina used to say, 'Don't grow old Annie dear, it's no fun', I do miss her."

"I don't think mother was ever aware of old age," said Anthony with a sigh, "her mind drifted back in time so while her body aged, mentally, she believed herself to be a young woman and events from many years earlier engaged her thoughts constantly, irrational and allowing us no means of sensible communication, we were strangers to her at the end."

His gaze travelled about the cellar walls, the boxes of stock so much less than before the outbreak of war. Annie imagined he was surprised at the lack of volume. At one end an old blanket box provided seating and Annie kept a small mattress there for Samuel. Thankfully Charles had seen fit to have a light fitted in the cellar, having no window, when a raid took place the low wattage bulb allowed them to see one another's faces and Annie could reassure Samuel with a smile, at least until the power went off, which so often it did.

"How is your sister Margaret?" Asked Annie, if she must share this unsettling space with Anthony Hemsley, then sensible conversation could only make her situation more tolerable.

"Well, thank you, the last time I heard at any rate, we don't speak often I'm afraid and yet I sense the passage of time, since mother and father died, has allowed a mellowing and there is now no actual impediment, we have simply developed an unfortunate apathy." He unfastened the buttons on his overcoat and reached inside the pocket of his jacket. "She sent me this, with a Christmas card, perhaps I am on the road to forgiveness." He passed to Annie a small photograph, "Two of her grandchildren, I thought when Gloria died Margaret would likely disown me altogether."

Annie was surprised, she interrupted him. "I'm sorry, I wasn't aware that your wife had died, I know that you lived apart but nevertheless."

"My dear sister is so thoroughly moral, so correct, I truly expected to be blamed entirely for Gloria's death as I was for mother's. Whatever has brought about the lessening of my sentence I don't know but to be sent a photograph of Margaret's grandchildren must surely suggest a measure of leniency. I wrote immediately to thank her of course and to express my genuine pleasure at receiving it." He leaned forward with his hands on his knees, as though easing a discomfort in his back. "Gloria died suddenly, I assume heart failure must have been the cause, not having lived under the same roof for so long I felt I could not be entitled to ask details, whatever it was happened without warning and in an instant. Apparently she had company at the time, a neighbour, shocking for the poor woman, one can only imagine. I was notified by the police the following day. It must sound incredible, false even, yet the news shook me, I sat for hours, incapable of collecting my thoughts sufficiently to propel myself beyond the door to the street outside."

Annie hardly knew how to respond, here was a different Anthony Hemsley, there was a tenderness about him, a fragility, his bowed head denied her any sight of his face but Annie imagined if she could see his eyes, they would reveal hurt. She handed back the photo of the two young boys, he raised himself, smiled and put the small picture safely back inside his jacket pocket.

"What made you buy the house in The Park Anthony? It's such a big place for one person but with Margaret's family expanding I'm sure you will have visitors."

Annie felt she must try to encourage his hope of Margaret's wish to restore closeness between them.

He gave Annie a curious look, he appeared anxious, uneasy and it was with some hesitation that he spoke again.

"I have a son Annie, and yes, to save you the awkwardness of asking, I sired a child by another woman, not from my union with Gloria but the result of my weakness, my wandering eye as Margaret, many years ago described the downfall of this womanising philanderer she has the misfortune to call brother. Not quite on par with the seaman, a woman in every port, but travelling light of loyalty, carrying little baggage as it were. Margaret knows nothing of Donald, he's twenty five now, serving abroad with the army, a young wife, one child, a daughter." Anthony stood up, suddenly and urgently. "Are you afraid of spiders Annie? There's a beauty, just came out from under that box."

Annie looked to where he pointed and realising it was his intention to tread on it she cried out. "No, don't kill the poor thing, you must know the old rhyme, 'If you want to live and thrive, let the spider run alive'."

He laughed and sat down again. "I remember Gloria was petrified of spiders, and moths, and mice," he paused, "and men." He fell silent.

Annie felt awkward but needed to relieve the tension such silence created. "How did you meet Donald's mother?" She asked nervously.

His features relaxed and he leaned back against the cellar wall, a faint smile suggested Annie's question had evoked pleasant memories.

"It was the most unlikely beginning to any romantic episode. I took a room for the night at a house close to the pit, a card in the window read, 'single room available'. All that afternoon I had been tormented by the most relentless ear-ache, I ventured to ask the landlady, if by any chance she had some drops, anything which might afford me some relief. She told me to sit down on a chair by the scullery table. I watched as she put a small pan of water over the range to heat, then as she opened a cupboard and took from it a bottle, some kind of oil. After a few minutes, when the water was hot she told me to put my head over on one side so she could let a few drops of warm oil slip into my ear. She dipped a teaspoon into the hot water then poured oil into the bowl of the spoon and stood right by me to drop the soothing oil onto the cause of my pain. Almost at once I felt the benefit. She did it with such care, her body when she leaned over me barely glanced my own and there was nothing at all improper about her actions, it was done purely through kindness, but I went to my bed reliving the moment, how absurd was that? I left the following morning and twelve months passed before I found myself again at Skipton needing a room for the night. It was the obvious place but there was no card in the window so I knocked. Donald was conceived that night. The single room was already taken.

Don't you find it tragic Annie? Her husband had been killed in France, 1916, can you imagine the shame, the cruel lashings she was dealt by tongues, careless and without compassion. I was married, a selfish philanderer with a wandering eye, she would surely meet someone, a good man who would care for them both. Tragic indeed Annie, she never remarried and I never divorced, hopeless, hapless individuals afraid of our own shadows, shadows that ever follow us year in, year out. One day the house will be his. She told Donald that his father was dead, easy to believe given that so many young men perished in the Great War. She bore me no animosity, just the one hurt, I was to remain unknown to my son." Now Anthony sat upright, he looked intently at Annie. "On my death he will come to know, Donald will inherit all that I have. When father's Estate was proved and Margaret and I inherited, the money enabled me to buy into the project at Mapperley. My investment paid well, gave me a good return, when I sold the majority of it, early last year, it was with the sole intent of buying a property to leave to Donald. Mrs.Wright's house at The Park seemed to me entirely apt, not only had it been the home of mother's dearest friend but it stood just a short distance from where I grew up, where my life began."

Annie had listened without utterance, shocked but equally saddened. "It is indeed tragic but surely the greatest tragedy is the fact that Donald cannot be aware of who you are until after your death, he may not wish to acknowledge you but at least he would have the chance if you were still alive, beyond your death he is denied."

"So Annie, you believe a man is entitled to know the identity of his father regardless of circumstances."

His remark flustered her.

"I don't know, I'm not sure, it's really nothing to do with me, I should not have commented."

At that moment the forgotten spider ran across the floor at their feet, disappearing beneath the blanket box and in the same instant the all clear sounded. It brought such a degree of relief to Annie that she was on her feet, across the room and at the foot of the steps before Anthony stood up. He fastened the buttons on his coat, sighed and followed her.

"It must have been a false alarm," said Annie as she unlocked the shop door. The street was in darkness but the rain had stopped.

"I know you will keep my secret Annie," said Anthony, "I believe we are both able to maintain a confidence." He picked his bag of groceries from the counter. "I'm sure Charles and Samuel will be home very soon. Goodnight Annie, thank you for the shelter, take care."

She could do nothing to escape the kiss he planted on her cheek yet strangely it felt harmless. She watched him for several yards before closing the shop door, the clock showed it to be a little after seven, she should begin to prepare a meal but before she even reached the counter the shop doorbell clanged and in came Mrs.Rashleigh.

"Have you ever known rain like it Mrs.Eddowes, water wer' flowin' down the entry like a tributary o' the Trent, me feet got wet through runnin' to the shelter, I wish Jerry'd make up 'is bloody mind, it wer' a false alarm last time an'all. I 'ad bread dough in a bowl then, an' by the time I got back to tend to it the soddin' stuff wer' stuck fast me tea towel, yer can't win, get to the shop late an' there's no bread left, try to make your own an' arf a loaf gets scraped of tea towel full o' tifflin's, yer can't put it back wi' the rest for fear o' chokin' somebody. Mind you, I could 'appily choke Bill sometimes, that's why I'm 'ere now, I need some washin' soda, I've run out an' 'is trousers get that ditched in dirt. Him an' Harry Marsh from next door 'ave been tinkerin' wi' an old motorbike, to look at Bill you'd think somebody 'ad run over 'im wi' the bloody thing, I've no hope o' cleaning 'is trousers wi'out soda. I told 'im, where there's muck there's supposed to be money but it don't apply to our house, I never find as much as a farthin' in 'is pockets, 'e makes sure they're empty afore I get hold of 'em, 'e promised we'd 'ave a new mattress, more than forty years we've been sleepin' on same one an' it wer' 'is aunty Maude's afore that. It's like layin' on cobbles, when I get up of a mornin' me back feels like it's been thrashed, I told 'im, I'll be pushin' up daisies 'afore 'e cough's up, 'e'll spend money on axle grease an' spark plugs, thinks 'e's goin' to sell the damn thing, make a few bob, well by the time 'e's split 'is gain wi' Harry Marsh an' ruined the only two pairs o' trousers 'e's got we'll be lucky if there's enough left to pay for a Sunday paper to go under the sunken mattress that come from aunty Maude's let alone a new one. Moffat's 'ad one the other week, but it wer' soon gone, owt that's good is never there long, I said we should nab it quick but silly old fool takes not a blind bit o' notice of anythin' I say, I'll take a candle while I'm here an'all, there's no more than an inch left on the one at home. How's your Hilda gettin' on, I've heard she's expectin' again, oh an' a box o' sulphurs then that'll do me?"

Mabel Rashleigh delivered conversation at such a rate it was almost impossible to respond in any sort of order so Annie placed soda, a candle and matches on the counter, thanked her for asking after Hilda, put the money in the till and sped through to the back before the woman could launch into a further chapter from 'tales of Rashleigh'. Edna likened it to the rapid gabble of the auctioneer at Monsall Street auction rooms, Billy had one day come home with a stirrup pump after believing he'd bid on a fireside chair. 'That woman's tongue could put yer in a coma', Edna had declared one afternoon after waiting for Mrs.Rashleigh to complete her purchases, 'if I wer' the poor man married to 'er I'm stop up me ears wi' sealin' wax'.

Confident that Charles and Samuel would return at any moment, Annie put a pan of potatoes on the stove to boil and three apples in the oven to bake.

The heavy blinds over the door and windows of the shop, after dark along with a low light behind the counter, enabled trade until half past seven, Annie made no delay in locking up, enough was enough for one day!

Anthony Hemsley was in no real hurry to reach The Park, an empty house stretched the hours, the streets offered some diversion at least. In the gloom he could make out two figures approaching.

"Hello Charles, Samuel, I have been sheltering in your cellar, Annie kindly suggested I remain there until the all clear." He held up his bag as if to justify the privilege.

Charles nodded, unlike Hemsley he was in a hurry, Celia's blocked drain, their time spent in the Batemans' Anderson shelter, the drenching weather, all had tried his patience and to get Samuel home now dominated his mood and the rate at which he walked. He hurried Samuel along, leaving Hemsley to proceed in the opposite direction.

'Surely the greatest tragedy is not knowing until it's too late'. The irony of Annie's words was not lost on Anthony, but for Charles it was already too late. He pulled up his collar against the elements and made his way home, to the house, to his attempt at redemption, pondering over the last hour spent in the cellar at Gregory Street. How sheltering from danger could bring about such relief, for overwhelming relief was what he felt, he'd spoken of his son, something he could not normally do, and to Annie, who had shown no condemnation. He smiled to himself, neither had she shown fear of spiders, moths, mice, nor men.

"Come on Gabriel, flap your wings, switch on your halo or summat, give us a clue, if yer come out now I'll buy yer a pint." Bob Budgeon, wet, cold and fed up called out in the darkness. "Creepin' about under drippin' trees an' squelchin' through soddened fields, a bloody goose chase, that's what we're on, a wild bloody goose chase, she's just a crank, angel my arse."

The Home Guard had been called out to search an area around Clifton. A woman in an agitated state had walked into the police station claiming to have seen an angel, with wings outstretched, float to the ground. While considering this unlikely event the sergeant on duty had calmed the woman, ventured to ask if she had seen angels before and on hearing her adamant 'no', mobilised the Guard to search for any sign of a parachute.

Charlie Jones, several yards behind Bob, prodded the hedgerow with his rifle. "Mrs.Gillet at No.19 goes to them spiritualist meetin's, reckons the dead float up an' down regular. Told me mam that if she went with her one evenin' they'd try to reach granddad, poor mam, just the thought of it give her a migraine, besides, reachin' granddad when 'e wer' alive wer' hard enough, yer didn't need to go to pantomime if yer lived at our house. Like fate a rat found its way into roof space, the sound o' the damn thing crossin' the boards at night played tricks wi' mam's mind, not until me dad come down from the loft wi' it hangin' by its tail from his fingers did she believe that granddad 'adn't come back. How she could 'ave thought that granddad wer' in the loft God knows, 'e never moved from the chair, last six months 'e slept in it an'all, poor old bugger, his leg got that bad wi' ulcers it would 'ave took a miracle to get 'im up to bedroom let alone the roof space."

"Well one of us better fetch Mrs.Gillet then," said Bob, "perhaps she can rustle up Gabriel. How could there be a bloody parachute if there 'asn't been any planes, an' what self respectin' Kraut 'ould land here in this quagmire."

"Stop moanin' can't yer," said Charlie, "we'll give it another arf hour, perhaps the others 'ave found summat."

The field was planted in winter barley, the ground so wet under their feet from the day's heavy rain that progress was slow and shining the torch briefly across the crop yielded no evidence of disturbance.

"Sod it, I've 'ad enough." Bob stretched his back while he waited for Charlie to catch up. "We'll tell Nias that we spoke wi' Gabriel, it wer' only a flyin' visit an' now 'e's gone back up."

"Yer daft sod Budgeon," said Charlie, but he too was wet and unconvinced and while he held no actual desire to find one, the fact that it was now into February, almost three and a half years since war began and he'd not clapped eyes on a single German, tested his self belief. How small his contribution had been when put alongside Jack Wainwright's. The number of dead and injured in the deserts of Africa made this field of barley seem like a kiddies' playground in comparison.

The Clifton angel was to remain a mystery, as a thorough search of the area had produced nothing, apart from a dead sheep, which Paddy Bolan stumbled over in the dark, his ensuing description of the unfortunate animal was so fluent in broad, Irish damnations that when Charlie roguishly asked, 'what sort o' sheep did yer say it wer' Paddy', the night patrol ended in raucous laughter.

Unbeknown to them however, on the other side of the city, a tragedy was taking place, which would cause grief and shock and furthermore the realisation that battles were won or lost, not only on battlefields, but on war torn, ravaged plains of man's mind.

Annie had sent the paper boys on their rounds, most customers through the door at this early hour were men on their way to the factories, buying smokes, it was as if the women regarded the hour between seven and eight as set aside for the male routine, the only exception being those occasions when a woman was 'sent' and her need to fulfil the set requirement as quickly as possible was ever obvious to Annie, as the poor woman's fingers scrabbled hastily through her purse before thrusting the tobacco or cigarettes into her pocket and dashing back to hand her man his dinner bag!

She was surprised to look up at the sound of the door bell and to see Billy, she knew at once that something was wrong. He sat on the chair by the counter, let out a long, troubled breath, and told Annie the news, which twenty minutes or so earlier had been told to him.

The driver of the lorry that ran over Myra had been found dead.

The court hearing earlier the previous year had resulted in him being charged with gross negligence while at the wheel of a heavy goods vehicle, leading to the bodily harm of a young woman. He had been duly sentenced to serve twelve months in prison. Released six weeks ago, he had last night taken a shotgun, sat on the seat in the outside lavatory with the gun between his legs, placed the barrels beneath his chin and fired.

Billy was physically shaken. "Even our Myra forgive 'im Annie an' me an' Edna, we couldn't condemn the man. It's the war, this bloody war, their son wer' shot at Tobruk, now of despair, the father's shot 'isself. It wer' 'is wife found 'im, heard the almighty bang, she'd already gone to bed. It's enough to turn the poor woman's brain. 'E must 'ave dwelt on nowt else, stuck in that prison, what good did lockin' 'im up in there do? 'E weren't a criminal. I dread 'avin' to tell Edna, part of me hopes that by the time I get home she'll already know, but the rest o' me 'ould rather be there, it'll upset her Annie, an' it'll bring all the horror o' that day back to Myra, just as the lass wer' pickin' up, movin' on."

"Come through to the back Billy, let me get you a cup of sweet tea, Charles is having his breakfast so there's tea in the pot."

"No, it's alright, ta anyroad. I wonder if you could come round this afternoon, spend an hour wi' Edna?"

"Of course I will Billy."

Just then Charles appeared, Annie felt the atmosphere tense.

Billy got to his feet. "How do Charles."

Seldom did the two meet, their characters so different there was little to inspire any comfortable dialogue between them. Annie felt she must speak.

"Billy has bad news, upsetting news," she briefly explained.

"Happy release more than likely," was the extent of Charles' response before turning his back to Billy as he made a contrived check of the cigarette shelf. Billy gave Annie a brave smile and left.

The entire morning was dominated by events, almost every customer preoccupied with the suicide, committed through such violent means. By midday Annie's head ached from the succession of reports until finally, Mrs.Rashleigh's interpretation pained not just Annie's head but assaulted her stomach too. She hurried down to the cellar where Charles had retreated to supposedly check the meagre stock and told him if he didn't serve at the counter for a while then she would likely be sick over it.

Mabel Rashleigh could always be relied upon to impart graphic details, George used to say that any account given by her was like a 'pop up' picture book, that she spoke in 3D. This morning it had been more than Annie could stand.

'Blew 'is brains out 'e did Mrs.Eddowes, splattered 'em all up the walls, carnage it wer', carnage, like a scene from the Somme. It'll take more than a pot o' Vim to scrub that lot off an' two coats o' lime wash I shouldn't wonder'.

Annie was glad to be out in the air, walking to the bus stop eased the unrest in her stomach. She took deep breaths, Harold used to stand still sometimes, especially in the arboretum, or at The Meadows. 'Fill your lungs' he'd say, 'out with the old in with the new'. The memory took her mind to a letter that had arrived two days ago from Jean, it confirmed that she was well and keeping busy but gave little away. Annie felt someone from the family should travel to London and visit Jean, if only briefly. Nora had the most opportunity, living alone as she did, but her work for the Hymers had cocooned her, kept her apart from the jostling, bustling throng and all the challenges they created. The streetwise learned how to avoid obstacles and if there was no diversion, then how to get over them, Nora's confidence paled within just yards of 69 Mitchell Street, to board a train and travel to the capital was no more likely that Nora travelling to the moon.

Annie reached the stop as the bus was pulling in. Talk among the passengers was little better than had been the nature of conversation at the shop. She closed her mind to it and instead thought of George and John, each day she hoped for a letter, to read words written in their own hand, to be reassured.

Samuel had suddenly shot up by a good two inches and now filled out the trousers that Mathew had outgrown. The old box camera that George brought when Charles came home from Egypt, for whatever reason had decided to no longer perform its purpose. Despite asking Charles if he might buy another, so that Annie could take a photograph of Samuel to send to his dad, and of Mathew and Emily for Celia to put in with her letter to William, her request had so far been ignored. She had looked regularly in Moffat's but there seemed never to be any type of camera available and the cost of a new one was beyond her pocket.

Annie reached Edna's without any hindrance, thankfully meeting no one on the way intent on drawing her into the general hive of animated discussion.

"Are you on your own?" Annie was surprised not to find Billy and Myra present.

Edna drew on a cigarette sending smoke swirling up to the ceiling with the sudden rush of air that entered when Annie had opened the back door.

"I've sent 'em to Susie's she's at home this afternoon, we've finished another blanket so she can hand it in tomorrow. Myra needs to be somewhere there's a bit more life, the girls'll be back from school in a bit, there's no chance o' maudlin when they're about an Billy can forget about things when their chatter takes off. Cathy is learnin' poetry, teacher told Susie that she's ahead of 'er age at English. Billy taught 'er a new rhyme last week but I don't reckon it's the sort o' thing the school puts the class to read."

Edna stubbed out her cigarette on the old saucer that she used as an ashtray.

" 'Ave yer seen our Sall's new bonnet,

It's a stunner in' no mistak',

Got red roses all the way round it

An' feather int' back."

Annie slipped off her coat and sat down by Edna.

"Are you alright?"

Edna sighed deep and long. "What was it Winnie Bacon used to say, 'every day the same, never two days alike'. So much happens, I try to think back to when we were young, to when we worked at Saul's, sewin', day after day just sewin'. Nothin' seemed to happen then, I used to think if I had to stitch another badge on a Blackmore's uniform blazer I'd scream out loud. Now I wish I could spend the rest o' me days, quietly stitchin' them gold acorns onto navy blue breast pockets wi' nothin' happenin' that required me to think."

Annie squeezed Edna's hand. In Annie's memory a great deal had happened in those early years of their friendship, but if Edna had managed to erase from her mind events that to Annie remained vivid, then given this day's trials that could only be a blessing. So Annie sat quietly, content simply to be a listening ear.

"They're sayin' some woman reckons she saw an angel in the sky last night." Edna moved the saucer of ash further away from Annie. "Do yer believe we go somewhere, yer know, after, or do we just rot in the ground?"

Annie looked at the three butt ends. "You shouldn't smoke too much Edna, it's not good for you. Whenever I think of Danny I imagine him to be in a good place, a happy place."

Edna burst into tears. "I'm sorry, of all folk I shouldn't have asked you that, I'm sorry Annie." Her shoulders shook from sobbing, so close was their friendship that Edna's pain passed to Annie as she tried to give comfort. Eventually they found relief and Edna sniffed the wateriness away from the end of her nose before she spoke again.

"It wer' about two weeks after Victor's funeral, I wer' here on me own, Myra had already gone up to bed an' Billy wer' at the Exchange. I'd boiled a cup o' milk an' sat sippin' it, there wer' nothin' particular on me mind. I heard footsteps comin' across the yard, the back door wer' bolted, it wer' late. They come close, I expected any second for someone to knock at the door but they didn't. I stood up, yer know me, too bloody nosey to feel frightened. I went to the door, opened it, looked around the yard, in the privy, the coal shed, nobody, there wer' nobody. It's too daft for words I know it is, but Victor come to our house that night. Victor 'ad a certain tread, different to everybody else, I could allus tell when it wer' Victor comin' across the yard, 'e walked same way as 'e talked, in fits an' starts. I know' what I heard an' it wer' Victor's tread. I've never told anybody, they'd only scoff an' Billy wer' grievin' so. But I've thought about it a lot since an' I believe Victor come to let me know that 'e wer' alright. 'E 'ad a strange way o' makin' yer feel better. I could be really fed up sometimes but in would come Victor wi' that soppy grin an' before too long I'd perk up. Well even after death 'e managed to do that, yer see if 'e's alright then so will be me mam, your Harold, Danny, all of 'em, that's what Victor wer' tryin' to tell me, for me to feel better."

Annie could hardly speak her throat was so tight with emotion, but then a loud knock at the front door, in an instant brought Edna's thoughts back to the present.

"You go," Edna's reddened eyes pleaded. Even Annie felt trepidation as she turned the catch on the front door but was immediately relieved at the sight of a pleasant faced man holding a lovely bouquet of flowers.

"The Dodds household?"

Annie answered his enquiry with a nod and a grateful, "Yes."

Carrying them through to the scullery where Edna sat nervously, Annie was amused by the change of expression on her friend's face.

"Who sent them? Are yer sure they're for this address?"

Annie chuckled, "Read the card, then we shall discover who has sent them."

Edna's eyes scanned the small white card, which had been tucked down among the blooms. She held it out for Annie to read.

"Andrew Smithfield, what a thoughtful gesture," she said, truly surprised by such kindness.

“ ‘E must ‘ave heard,” said Edna, she hesitated. “I told him off once, give ‘im a right mouthful. ‘E’d been walkin’ round lookin’ miserable as sin for days, so I told ‘im, ‘e should count ‘is blessin’s an’ think a bit more about other folk’s troubles, ‘e wer’ gettin’ on me nerves. I thought ‘e’d sack me there an’ then but instead ‘e gathered ‘isself together, drove me an’ our Annie wi’ Janet, to the hospital for the poor mite’s first operation. Then ‘e went to Skegness an’ give your Charles a lift to Freddy’s. ‘E’s a good man goin’ to waste, ‘e deserves a good woman but if you ask me, whoever it is ordains these things, more often than not makes a right mess of it.”

Annie was taken by surprise, Edna spoke with such conviction. “I think it’s true of a good woman too, she equally deserves to have a good man.”

For a moment Edna dared to think that Annie’s remark was a veiled expression of her own regard for Andrew Smithfield, but then she continued.

“I have come to know Florence Stanford very well, she is a truly good woman and entitled to some happiness. Her life with Basil left much to be desired and I have actually found myself considering how suited Florence and Andrew would be as company for each other.”

“Bugger the company,” said Edna, “you better make haste an’ introduce ‘em, we’re no spring chickens an’ they’re older than we are. Whether posh or poor, if yer live long enough there’ll come a time when yer won’t manage to get up on the perch!”

“Just fetch a vase and put these beautiful flowers in water,” said Annie, inwardly pleased to hear Edna in more familiar tone, the sadness was easing. “I’ll make us a brew.”

“Good idea,” responded Edna. “Have you heard from George yet?”

If Annie’s hopes were for Florence Stanford then she may as well give up on any thoughts of Annie sharing Smithfield’s roost and change the subject. She placed two stems of spray chrysanthemums in the vase, one yellow one white, they complemented one another perfectly, just as Annie and Smithfield could do if only circumstances were different, but they were not. Edna arranged the remaining flowers in the vase, smiled down on them and whispered, ‘God bless’, swallowing a lump of heartfelt pity for the lorry driver as she carried them carefully to the sideboard in the living room, placing them right beside the photograph of Victor.

Annie peeped in through the shop door, it was empty of customers and Charles appeared to be reading the newspaper. He looked up as she entered.

"The Germans have surrendered to the Russians at Stalingrad, it says here that it was a decisive victory and they're calling it a turning point, the focus is now on Mussolini." Before Annie had chance to respond Charles lowered his voice to say, "There's a young woman in the back, friend of John's, Samuel is chatting with her. I said you wouldn't be long, she has to catch her train at 5 o'clock."

"Laura," said Annie, "Laura Innes. I wrote to her at Christmas and in her reply she said she would visit when she could."

Annie hurried through, Samuel was proudly showing Laura the RAF cap badge which John had given him, conversation between the two appeared to be flowing easily, Annie smiled at the scene.

"I am sorry I was out when you arrived Laura, I shall make some tea for us all, Charles tells me you have to catch the 5 o'clock train."

The young woman stood up obviously amused by Annie's urgency. "John did say 'the first thing mam will want to do is feed you'. I am so pleased to meet you at last Mrs.Eddowes but I shall be home before seven so there really is no need to worry about getting anything for me, I simply wanted to meet John's family."

"Well do sit down Laura, we have a little time before your train."

Annie hung her coat behind the door, Laura Innes was a pretty young woman with a confident manner, Annie imagined that confidence was a requirement of teaching. To have the responsibility of a classroom filled with children must surely demand abilities beyond simply imparting the three R's.

Laura felt she should explain the reason for her being in Nottingham and the fact that not knowing how long her interview might last, she was unable to do the polite thing and write in advance of her intention to visit, just in case not enough time remained.

"There is a teaching post available here, at Harrow Road School. So many children have been evacuated from Castle Bromwich that class numbers at the school where I work are now too low to warrant a full complement of teaching staff. It is understandable after all, the factories are a target for bombers. I've been offered the post at Harrow Road," she paused for a second, "and I have accepted it. I begin work there at the end of the month." She smiled nervously as though anxious that Annie might not approve.

"Your mother and father will be torn I'm sure," said Annie, "pleased for you but disappointed that you will be living further away from them."

Laura sighed, "They've been fretting ever since I moved to gran's. I don't know why because the bombing has been bad at home as well. The close proximity of the aircraft factory I suppose is what troubles them, gran's house isn't very far from the factory. Anyway they will have no time to worry about me, gran will be moving in with them, over the post office, that is what we all agreed would happen if I got the job here in Nottingham."

"But where will you live Laura?" Asked Annie.

"Laura could stay here couldn't she Grandma?" Samuel's spontaneous response caused both women to laugh. "No one sleeps in aunty Hilda's old room."

"Bless you Samuel but I'm sure I'll find lodgings without too much difficulty, your grandma has quite enough to think about as it is, there is the shop, besides, your granddad must surely be glad to close the door on people outside of family by the end of the day."

"Granddad won't mind, especially if you help me with my homework so's he doesn't have to. Poor granddad gets stuck on isosceles triangles."

"Really Samuel, that is not at all fair, Laura must be shocked to understand that the room is offered with such a condition attached." Annie turned her face to Laura and winked.

Samuel felt he must redeem the situation. "I could show Laura the arboretum and the park at the weekends, aunty Celia might come with Mathew and Emily, then we could throw sticks for Tilly."

“I shall speak to Charles, I see no reason why you should not stay here, at least for the time being and it might relieve some of your parents’ anxieties to know that you are with John’s family,” said Annie.

Samuel’s face broke into a big grin at the wink, which Laura gave him, it must surely offer hope, Charles’ patience could very quickly grow thin when faced with school exercise books, but to have a teacher, actually staying, what a coup that would be.

Samuel was getting ready for bed, Annie had served the last customer and Charles was now about to go through to the shop and cash up. He’d observed his usual practice of sitting with The Evening Post after his meal.

“Birkett is retiring from the bank, there’s a piece in the paper. It doesn’t give any indication of who his replacement might be. They come and go, Rothero finished at Barclays, now Birkett, he had a good innings. They say the fellow who took over from Rothero has a speech impediment, an unfortunate stammer, someone in the shop put it, that never has there been so many p’s to the pound! Birkett is retiring on health grounds apparently, probably consumed more gullible clients than was good for him.” Charles folded the paper, stood and let it fall onto the chair where he’d sat. “There’s a piece about the suicide as well, if you want to read it.”

Annie watched him walk through to the shop with a feeling of surprise, so he too recognised Gerald Birkett’s appetite for gain. There were times when Annie felt that despite all their years of marriage she had little knowledge of what went on in Charles’ mind and she had yet to speak with him about Laura. Annie cast a glance towards the newspaper, it held no interest, the war, Birkett, the dreadful suicide, she would be glad to lay in the fire with it. To read letters from her sons was all Annie craved. She sighed and climbed the stairs to Samuel, pausing for a few seconds by the door of the spare bedroom.

‘Get to know her mam, she’s lovely is my Laura’. For John, she must persuade Charles that it would be for John, isosceles triangles apart.

CHAPTER TWELVE

Mid May 1943

Celia sat for a moment on the arm of the chair, even with the windows and back door open, the air was oppressive, all morning it had been humid, the washing hung still on the line and the dog clung to the shade offered by a low growing branch of the pear tree. Just a few more items remained in the ironing basket, sometimes when she ran the iron along the collar of Mathew's shirt a rush of anxiety induced a shiver, the expression 'sends a shiver down your spine' seemed not to describe sufficiently the extent of fear, which coursed through her entire body when she imagined the shirt on the ironing board not to be her son's but William's, to be her husband's shirt. Celia longed for nothing more than to be tending her family, all of her family, yet the contrary illusion that transformed one of Mathew's shirts to one of William's gave fleeting comfort, for reality took her happy dream and swathed it in sadness. His letters she read over and over, so familiar became the passages that at night, in bed, she whispered the words to herself. Yet William wrote in such sober terms, despite her letters to him being purposefully filled with accounts of their children's progress, of only uplifting dialogue.

Celia had one day taken the atlas from the book shelf and studied the map of Africa. A continent so big, vast when compared to 'the man riding a pig', that odd shaped little land mass that made up Britain. The deserts of the north, lands which for months into years had devoured men by the thousand and somewhere among those resisting still, William, her own William, a tiny speck of humankind. This was how Celia perceived it to be and nothing in William's letters caused her to believe that in North Africa was there any goodness, any joy, any worth to justify such Godless destruction of life through defence of it. She sighed and forced herself to get up from the arm of the chair, determined to finish the ironing.

"Cooee, it's only us."

The welcome sound of Rosie Spooner's voice raised Celia's spirits at once.

"Tell aunty Celia what you've been doin'."

Rosie held Beryl by the hand, the child, wearing only a vest and knickers gave Celia a big grin and called out.

"Splash, splash."

"We've just come from me mam's." Rosie looked down at Beryl. "Grandma put water in the old bath pan out in the yard didn't she, so you could paddle an' little Tony Gaskin from next door come round to paddle an'all didn't 'e?" Beryl nodded, jumped up and down on the spot then ran outside to see Tilly. "Don't you torment that poor dog, Tilly's too hot to be bothered wi' you today."

Rosie flopped down onto a chair, pulled open the front of her blouse and blew into it. Celia smiled, Rosie's ample bosom on days like this, could only add to the sticky discomfort, which Celia herself was experiencing and that with considerably less overhanging flesh to keep in the heat.

"Have yer heard the news, it was on the wireless at dinner time, Rommel's lot 'ave surrendered, mam dunked 'er bread into the Bovril like she wer' drownin' the bugger, just to make sure 'e wer' done for, good an' proper. Your William'll be alright now won't 'e?"

Celia looked at Rosie with disbelief.

"It's right enough, me an' mam heard it wi' our own ears an' there's no mistakin' what them newsreaders say, they speak so proper, as mam says, the likes of us don't hear correct English spoke much, although one o' me cousins went to elocution classes, his mam's a bit above 'er station, if yer know what I mean, but she reckoned that when 'e got tonsillitis an' doctor come an' put the spoon handle on Percy's tongue an' told him to say, 'ahh', 'e wer' tone perfect. 'E had a barrow at Arnold market for years, folk used to say that listening to Percy Potts workin' the crowd wer' an experience not to be missed, 'e wer' the only one sellin' ripe 'baaa-naa-naas' an' King Edwaaard potatoooes!" Celia had become transfixed. "If yer don't take the iron off that pillowcase it'll scorch," cried Rosie, before blowing one more time down the inside of her blouse then letting it back into place with a sigh.

Celia laughed, a bewildered, random laugh, then she turned off the iron, folded the pillowslip, put it on top of the ironing that she had already done, and burst into tears. A little voice at the door called out.

"Why's aunty Celia cryin'?" Beryl stood holding up the front of her vest while Tilly licked her stomach, giggling each time the dog's tongue passed over her belly button. Rosie let out another, lengthy sigh.

"Aunty Celia's cryin' 'cause she's happy." The child looked puzzled. "But it's a funny sort of happy. There's a sad pain an' a happy pain an' every once in a while yer get 'em both at the same time. It's not like havin' earache an' toothache, they feel like they're on the outside of yer, but a funny happy pain is deep inside, at the cockles of your heart. It makes yer laugh an' cry together an' yer don't know why you're doin' either." Rosie cast an understanding look to her friend and Celia dabbed her eyes with a hanky before walking over to where a mystified Beryl stood wiggling a finger in her belly button.

"All better now," said Celia, "would you like some cold milk?"

Beryl nodded her head and let the vest fall over her tummy. "Want to wee."

"Now do you really want to go or do yer just want to look at aunty Celia's posh bathroom?" Rosie's frankness made Celia smile.

"I'll take her, you pour some milk and put the kettle on." Celia took Beryl's hand and looking into the child's eyes said, "We're all happy now aren't we, look, even Tilly's happy."

The dog lay on its back over the polished clay tiles at the hearth, gently moving from side to side, relishing the relief offered by their cool surface, before finally rolling onto its stomach and resting its head on the fender, closing its eyes in sleep.

"I saw Hilda Haynes this mornin', I did feel sorry for 'er, she must be due any day, carryin' so low an' in this heat." Rosie sipped her tea.

"The due date was yesterday," said Celia. "When it happens Samuel will come to stay here with me for a day or two so Annie can be with Hilda and the baby. I can't imagine Charles will be too enamoured with the idea, he leaves so much of the shop to Annie, but it's hardly hectic, with rationing putting everything in short supply no one is able to make a big list. But being there throughout the hours of opening is something Charles is not used to. When David was born poor Annie was rushing between the shop and Forest Road, doing her best at both and Charles' mood grew more sullen by the hour. Now of course, there's David to look after as well as a new baby but Hilda was stoic the last time and God willing, nothing will prevent her from being so again. Knowing Annie she will have organised meals and now that John's friend, Laura Innes is staying at Gregory Street it should be a little easier. I'm sure she will help, Laura is very nice and more than capable of preparing food for Charles and herself. Perhaps he'll feel obliged to contain his grumpiness with Laura present."

Rosie huffed her disapproval. "Sounds to me like there's a funny, happy pain, a sad pain an' there's Charles Eddowes!"

Celia smiled but inwardly recognised the irony of Rosie's remark. There had been many times when she'd seen pain in Annie's face and observed a corresponding tetchiness in her father in law, Charles Eddowes. Annie never spoke of her troubles but Celia felt a sympathy, William too could be difficult. Moods, it was the changing moods and cutting remarks that hurt, yet Celia longed to see him walk through the door.

Rosie interrupted her thoughts. "Look at them two." Beryl lay asleep on the hearth rug, her hand resting on Tilly's back. "It's one o' Tommy's expressions, 'e'll look at 'er sometimes, when she's fast asleep, an' there'll be tears in his eyes, 'e'll blow 'er a kiss an' say, 'don't it warm your cockles Rosie'. I know exactly what 'e means, Tommy sees so much of life's sadness that the sight o' Beryl, safe, content, asleep in 'er bed gives him that funny happy pain." Rosie sniffed up a stray emotion, while Celia hugged tight a cushion.

Three magazines lay on the table but Celia could not have concentrated sufficiently to have read beyond the open page of the one closest to her. It was out of date by three years, 'Country Life', displaying a portrait picture of a young woman, her neck long and slender, a string of pearls so precisely poised an inch above the neckline of an evening gown, the waves of her hair, silk like, her eyes free of the slightest shadow from weariness and the degree of smile at her lips, just so. Sitting alone in the reception area of the solicitors' offices Celia's nervousness advanced with the ticking of the heavy cased clock, which seemed to look down on her from the opposite wall, she wished she had applied a little makeup and pinned a brooch to the front of her cardigan. She had received a letter from Nigel Caffin requesting that she attend an appointment at 11o/clock on Monday May 17th. It gave no indication of what it might concern and as she waited her thoughts inevitably, were of her brother Edmund. But why was Caroline not here for surely it must be to do with Edmund's affairs and his wife, first and foremost, would be consulted. The large, panelled door suddenly opened and Nigel Caffin with a broad smile, greeted Celia warmly.

"Come in my dear, it is good to see you, the family is well I trust. Good news from the front, your husband is with the Allies in North Africa I believe."

"Yes, his latest letter confirmed that he was well, at least as well as I imagine one could be in such a situation, but the children are thriving, in spite of everything." Celia smiled but still an anxiety lay behind her response.

"Please, do sit down Celia, it will take but a few minutes." He turned over some papers on the desk in front of him, glanced at them, cleared his throat and said. "It is regarding your mother Mrs.Gwendolyn Tozer. It was typical of Edmund, over the course of time that he worked here Edmund and I became good friends, I think it would be true to say that we had complete trust in one another's diligence and integrity. Soon after your father died Mrs.Brewer was appointed housekeeper, your mother had a degree of dementia and needed someone to help." Nigel Caffin paused for a moment, fingering the edge of one of the papers. "Just before Edmund left to join The Air Force he came into this very room to speak with me, he was anxious over possible events, the nature of what he was about to begin he knew was dangerous, pilots could envisage only a precarious future. Your mother's condition was worsening and he was preparing to become involved in war, he asked me to accept 'power of attorney' over your mother's affairs, her finances in the main. Edmund felt it would be unreasonable to place such responsibility on Caroline or your husband William and he was unwilling to burden you. I have continually sought the best rate of interest on the capital left by Jessie Tozer but unfortunately it has reached a point whereby I can no longer put off consulting you. If further funds are not found then within three months there will be no money remaining to meet Mrs.Brewer's wages."

Celia was taken completely by surprise, naively as she now deemed it, her thoughts had been solely for her mother's unpredictable behaviour and for Sybil Brewer's lasting patience, but not once had she given any thought to the financial situation. The sudden death of Caroline's father, the devastating news that Edmund was lost, William's call up, her constant watch over Mathew and Emily in their dad's absence, all had achieved to occupy her mind to such an extent that the day to day expenses of her mother's household had at no time entered her head. Nigel Caffin spoke again.

"There is of course a value attached to the house, your father left it freehold. I could arrange a standing charge against the property through the bank, so as to enable the continued employment of Mrs.Brewer but it would erode substantially any sum, which the property might yield in the future and the interest it would incur must be a consideration," he sighed.

Celia was on the verge of tears. "I don't know what to say, what to do. I can ask neither my brother nor my husband."

"We have a few weeks in which to find a solution, perhaps you could write to William, most certainly the conflict surrounding him would make this dilemma seem mild indeed, he will offer advice surely."

Nigel Caffin was aware of the inheritance William had received from Davina Wright but now suspected that William's wife held little knowledge of her husband's finances. Through his meeting with Annie Eddowes, Caffin was further aware that the money had saved William from failing on his mortgage, however some funds, over and above the crisis, remained. Whereas Edmund's estate, whilst leaving Caroline comparatively safe after clearing all charges against Moreleigh, provided only a modest sum. None of this knowledge could he reveal to Celia, ethics, the nature of his position as solicitor dealing with last Wills and testaments, bound him to complete silence, total discretion, it complied with his professional undertaking but frustrated him as a caring individual.

Celia clutched the handbag on her lap as though it were a lifebuoy to save her from drowning.

"Perhaps you could seek advice of your mother in law, I have found Mrs.Eddowes to be a most capable woman. Try not to worry too much my dear, the important thing to remember is that William is well. Our son too is somewhere in North Africa, his mother thinks of little else. I am fortunate, my work can take my mind away from the conflict, but when I leave here each evening my thoughts are immediately transported. If a solution can be found to the manifold problems that divide the world, then the small matter of Mrs.Brewer's wages can surely be remedied. Take some time to consider, to speak with family, then let me know what you decide."

He led Celia to the door.

"I remember clearly the last meeting I had with your father, I took from him instructions over his Will. Obviously it would have been improper for him to instruct his own son, although Edmund, in his capacity here, dealt with matters of probate. Mr.Tozer was a mild mannered gentleman, as he shook my hand that day he said, 'I am a lucky man Mr.Caffin, I have a son and a daughter, a perfect pair'. I realised of course that it was a reference to his work as a shoemaker but the remark lodged in my mind. We too have a daughter you see and as yet, we still have 'a perfect pair'."

His voice faltered and Celia, in that instant, saw evidence of the funny happy pain in Nigel Caffin's eyes. This war spread it like an infection to which no one was immune, it reached even the cockles of a solicitor's heart and as Celia walked across the reception area to leave, the ticking of the clock had found more mellow tone and from the page of the magazine, the young woman's smile had spread beyond 'just so'.

Celia had given herself time to think, to conceive of possibilities and this morning she had watched Mathew and Emily as they left for school, realising how much they had developed, both in size and good sense. Before pursuing any notion she had decided to follow Nigel Caffin's suggestion and seek advice of Annie. Now on her way to Gregory Street she felt altogether more positive. Charles may or may not be there but even if Annie was serving in the shop it should be quiet enough to enable them to chat, if only between the comings and goings of customers.

She peeped in through the door, Charles was behind the counter serving Mrs.Glasson. Celia was relieved, she could talk with Annie more freely at the back of the shop. She tapped at the back door, opened it, expecting Annie to be in the scullery but there was no one. An envelope with 'Laura' written on it in Annie's hand had been propped up between the salt and pepper pots at one end of the table. At that moment Charles appeared, clearly agitated.

"I was going to send Laura to your house with Samuel after tea, but now you're here you can take his bag with you and meet him at the school, he knows his grandma's not here. Word came 5 o'clock this morning, Hilda's pains had started, I suppose it was Haynes who fetched Annie."

Charles' words were heavy with resentment and Celia felt like challenging his attitude but that would never do, she could imagine the scene Annie had faced on leaving Charles with the shop as his persistent animosity towards Jack Haynes could drive his manner to extremes of unpleasantness. Celia was disinclined to linger, a small holdall sat on a chair by the scullery table.

"Is that Samuel's things?" She asked.

Charles replied with an abrupt, "Yes." The clang of the shop doorbell caused him too mutter something under his breath before lifting the holdall onto the table with a less than gracious, "Enough to last him several days I dare say," then he went to serve the next long suffering customer.

Today there would be no kindly conversation to compensate for the lack of stock but an unlimited amount of ill humour, unfortunate though it might be for those concerned, Celia considered the doorbell to be a welcome, saving grace! She gathered up Samuel's bag and left, the problems of her mother's finances would have to wait, the safe arrival of Hilda's baby must be the priority now.

The billboard outside the shop, which displayed current headlines from the papers, caught her eye as she passed by.

'Mohne and Eder dams breached by British bombers'.

That shiver, which went far beyond Celia's spine, caused her to tighten her grip on the bag and to hurry along. The previous evening she had begun a letter to William, a cheerful account, as always. Her hand had held the pen above the notepaper several times and at each one, defied the temptation to write of her meeting with Nigel Caffin. Instead, lines of random, everyday trivia from which William could extract no hint of bother. Surely there would be news of Hilda's baby very soon, not until she could include that in her letter would Celia mail it. A baby, a newborn baby was just what she needed to look upon. Mathew would be fourteen in November. Thomas and Samuel, Rosie's twins, would be fifteen in just over three months, they were to begin work at Raleigh in the autumn. Even Emily at eight years old was gaining confidence. Celia's mind, in recent weeks, had pondered on finding suitable employment for herself, it would need to be within a sensible distance of Wollaton because of Emily. While Mathew was a responsible youth Celia would not feel comfortable if she were absent when Emily was home from school and although the air raids had been less frequent of late, not to be there when the siren sounded was too disturbing to contemplate, yet now, more than at any time before, Celia needed to earn.

At school she had achieved well at English and displayed a reasonable grasp of mathematics helping her father with his accounts from time to time. Perhaps Andrew Smithfield would know of an opening for her. Brassington was too far away from Wollaton, for William it hadn't been a problem but for Celia, to be that distance from home would not allow her peace of mind. Smithfield was a man of commerce and above all else, entirely approachable, he might point her in the right direction. At the first opportunity she would ask Annie's opinion, after the baby's safe arrival. Perhaps that remedy, of which Nigel Caffin had spoken, would not prove so difficult after all.

"Thank you doctor," said Annie as she lifted his jacket from the back of the chair and held it out for him to feed his arms through the sleeves.

"She is a strong baby, eager to enter this world, hence a stitch or two, but mother is equally strong, so I do believe Mrs.Eddowes that you can look forward to a steady progress in them both." He was about to pick up his bag, then, as if a sudden thought had changed his mind, he turned to Annie and said, "How is your family, I imagine that like so many, your sons are serving abroad. I bumped into Jack Wainwright the other day, tells me he's working at Bonham & Turners. I can recall him coming to my door singing carols with Charlie Jones, strange how some individuals lodge in one's mind. I had occasion to lance a boil on Jack, never as much as winced. As for Charlie, I've observed him on the dustbin round, what he lacks in digits he makes up for in muscle. Saw him lift the wheel of a rag n' bone man's cart out of a pothole on Witford Hill when the poor old horse was near out of steam! Gritty young lads, now gritty young men.

I've been a doctor for nigh on forty years and I have seen it many times, the human body overcome more than any text book maintains to be bearable and when it comes to the mind, that mysterious unknown, which keeps a medical man at perpetual study, it appears capable of enduring beyond height, depth, breadth and length of possibility. I sometimes feel that we doctors, despite our years of reading and practice, have but scratched the surface. Have faith in your sons my dear, and try to get hold of some liver, you look a little pale, top up your iron levels, I shall see myself out." This time the bag was grasped firmly.

As the front door closed behind the doctor, almost simultaneously the back door opened and in came Celia.

"Any news yet?"

Annie was pleased to see her, the morning had granted little time to worry about anything other than Hilda and the baby, but now that anxiety was eased Annie's concern had moved to Samuel. It had been too early to wake him before she left and too early to disturb Laura. She had packed a bag for Samuel more than a week ago, anticipating a call in the early hours of any day soon and this morning she had hastily written a note to Laura. When she had roused Charles and told him it was time, she must go to Hilda's, the fact that God willing before nightfall they would have another grandchild seemed not to register with him. His response was careless.

'I found mouse droppings in the cellar yesterday, I've set three traps, couldn't use cheese, there's not enough of that to make a decent supper let alone waste it on a mouse so I've used carrot. You'll have to warn your friend Hemsley if he seeks shelter again, he hasn't paid his paper bill for three weeks'.

It had been the thought of Samuel struggling with Charles' irritability that preyed on Annie's mind, seeing Celia was reassuring, it must mean that she had spoken with Charles and was aware.

"A girl," said Annie, "nearly 9lbs, all is well, you've only just missed the doctor, Hilda needed a couple of stitches. Come on, we'll go upstairs and see them."

Hilda sat upright in bed, the evidence of exertion clinging to her features but with a smile that radiated beyond all weariness.

"Jack now has a daughter," she said, "his mam hoped for a daughter but seven boys came. Her name is Rosemary, Rosemary Alice Haynes."

Annie had been touched by Hilda's desire to call her daughter Alice and George too would appreciate the kind thought.

Celia planted a kiss on Hilda's cheek, squeezed her hand and gazed into the crib by the side of the bed. A mop of dark hair, that brand new, pink skin, which looked as though only minutes earlier it might have been still at the hand of its creator, his final touch lingering at the spot just above the infant's tiny mouth.

"She is beautiful Hilda," said a beguiled Celia, not taking her eyes off Rosemary, "a son and a daughter, a perfect pair."

The three women chatted happily until the baby stirred. Annie lifted her from the crib into Hilda's arms, to be fed.

"I should be off," said Celia, "I told Charles I would fetch Samuel home from school, I called at the shop quite by chance, I wanted to talk to you about something but of course you were already here. I was able to gather up Samuel's bag so Laura won't now need to bring him to Wollaton after tea."

"I'll come down with you," said Annie, "I need to make Hilda a drink, you surely have time for a quick cup."

Annie sensed a problem lay behind her daughter in law's pensive look, her quietness while Annie was making the tea.

"What did you want to talk to me about? Have you heard from William?"

Celia let out a long sigh. “I shouldn’t bother you, what with the shop, Charles and events here, you have more than enough to think about as it is.”

Annie sat at the table beside her, simply smiled and said, “I’m listening, tell me.”

Celia related, in not too much detail, the situation of her mother’s finances and her own need to find work, which was not altogether a result of these developments but something she had been pondering upon for a while.

“I thought I might ask Mr.Smithfield if he knows of a possible job for me, Brassington is too far from home to be a sensible option but he may be aware of a vacancy with another employer. What do you think? Should I or should I not trouble him?”

Annie was thoughtful for a moment, other than when he called at the shop there had been few conversations between Andrew Smithfield and herself for some time.

“I don’t believe Mr.Smithfield would consider himself troubled and as you say, he may be able to suggest something. I see no harm at all in asking him, he has a genuine kindliness, since Myra’s accident he has shown great concern, Edna quite rightly describes him as ‘a good man’ and you know how sparing Edna can be with compliments.” Both women chuckled at the notion. “Other than your mother’s affairs, your own finances are without problem surely Celia?”

“Oh yes, William sees to all that, besides, there’s little availability of anything so I don’t need much money to spend, his army pay is adequate.”

Annie smiled but felt dismayed that William had not seen fit to let his wife know the extent of Davina’s generosity, Celia was always sincere and refreshingly open when talking with Annie, if she had full knowledge of William’s financial situation, then to Annie she would have declared it. Yet it was not really surprising, William seemed never to learn from his mistakes, to recognise his need of others.

“If all else fails Celia, you must come to see Charles and me, Mrs.Brewer’s wages will be found somehow.”

It was about half past five when Jack got home, Annie had met David from school, telling only two young mothers of the new arrival yet Jack already knew. His dinner bag was cast over the scullery table, his face and hands scrubbed clean at the sink, words tumbling from his mouth in his excitement.

"Bill Rashleigh told me, I met him as I got off the bus, his missus had told him just ten minutes before, 'you've got a lass Jack' 'e said, 'you lucky bugger, a bonny little lass'."

Jack grabbed at the roller towel, hurried across to where Annie stood, took her in his arms and squeezed her tight then raced up the stairs to his wife, his son and now his daughter too.

Annie could not have explained to anyone why, for she didn't really understand herself, she was happy, the house was filled with happiness, yet she wept, from a hurt deep within, silently so as not to be discovered, Annie wept.

Word soon got about and almost every customer to the shop on Wednesday morning made mention until by midday Charles' irritation was beyond containment. The unfortunate recipient of his released annoyance happened to be Anthony Hemsley. Well meaning, he offered his sincere congratulations on the birth of another grandchild, further making the mistake of saying, 'you must feel proud Charles' and remarking on the help Laura Innes must be in Annie's absence, referring to his own tiresome ritual of preparing a meal for himself. If he'd stopped there, Charles' intolerance might have simmered but not boiled over. When Anthony went on to say that Harrow Road School, where Laura taught, he had attended as a boy, following his earlier lessons with Annie's aunt Bella, Charles let go his frustration. It was as pitiful as it was inexcusable.

"That cantankerous old maid, what joy your lessons must have been," said Charles, his voice raised, his forehead turning red with temper. "Had it not been for the sanctuary of my father's workshop I doubt if Annie could have claimed any sort of life for herself, she was nothing more than a chattel to Bella Pownall. I didn't realise you were desperate, I dare say Laura would attend you at The Park, your big house at The Park, cook you a meal, John wouldn't know would he? I have two sons and a stepson, God knows where, eating God only knows what, don't you think I might be more worried over them than I am overjoyed at the birth of a Haynes. But what could you know of such things, you have no one other than yourself to bother about, which begs the question of how you could overlook the fact that you owe for three weeks papers."

Anthony Hemsley did well to hold in check his own response, how tempted he was to lean across the counter and shout into Charles' face, Saul Eddowes was not your father, you are Nathan Wright's bastard son. To reveal his daily anxiety for his own illegitimate son Donald. Instead he took money from his pocket and placed it on the counter.

"That should cover it, anything over will leave me in credit."

As he walked away from the shop his initial anger turned to an inexplicable sadness. What sort of life could Annie have with such a husband, was it no less fractured than his own, broken in so many places, stuck together, best side out for appearances. His memory of Bella Pownall was vague after so many years but it nevertheless reminded him of a kindliness, of a happy childhood. Happiness and sadness drove a pain deep inside him, a curious, wounding pain like no other.

The bus was busy and on seeing several people waiting at the stop, Celia edged closer to the window, anticipating company in the seat beside her. The usual patter from the conductor and the way in which he virtually sang out the various destinations as he dispensed the relevant tickets, orange, green or blue, depending on the fare, drifted through Celia's head, an insignificant background noise. Her concentration was for the conversation she would have with Andrew Smithfield.

Whenever she called on her sister in law, Caroline, Celia found herself thinking of William's determination in those early days of his job as 'Stanford's man', to impress Basil Stanford, a man who by reputation was difficult to satisfy. Caroline rarely spoke of her father and if Celia brought up his name in conversation she noticed Caroline's expression change. William had left his job at Brassington to pursue what Celia had considered an ill conceived fascination with Stanford, turned his back on Andrew Smithfield after years of fairness, of kindness. Yet when William needed employment following Stanford's death, Smithfield had created work for him, borne no grudge. Now Celia was seeking his help, was it an audacity, would he think less of her for making the approach. Annie had not thought so but Annie saw only the best in everyone, she would not have acknowledged any possible impatience in Mr.Smithfield's nature.

Movement beside Celia and a hand appearing on the grip rail at the back of the seat in front as the individual lowered themselves to sit by her, automatically diverted her thoughts and turned her eyes to the man, the hand showed it to be a man, the fingers stained from nicotine. He smiled and after a few seconds he spoke.

"You don't remember me do you, it's Celia isn't it, Celia Tozer?" His voice was gentle, almost frail sounding. "It's not surprising, I used to see you often, when I delivered leather to your father from the tannery, you were only a girl then. I did see you again but even that occasion was years ago. I showed you and your friend, with some children, to your seats at the theatre, the pantomime I believe it was."

"Yes, I do recall, your face was familiar to me that day, but I suppose the children's excitement and with so many other people all awaiting the performance, there was no chance to dwell on it long enough to remember who you were and where I had seen you before. Give me a minute to think, to bring back your name."

Celia desperately tried to remember but despite picturing a young man in her father's workshop who would sometimes give her a toffee, a name just would not come.

He was amused by her obvious intense, concentrated effort to remember, he chuckled.

"It's Stan, though your father always called me Stanley," he sighed, "the war, first one I mean, it took me away from Nottingham and by the time I got back, well, so much had changed I had to find different work then, folk had moved on. Ended up doing all sorts of jobs, one of them being an usher at Theatre Royal." He hesitated before adding, "Your mother and father, are they alright?"

"Father died a while back, mother is alive but sadly, she has quite advanced dementia. Do you remember my brother Edmund?"

“Didn’t see much of your brother, although your father spoke of him a lot as I recall, I suppose he’d have been at his schooling when I came with the leather.”

Celia’s fingers clutched at her handbag nervously.

“Edmund was killed, his plane was shot down, this horrible war, he leaves a widow and two young sons. My husband William is in North Africa with the army, we have a son and a daughter.”

Before Celia could continue Stanley spoke again.

“When you were with him in the workshop, Mr.Tozer would hold up a pair of boots or shoes that he’d completed, a lovely polished pair of chestnut brown hand crafted shoes and he’d say to me, ‘Stanley, a perfect pair, a man can do no better than a son and daughter’. He was so proud of his children, you and Edmund. I don’t wish to speak out of turn, but I got the impression that he struggled a bit with your mother.”

“We all struggled a bit with mother, bless her,” said Celia with a chuckle, “she intended no harm I’m sure and I don’t believe she was ever aware of how testing she could be. Now her mind is so confused, she lives in a curious world of her own, yet we glimpse logic, briefly, out of the blue, it’s impossible to fathom how her sense can come and go so swiftly. But the strangest coincidence is that I should meet you today, when the purpose of my bus ride surrounds mother and that you should tell me about father’s ‘perfect pair’, only the other day someone else spoke of that very same memory.”

“Did Mr.Tozer die before his son?” Stanley looked genuinely troubled.

“Yes, thankfully he did.”

Stanley nodded and whispered almost inaudibly, “Thank God.”

“I get off at the next stop,” said Celia, “it has been good seeing you again Stanley, take care.”

He stood to one side, to let her down the aisle of the bus and as he slowly lowered himself onto the seat he pondered the coincidence. Earlier in the morning he had attended an appointment at the hospital. Since failing his medical a little over a year ago and undergoing the treatment that followed, Jessie Tozer had taken up a gentle dwelling in Stanley’s mind.

In 1915 he had enlisted, answered Kitchener's call, 'Your Country Needs You', by some miracle survived the hell of the trenches, found himself alive at the end of hostilities and with no physical injuries beyond cuts and scratches. But anger raged within him, the treatment of his comrades, shell shocked, driven to madness by a grotesque evil, shot for cowardice by a command, which paraded its authority behind the banner of top rank and that rank not necessarily military, but of breeding and blood. His scurvy, scab ridden skin hid a soreness, an ugliness far greater than the blemishes visible on the outside. Stanley was a disturbed young man and as the months went by, with no work, no prospects and everyday more likelihood of him venting his anger on someone not deserving of it, he went back into the army, signed up for ten years, 'better the devil he knew'. During that period he somehow managed to rid himself of the demons, returned to civilian life with no axe to grind. Throughout those army years he had often thought of Jessie Tozer, when pulling off his boots and polishing them, putting them down by his bunk, a perfect pair.

When he'd been recalled in 1941 any doubts he'd harboured had been rendered pointless. At his medical the doctor had found abnormalities in his testes. Last year, in the hospital, a surgeon had explained to him the need to remove them. The irony of Jessie's expression of pride had not been lost on him, 'a perfect pair'. If anything, it brought it closer to mind, the children he would never have.

He had not married, always feeling that little bit uncertain, were the demons truly gone or were they simply keeping their heads down, waiting their time. He knew of men who used their wives in the most alarming way as they wrestled with merciless torment. The cancer had spread to his prostate, this morning, at the hospital, they had explained with carefully chosen words. He felt calm, remarkably undisturbed as he fingered his bus tickets, one blue one green, he had paid to the terminus.

"Come in." Andrew Smithfield looked up from his paperwork when a light tap came at the half open door of his office. "Celia, Celia Eddowes, my dear, how nice to see you."

Then a pang of anxiety caught at his throat, William, surely not William. It was curious how when William received his call up papers and Andrew had shaken his hand and wished him well, he had felt entirely confident in the belief that William Eddowes would return, intact and with the most colourful accounts of battle, which at each and every one William had triumphed! Celia's happy smile allowed his throat to relax.

"Do sit down Celia, tell me, is everyone well?"

She found conversation with him to be so easy and his interest in the family so obviously genuine.

"A daughter for Hilda and her husband, I am very pleased for them."

They chatted for several minutes until Celia felt obliged to declare the purpose of her visit.

"Do you hold any typing skills Celia, or experience of accounts?"

She must be truthful, there was no point in claiming abilities beyond the comparatively simple ones she had.

"I did help father with accounts sometimes but I've not used a typewriter. I am quite dexterous, I mastered basic tunes on the piano without tuition."

Andrew was amused by her honesty, it was endearing. "If you were to attend a short course in secretarial work then I think some hours might be offered you at the council offices. I'm afraid the pay is not the best that is why a number of young women have abandoned clerical work for the factories, where the hours are longer and the physical demands much greater but the financial rewards significantly more inviting. I believe secretarial courses can be studied at Clarendon College, being a mature student there would no doubt be a fee but if that creates a difficulty, then please permit me to arrange it. William is not here because of the war, whereas I am, through age and uselessness. I would attend to it in his absence and consider it my privilege."

Celia felt more gratitude than she could adequately express, thank you seemed to fall short.

"Annie sends her regards. I confided in her my intention to come and see you, I sought her opinion."

"And what did Annie say." Asked Andrew, trying to sound amused at Celia's apparent need of reassurance but inwardly seeking more mention of Annie, further conversation to perpetuate her name."

"She said she could see no harm in asking your advice, that you would not consider it a trouble."

"Correct, as always," he said and laughed light heartedly. He walked Celia to the factory gates, charging her with extending his very best regards to all the family. As he turned to walk back inside, a feeling of happiness at this renewed association with William's family, with Annie, spread over him, a glorious warmth, a purpose beyond the daily routine of the factory. But happiness was so soon joined by sadness, a deep hurt, a pain, which came from no part of him he could by name identify and it intensified as mentally he spoke the name, Mrs.Charles Eddowes.

He sat once more at his desk, staring down at cold reality. He took a pen from the old tea caddy, applied his signature to the typed sheet in front of him, sighed long and placed it in the tray marked 'out'.

CHAPTER THIRTEEN

Late August

"Looks like it's well alight downstairs, at least the hydrant's close by. Right 'ere we go lads, force the door an' get some water on it, fast as yer can, it's showin' too much light from above, the place is supposed to be unoccupied but we can't rule out squatters, I'll put a ladder up to the bedroom window."

Jim Caddick, leader of the Shakespeare Street crew had felt dismayed when given the address, 41, Garland Street. He'd known the family for years, went to school with Louis Mazarelli. Folk hadn't given it a thought, the Mazarellis made their ice cream, sold it and made some more, year in, year out.

On the football field Louis would burst into wonderful, excited Italian each time the ball came his way and cry 'Mama Mia' when Joe Shields' bull terrier, Dribbler, jumped the fence to join in. When they beat a team from Grantham at a friendly, Louis insisted they take the dog to the pub with them and it was Louis who bought Dribbler half of bitter, it lapped all but an inch in the bottom of the glass and Louis poured that, little by little into his cupped hand so the delighted dog could drink the lot.

When the police came to take away the Mazarellis folk were in a state of disbelief, while the Allies had been battling in North Africa, despite Italian units making up the Axis it had seemed a world away from the familiar sight of Mr.Mazarelli with his ice cream cart at the embankment. Then came the Allied advance on Sicily, British troops were fighting in Europe and even those with a limited knowledge of geography had come to view Italy, so much more of an enemy. Jim Caddick dared to hope this blaze would prove to be the result of some accident, but malice rose up from ignorance and fear, finding squatters huddled in an upstairs room of the Mazarellis' house would be a relief, arson would be sickening.

It was now almost 10 o/clock. A neighbour had called the brigade and that had been a stroke of luck. Normally Colin and Evie Morgan would have been well ensconced behind the black out, thus unlikely to have seen the glow from a fire at

No.41, but having attended a funeral in Derby and stopping at the chip shop before returning home, they had been alarmed by the light coming from what at first they had thought to be their own house. On finding it was in fact the Mazarellis' next door, they ran to the nearest phone box and called for the brigade.

Jim Caddick rapped with his knuckles at the bedroom window peering in between the tapes, there was no response from within. Hastily scrambling down the ladder he hurried to the entry and round to the rear of the property. Curious folk had gathered in their back yards, the low drone of speculation hovered about Jim's ears as he raised the ladder to the bedroom window and repeated the process. Again no response from within. He should try the back door, see if there had been a forced entry. As he stepped sideways across the cobbles his boots found something, he stooped to look.

"Rotten buggers," he muttered under his breath, horse manure, somebody had tipped a bucket of horse manure over the step at the back door. He called out. "Did any of yer see anythin', hear anythin'?"

But for one voice, which answered, "Not a bloody thing, can't hear owt over the sound o' me stomach rumblin'," no one else uttered a word and not wanting to be involved in questioning by officialdom one by one they disappeared inside their abodes.

One of the crew called from the mouth of the entry.

"You best look for yourself Jim."

Caddick sighed, gathered up the ladder and followed him to the street. Just inside the front door the men had found what looked like burned paper, now wet and trodden into what remained of a doormat, it made for a depressing sight.

"Could have been mail, put through the letterbox by the postman," said one of the crew, able to read the despairing thoughts of his leader, "if the fire started accidentally any post would have burned."

"Did the postman deliver a bucket of horse shit an'all, did he tip it over the Mazarellis' back step, did he summon a thunderbolt from the heavens to set the place ablaze? Makes yer sick." The crew men knew only too well just what the charred paper meant, probably soaked with lighter fuel and like Caddick they didn't want to believe it.

The smell of scorched wood, of charred, wet matting, that potent smell of burned paintwork that reached the very back of the nose clinging there until spittle tasted of it, all offended their senses and most acutely, their conscience. Someone had purposefully set out to destroy the Mazarellis' home and while the fire crew had tackled the blaze with every determination, just the fact it was likely to be someone with whom they shared the streets locally, made it personal.

Jim Caddick stared at the glass shade that hung by three chains from the ceiling, now blackened, suspended above a scene of wanton vandalism, mindless aggression, it deepened his disgust.

"Gather up the gear, the police will have to take a look, I'll stop off at the station, they'll need somebody to board up the door when they've finished in here."

In his head Caddick could hear old Mr.Mazarelli calling to the people at the embankment, scooping his ice-cream into the waxed tubs that bore the family name, handing the cornets to children with a smile on his face from ear to ear, he sighed, if this war prevailed for much longer then a man would be in danger of losing his instinct, his ability to sensibly consider, to identify the true enemy. Folk were hungry from lack of food, weary of the blackouts and thirsty for peace, but maddened by endless reports of strife and bloodshed.

Taking a shovel from the tender Jim Caddick returned to the back yard, where in darkness he cleaned the mess from the doorstep as best he could. As he cast the last shovelful over the small patch of garden, a memory came, sharp and clear in his mind, the horse manure was gone, 'all gone'. He called out to his old friends, wherever they might be.

"Tutto perdutto, tutto perdutto."

Messina, Sicily.

"Oh I do like to be beside the seaside,

I do like to be beside the sea."

"Has anybody ever told you Parker that you can't bloody sing, yer couldn't carry a tune in a bucket?"

Parker picked up another stone from beside his feet, not lifting his chin from where he rested it on his knees, he chucked it into the water idly.

"For months we had sand, mile after mile o' the soddin' stuff but no bloody seaside, now we've got seaside an' no bloody sand."

"Well it's all to do wi' Etna," said another, "every so many blackberry seasons it erupts, spits an' spews its guts up an' like all spew it comes out hot an' sets when it goes cold. I'd had a skinful one night, 'ad a win at the dogs, fluke it wer', the favourite come nowhere near, I just backed which ever name took me fancy, Mister Twister, trap No.5, never forgot it, strange really cause I couldn't remember owt else about that night. I woke up wi' me legs down the sleeves o' me pyjama jacket an' our mam hollerin' blue murder. I must 'ave threw up when I got in, it wer' all down the front o' sideboard, set there, lookin' like one o' them glaciers yer see pictured in National Geographic'. Anyroad, this lot's dear old Etna's aftermath."

He picked up a handful of smaller stones and cast them into the sea. He gave an involuntary shudder, for in that instant, as he'd watched the stones plunge through the surface of the water, he'd imagined a scene, men, struggling for breath, their heads just above the surface, calling out, a hail of machine gun fire sending plumes of water rising up around them.

U boats torpedoed the convoys, destroying the ships and machine gunned the water to destroy men who might otherwise survive to defy their aggressor and battle on. When he'd first heard of it he'd imagined such talk to be intended as a spur to flagging strengths, a bit of government propaganda to swallow with breakfast porridge but then a letter from home confirmed the God forsaken truth of it.

"What's up Skinner?"

The others had noticed his changed expression, his sudden silence. It was something war did to men who spent their days and nights united in fear and misery, which they disguised behind tales, yarns, bawdy songs and random items of obscure knowledge, when desperation seemed to concentrate the mind away from whatever assailed it. They developed an instinct for one another's needs, sometimes it was a boot up the backside or simply a minor affront to get the juices flowing again, then there were times when a memory, a gremlin inside the head momentarily weakened him, instinct knew when not to drive, but to lead, to lead him away from that moment.

"Me nephew, I wer' thinkin' about me nephew Tom," said Skinner, "his ship wer' torpedoed, last November. He never learned to swim, used to get ear infections, aunt Kitty wer' convinced it wer' the water at baths, so she stopped him goin'. I've widdled in the baths, I reckon most of us did so perhaps she wer' right. Seventeen, just seventeen, poor kid."

"Come on," said Parker, "let's go see if we've got another rabbit, fresh meat for cook to stick in wi' the beans. Bunny hotpot. I don't know what bit of it I had last time, could 'ave been its knackers for all I could tell but it tasted good enough to me. Any day now we'll be headin' across the strait an' up the wops' big toe so let's catch ourselves a long eared, fluffy little bugger while we've still got chance."

Norman Parker got to his feet, rubbed his hands down his backside and was off.

"I do like to stroll along the prom, prom, prom,

Where the brass band plays tiddly omm, pom, pom."

Scrambling over the boulders and up the rugged ground, singing in his usual dire fashion, Parker led. The others looked at each other, grinned and followed.

"Ere you are Sarge, a mug o' the old Rosie Lee."

George looked up from writing his letter. "Thanks Bayliss, is all quiet?"

"Aye it is, except for Carter, 'e's 'avin' a tooth pulled, Doc reckons there's an abscess underneath."

George winced. “Oh dear, perhaps we could find something a bit stronger than tea for Carter, when it’s done, it would help sterilize the cavity.”

“I reckon the men’d welcome that Sarge, there’s been days when Carter’s arse has near choked us all, flatulence, to be polite, never known the like of it. Do I ‘ave your permission to tell ‘em that we’ll be sterilizing Carter’s cavity then Sergeant?”

George sighed. “Show a little compassion Bayliss.”

“Right you are Sarge, I’ll be compassion itself.” Bayliss winked and hurried off.

Sergeant Boucher as George now was, gave a resigned smile, that was the irony, they wouldn’t hesitate to laugh at some poor sod’s expense, yet defend each other to their last breath. They deserved a period of respite, the progress from Syracuse had been slow and gruelling, the terrain hazardous even apart from the stiff resistance they’d met with. Enemy fire rained down from the hills south of Etna, perfectly hidden from sight at lower ground, burrowed into the brush and outcrops of rock, the Italian forces proved hard to rout and the Eighth army had suffered heavy casualties. The American and Canadian armies had forged their way across country to Palermo where they had cut the coast road, amphibious landings had reinforced their strength and they had entered Messina shortly before the British. The German and Italian forces had been driven back resulting in the island falling to the Allies, most however had been successfully evacuated to the mainland. Now the coalition forces awaited orders from High Command. For some it brought relief, a welcome interlude, for others a nervous tension. One man referred to the joint Allied forces not as the coalition but as the ‘constipation’, too many chiefs at the ‘pow wow’, his need to keep on moving made this period of waiting a torment that increased day on day.

Word would surely come soon and George was aware that when it did, the opportunity to write a letter home might well be fleeting. He read the first few lines so as to begin where he’d left off. Just speaking aloud their names brought a lump to his throat, yet he so needed to hear the sound.

Dear Mam, Dad and Samuel,

The sun is warm here and we are able to look out at some greenery, I imagine that is why my thoughts have been with Freddy. Not until seeing other parts of the world did I come to realise just how beautiful is our own England. How proudly Freddy would speak of 'the land', now I understand so much better his actual sentiment. While Sicily displays a greater diversity of landscape than does the desert, it nevertheless failed to win the creator's attention to detail, which he applied so diligently at every turn while at his design for England.

Mount Etna rises above the ground, mysterious in the early dawn, shrouded in mist, ominous through her unpredictability. I say 'her' as the men, not altogether surprisingly, have given the volcano a more British feel. Parker blows a kiss every morning and says 'how's our old lass Edna today'? Of course my mind goes immediately to our own dear Edna, I do hope that Myra is progressing well, Jack Wainwright is probably better than most at providing encouragement, he's seen the need of it many times.

I was delighted to hear of Rosemary's safe arrival. One of the men became a granddad in June, twins would you believe, he didn't find out until last week. The mail can sometimes be held up for weeks then we get several envelopes at the same time, so we must first check the dates so as not to read them in the wrong order, that's what happened to Private Withers. He was confused by a letter from his mother that spoke of a Gracie and a Vera. At first he presumed that they were two evacuees, as his family live in a small village in Derbyshire, but when the letter went on to describe Vera as determined to pick Gracie's backside bare and that perhaps her agitation was due to red mites, that had infested their legs, he sought explanation in his other letter. That one of course predated the one he had just read. Gracie and Vera two Light Sussex hens, had been installed in the redundant dog kennel and were doing their bit to add to the nation's egg supply, feeding on Mrs.Withers' vegetable scraps, which she boiled up with Mr.Withers' sawdust, a bi-product of his work with the Forestry Commission. Miss Innes sounds to be settling in well, I hope Samuel, that you won't pester her to help with your homework too often when term starts.

There have been a number of airborne landings here and I imagine that the airbase will be of strategic importance over the coming months, but that is only my unqualified interpretation of the situation. Inevitably I think of John and wonder if he will find himself on Sicily at some point, we will have moved on long before then I'm sure.

We have enjoyed some tasty, rabbit flavoured beans in the last few days, I say flavoured as a little, of necessity, has gone a long way. Some of the lads have contrived make-shift traps and though their success has been limited and cook's ability to stretch the catch challenged, I think everyone has entered into a spirit of enterprise and I've heard rumours that the next endeavour will be fresh fish.

I have not yet come across William but that's not surprising, one day, God willing, we shall find ourselves in one another's company. The world is a big place and the powers that be determine which way we head, but it is logical to suppose that as we all strive for the same end then at some stage our paths will cross or merge. Like the rabbit, the notion goes a long way.

I shall close now, I need to find Lieutenant Carlisle, one unfortunate man has had a tooth pulled to relieve an abscess beneath, I hope the modest request of a tot of brandy might be approved, it would act as an antiseptic for his mouth first and foremost, a strengthener until the fish arrives, a secondary benefit!

Give my love to everyone and tell Hilda that I am proud my niece is to have Alice for her middle name, perhaps Jack can take a photograph, I remember you mentioned in one of your letters the fact our old camera will no longer work.

Thank you for taking flowers to the cemetery, which I surely know you will have done.

Be good Samuel and helpful to your grandma and granddad. Be sure and tell Edna Dodds that Mount Etna has been renamed in her honour, I'd like to be a fly on the wall when her response 'erupts'.

Take care, and keep safe and well,

Always in my thoughts, George.

He read it through to check that his tired mind had made no spelling errors, folded it and put it in an envelope. If they could only know just how much love was sealed inside. A tear was too close, he quickly got to his feet, there must by now be an urgent need to sterilize Private Carter's cavity. George smiled to himself, that saving grace, so often clutched at, could come from the most unlikely source.

“The police are takin’ it very seriously an’ so they should, as if the bombin’ weren’t enough, we can’t ‘ave folk settin’ fire to other people’s houses.” Edna began putting the shopping into her bag. “What’s the damage? Oh, before yer tot it up I’ll take a tin o’ Zeebo for the grate, thinkin’ about the fire reminded me.”

Annie reached up to the shelf. “Have you heard from Liza lately?” She asked.

“Not in a while but I suppose this time o’ year must be one o’ the busiest in the fields. Just what did they imagine Mr.Mazarelli wer’ goin’ to do, send a coded message to Mussolini in a tub o’ Neapolitan, the world’s gone mad.”

Annie added the cost of Zeebo to Edna’s list. “Florence Stanford has been worrying over her daughter Julia, if the authorities here detain Italians then she’s probably correct in thinking Julia has been put under some sort of house arrest or transported to a place where foreign nationals will be held for the duration, her marriage to Luciano may not protect her from discrimination. To us it does feel that the world is beset with madness because we know so well the Mazarellis and Florence’s daughter, they are entirely innocent of any supposed political activity.

The police will make every effort to find whoever did such a dreadful thing to the Mazarellis but when the family eventually return, how will they manage to put the house back into good repair, I understand the downstairs is very badly damaged. I shall start a collection, here at the shop, simply a jar on the counter into which customers can drop small donations.”

“Fetch one now an’ I’ll start it off,” said Edna, “rattle it under Hemsley’s nose when ‘e comes in for ‘is ration, ‘e’s not short of a bob or two. Why one man needs such a big house God knows, it could only be snobbery.”

Annie felt compelled to point out that Andrew Smithfield also lived alone in a large house, remembering Anthony’s revelation, told to her in confidence, she found herself defending him.

“That’s different, it came to ‘im when the old aunt died, ‘e didn’t buy it out o’ notions o’ grandeur an’ anyroad, ‘e’ll give a generous donation wi’out bein’ pressed, a good man is Smithfield.”

"I suppose you'll tell me in a minute that he is sadly going to waste." Annie gave Edna an old fashioned look and they both chuckled.

"We had a long letter from Francis yesterday," said Annie as she wrote the total at the bottom of Edna's list. "They've been having a difficult time, one of the land girls became very ill, she was in agonies of pain but had gone to work in the fields regardless, saying nothing to the others. It must have been frightening, she apparently collapsed. They called for an ambulance and Francis said it came within no time at all, although it felt like an age. It turned out to be a burst appendix, she was in hospital for a fortnight, of course they had to let her parents know, she's from Manchester.

Freddy's taken in more land by demolishing three hedgerows between fields, enough to put in mangolds for the cows. Faith proved a wonderful help, they'll miss the extra pair of hands when she goes back to school. Another young woman was due to arrive that evening, Francis said that Freddy was to meet the train at Steeping and he would post the letter on his way.

"Your Freddy's surrounded by women," said Edna, "like my Billy. Yer can tell a lot about a family from their clothesline.

When I wer' workin' at Brassington, if I missed the number 16 bus then I'd cut up through the houses on Thorpe Street an' it'd bring me out at the junction wi' Melbourne Road where I could catch the 53. There was a backyard halfway along an' I counted the socks on the washin' line there one day, all mens an' boys, thirty two socks. So then I counted the pants, four pairs o' long johns an' a dozen Aertex trunks, but only one brassiere, one pair o' stockin's an' one pair o' knickers. I thought to meself, the poor woman, can you imagine what she must 'ave put up with? All that talk about football an' cricket, fishin' rods stuck at the back o' the privy, in 'er way every time she scrubbed it out. Toe nail clippin's over the bedroom floor an' all them combs clogged up wi' scalp grease, waitin' for 'er to perform a miracle on wi' the last o' the water from the boiler after she'd washed all them pants an' socks. There should be some sort o' medal awarded to women who live surrounded by men."

At that moment the shop door bell clanged and in came none other than Anthony Hemsley.

“Ey up, time I was off.” Edna hastily paid for her purchases, lifted her bag from the counter and offered him a “ta very much”, as he held the door for her. She would donate to the Mazarelli fund next time.

Annie was pleased to see him, he had called at the shop much less frequently of late, she wondered if all was well with Donald but it wasn’t possible to ask if others were present and on the one occasion that he’d come to the shop, when apart from him there was no other customer, Annie had felt strangely awkward in raising the subject of his son, surely if anything untoward had transpired he would say.

“Hello Anthony, are you well?”

“I have just witnessed an unusual sight Annie, military vehicles, at least nine or ten, not British but American I think. Something must be happening or due to happen, have you heard anything?”

“No, nothing at all,” said Annie, “but would the public necessarily be told I wonder?”

“Uhm, you’re probably right, they do keep all things military under wraps, understandable I suppose. Anyway, I would like to pay my paper bill and take a loaf, if I’m not too late please Annie.

All is well with the family I trust. For me it is the old adage, ‘no news is good news’ that most encourages, I’m sure his mother would write to me if.........,” he hesitated. “Well, you know exactly what I mean.”

“Annie took a loaf from the bread shelf, “its brown, will that be alright? And yes, I do know, we heard from John two days ago but not from George for some time. Laura must have read John’s letter over and over a dozen times. He does write letters addressed only to Laura as one would expect, then she disappears upstairs for ages, sometimes I sense she’s had a good cry before coming back down, she wouldn’t let Samuel see her upset, my heart goes out to her. It was good that she went to see her parents in Birmingham for a fortnight, at least when school starts again her mind will be fully occupied. Laura certainly gives all of herself to those children, every evening she is planning lessons.”

A sudden sound from the back room drove urgency in Hemsley to leave, but Charles appeared in the doorway almost immediately. He spoke to Annie.

"I've left Samuel with Mathew and Emily, Celia will be home from her work by now, they were playing some sort of board game, it seemed silly to disrupt it, Samuel will come home later. I saw military vehicles, they drove into Wollaton Park, American personnel, no mistaking the markings on the trucks, U.S. army." Charles turned his face to Anthony Hemsley. "What do you know about the Yanks Hemsley? I've heard they have a reputation for attracting the women, you should take a stroll along Lime Tree Avenue, sample the air in the park, observe those multi talented G.I.'s, you might pick up a few tips if nothing else."

He turned and walked back to the scullery. Annie was embarrassed but before she had chance to utter Anthony smiled, he appeared quite genuinely amused.

"I am indebted to Charles, he has after all furnished me with a little information regarding the Americans, enough to answer some of my curiosity at any rate, I now know their destination as being Wollaton Park and most interestingly, I am apprised of their enviable ability to charm the ladies. I shall go home right away, to cultivate a convincing American accent."

Annie was grateful to him for making light of Charles' rudeness, she could no longer account for it and was weary of making excuses for him. Unaware of the sharp exchange, that had taken place between the two men whilst she was with Hilda and the baby, Annie put Charles' unfortunate behaviour of this afternoon down to his usual moodiness.

Annie looked up at the clock, it displayed the time as being half past ten, Samuel and Laura had gone to bed. Charles sat with his eyes closed in the armchair.

"When do you think the Allies will advance into Europe?"

Annie had been quietly thinking of George and William, the presence of American troops must surely suggest something was about to happen. Charles opened his eyes and seemingly stared at nothing as he spoke.

"The politicians and generals will be thrashing out the plan at Allied headquarters, they won't want to delay for too long, it would allow the enemy to reinforce, to dig in, but now we've secured Sicily the logical move would be up through Italy. Airfields and ports will be the main objective, there must always be a route of supply."

"I've not asked you before but what happened to your friend Clem?"

Charles was silent for several seconds, now he lowered his gaze to the floor.

"He was driving the truck, I was in the passenger seat with a rifle. It was over in an instant, I saw no one. If it had been the other way round and I'd been driving then it would have been me who took the bullet, or bullets I should say, they fired twice. Clem was never afraid of dying, only of not having lived first." Charles now looked intently at Annie before continuing. "If Charles Eddowes could come home from the last lot," he sighed. "You must know that George is more of a man than I have ever been, believe that, hold on to that."

"I was thinking of William too," said Annie, "of all of them. I know women who come into the shop with sons serving abroad, Gertie worries herself ill over Henry and furthermore, that judgement of yourself is far too harsh."

Charles got to his feet, "Always loyal, how can you be always so loyal, so proper? I see the way they look at you, Hemsley, Smithfield and I know you did nothing with Edwin Garbett, but I'd guarantee he hankered for it, with you."

Annie was mystified by his remarks.

"You can't really believe such nonsense Charles, for goodness' sake keep hold of reality."

"The reality is my dear, we can be here one minute and gone the next, alive, then dead, within the blink of an eye. 'Live Charlie boy, live while you bloody well can'. Clem would say that while we worked in the stores, never afraid to die but determined to grasp every moment of however much life was to be granted him." Charles sniffed and the tension across his shoulders gradually relaxed. "Apparently the police are questioning somebody about the Mazarelli affair, two youths from Radford is the rumour." He walked away to the foot of the stairs, paused and without turning to look back at Annie said, "Come to bed, it's late."

The topic of conversation between most folk following the arrival of American personnel was speculation over 'something big', the likelihood of an imminent Allied advance. It eclipsed the previous week's topic completely, the arson, as it was established to have been, was now overwhelmed by a much greater curiosity. Billy had come home from his shift at the Exchange with mixed feelings.

"Yer can't help feelin' sorry for the Mazarellis, folk move their concerns along so quick, they do say that the Yanks have a way of takin' over an' they've certainly done that but wi'out them we'd be buggered, we need their weaponry an' their numbers, no two ways about it. Them as 'ave already arrived at Wollaton are only the first of many you may depend. They'll 'ave to set up camp, it won't be done overnight, the Americans are known for providin' their troops wi' decent facilities, these'll be the vanguard."

"Annie is goin' to put a collection jar on the counter at the shop, for folk to drop whatever they can afford into a fund to help the Mazarellis when they come back," said Edna, herself doggedly determined not to be swayed from her deep sense of loyalty to the Italian family and her condemnation of what she deemed to be an attack on their home, for which they'd worked so hard.

Billy was approving, "You tell 'em Edna, you an' Annie Eddowes are a force to be reckoned with."

"Are you bein' sarcastic Billy Dodds?"

Edna's hackles were up! Billy kissed her on the cheek then on the lips.

"Every word is true, I'm proud of yer, allus 'ave been. Now what about some porridge."

He gave his big grin that ever softened Edna's heart, she could have no way of knowing how much this day was going to test her.

The morning had been like any other at the Dodds' household, Billy had slept for a few hours, eaten his dinner and gone to see his aunt Jessie, who at ninety one seemed indestructible. Myra had been keen to make a cake of some sort as Jack had said he would call after work. When a knock had come at the back door early in the afternoon, Edna expected it to be Minnie Bishop from two doors down, returning a cup of ground rice she'd borrowed the day before.

The sight of Archie Medlyn's mam, that tell tale blotchiness about her eyes, the trembling fingers, had sent Edna's stomach tumbling. The next hour had been desolate and now Edna could not bear the sight of Elsie Medlyn's distraught figure walking away from No.24. She had taken her arm to support the poor woman as far as the street end of the entry, making her way, an image of utter despair, Elsie represented the suffocating misery perpetuated by war and through it, reduced Edna to an agony of compassion, her breathing so short that as she turned to seek sanctuary indoors a giddiness came over her, she leant against the wall and begged the world to stop spinning. Finally it passed and her eyes found focus at a spot on the wall where crude lettering spelled out a message. Scratched onto the surface of the bricks,
JS loves SD. Joe Spooner had declared his feelings for Susie when in Edna's mind they had been no more than children, early teens, 'still wet behind the ears', as Billy would say. Yet years on Joe's sentiment remained true and this moment made Archie's letters to Myra, his unfailing devotion, declared through words written amidst the uncertainties of battle, all the more tragic. Edna had observed her youngest daughter's increasing detachment, while an attraction, which grew steadily stronger, tormented Edna's thoughts each time Jack Wainwright called. She had broached the subject one evening, when sitting quietly knitting squares with Myra. 'What do you want me to do Mam', write back to Archie and tell him that's an end to it, send a letter to the front spelling it out, I've met somebody else'?

Edna had been unable to answer. Now Archie was dead, killed during the Allies' struggle to take Sicily and rather than relieve her anxiety, knowing he would never need to be told, the news brought to the house by Archie's mam, drove a torment of loyalties that caused Edna to feel as though the light at the end of the entry was directed at the Dodds' household, to illuminate their weakness, their wanting behaviour. Edna had held Elsie Medlyn to comfort her, Edna's tears were very real, they stung with true hurt, her heart ached with soreness no less intense, but it wasn't enough, how could it be enough.

The sight of the forlorn figure walking unsteadily along Winchester Street filled Edna with despair and regret, the message on the bricks induced a sickness to the pit of her stomach. This war, this bloody awful war.

Myra sat in silence at the scullery table, not even raising her head when Edna entered. When Mrs.Medlyn had read out the content of the telegram Myra had wanted to run upstairs, to hide away, but run she could not, one step at a time was the only pace her damaged leg allowed. Myra waited for her mam to close the back door.

"If I have to knit even one more square I shall go mad. School starts again soon, I've told Susie I want to join the WVS. Cathy and Gillian can either come here to you and dad after lessons or go to Rosie Spooner's and Janet is old enough to look after herself when our Annie isn't at home, I might have a gammy leg but there's nothin' wrong with the rest of me."

Edna lowered herself to the chair beside Myra.

"It'll be hard for Jack," she said, "if yer love 'im, you'll let 'im be for a bit."

Myra picked with her restless fingers at a worn patch of oil cloth.

"Susie told me yesterday that Stella Caffin's son has been killed, he was in Sicily like Archie."

Edna looked puzzled, she tried to recognise the name.

"You had Mr.Chaucer," said Myra, "Stella is Nigel Caffin's wife, one of the other solicitors."

Now Edna recalled, Chaucer, Caffin and Holt, the names written in gold and black across the window of the solicitors' offices.

"Two hundred pounds Mam, what am I supposed to do with it?"

The first sign of tears appeared in Myra's eyes. It was yet another question to which Edna could give no answer. Her hand reached out to her daughter's nervous fingers and held them tight, the worn patch of oil cloth, now too big to be covered by the salt pot.

"We'll go to Halam to see Liza," said Edna. "Thursday we'll go on Thursday."

Myra sniffed a grateful, "Yes." Picked up the needles and began to knit. Edna fetched her own knitting from the dresser where she'd abandoned it when Elsie came.

Clickity clack, clickity clack of their industrious needles the only sound and their every stitch, impassioned.

CHAPTER FOURTEEN

January 1944.

"Breathe deep, long breaths, keep your head up an' close your eyes, listen to me, you're alright, again, breathe deep."

Jack Haynes' confident voice at last began to calm the young man. This was the fifth time in as many days that Stuart Adler had been overwhelmed by panic, almost stifling when his lungs became literally petrified, refusing to respond to the frantic demands coming from the rest of his body.

Now his head fell forward and his shoulders followed as exhaustion sapped all strength from his frame. In the gloom Stuart Adler created an image before Jack's eyes that he could describe most accurately as the sight of a man dying on his feet. Claustrophobia to this degree Jack had not witnessed before, over the years he had seen men tense, tighten up and retreat into a self protecting silence before eventually accepting life underground, but Adler was different.

The first time it happened cries of derision erupted among the others, their feelings strong, if they had to do it then so must he. It was the same on the second day, noticeably mixed on the third but on both yesterdays shift and in the tunnel today, a genuine fear gripped the men, young and old alike. No one wanted to see death, while ever they all walked away from the gates at the end of shift the pit was just a place of work, that was how they coped. When a death occurred, through whatever circumstance, then for days following, the pit became a bloody black tomb for which they had all been measured.

Jack sighed, "Come on, Eddie Wills keeps brandy in the office, it'll be no more than a sip but your heart needs it."

The 'Bevin Boys', as they had come to be known, arrived early in December. Lodgings had been found through an appeal for those with any room, to offer board to these young men conscripted into Ernest Bevin's 'underground' army. Stuart Adler, previously a bank teller from Cheltenham, had moved into No.67 Forest Road, sharing a bedroom with David Haynes. Quietly spoken, almost shy, his character had been perceived as feeble by the other conscripts even before the first incident, but Jack consciously avoided making early judgment of any man and as he'd observed Adler through the period of training, it had been this young man's readiness to listen, his concentration and genuine desire to 'get it right', which influenced Jack's regard for him. Not until the first day of actual work, deep in tunnel 4, in places so denied of headroom a man couldn't rise from his knees, did the powerful claustrophobia engulf Stuart Adler, creeping out from the darkness like a strangler, circling his throat and neck, tightening, ever tightening 'til his chest became solid, his eyes fixed as in that moment when the very last breath halts in passage, setting the features in their final expression. For the other men this phenomenon smacked of charade, a devious sham making Adler worse than a conchie, but as the days followed Adler's plight became everyone's dread for surely no individual could survive many more of these attacks. Deep in the chambers of the mine that's what they were and not confined to Adler, the attacks threatened them all, weakened their concentration, rendered them all vulnerable.

It could not continue and it was Jack's responsibility to take the problem to Hugh Porter in the hope that their instincts would coincide. Porter was not an unreasonable manager, in the main he accepted observations brought to him by the foremen.

Leaving Adler in the pay office, his crumpled frame deposited on a chair, with a sip of brandy in a cup being placed in his coal black hand by the kindly Eddie Wills, Jack knocked at Hugh Porter's office door.

As Jack entered Porter smothered a sneeze with his handkerchief and rubbed one hand up over his brow with a display of weariness, suffering from the ravages of a bad head cold, his eyes appeared glazed and desperate to close on all about him.

"What is it Jack, I'd make it quick if I were you, before I give you this infernal cold." He had barely finished the sentence before the eruption of another, almighty sneeze.

"We've a problem Mr.Porter, it's genuine enough, I wouldn't trouble you with it otherwise. Adler, one of the young conscripts is claustrophobic. The lad's not puttin' it on, I've never seen a man so stifled, I'm convinced he can't take any more, it'd finish him. It's affectin' the others, they're more frightened by Adler's attacks than they are of anythin' the pit threatens 'em with. I don't want a death down there Mr.Porter, especially one as futile as Adler's would be if we made him go down again. It wouldn't produce a single nub o' coal, he's out there with Eddie, shall I fetch him in?"

"What's the point, I'll contact the authorities, they'll have to reconsider Adler. They won't like it, 'stiff upper lip' and all that two faced rhetoric they chant by rote. They may simply cast the problem back, he's a number you know, just a number. Send him to his lodgings but warn him, I can't make miracles."

Jack sensed Hugh Porter would have little spirit of opposition in his current poorly state, not likely to put over too much of an argument when dealing with the Ministry.

"I have a suggestion," said Jack. "I'm a simple man and work with a simple logic, I believe we could solve the issue without the need of approaching the authorities. You must know Hollingsworth, manager at Mapperley, ask him if he'll do a straight swap. Adler to go there in exchange for one of their Bevin Boys to come here. Open cast mining Adler will cope with, he's not afraid of hard work, he listens and learns, probably one of the brighter ones if truth be told. The fact that each day for the past week he's gone down, despite everything, proves to me that the lad's got mettle. But to force him into that tunnel for the sheer sake o' satisfyin' officialdom makes no sense an' I've not worked this pit all these years to be mindless at my age. Adler's been lodgin' at our house, we'll afford the same hospitality to a lad from Mapperley provided he produces his ration book, an' whoever's been accommodatin' him can be confident in the knowledge that Adler will be nothin' but pleasant an' respectful. He's been with us three weeks an' caused not a minute o' trouble. Our David shares the bedroom with him, he's good with kids, I reckon he must have younger siblings, David likes him, Hilda finds Adler a real help, he'll read with David, do a jigsaw, he's not the pub type."

Hugh Porter remained silent for a moment, thoughtful, then with a cautious wipe of his sore, reddened nose he spoke again.

"I'll talk with Hollingsworth, if he's agreeable then Eddie can take Adler to Mapperley on Monday and bring back the replacement. Let us hope for a reasonable exchange Jack, they none of them come with a pedigree. If Hollingsworth refuses to co-operate then I'm afraid Adler will be at the mercy of the Ministry, God help him." Another powerful sneeze near doubled up Hugh Porter. "Damnation, why must a man be so tormented." He paused and took a deep breath, letting it out like he cast it over an advancing irritant. "It offers only one blessing Jack, Mrs.Bradshaw will give me a wide berth while I am so abundant with germs, not so small a mercy for which to be thankful!"

Annie waited patiently for the two men to finish their conversation, Albert Hickling, one hand still in his coat pocket where presumably the loose change to pay for his cigarettes awaited its purpose, had brought up the subject of Bevin Boys and their lodgings. He and his wife were accommodating two and the fact that Patricia Bradshaw, living alone in the large house on Castle Road, had not opened her door to a single one made him vociferous in his indignation. The exchange continued for a few more minutes until Joyce Haynes entered the shop, it prompted Annie to politely say.

"That will be 1/2d Mr.Hickling please."

At last the two men left and Annie was able to ask Joyce if there had been any recent news of her husband William.

"Yes, he's been moved again, now they're holdin' him in a Stalag at Limburg. He says it's cold as charity, they spend a lot o' time flappin' their arms to stop the'selves freezin' an' nobody complains about the crowdin', 'tis only the next body that generates any warmth. He's still with a chap from Ilkeston, younger than William, readin' between the lines I reckon that most o' the men he wer' taken prisoner with have been spread around the camps, Jerry don't want 'em together long enough to hatch any plots you may depend. I've sent him thick socks an' gloves via The Red Cross but God knows whether or not the guards'll let him keep 'em. You feel hog tied, useless, desperate to do summat." Joyce hesitated. "I thought about offerin' lodgin' to a couple o' Bevin Boys meself but yer know what folk are like, twist things about to suit their purpose. Surely they recognise that the young men need some kind of home, the clue's in the title, Bevin 'Boys', eighteen or nineteen most of 'em, I'm old enough to be their mam but that wouldn't stop tongues waggin', spare room could do wi' havin' some life in it, if only to drive out the damp."

"You can't forever allow the past to dominate what you choose to do now Joyce," said Annie. "The country is at war, we all must pull together, victory at The Front can only be achieved by constant, unlimited supplies reaching the troops, in that we are each and every one of us obliged to do whatever we can. Samuel is sharing his bedroom with one of Mr.Bevin's conscripts, Ted, nineteen years old, working as a chimney sweep before getting his papers. He jokingly says, 'I'll be okay Mrs.Eddowes, coal is only big soot', but I think he's finding the work hard, he nodded off at the table two nights ago. At least Charles seems to like him and Samuel is delighted when he agrees to play dominoes. Laura has lent him a book, 'Far from the madding crowd', we can't replace his family but while ever we have room he will hopefully know some sense of home.

If you feel able to tend a couple of Bevin Boys with food and clean bedding then don't be deterred by silly doubts, do it for William, every nub of coal they produce will serve the war effort and help bring William home."

"You sound like Tommy, he said more or less the same thing. Anyroad, I best have a packet o' ten Weights an' be on me way, it's been eight o'clock start all this week."

Annie took the cigarettes from the shelf and passed them to Joyce.

"Hilda told me they're likely to have a different lodger next week, the young man who's been staying with them suffers with severe claustrophobia and the likelihood is that he'll go to the opencast mine at Mapperley and one from there will simply swap place."

"I'll go to see Hilda an' Jack for an hour tomorrow, I haven't seen the kiddies since before Christmas. Raymond wer' there an' the men were discussin' the pit an' the factory, they've both got a lot on their plate I know, but I couldn't help meself from thinkin' how much my William, their brother, would give to be gettin' in the winch cage wi' the others at Birchdale or clockin' on shift at Players instead o' flappin' his arms like a soddin' penguin in a freezin' German Stalag."

Suddenly the shop door opened with such urgency that the bell jammed and Annie hurried across to remedy the situation. Mrs.Glasson, breathless and obviously in receipt of some news that she could barely wait to impart, sped across the floor and flopped down onto the chair by the counter, patting her chest and saying.

"Oh dearie me," repeatedly.

Joyce cast her eyes to the clock and smiled sympathetically at Annie, knowing she must leave her to deal with the harassed Mrs.Glasson.

"It's Mabel Rashleigh, I can scarce believe it, have you ever known a more robust woman Mrs.Eddowes? Dead, gone, her husband woke up this mornin' an' there she wer' dead in bed beside him, an' it wer' only a fortnight ago they took delivery of a brand new mattress, from Burtons if yer please. Ida Cowling saw 'em carry it in, a good six inches thick she said it wer' an' sprung, a proper sprung mattress, it's tragic don't yer think Mrs.Eddowes, tragic?" She continued to pat her chest with another, "Oh dearie me."

Annie felt dismayed, Mabel Rashleigh was one of those people never to be doubted, a constant who rose with first light and saw each day through to its end with eyes wide open, a living, breathing calendar recording all events. Poor Bill, his wife's illuminating dialogue, how would he ever fill the void, a chasm of nothing after an entirety of so much.

Mrs.Glasson had obviously recovered steam.

"I reckon it wer' shock that weakened her heart, all the years she's chivvied him to get another mattress. I know he wanted to surprise her, what with it bein' Christmas an' that, but Glory be, a new one! I reckon if it'd been second hand she'd still be here. Yer can only hope it hasn't took too much stainin', bein' so new the coverin's likely to be stiff wi' dressin'. I never think brand new curtains hang right, not until after the first launderin' can yer get 'em to fall neat an' proper. He must be beside hisself, it is a shame."

"What can I get for you Mrs.Glasson?" Annie could not be rude but surely the Rashleighs were deserving of a little more reverence, Mabel's children and grandchildren needed condolence, not inappropriate speculation over a mattress, brand new, six inches deep, sprung or otherwise.

"A loaf o' bread, it don't matter if it's a bit stale, in a basin of Oxo yer can't tell any different. Do any o' them Americans come to the shop? Some of 'em are black so I've heard. I've never seen a black man, except in books, though one did come to the Mission years ago, stayed with Esme Tutin. I wer' bad wi' shingles at the time, all the way up the back o' me neck, over top o' me head an' down me forehead, stopped short o' me eyes thank goodness, but by the time I wer' fit to go to the Mission he'd gone back to Africa, or someplace t'other side o' world. Are they black all over do yer suppose or are some bits of 'em paler, the parts that don't see daylight, like the buried up bit of a leek? I've heard they're good dancers, got natural rhythm. Perhaps I'll go down Palais next time the band comes, just to sit an' watch, me rheumatism wouldn't let me jitterbug now, be we none of us can tell what's in store an' I'm only a few months younger than Mabel Rashleigh, I ought to have a black man smile at me afore I snuff it, like the picture in 'Uncle Tom's Cabin', a proper smile. Folk these days can't be bothered to crack their face. I best take a box o' matches for the gas an'all."

When Mrs.Glasson finally left Annie sighed with relief, although concern over how quickly Mabel Rashleigh's shoes seemed to have been filled she found unsettling. Mrs. Glasson had closed the door firmly behind herself and no other customer had entered yet a curious aura lingered about the shop, Annie without aforethought spoke out loud.

"Goodbye Mrs.Rashleigh and thank you."

Hilda put the knuckle of her finger between Rosemary's gums and willed her to cease from crying. "Please, please stop." There remained some fire in the grate but still the air was cold and when Jack appeared in the doorway, tiredness and tension finally reduced Hilda to tears.

"I'll make up the fire then you go back to bed, I'll sit with her." He fetched the coal bucket from the scullery and put a shovelful over the embers.

If Edgar Perry, the Bevin Boy from Mapperley was not upstairs, wakeful through Rosemary's relentless crying then the situation would be less stressful, but knowing sleep was surely impossible and seeing the young man's obvious tiredness when at each of the last three mornings he'd sat over his bowl of porridge, endeavouring to eat it between yawning, the situation had become unbearable. For any man new to the work, alertness was vital, the mine could be unpredictable and even the most seasoned needed to have their wits about them.

It was ironic that just two days after Edgar's arrival the infant became troubled with teething and the previous three nights had been no better than this night. Rosemary had kept Hilda pacing the living room floor, yet in the night hours, even taking the child downstairs did little to relieve the disturbance to those above desperately seeking sleep.

"Shush, shush, please be quiet." Hilda tried the teething ring but it was immediately rejected. "I can't give her another powder, she's not long had one, if it wasn't the middle of the night and pitch dark I'd put her in the pram and push her round the block."

Jack lifted Rosemary from Hilda's arms and gently blew over her forehead. "Hush little Rosie." His tone low and soothing, he again sent a waft of breath over the child's head. Her crying eased, her fingers pulled at the neck of his vest, she let out a sigh far too big to be coming from one so small, then, like a miracle her eyelids closed.

"Fetch my jacket from back o' scullery door," said Jack, "put it round me shoulders then you go back to bed, we'll be alright."

He lowered himself into the armchair by the hearth, Rosemary slept in his arms, her warmth found his chest and when Hilda wrapped the jacket about him Jack felt his own eyelids defy the urge to close as she knelt by the arm of the chair to whisper something.

"When Joyce called last Sunday she told me that she'd thought of offering lodgings to a couple of Bevin Boys, they could share her spare room. It would make sense, the space sits empty and wasted. If Edgar was to go to Joyce's he'd have undisturbed sleep and there are sure to be more young men arriving to work the mines so she could take another then, company for Edgar. I can't imagine he would raise any objection, in fact he'd probably jump at the chance to leave here the way things are. I worry for you too, you need rest and sleep as much as he does but I couldn't bear it if you went to Joyce's as well."

Jack smiled, "I don't reckon our William'd approve o' that arrangement neither."

Hilda leapt to Joyce's defence. "I know what happened but that was years ago, Joyce is a good woman."

Alarmed at Hilda taking the wrong impression from what he'd said Jack responded with, "Good God, I didn't mean that, I only meant that William would take a dim view of his brother leaving his sister in law to struggle alone with their teething baby."

"Oh, I see, well I think I should be the one to stay down here with her anyway, I don't have to go to Birchdale in a few hours time."

"She's settled now, look, out to the count, we're both warm, the fire's recovered, go back upstairs and get some rest, I shall be fast gone 'afore you've even put your head on the pillow. On our way to work Edgar an' me'll call at Joyce's, if the two of them are agreeable then after tea tonight I'll go there with him, see him installed, make sure Joyce has everythin' she needs then leave 'em to it. Now does that make yer feel better?"

Hilda got to her feet, kissed his cheek and whispered. "I love you Jack Haynes." She tiptoed across the room, turning to look back before closing the door behind her.

The fire flickered sending a curious, dancing light about the dimly lit room, peace had descended over the household, little Rosemary's breathing was at last deep and easy. Jack's tired mind drifted in and out of awareness, his brothers, miles away from home, 'home', that word, which tormented him. A house on Valley Road was for sale, the bus passed it on the way to the pit. He'd made a tentative enquiry, three bedrooms, a bathroom, small garden front and back. The agent had revealed it to be an executor sale, the elderly lady owner having died and her family needing to sell the property, not dissimilar to the circumstances of Davina's passing. What to do?

Jack fought with weariness over 'what to do'. If his mam were there she would likely tell him, 'forget this place Jack, it's only bricks an' mortar'. But his dad and mam both died under this roof, Victor fell into his last sleep in this simple terraced dwelling, perhaps for that very reason Florrie Haynes would say, 'leave it Jack, leave 67 Forest Road to its echoes, find life, make life for your children in a different place'.

The flames in the grate now lost their energy, sinking once more below the embers. Whatever occupied Jack's mind, it now did so behind his closed eyelids, in unison father and daughter breathed deep and easy, morning would come all too soon but for a little while at least, troubles lay still.

"I never give a thought to bein' wi'out 'er, always imagined it'd be me as went first, it wer' 'er heart, the post mortem thing they did showed summat wrong wi' Mabel's heart."

Bill Rashleigh sat on the chair by the shop counter, a sad, broken figure. Annie felt such sympathy for him, the shock, the sudden nature of his wife's demise had certainly taken its toll.

"She wer' a good lass, 'er tongue could rattle on, and on, but it wer' harmless, there wer' never any malice in it. What shall I do now Mrs.Eddowes? Yer see, that wer' what held it all together, Mabel's chatter ran like a thread through the days, binding 'em one to the next, now there's nothin' to hold today fast o' tomorro'."

I think it's best to look back for a while Mr.Rashleigh, let the tomorrows be random, all those yesterdays are bound together still by Mrs.Rashleigh, that's what memories are, a passage of time through which thread all those things that matter the most to us. Your family will eventually find a way of securing the tomorrows, for now it is enough to simply value the pearls your wife strung together, pearls of wisdom, of humour and loyalty that become ever more valuable with age, a legacy, handed down by Mabel."

Bill Rashleigh dabbed at a tear with his frayed handkerchief. "She liked you, said you wer' copper. It wer' one of 'er mam's expressions, for folk she respected, them as 'ad a bit o' somethin' about 'em, decency I reckon it wer'. Will yer come to funeral, it'd make the lass proud if you were there. It's at Methodist Chapel, next Tuesday 2o/clock. Tommy Spooner's been good as gold, sorted everythin' out for me. It's cemetery after, she wouldn't want yer to go there, Mabel reckoned that cemetery were no place for the livin'. She'd go there once a year, 22nd April, her mam's birthday, put daffodils on the grave then come home an' start spring cleanin'. Happened every year the same, what wer' goin' through her mind I don't know but the curtains'd come down an' the rugs'd come up."

"Of course I will come to the funeral Mr.Rashleigh," said Annie.

"Bill, call me Bill, our families have known each other for a long time. How are your boys? I recall that night young Freddy sat in the pub despairin' over Bobbers Mill, I thought that wer' bad enough but when your George lost his wife an' 'er so young, I shed a tear for the lad, it's God's truth I did."

Annie was touched by his concern. "We get letters as often as they find it possible to write. George and William are in Italy, John is regularly moved to wherever the need of his skill arises. Freddy works day and night on the farm, I sometimes wonder if he sleeps at all."

The sudden clang of the door bell prompted Bill to get to his feet.

"Remember me to 'em when yer write, no need to mention owt else, Mabel weren't one for maudlin'. Perhaps that's what I'll do next Tuesday when it's all over with. That'd set 'er tongue goin' up there." He pointed to the ceiling above. "All of Heaven in the space o' five minutes'd know that Bill Rashleigh wer' spring cleanin'." He nodded politely at the next customer and left.

"Do you keep chalk ma'am, plain white chalk?" Asked the stranger with a strong American accent. "And a deck of cards if you have such a thing."

"The chalk I have but not the cards I'm afraid," said Annie, "although we have several packs out the back, seldom are they used these days, with our sons being away. You would be welcome to one of those if you don't mind the fact that they've been used before."

"Well that's real kind of you ma'am and I gratefully accept, I see you have some kind of collection going on." He pointed to the large jar on the counter and read aloud the words on the label, "Donations to help the Mazarellis."

Annie had kept the jar there as people continued to drop money into it, mostly small change but over the course of months the total grew significantly and in a strange way Annie found it to be a source of hope, a reason to be optimistic.

"For the Mazarellis." The American pushed a folded ten shilling note through the slit in the lid, "With a name like that I guess they must be Italian."

Annie felt she should explain the circumstances, he listened intently and his smile when she finished speaking eased the nervousness she'd harboured at trying to impart everyone's regard for the Italian family, after all, he was not from Nottingham, not even from England and perhaps his distance would prevent him from considering the Mazarellis any other than enemy. She hurried through to the back room to fetch the cards.

"Ma'am, if they turn out to be a lucky deck then it will be my pleasure to help the Mazarellis some more." His broad grin was so spontaneous it could be nothing but genuine.

As he closed the door behind him Annie found herself likening him in age to George. She did indeed hope that the cards would bring him luck, he was some young woman's husband, a mother's son.

The ten shilling note sat proudly with the coppers and sixpences, the world felt a little less divided as Annie carefully moved the jar closer to the front of the counter, where customers couldn't fail to notice the generosity.

"Joey, come 'ere a minute."

Mrs.Spink called out forcefully, she made for an imposing figure, solid, one way of putting it, and a good face to fight a bull with, as Charlie's dad would say of the more dominant female example.

"How long's 'e been gone?"

"I don't know exactly," said Charlie, "but long enough for his mam to be despairin', she had to tell him, the telegram come this mornin', yer can imagine what it's like at their house now Mrs.Spink. When Colin got in from work his mam let him read it, he's not a kid anymore, she thought 'e wer' entitled to read it for 'isself. They thought he'd gone to the privy, to be on his own for a bit, but after a while, when he didn't come back indoors, Maureen went to look for him an' the place was empty, no sign of him."

Joey appeared at the doorway behind his mam.

"What's up? Whatever it is it weren't me as done it."

"Shut up an' listen to Charlie Jones," cautioned Mrs.Spink, a woman not to be messed with, her air of command caused even Charlie to tense.

"Have you seen Colin, I know you and him are best mates so I thought he might have come round here to tell you."

"To tell me what?" Said a perplexed Joey, disgruntled at being called away from the table, he had a winning hand and the 'pot' stood at five bob, now the others would know exactly what cards he had.

Mrs.Spink clipped his ear. "You mind your manners, show a bit o' respect, yer might be at factory now but I'm still bigger than you."

Nora Spink was wasted keeping house on Monsall Street, was Charlie's immediate thought, she made Captain Nias look like Tinkerbelle.

"Colin's dad has been lost at sea Joey, his ship wer' one of a convoy carryin' supplies, North Atlantic, U-Boat got 'em." Charlie spoke the words with growing contempt. "Soon after Colin read the telegram he ran off an' we don't know where he's gone. I could do wi' your help lad."

Joey's eyes filled with emotion.

"'E's not 'ere but I'll go with yer to search for 'im, I know some likely places."

Joey would have gone right there and then but for Nora.

"Put your jacket on first or we'll 'ave another catastrophe, you'll catch your death, look at yer, standin' there in your shirt sleeves covered in goose pimples."

Joey grabbed his coat from the hook. "Give it a rest Mam will yer." He ran past Charlie and down the yard beyond his mam's reach.

"Sorry to have bothered you Mrs.Spink, I hope we won't be too long." Charlie touched his cap.

"Give my condolences to his family, I wer' at school wi' Colin's mam. I used to envy Lizzie Sugden, allus so neat an' pretty, all the boys followed Lizzie down the street, 'tis no wonder Ernie Talbot took a shine, they married young, Ernie could lay on the charm mind you, had that way about 'im, not cocky but sure of 'isself." Nora sniffed up a distant memory and quickly closed the door.

Joey was waiting by the entry. "Have yer tried the brickyard? We don't go there as often now we're at factory but 'e'd be out o' sight there, yer know, if 'e wer' upset 'e'd not want folk to see 'im cryin' would 'e?"

"That wer' first place I looked," said Charlie, "an' I've been to railway arch, round the back o' your old school, even looked in churchyard but not a sign of him."

Joey thought for a moment. "We'll try the allotments, 'e might be sittin' in 'is uncle Cedric's pigeon loft wi' the birds, Colin's favourite's called Monty, it used to be called Mosley 'cause o' the unusual black plumage over its breast but they renamed it after Alamein."

Hurrying through the streets in the darkness, looking in all likely places on the way, Charlie clung to the hope of finding Maureen's young brother seeking comfort with Monty in his uncle's pigeon loft, but it was not to be.

He'd been searching for more than two hours, the family would be worried sick, he'd told Maureen and her sisters to stay with their mam, Colin's older brother was on night shift at the pit. His instinct told him to send Joey home but should Colin turn up at Monsall Street then hang on to him and get word to Mrs.Talbot right away. Colin was fifteen, funny age, Charlie could remember how life was at fifteen, some days you could feel like a yo-yo, up and down, pulled this way and thrown that, wound up, toyed with. Daft fantasies passed through the mind like flickering, silent movies, one day you were a valiant leader of men, about to create history, the next, a frustrated youth with unrealised potential languishing between the loins. Yet maturity was subtle, it didn't arrive in a blaze of light, a sudden life changing spectacular moment of ascending, of reaching freedom, freedom to enter the pub, the institute, the female form, heaven on earth. Maturity was recognising the face of the 'Man', looking back at you from the mirror and knowing, that what that man would make of himself was down to you and you alone.

Charlie wanted to make a good life for Maureen, when the war ended he would ask her to marry him, if this bloody war ever did end. He was almost at the entry to the Talbots' back yard, perhaps Colin had already come home, Charlie let out a long sigh. Just then a voice called out from further along the street.

"He's alright."

The blackout made everything so grim, figures loomed out of darkness, folk had begun to ask, 'who goes there, friend or foe'? Always the answer was 'foe', only to prompt the response, 'right you are then, goodnight', from the first to speak. Common sense dictated that no actual enemy would admit to being such and so everyone secretly dreaded hearing 'friend' declared. It was a nonsense, one of many that cocked a snook at Hitler, but it served to drive the spirit and reassured those who must walk the streets in blackout among shadowy figures and the anxieties they created.

"Jack, is that you Jack?" The sight of his mate Jack Wainwright, with Colin by his side, sent a tide of relief over Charlie. "Thank God, they'll be desperate by now, come on, let's show 'em he's alright."

Jack spoke quietly. "I'll not come in Charlie, they need their peace tonight." Jack put his hand on Colin's shoulder. "Be strong for your mam. Perhaps you, me an' Charlie can get together at the weekend, do somethin' manly, I'll think o' summat." He winked at Charlie. "A chap needs a bit o' time to think, explain that to the family Charlie, especially the women, you know what to say an' if yer don't, then you'll think of it afore you reach the back door."

"Thanks Jack, thanks a million." Charlie's gratitude was beyond words.

As Jack walked home his thoughts became bound in war, the consequences of war. When the knock had come at the back door and his mam had called out, 'its Colin Talbot for you Jack', one look at the youth's face told him at once what had happened. Jack had walked him to the arboretum where they'd sat in the bandstand and held him while he'd broke' his heart. Between gulps of air and those involuntary eruptions induced by sobbing, Colin had spluttered out the words. 'He wer' brave, me dad, you know don't yer Jack, you know all about bein' brave, you said that the

Merchant Seamen were among the bravest, my dad, Ernie Talbot, Merchant Seaman, bravest o' the brave', that's right innit Jack'?

Colin's words had echoed about the bandstand, the horrors of war had invaded the sanctuary of that old, familiar place as images of bloody battle, graphic in detail, drove out the present and installed the past to Jacks' still haunted mind. But Colin was the reality now, one of the casualties, left behind when the line advanced.

Jack had known so many brave men, their actions, their deeds, could be described as nothing less, gallant, heroic, stout hearted. Yet truly knowing a man enabled insight, they weren't ready to die, they wanted to live, to watch their children grow up. To grow old alongside their wife and to be there to do right by their mam at the last. Bravery was on the outside, real substance lay within.

The news that his dad was dead had done to Colin what that same shock had done to so many others, it took a youth straight to the threshold of manhood far too soon, without preamble and cruelly left him there, alone, afraid to move forward yet unable to turn back. Colin Talbot needed to be a man, he was desperate to be a man but he did not want to cross that threshold on his own.

"Somethin' manly." Jack spoke the words out loud. A letter, which had come from his brother Henry, consisted of half a dozen lines, simple benign words for their mam to hold to her as she cooked, cleaned and washed, words which spoke virtually nothing of war. That was manly, keeping everything within.

When finally this war ended and people asked, 'what was it all about'? That would be the answer, 'nothing', a great big nothing, too immense to be spoken of.

No matter how many fell, death never became familiar, it shocked the senses, like a strong current causing every sinew to shudder, leaving an unnerving twitch that only passed with exhaustion. Now Ernie Talbot was gone, but Jack's nerves shuddered still from the news of Archie Medlyn.

'Archie'. Something manly.

Jack loved Myra Dodds, he'd loved her for years, it was hard to think of something manly when deep down he felt anything but.

They could simply chop off a mangled limb and replace it with a length of metal, non-feeling, impervious.

Jack made his way through the darkness, in the distance he could vaguely make out an approaching 'foe'!

To hell with Hitler, Adolf could go to hell.

CHAPTER FIFTEEN

Late April.

The winter seemed to have dragged on and on, at home the sky had hung low and grey making the news from the Fronts seem all the more bleak. 'Anzio' a word, that in peacetime would likely roll off the tongue so lyrical were its syllables, now could not be spoken without a bitterness coating the lips and the classical sounding Monte Cassino lost all attractiveness as day on day, week on week it spat venom at the Allies and linked arms with the devil.

Places had taken on identities, they were considered as living, breathing tyrants, devious, ruthless, thirsting for blood. Reports of fighting in Burma, the ability of the Japanese soldiers to literally thrust, like the sharpest blade, through any life and limb in their path sent nauseous revulsion deep into stomachs too empty to resist it. Tiredness allowed the mind to stray, then brief spells of recovery reined it in so fast it became disorientated and confused, it was why people wept but could offer no reason for doing so. Normality could not compete with so many influences, it had given up, withdrawn to some far distant place unknown to man. This was how Annie perceived it to be, her own weariness pulling her thoughts this way and that. A forced cheerfulness when with Samuel or the other grandchildren but a preoccupied quietness when pretence was not required of her.

Charles too sat through lengthy periods of silence, those customary remarks he would oft' times cast into conversation from behind his newspaper, to 'stir the mix', he no longer deployed. Even he had ceased to find amusement from his cynical provocation. There was little now to amuse anyone and despite the efforts made to shield youngsters from anxiety, inevitably they sensed it. Mrs.Hickling had declared even their whippet to be so sensitive of 'upset', that it had begun to bite its nails and she'd twice painted them with mustard to curb its habit. 'The daft thing lies there on the mat grindin' away Mrs.Eddowes 'til me nerves can't take no more', words delivered across the shop counter along with the request for a tin o' Colman's.

There had been no word from the boys in weeks, activity, to be constantly busy was Annie's way of coping. This Sunday afternoon she and Samuel were on their way to Purbeck Road, to see Caroline, Florence and the boys. Annie felt much admiration for Caroline, bolstered by her mother's company she had shown great strength and for some time had volunteered as many hours as she could at the hospital, relieving qualified nursing staff to attend the most serious cases.

Celia had made no mention to Caroline of Gwendolyn's financial situation, for which Annie felt equal admiration. When Anthony Hemsley had come to the shop to ask Annie if she could recommend someone to help, just a few hours a week, she had been puzzled. Living on his own and preparing meals for himself, as he often declared he was happy to do, it had seemed odd. But when he'd gone on to explain that sitting alone, passing the doors of unoccupied bedrooms every night, acknowledging the selfishness of such a sheltered existence had rendered him duty bound to offer lodgings to three Bevin Boys, Annie had understood completely.

'Just a little light cleaning', he'd said. 'I have told the young men they must attend to their own laundry and make a conscious effort to be tidy. I have little else to do so cooking for all I am more than happy to undertake'. Anthony had then produced three ration books in addition to his own with a flourish of pride.

Annie had no doubt in her mind that he would be nothing less than a fair and thoughtful employer. Knowing that Celia, while working at the council offices four mornings a week, would welcome a flexible arrangement to enable her a little further income, Annie had ventured to suggest Celia as a possibility. Then it had been Anthony's turn to feel puzzled, he was aware of what had been Davina's wishes. Annie had felt obliged to explain, in confidence, Celia's determination to support her own mother. If in his mind he questioned the need, given William's inheritance, then he chose not to voice it. Celia had been happy at the chance of working for Mr.Hemsley, after all, the house at The Park was familiar to her and he'd been generous when setting her hourly rate of pay and entirely agreeable to her working whatever hours she could or could not manage, as the case might be.

Accommodating the influx of young men to work the mines had produced a somewhat unexpected outcome. A number of women, perhaps not surprisingly, wrestled with the torment of keeping an empty room. But what if their son returned, injured, crying out for home. Some had given in to the needs of the war effort while others clung helplessly to that place, the unoccupied bedside at which they wept and prayed, ever holding it in readiness.

Like Anthony Hemsley, Andrew Smithfield too had opened his house to the anxious young men, about to spend their days deep down in the mines. A woman local to Brassington now worked as housekeeper for Smithfield. The factory was severely affected by clothes rationing and the lack of material, Annie wondered how long he could continue without laying off more of his employees. Young women applied themselves with less difficulty to those jobs traditionally held by men, but older ones struggled to adapt. The women who worked the machines at Brassington were mostly middle aged, highly skilled at their task but less able to grasp the demands of precision engineering and heavy metal work. Andrew Smithfield seemed always too compassionate for the cold principles of industry. 'A good man going to waste'. Annie had chided Edna for making the remark, yet its truth she could not deny.

"Look Grandma." Samuel pointed across the street. "It's Jennifer," he waved to draw his cousin's attention.

She called back to him. "Stay there I'll come across." Jennifer Hillier hurried over to where Annie and Samuel stood. Her face was pale from tiredness, still in nurse's uniform Annie thought it an unusual time to be coming off shift, "It's all a bit fraught, I can't say too much." Jennifer lowered her voice. "They're going to be alright but there was an accident at Ranskill yesterday, two women suffered burns, don't repeat it, we're not supposed to say anything."

"Of course not," said Annie, "we're on our way to visit Caroline and the boys." She was about to add, and Florence too but Jennifer revealed that Caroline wouldn't be there.

"She's still at the hospital. I was meant to finish at eight this morning." She looked at her watch. "It's gone two now. I think Caroline intends staying for another hour. There was some kind of gas related incident at the pit yesterday afternoon, the rescue team got the men out fast. They've all been given a thorough check, don't worry, Hilda's Jack wasn't among them. Uncle Steve was with the rescue team. 'I'm gettin' too old for this Jenny', he said and gave me a kiss on the cheek. I'm not sure whether he meant too old for the pit or too old for the kiss but his grin was all mischief, dear uncle Steve. I best get on, I've told mam never to worry when I'm late, sometimes it's unavoidable but she still frets, especially if dad's out with the guard. I would have got away an hour earlier if they hadn't brought in a German prisoner but the ward was so busy and his problem was difficulty in breathing too, a collapsed lung."

Jennifer began to hurry along, calling out as she went, "Love to everybody," then, as if suddenly remembering something, she turned to look back and blew a kiss to her young cousin, Samuel laughed, he liked Jennifer, she was always bright.

Annie sighed, poor Gertie, having Jack back home must be such a relief but Gertie anguished over Henry and the incident at the pit would have distressed her. Thankfully all were safe and checked over at the hospital. Ted hadn't mentioned anything, perhaps he didn't want to dwell on it, Annie could imagine that such events might prove unsettling if allowed to occupy the mind for very long.

When Annie and Samuel reached Moreleigh they found Florence in the small front garden lamenting the fact that sparrows could not resist picking off the crocus petals, but her spirits were instantly raised by their arrival.

"Come in my dears, Jonathon and Gregory are working on a puzzle, the Tower of London in 500 pieces, well, 499 to be exact, although we have carefully examined every piece on the tray we cannot find the last straight edged bit of the border."

Annie explained their meeting with Jennifer, making no mention of disasters, Florence didn't need to hear of troubles, more than enough had come her way in recent years.

Within the space of five minutes Florence had washed her hands and put the kettle on the stove to boil. Samuel at once joined the boys at the jigsaw, all three showing deep concentration.

"I don't know who it was first devised the notion of a picture puzzle Annie but their service to mankind, especially its young, should be recognised and acknowledged through the dedication of a medal and be pinned to their chest at the end of hostilities by the King himself." Florence fell very quiet for a moment, obviously deep in thought. "I am glad you've come, I can talk to you Annie and feel relieved. I can only hope that my silly ramblings don't burden you for I'm sure that is really all they are, foolish concerns of an old woman."

Annie chuckled. "You are only a few years my senior Florence so if you are an old woman then so am I. What is it that worries you?"

"Patricia, it's Patricia. I can't speak about it with Caroline, that wouldn't be fair, her days are filled with challenges as it is. When I called at Castle Road the other day I found Patricia in a very strange mood. Not obnoxious as she can so often be but subdued. The business of Colver is all settled, it's not that, her demeanour was too quiet, normally she thrives on contrariness, confrontation suits her, she excels in debate and invariably wins any argument. Yet that day there was no spark, nothing to ignite her defiance, she displayed indifferent accord which unsettled me then, and now. I do believe Patricia is desperately lonely and feeling out of her depth. I asked if she had heard from Anthony. Her reply was bitter and yet sad. 'If he calls my name then it is in vain, as I hear nothing', those were her very words."

"Patricia hasn't considered offering lodgings to any Bevin Boys? Surely the company, some movement about the house would help."

Annie could do nothing but offer a practical solution, while knowing who she was and able to recognise Patricia Bradshaw if she saw her in the street, not once had they ever conversed.

"I asked her that myself," said Florence, "goodness knows, the house affords plenty of room. Her answer was almost childish. 'They all hate me at the pit Mother', she said, 'I won't be hated in my own home as well'. I sensed she was close to tears. She misses Anthony, I can only hope and pray that she's not left it too late. Whether Cynthia Woolascroft would tell Patricia if she received a letter from Anthony I don't know, I imagine he might write to his sister. I remind myself that Patricia remains Anthony's wife so surely any official word would be sent to her, thank God there has been nothing."

"Found it."

A triumphant cry erupted from Samuel. the missing jigsaw piece must somehow have been lifted from the tray by Gregory's rolled up shirt sleeve and had lodged itself in the folds of cloth, only coming to light when Samuel tugged at the sleeve in his glee on completing one of the turrets. The afternoon passed pleasantly and Caroline returned home in time to see them before they left.

Walking back to Gregory Street Annie thought about Florence's eldest daughter. Perhaps it was something to do with being first born, eldest. William could display that same confrontational attitude when there was no call for it and like Patricia, it distanced him from those who simply dwelt within their own skin, to the best of what God had given them.

Charles was down in the cellar, Laura was doing her patch work, a cushion cover for a work colleague due to be married in June and Ted was out with friends. The room settled to a peaceful evening as Annie prepared their evening meal, tinned pilchards on toast. A knock came at the back door.

"I'll go." Samuel was on his feet and across the scullery, curious as to whom it might be at this hour on a Sunday, Ted would just come in, he didn't knock anymore. Annie heard only two words. "Uncle John."

She felt her knees buckle, but Samuel's voice was vibrant, excited and when John stepped inside calling out, "I wanted to surprise you all," relief near' sent her falling to the floor. With tears in her eyes she watched him walk towards her, felt his arms enfold her, neither of them uttered a single word. Annie let the happiness, for which she could not find sufficient words to adequately express, abide until more would have been selfish. Laura stood by the hearth, tears streaming down her face.

"Fetch granddad Samuel." Annie looked into John's eyes and whispered, "Thank God," then directed her gaze at Laura, in her motherly way letting him know that she understood his need. The young couple melted into one, so tight was their embrace they appeared to fuse together, even Charles, emotion straining his features as he struggled to remain composed, waited patiently whilst true love clutched at lost time. Samuel's glorious smile reached every corner of the room and still no one spoke.

Finally John crossed the room to where Charles stood, extended his arm and said, "Hello Dad," his voice soft and warm with affection. Charles ignored the offer of a handshake and instead took John to him and hugged him tight. The only sound Annie could hear was the release of Charles' breath as all his pent up dread poured out over their son's shoulder. Samuel gave a gentle tug on Annie's sleeve and whispered.

"What about Ted Grandma?"

She whispered back, "He'll go to aunty Hilda's."

Samuel's big grin in response was evidence of the boy's delight at having his uncle John back, in fact the entire home was filled with delight. For how long it might remain so Annie felt unsure, her instinct told her John's stay would likely be brief. A few moments later the back door opened and Ted walked in, he looked surprised, the man in RAF uniform sitting at the table must be Mrs.Eddowes' son John. His own situation would now change, Ted was aware, they had discussed such a possibility at the outset.

Annie knew she must speak. "John this is Ted, Ted Furniss."

John shook Ted's hand firmly. "It's good to meet you Ted, mam wrote that you'd come to stay at Gregory Street while working at the pit. I admire you for that, any man who says goodbye to daylight and sweats his way through the bowels of the earth for hours at a time is a hero in my book." He turned to look at Annie, "Your letter only caught up with me three weeks ago Mam, you'd never believe how much word from home helps."

She noticed John's eyes, when he spoke the last word, travel instantly to Laura.

They had all sat around the table to eat their meal and despite John's long absence and the limits imposed on him still as to what he could tell them of his work, conversation flowed freely and comfortably.

Ted rose to his feet. "I'll fetch my things now Mrs.Eddowes and go to Forest Road, if you're sure your daughter won't mind."

"Good grief no," said John, "I've only tonight, I've to be at Newark by nine in the morning. Some of the lads had no chance of seeing their families, too far away, but an overnight at Newark, well, I couldn't let a Godsend like that pass me by. We'll manage Ted, you don't need to disturb Hilda and Jack, does he Mam?"

Annie knew John's mind, his heart too hid little from his mother's instinct, where else would her son choose to lie for these few precious hours but alongside his lovely Laura. Yet would Charles sanction it, over the years they had all heard him deliver his authority through the customary reminder, 'while under my roof'. Looking across the table to where Charles sat Annie willed him with her eyes to speak, it would be so much better coming from him.

It was fortunate that Samuel excused himself to go outside to the privy, Charles took advantage of the moment.

"Nine o'clock tomorrow morning will come around too soon, grasp life, live Son, live." Then as if to acknowledge a regard for Laura's parents. "Laura will know best." He offered a sensitive smile.

Ted's expression confirmed his absolute approval.

Annie recalled Charles' words. 'The reality is my dear, we can be here one minute and gone the next, alive then dead'. Silently, to herself, Annie too charged John, 'to live, live, please live'. Charles stared at Annie from across the table, she mouthed the words 'thank you', and she did so thank him from the depth of her soul.

"What's the matter can't you sleep?"

Gertie was disturbed by movement at her side, Steve sat up in bed, pushed back the covers and put his feet on the floor.

"I'm alright, just need to sit up for a bit, couldn't catch me breath, it'll ease in a minute. Steve glanced at the clock, twenty past four. He'd felt a tightness in his chest all the previous afternoon. His lungs weren't good at the best of times, the hospital had checked him over after the incident at the pit and he'd felt no different to any other day. Forty five years at the mine, forty of them below ground would make any man's lungs complain, but now the old bellows seemed reluctant to work at all and he felt strangely lightheaded. Gertie was speaking, she sounded so far away, faintly he heard her say.

'You're not goin' in today, I won't have it'.

Steve lurched forward and fell to the floor. Gertie cried out to Jack.

"Come quick Jack, it's your dad, make haste Jack."

In the other bedroom Jack awoke with a start, confused, what was it?

"Quick Jack, it's your dad."

The sound of his mam shouting almost hysterically rallied his senses, grabbing his artificial leg from the floor his fingers trembling over the fasteners, he got to his feet, steadied his balance and made haste to his mam and dad's room. The scene within, his eyes were loath to look upon, his mam clutched his dad's hand, she seemed to shrink before him, consumed by dread, her nightgown fell about her in loose, unoccupied folds.

"I can't tell if he's breathin' Jack, he sat on the edge o' the bed, spoke half a dozen words an' fell forward." Gertie was frightened, it was only intense fear that held back the tears.

Jack couldn't stop himself shaking. 'Damn an' blast the bloody thing', he cursed his disability, muttering under his breath as he struggled to kneel by his dad, the false limb defying his urgent attempts to lower himself to the floor where his dad's body lay crumpled, half on and half off the rug by the side of the bed. He felt for a pulse, for the slightest rise and fall of the chest, for breath at the lips, for any sign at all.

"Get dressed Jack, go to the phone box, call for an ambulance, quick as you can."

Jack knew his dad was gone, so many times he'd willed breath to come, a pulse to throb, stared at death, yet been in denial of it.

The street was empty of all but a determined darkness, the desert was like that, not a sound, nothing but darkness, intent on stealing up on a man, throttling him if he dared to sleep. Jack reached the phone box, the door closed with a thud behind him intensifying his sense of isolation. Trying to control the trembling in his voice he gave the address to an operator, it wasn't Billy Dodds, he needed to see Myra, if only it could have been Billy then in the morning Myra would know, she would come.

Jack walked back along the street but saw no houses, felt no chafing from his dummy leg.

'This one's a gonna', 'you'll be goin' home now lad', 'that's right son your mam's just over there', 'dyin', 'course you're not dyin' I've got yer now ' aven't I'? In his head Jack could hear the stretcher bearers, their voices replacing the sound of battle, the air thick with spent explosive, smoke, charred flesh, ripped entrails, shite, always shite. He found himself at the back door, he leaned against the wall as tears streamed down his face.

"Mam, Mam." There was no one there to see his despair, to know his need. He wiped his face with his sleeve, raised his head to a glimmer of first light above the roof tops, darkness was retreating, driven back and Jack lived still. He sniffed away the last remaining salty tear and made his weary way to the reality awaiting him in that room above, calling out. "I'm comin' now Mam," as he dragged his leg up each tread of the stairs. Jack was tired, tired of hurting.

CHAPTER SIXTEEN

August. Florence, Italy.

"We've found an English woman Sir, she claims to have been held under house arrest, what do you want to do with her?"

"I'll see her, where is she now?"

"Back there with Lieutenant Saywell Sir."

Captain Styles thought for a moment. "Does she appear to be in reasonable health?"

"Not a lot o' flesh on her bones Sir an' a bit pasty around the gills as me mother'd say but in possession of her senses I reckon."

"Bring her here, always with consideration Private when dealing with any female. The war forces us not to spend time with women, for too long, man to man we can become a little lax with our manners, so a conscious effort Private, we are still gentlemen despite everything."

Private Ridley saluted. "Yes Sir, despite everything."

Styles raised his eyebrows but Ridley turned on his heel and was gone. 'Everything' was a sensitive word, in a previous life it could embrace the good, the pleasant, but in this incarnation its inclusions seemed only to be bad. The men were tired, for months they'd battled through mountainous terrain, encountering stiff resistance from the Axis forces, dug in, concealed, so as their fire erupted from bunkers known only to the wandering wild creatures evicted in the process of their construction. No rock, bush or tree could be considered an innocent design of nature. Guns and men to fire them, invisible behind screens of verdant foliage and lush grass banks, giving no hint of interference from man or any suggestion of his contrivance. Only the news of the Allied landings at Normandy and their advance across France, which filtered back to the Eighth Army, struggling its way up the spine of Italy, allowed any sense of hope. The weeks merged into months and the recurring theme was death or hideous mutilation. Florence was now cleared of enemy troops but Italy was becoming a cyclone of conflicting elements, Mussolini, freed by the Germans, controlled the Italian army while partisan groups fought independently of the Allies in their opposition to the fascists and the independent state of San Marino, sitting amid Italian territory, stared at the ever growing likelihood of being surrounded by and subject to, the ravages of a civil war.

Styles looked up as footsteps approached the door, Ridley stood alongside the woman, anticipating his dismissal.

"Bring over a chair Private."

Styles indicated to Ridley with a sideways movement of his head, the chair in position, Ridley saluted and left.

"Please sit down." Styles smiled to reassure her. Yet to question the woman, to establish the truth of her story, it was the sight of her frailty that moved him to the kindly expression. "What is your name?" He asked, pen and paper at the ready to record her details.

"Julia D'elia, I came first to Italy many years ago, to work at the Consulate. I met Luciano and in due course we married. No children, we had no children." She paused, "I've not seen him for twelve months, I don't know if he is alive or dead. He progressed at his work, although I don't believe his post within the Government was senior, Luciano held a position at The Ministerio Affari Esteri." Styles looked puzzled, she translated. "The Foreign Office, he never did speak of his work in any detail but as the likelihood of hostilities mounted, to me he spoke of it less and less. Two years ago I was taken from our home in Rome and brought to a house here in Florence. I was allowed books to read but no wireless or newspapers. I've received no letters nor was I permitted to write any. I was brought food and one day, embroidery threads and linen, I think they must imagine that all English women sit with needle and thread, diligently and obediently embroidering away any notions they might have of being significant individuals. However, no one has been unkind but no matter how many times I enquired after my husband they would tell me nothing."

Styles felt fidgetiness in his legs and stood up, he walked across to the window of their makeshift headquarters within the town hall. It was impossible to tell how many citizens of Florence were loyal to Mussolini, the army had been routed and

Italy's government now paid allegiance to the Allies but what lay beneath the skin of ordinary people it was impossible to know, even uniform, while identifying a military order, could not confirm just where a man's beliefs actually lay.

"Is your husband a fascist Mrs.D'elia?"

Julia took a deep breath. "Could I have a drink of water?"

Styles returned to the desk and poured water from the carafe, handing it to her he said, "Italy is a confused place, if I am to locate Luciano D'elia then anything you can tell me would be helpful."

Julia took several sips from the glass. "I believe he bowed to Mussolini's authority, why else would he choose to tell me so little of his affairs. I like to think that he was trying to protect me in his simple way. I am not at all political Captain, my father would frequently tell me that I was ill equipped for the rigours of a man's world and rightly or wrongly I have always considered politics more the domain of the male. I'm sure some women would have me publicly flogged for such apathy but throughout adolescence I was constantly told of my limited abilities and so I have followed a subject for which I do have aptitude, languages, Italian, French and German."

"Regardless of whereabouts your husband may be the fact that for twelve months he's not visited you suggests his own life is not without complications. Neither can we rule out the possibility that he's dead. I'm sorry to be so blunt but in these circumstances time dictates our actions. I am duty bound to arrange your passage back to England. You have papers I presume?"

"I have proof of my work at the Consulate but my passport was confiscated."

"What family do you have in England?"

"Mother, father and two sisters."

"One of my men will escort you back to the house to collect your things, and then he will bring you back here, where for your own safety you must remain. I anticipate our time here will be brief so I must pursue arrangements for your evacuation with a degree of urgency."

"Thank you Captain, I don't wish to hinder you but I would clutch at the opportunity to discover what has been happening. Having been entirely cut off from all reports I know nothing of our progress. Existing in such a vacuum produces the strangest sense of loss, of being bereaved. That must sound pathetic to you as I can only try to imagine the actual loss you have endured."

Styles expression for several seconds was remote. "The Eighth' has been battling in this country since last September, since the June if you include Sicily. Most days the loss has been necessary to achieve the gain. I refer of course to military gain, bereavement is human, bereavement applies to flesh and blood, I don't believe this erupting world has any established measure for that loss. We calculate land mass, we add and subtract it, in some cases divide it yet flesh and blood we leave for the Almighty to count." He sighed and Julia noticed his fist momentarily clench. "Even my knowledge is limited, we act upon orders and if a communiqué comes through informing us of progress then we use it as a spur. The Allies are advancing across France, the Soviets have reclaimed significant territory and we have secured the western deserts. But the further you drive the beast and the closer to exhaustion it finds itself, then sheer desperation can unleash unimaginable fury, it becomes neither the hunted nor the hunter. I'll call Private Ridley, gather your belongings as quickly as you can."

"So Captain's dinin' with a woman tonight, I suppose we're considered unfit company, likely to forget our table manners after all this time o' livin' like navvies, we might eat our beans off the wrong side o' the fork."

"Give it a rest Smithy," said Ridley, "if she wer' your missus or sister where would you want her to be, in here with us feelin' overwhelmed or with Styles, feelin' a lot less outnumbered."

A voice from the far end of the room, where they randomly sat to feed on the usual monotonous ration of bully beef and beans, enquired after the English woman's name. Private Smithy, having most to say, called across to the mild mannered Ridley.

"Remember her name can yer Ridley? Bradshaw over there needs a bit o' stimulus to give some tingle to his fantasy, summat to call his heroine," he laughed carelessly.

Ridley scraped the last morsel from his dish. "Yes, I can remember. When I was a kid I enjoyed the poems of Edward Lear, nonsense rhymes, limericks. When she told me her name was D'elia it stuck in me mind, bein' similar, the last letter of Edward and the same pronunciation, 'D'elia'."

Bradshaw got to his feet and without speaking, walked out from the room.

"What's up with him?" Said Smithy, "Can't the miserable bugger take a joke for God's sake."

"Yes Bradshaw, what is it?" Anthony stood before Lieutenant Saywell.

"Sir, I've reason to believe that the English woman with Captain Styles may well be my sister in law."

"Good heavens, you best wait here for a minute, if that is the case then many of the questions Captain Styles is required to ask can be answered right here and now. It would save valuable time, what a stroke of good fortune, quite incredible."

Saywell hurried off, aware that Styles, through the course of supper was to gather more information from Mrs.D'elia, which he must then have confirmed by the authorities in England prior to arranging her transport.

Anthony had last seen Julia when she brought Luciano to England to meet the family in the summer of '32. Julia on her own had made a short visit to her mother and sisters again, a couple of years later but on that occasion he'd not been present.

"Hello Anthony." He turned around, a curious anxiety at the pit of his stomach. There she was, the English woman, paler, thinner, older but it was Julia. "I don't know what I'm permitted to do." She looked directly at Captain Styles. "I want to embrace this man, my brother in law, to kiss his cheek, even to shed a tear."

Styles' smile, as he gestured with his outstretched hand towards Anthony, was all the endorsement she needed. Anthony felt the slightness of her body, Julia noted how much thinner he felt in her embrace than in years previous.

"I think I have understood correctly Mrs.D'elia's impatient explanation of your relationship Private Bradshaw, not surprisingly her reaction was one of immense relief and urgent desire to see you, the husband of her elder sister Patricia."

Now standing side by side, remnants of war as Styles perceived them to be, he found the image touching.

"We shall leave you alone for a little while, there must be a great deal of family news for Mrs.D'elia to catch up with, but then I'm afraid, we must resume the serious and pressing matter of getting her safely back to England. At least I have sufficient information to radio back to command H.Q. You should be prepared for movement possibly as early as tomorrow Mrs.D'elia."

"I know so little Anthony, for two years I've been denied any news from beyond the house in which I was held. Your Captain has told me as much as he felt it proper to relate of Allied activity and progress, but now, seeing you, it's word of home that I seek. Mother, Caroline and Edmund, the boys, Patricia and father, even father."

She laughed, her happiness pained him, how things had changed. He must tell her, to allow Julia to go home to Nottingham unaware of Basil's death, of Edmund's death, of his own unfaithfulness to Patricia and the ramifications that followed would be unkind, cowardly with regard to the latter revelation.

Julia listened while he explained the nature of her father's death, a haemorrhage in the brain, very sudden. She displayed shock but no grief. When he revealed that Edmund's plane had been shot down in '42 with no survivors, she had wept despairingly but on hearing of Anthony's infidelity she took his hand, smiled and said simply. "Tell me about mother, I need to know that mother is safe and well."

"Mother is living with Caroline and the boys, you can imagine the distress at Moreleigh when the telegram came. They are strong and coping well."

Anthony would say no more, the outcome of Basil's will Julia must discover for herself.

"Now you must tell me what has happened here, where is Luciano?"

Anthony tried to appear neutral on the subject of Julia's Italian husband, but permitting two years of house arrest to be inflicted on the man's own wife did little to endear him, unless of course he was dead prior to her detention and thus could do nothing to prevent it. Yet Styles' need of question and answer, whilst not taking the form of rigid interrogation, nevertheless suggested to Anthony that D'elia saluted the fascist flag and embraced dictatorship. 'Beware Prussian unrest'. How often Anthony had heard his own father deliver those words when the topic of world order entered any political debate. Now Nazism had replaced the old threat and if 'beware Nazi unrest' was not to become the first line of any future political exchange, then Hitler, all that he stood for and those who stood with him must be defeated. Yet what sacrifice in bloodshed was made through this need to vanquish and what would remain of the world when it was finally done? Anthony had long told himself that he would surely be killed before then so it was not for him to ponder. His distance from Patricia, not in miles, but in understanding, gave him no cause for hope. They had parted with a deep sense of closure, his wife seldom thought twice. Cynthia, his sister, his only sibling, her overbearing, manipulative husband, Fred Woolascroft and his back hand followers, sickened him with their self importance. The way his father in law Basil Stanford, with not a trace of conscience, achieved to pull so many strings to further his own ends, galled Anthony's stomach. Caught in the middle of their conniving, knowing that to blow the whistle would damage his sister whom he loved in spite of it all. Would wound terribly his mother in law Florence, a thoroughly decent, kind woman for whom he had a great deal of respect and cast a shadow over Julia and Caroline that would take years to fade. Aware of all this he had chosen to ignore duty and instead, taken the easy option. At the very least he should have walked away from his post at the council offices, found self respect elsewhere. But no, he had sought comfort, solace, diversion, call it what you will, in the arms of an understanding, undemanding, warm woman. His 'other woman', that damning judgement cast as the first stone. Exposed, ashamed, he had come to view war as the inevitable fate, the end of his miseries and resigned himself. Now, seeing Julia, feeling her warmth, recognising her need of the family, restored his desire to survive, to be alive when the last guns fell silent across whatever might be left of the broken, wasted world.

Julia looked pensive, intent on choosing her words carefully. "When Luciano and I first met he was charming. You know what life could be like under father's domineering, 'head of table' mastery. Suddenly I felt valued, considered worthwhile as this bright, kindly man actually wished to spend time with 'me', listen to 'me'. Happiness grew in those early years. But as Luciano progressed at his work his character changed, never consciously uncaring, I do believe that, yet something or someone occupied his mind. I began to have silly notions but looking back I'm convinced it was a doctrine, a driven belief, which took him away from me and put him among Mussolini's stalwarts. When they came for me that day, to take me away I felt no surprise, nor did I feel in any actual danger, despite Luciano's increasing remoteness I didn't doubt his protection. The hardest element of it all was the imposed ignorance, I was told nothing. He came to see me just twice in the first year but any questions I asked, however mild, he dismissed and stayed but briefly. 'It will end one day soon and we will go back to Rome', that was the last thing he said to me, since then there has been no contact. For months I've not felt married, two years is a long time and that probably accounts for my feelings but it was only two years of twelve after all. But still I have a sense of widowhood and I wish one way or the other it could be confirmed."

The sound of footsteps announced the return of Captain Styles. "We have prepared a place for you to sleep Mrs.D'elia. I have no doubt that the details you have given me will in the morning be proved correct and I shall receive clearance to arrange for you to be put on a train here in Florence, which will carry you to Rome. There you will be met, taken to an airbase and flown back to England at the earliest opportunity. Bradshaw, you need to return to your quarters, I imagine there might be some speculation over your absence, I see no reason why the men should not be told of this unexpected but encouraging discovery. Any happy event we must share, God knows they've been few enough."

"Yes Sir." Anthony saluted. "Goodnight Julia and thank you Sir."

Even as Styles walked Mrs.D'elia to her accommodation he was aware that an order to mobilise his company was imminent, they were to return to the Adriatic coast, pushing north to force the Gothic line. Winter would come all too soon to this land of extremes. The Eighth had shivered through blizzards and drifting snow at the last one. Cold was a big threat, it weakened not only a man's ability to function but his determination to one day see beyond the icy world closing in all around him. So curling up there and then, in one piece, rather than being dismembered on another battlefield later, he deemed favourable.

"The whereabouts of your husband will be pursued through appropriate channels and any verified information will be given you by the authorities in England," he said.

"Luciano was raised a Catholic. I didn't convert and no offspring came along. If he is found to be alive I shall be grateful for these past blessings. However, in my bones I feel he no longer lives. If tomorrow events should become rushed and time for goodbyes is slight, then as a precaution I shall thank you now Captain. I pray that one day I shall talk with Anthony in England, but for this day alone I shall be eternally grateful and I look forward, more than I can put into words, to seeing my mother again. At home there is now a freedom to be enjoyed aside from that for which you all fight, a simple freedom, one of no military or political importance but I relish the thought of it."

As Styles returned to his desk he puzzled over Julia's last remark, 'simple freedom', but looking at his watch more pressing matters hastened his pace. "Simple freedom." He spoke the words quietly to himself, did such a joy really exist?

"How much longer will Jean Tennyson stay do yer think?" Asked Edna, as she sewed a patch to the knee of Billy's trousers, working from the underside to render the repair almost invisible.

"I'm not sure," said Annie, "we've all been surprised at her willingness to remain in Nottingham all this time. I never doubted she would come to Steve's funeral and it's made all the difference to Gertie, having her sister's company, even as children they were particularly close. Nora too has enjoyed time with Jean, all our previous attempts at persuading her to leave London have come to nought, so for her still to be here perhaps signifies a change to Jean's state of mind. Randall's been gone a long time now, she may be able to live with her memories and allow herself distance from the cemetery, I do hope so, as much for her sake as for Gertie's. Of course she's still paying rent on her flat all this time and has her personal belongings there, I believe the flat was furnished when they took it over so I wouldn't think Jean has many large items of furniture to worry about if she decides to come back here for good."

"Umm," Edna's only response as she turned the material to check her work. "If I tell yer a secret you'll promise not to say owt to anybody?" She put down her needle and thread, looked directly at Annie, a big grin spreading across her face and revealed the source of her obvious, albeit secret, delight. "Yer know that Jack an' Myra are together again, they were never really apart, not in their heads anyroad. After the news come of Archie, it turned everythin' upside down, I could understand why neither of 'em felt able to cope wi' their feelin's, even my innards churned, never mind rationin' if somebody 'ad come along an' put a plate o' steak an' kidney puddin' in front o' me an' said it's for you Edna Dodds, from the Almighty 'isself, I'd 'ave choked at the thought, I felt sick for days an' empty for weeks so God knows what them two young 'ens wer' goin' through. Jack's visits were very random an' 'e only ever stopped for a few minutes, Myra hardly knew what to say to him when he did come. There wer' times when I wanted to shout at 'em, 'Archie's gone, remember him, allus remember him, love him for what 'e wer', a grand lad, but live your lives, you're not dead'. Even if Steve Wainwright 'adn't died sudden the way 'e did them two would 'ave got together somehow, yer only 'ad to look at 'em to know that." Edna hesitated for a second. "Our Myra's got not an inklin' but Jack spoke wi' Billy an' me and showed us the ring, a lovely little diamond in a simple gold band, from H.Samuel. Jack's goin' to pop the question on 'er birthday. I cried when 'e told us, couldn't stop meself, daft 'alfpeth, bless 'is heart, it's not for another month. But I can imagine 'im of a night, sittin' on the side of 'is bed, openin' up that little red box an' lookin' inside, dreamin' o' the day----- an' the night!" Edna laughed roguishly.

"I think that's wonderful news Edna," said Annie, "of course I'll not breathe a word, I wouldn't spoil the moment for them. Now we know we can start a bottom drawer."

"Well that's what I sit here frettin' about when I'm on me own. I've got to know Jack Wainwright by now, 'e reminds me a lot o' Billy, same ways, same big soft heart. While 'is brother Henry is God knows where an' with 'is dad gone, 'e won't leave 'is mam on 'er own. When me an' Billy first spoke o' gettin' wed 'e wer' all for livin' at me mam's but I didn't want that, I dreamt o' keepin' house in our own little place, it didn't matter how small or how simple, I just wanted to cook for Billy, bake for 'im, do 'is washin', look after me husband but in our own little abode. If Jean stopped wi' Gertie then Jack'd feel better about it all, knowin' 'is mam wouldn't be on 'er own. God knows I pray that young Henry Wainwright comes back safe an' sound, I really do but when all's said an' done, how much more sensible would it be for Jean to give up that flat in London an' all the loneliness that goes with it to be among the family again. Maggie's girls, Marie, your Samuel, they'd make Jean look forward instead o' dwellin' on the past, yer never know, she might get a job tutorin' at the school of art, she wer' allus good at drawin', I shall never forget seein' that picture she'd done o' the naked man, posin' wi' is hand over 'is wotsit. I tell yer what, I saw Billy in a different light after that. I tried to get 'im to pose in same way one night, I wer' feelin' a bit fruity like yer do but poor Billy, 'e reckoned it wouldn't look right wi' one arm, so if I waited 'til 'e lost the other then 'e'd stand in front o' the wardrobe like that famous sculpture an' let it all hang out an' I'd see 'is backside in wardrobe mirror at the same time."

Annie chuckled, but felt obliged to point out that the famous sculpture with no arms was in fact a woman, The Venus de Milo. It was Michelangelo's Boy David, which displayed the genitalia, but that did have arms although neither was employed in covering David's dignity.

"It'd be no use me tryin' to explain all that to Billy," said Edna, she giggled and blushed, "besides, we made a compromise." She burst into full blown laughter. "What were we talkin' about, I've come over all unnecessary, oh I remember, Jack an' leavin' 'is mam's. Now I'm not sayin' the weddin's likely to be any time soon but once yer get engaged yer can see what yer want in the shop windo' an' yer don't want to queue too long for it do yer? Billy says that's the whole point o' puttin' a ring on a lass's finger, so's the other blokes can read the sign, engaged, somebody already in there!"

Annie pointed to the needle and cotton that had become caught in the cuff of Edna's cardigan. "You best sort out that patch Mrs.Dodds before you lose the thread."

"I lost that years ago," said Edna. "You remember Violet, used to be at the workshop?" Annie nodded, anticipating Edna's next revelation. "Well I saw 'er last week, I heard somebody say that she wer' gettin' a bit confused, the fella she married weren't up to much, a bit of a drinker wi' a wanderin' eye. She wer' standin' outside post office, 'er blouse wer' fastened up on the wrong buttons. I spoke to 'er, said it wer' me, Edna. She looked right through me, 'adn't got a clue who I was. 'Is this where you get stamps'? She said, we were standin' right underneath the Post Office sign wi' bright red post box not two inches from 'er elbow." Edna pushed the needle through the material with a heavy sigh. "If I ever go doolally don't let me onto the streets for folk to pity me, I'd rather fade away behind me own front door."

Just then Billy arrived home, he'd been to visit Norman, a chap from work who was recovering from a hernia operation.

"I've got two bits o' news," he said, pulling out a chair and sitting down beside Edna. "I'll give yer the one off wireless first, Norman keeps it on for company I reckon, since 'is missus passed away 'e's been on 'is own an' I suppose the wireless can be a bit like 'avin' somebody else in the house, anyroad it come over the airwaves just after 3 o'clock, they interrupted the play to announce it. The Allies 'ave liberated Paris, God bless 'em, our lads, the yanks, the Canadians. The Allies 'ave got Adolf an' 'is cronies on the run. The other bit o' news is that Wollaton Park is goin' to be used as a POW camp now the Americans have gone. Makes sense, the yanks put up some sturdy accommodation blocks."

Annie felt concerned, immediately thinking of the park's close proximity to Celia and the children. Billy noticed her expression change.

"No need to fret Annie, they'll be well contained, most o' the poor sods'll be on their last legs by now. Rome, now Paris, the day'll come when our lads drive Hitler out of his own Berlin. For all their struttin' an' gesturin', Jerry can't hold a candle to our lads."

Annie shuddered, whatever the news from the Fronts it caused her entire body to tense.

"Stick the kettle on Billy," said Edna. Her repair to the trousers almost done she began to sing, the only bit of French she knew, in fact the only bit of French most local folk knew, the song they'd all learned in school. If Edna had been able to understand the meaning of the words then she would have recognised them as being most apt.

Frère Jacques, frère Jacques

Dormez-vous, dormez-vous

Sonnez les matines, sonnez les matines

Ding dang dong, ding dang dong.

"Is there any sawdust cake?" Billy called out cheerfully from the scullery. Paris was freed.

Patricia crossed the hallway feeling tetchy at being disturbed, not having much appetite of late she had drifted into a very haphazard way of eating. Breakfast seemed too insignificant to bother with, supper came too late in the day to warrant any real effort and so lunch had become the antidote to starvation, a tedious necessity, a monotonous chore. Today she had heated a can of soup in which to soften the dry remains of a loaf. Now, just two spoonfuls into her meal, the doorbell rang. Tempted to ignore it she had sipped the third, whoever it was persisted, ringing for a second time. Patricia huffed annoyance as she turned the catch. It was likely to be someone collecting. So many causes had sprung up and volunteers to pursue them. There was a sign on the gate 'No Hawkers', if it were not likely to place her name on the tip of every tongue in the parish she would have added the words 'or beggars', but even Patricia Bradshaw, née Stanford, was tired of being everyone's whipping post. What was her sin? With what was she charged? Yet sideways glances or open avoidance left her in no doubt as to people's opinion of her. She opened the door in advance of her prepared response to whomever or whatever this day's irritation might be. Patricia's breath, for that instant abandoned her, a panic, quite without reason prevented speech. The acid taste of tomato soup rushed the back of her throat, she swallowed hard to repel it, her fingers tightened around the door catch as shock threatened her ability to stand.

"Patricia? I didn't expect to see you here, Anthony told me that mother had gone to stay with Caroline, since the tragedy of losing Edmund, but I thought it only sensible to come to Castle Road first, just in case mother was back home." Julia smiled nervously and glanced down at her small suitcase on the step by her feet.

Patricia opened the door wide and stood to one side, Julia interpreted her sister's intention as best she could, given that no actual word of welcome had been spoken, picked up her case and stepped inside. It looked very different. The hall as she remembered it, had held a large oak hallstand just inside the front door on the left and a side table on which her mother used to keep a vase of seasonal flowers and framed photographs of Patricia, Caroline and herself. The rug that had lain at the foot of the stairs had gone, it had been showing signs of wear at her last visit but mother had always been loath to part with it since it came from their grandmother's house on Denman Street after she died. A deep plum colour with a midnight blue border. Its replacement, in bold green and blue swirls appeared a most unlikely choice for her mother to make, it was one of Florence's expressions when considering an outfit of clothes or curtaining, 'blue and green should never be seen'. The heavy hallstand had disappeared and in its place, a simple rack of hooks bearing assorted men's coats and jackets. Where the side table once stood was now positioned a chest of drawers, on top of which sat a row of books between two dark wood book ends, their titles in gold on a red spine revealed them to be volumes of text on legal matters. A man's hat rested crookedly over the back of an umbrella stand and the gamp shared its assigned space with two walking canes and what looked like some large maps or documents rolled and tied around with twine. An unattractive blanket box stood against the opposite wall, a pair of binoculars in a case on top. Lined up on the floor beside it, three pairs of men's shoes, each pair with laces tied together and perhaps most curiously of all, the portrait photograph of Anthony's father, Lionel Bradshaw, Julia recognised it at once, despite the pillowslip draped over the heavy gilt frame to obliterate the face. It was propped up against the wall as though destined for removal. In fact the entire area suggested the items were assembled in readiness of being collected and transported to some other place. Julia felt confused and uncomfortable.

"You best come into the sitting room," said Patricia. Now having lost what appetite she'd had for the soup, it sat forming a skin across its surface on the kitchen table, too much of an embarrassment to permit her sister the sight of. Even the most humble of folk made some attempt at creating nourishment from their meagre ration rather than abandon stoicism and submit to an easy option. Cussedness, stubborn determination were the saving graces of households under threat from war. Patricia no longer cared one way or the other and yet this sudden self consciousness in the unexpected company of Julia undermined the indifference she'd adopted by way of 'thick skin'. No longer able to contain it emotion spilled and Patricia burst into tears.

"Whatever is the matter? Please, please don't tell me that something has happened to mother."

Julia was overcome by dread, to be too late after enduring all the troubles in Italy, to reach home only to learn that her mother was gone was more than she could bear.

"Nothing has happened to mother." Patricia's voice was so woeful Julia felt some other tragedy must surely have occurred, a dramatic event of which dear, far away Anthony had no knowledge. "She's at Caroline's." Patricia at last began to calm. "Why didn't you write to say you were coming?" Patricia was regaining composure and her usual stern demeanour was fast returning. "We've heard and seen neither hide nor hair of you in years, then you just turn up out of the blue as though your absence has been no more than a weekend at Skegness, it's enough to shake anybody."

Julia sat down and let out a long breath of frustration, was Patricia's world really so small, her awareness of the struggle so pathetically deficient. Julia tried to make some sense of the situation about her, she was at the point of speaking when Patricia launched a barrage of questions.

"You say Anthony told you mother was with Caroline, when did he tell you? Where is he, where is your husband Luciano? Did your dear brother in law choose to tell you of his affair with some trollop from his work, I expect that bit of news he kept quiet about, but I bet he couldn't wait to inform you of father's wishes, 'The Will' that great debacle so much more heinous than Anthony's own two timing, two faced carry on."

Now Julia felt even more confused. When it came to the wishes of their father, she wouldn't care to predict or anticipate anything other than controversy. It had ever been his nature to 'stir', to incite unrest, then relish others' anguish before sitting back on his comfortable plump cushion of satisfaction. Julia could imagine that even beyond the grave he would make provision for the continuation of his life's endeavour.

"I need to know all that has taken place here Patricia, just as you must come to understand the many events that have brought me to Castle Rod unannounced and alone. But first, please, a moment to rinse my face and hands, a few minutes in which to gather myself. Explanations can begin after that."

Julia ventured a smile, while Patricia turned to walk away, to the kitchen, to the cold soup with its thick skin and to the hardening bread. She couldn't swallow it, wouldn't swallow it whatever Anthony's pathetic excuse might be, or countenance any distorted interpretation soft Julia might spit out from her own chewing of the cud.

In turn each had listened to the other's account, in Patricia's case, a partial explanation, adding that their mother would no doubt furnish Julia with every detail. Julia had tried to convey to her sister the confusion, the misery, the depth of strife prevailing Italy. The fractured society, which created mistrust among people of the same nationality, though divided by political dogma and opposing beliefs. When she declared Anthony to have been entirely open on the subject of his infidelity but silent with regard their father's affairs, Patricia had said simply, 'really', somewhat sarcastically but relaxed her defences, actually voicing the question, 'did he seem well'?

Encouraged by this mellowing tone Julia pursued the curious subject of the hallway, all areas of the house displayed a scene quite different to the one held in her memory.

"It's Anthony's things. When he returns they will be ready, in one place so he can conveniently remove them."

"And if he doesn't return?" Julia was dismayed by her sister's heartless actions.

"In that case I shall donate his belongings to the poor and he must equip himself anew wherever he chooses to lay is head."

Patricia's reply beggared belief and Julia could not ignore her sister's naivety.

"The Eighth Army is advancing on the Axis lines of defence in the north of Italy, what they must face, what they have already endured, you, in your realm of denial, could not begin to imagine. While you spend your life lining up Anthony's shoes, positioning his things at the threshold of departure, rehearsing the speech you intend one day to deliver over his weary frame does it never occur to you that more likely an event will be the arrival of a telegram, informing you that on some beleaguered battlefield Anthony met his death. And when that telegram comes, and you read those words, which will you do first, cast his chattels to the poor or weep from regret? In the past I've wondered if any warm blood flowed through your veins Patricia, if the coldness of your manner was a direct result of some cruel abnormality of birth. I didn't want to be distanced from you but your arrogance kept me, kept us, mother and Caroline, at arm's length. You and father so alike, pooled your strengths and how mighty became that joint strength. I acknowledged defeat long ago, Caroline too turned her back on the struggle but mother had no choice other than to bear it, to exist under the constant domination. Isn't it time you abandoned the Stanford whip that thrashed us into line, can't we at last be permitted some sway, just a little relief from the everlasting strain of remaining 'on the spot', every nerve taut, stretched to breaking point." Julia got to her feet. "I shall go to Moreleigh, I won't hinder you further."

"He doesn't write," Patricia's voice held a trembling, "not a word, not a single word. I've not known where he was, which regiment he joined, nothing, I've known nothing. He could be writing long epistles of desire to his hussy for all I know. What would you have me do? Pay her a visit, ask if she would kindly let me have Anthony's contact details so as I might send him my plea. I won't beg, not even for father would I beg."

Julia rubbed her hands up over her face, she was tired from travelling and wearied by the situation. "I have his regiment details and service number, to enable a letter, he gave them to me in the certainty that I, in turn would pass them on to you. Why don't you come with me to see mother and Caroline, what is there to keep you here?"

Patricia sniffed, "They won't want to see me but you may as well leave your case here, there's little enough room at Moreleigh as it is."

"Fetch a jacket or something, we'll go right away, I want to see how the boys have grown, our nephews."

Patricia's stomach rumbled from emptiness, too feeble now to argue she lifted her cardigan from the back of a chair and thrust her arms into the sleeves. So be it whatever 'it' may be, she would let the whip slip from her hand, shed the weight of it, the encumbrance, that burden of responsibility. In name she was no more a Stanford than Julia or Caroline, but in her head, how their father achieved to occupy her head, and how he would rebuke her for failing, she stood inert.

Julia took her sister's arm and steered her to the door. "Time to go forward," she said, "to advance."

Patricia opened it, walked through it, not once turning her eyes to look at her husband's life, assembled into lots, waiting on fate to decide their purpose.

"Let's walk," said Julia, "I don't want to ride again today, I'd rather feel England beneath my feet, the ground in Italy became very unstable and I think we will both benefit from an intake of 'fresh' air."

Patricia gave no reply and they made their way with an understood, long overdue sense of truce. Not yet a white flag but with every hope of a lasting peace.

"Show your daddy." Hilda prompted their daughter. Rosemary began to walk across the floor to where Jack sat, his arms outstretched, her progress a little shaky at the start but in her eagerness to reach him she covered the last yard like a trooper and chuckled her delight at being lifted onto her dad's knee with a kiss. "She's away now, David will have her kicking a ball about in the back yard by the weekend." Hilda held out a buttered crust from a fresh loaf and the little hand took it with glee. "What do you say?" the child beamed at her mam.

"Ta." Came the reply, then Rosemary lifted the crust to Jack's mouth, he pretended to take a bite.

"You eat it all up now, all of it, 'cause when you're a bit bigger I'll take you to Burton's an' buy you a party frock wi' lots o' petticoats an' frills, an' dancin' shoes to go with it."

Rosemary for now needed nothing more than love and her buttered crust. Hilda sat down opposite Jack, since Steve Wainwright's funeral events had preyed on her mind. More and more she wanted an end to Jack's work at the pit, but it was a touchy subject and she didn't want to upset him again. When she'd spoken of her concerns the last time Jack had rounded with, 'if you want me to quit the mine then there's only one alternative, I'll go with the others to fight, I won't turn soft, not now'. His response had alarmed her and since then she'd been silent with regard to Sylicosis, the main contributing factor in Steve's death. His lungs were already severely damaged and the night he collapsed, a lack of oxygen along with the residual effects of breathing gas caused his major organs to fail. All the years of exposure to the dust and that last rescue at the pit had finally done for Steve Wainwright.

"I've been thinking about things," she said. "When you came home from work that day and told me about the house on Valley Road and I said, no, mam's right, it's best we wait until after the end of the war, if I'm honest, I was tempted, part of me wanted to see it, to jump at the chance of having our own place, but now I'm convinced it wasn't meant to be."

Jack sat back in the armchair, Rosemary now having eaten all of her crust leaned back on his chest, her adopted position of total contentment. Hilda continued. "You are clever Jack, I see all the things you do to this house, repairs, painting, unblocking the drains, new roof on the coal shed. Like you always say, if we wait for landlord, we'll be waitin' forever. You were still at school when you started buying items from Abel's scrapyard, to sell on for a small profit. If you really put your mind to it, if 'we' put our minds to it, I see no reason why we couldn't establish a business of our own. We should use Davina's gift to set ourselves up, a house can wait, that would be the incentive, what we strive for. With your abilities Jack I'd wager that it wouldn't be long before you'd generated enough to warrant employing someone, then in time, perhaps one or two more. It's how most industries began years ago, the vision of one man would enable the furtherance of others. Not right now but when the war is won and I refuse to doubt our victory. News from the Fronts gives us reason to believe, if we don't, if we allow doubt to disable us then we let down those who committed all of themselves to the fight. Whether or not you clock on each day at that pit, the mine will continue, someone else will become foreman at Birchdale in your stead. But starting your own business puts something new into the workplace and Davina, bless her, has provided us with the means, now it's for us to declare the intent."

Still Jack sat quietly, making no immediate response. Then the sound of David playing out in the yard seemed to rouse him. It was a simple activity, kicking a ball and aiming for a bucket that lay on its side at the far wall of the yard, David never tired of it, more often than not Hilda had to call him in to save poor Mrs.Flowers from the noise.

"I used to dream of bein' me own master," said Jack, "not 'cause I wanted piles o' money but for the freedom, my decisions, my ways, me own satisfaction instead o' bein' a tool of some other man's design."

"I've scored ten goals Dad."

David's excited young voice carried his happiness in through the open scullery window and Rosemary started to wriggle her way down from her dad's lap to the floor.

"Time to stop now David, tea will be ready soon." Hilda smiled and got to her feet, ready to follow Rosemary.

Jack spoke again. "Haynes and Son." He laughed.

"What about your daughter, you might have to extend your sights, 'Haynes and Company," said Hilda, feeling relieved.

Now Jack stood, for a few seconds he observed Rosemary's progress across the room, he was about to go outside to David when he remembered something.

"There's a rumour goin' round at the pit that Mrs.Bradshaw's sister has turned up, didn't the middle one marry an Italian?" He caught hold of Rosemary's hand and led her to the back yard.

Hilda spoke aloud to herself. "I wonder if mam knows that Mrs.Stanford's daughter Julia is here. It must be true, how could anyone make up such a thing?"

Hilda sat down again and closed her eyes, their meal had lost importance. She pictured in her mind prospering business premises. J.B.Haynes and Son, sign written in bold black on white. An entry in the telephone directory and printed business cards. A trade account with the bank, respected, recommended and every element of the business conducted above ground where a man could breath as his maker intended. Jack had already spent twenty years working at the pit, Steve Wainright gave his life to it, she would not let Jack do the same. Her confident determination contrarily induced tears, it seemed obliged to remind her of her brothers, of Jack's brothers, of the unknown. 'J.B.Haynes and Son'. Hilda clung to the dream.

Florence looked at the clock for the third time, her mind would not be still. When a knock had come at the door yesterday and on opening it she had seen Julia standing there it was as much as her eyes could take in, poor Patricia, also standing on the top step, had faded into the background, a mere incidental. After all this time of not hearing anything, of not really knowing, there she was, Julia. The sound of Bill Stribley's Hallelujahs had filled Florence's head like a peal of bells proclaiming an event of great magnitude, calling for jubilation across the entire land. Tears, laughter, breathless shock, indescribable relief had swept across the threshold at Moreleigh filling the house with happiness. Florence had ushered her daughters through to the living room where Patricia sank onto a chair looking for all the world like a tailor's dummy, gradually losing its stuffing. The arrival soon after of Caroline, home from her work at the hospital and the boys, who had been on an errand, created a mix of emotion so potent that it stung the senses. Feeling exposed and vulnerable, Patricia had sniffed into her hanky and pointed out, 'It's all very well but she'll need a ration book and coupons'! Florence had put her hand under Patricia's chin, raised her eldest daughter's face and whispered, 'Let yourself be loved Patricia'.

Now the clock had ticked the hours and Florence was tormented with worry over how to tell her previously absent daughter of all that had transpired. Julia had explained the remarkable good fortune of seeing Anthony in Italy but gave no indication of knowing any part of the story, which had coloured so drearily the situation in Nottingham, the story Florence must as her mother now relate.

She turned the pillow to the underside, its coolness was soothing, yet her thoughts and concerns persisted. Surely now Patricia had news of Anthony she would grasp the chance to redeem the marriage. But Julia had seemed evasive when asked about Luciano, Florence detected awkwardness on her daughter's part and with Jonathon and Gregory present it had not felt appropriate to pursue the subject, always the war undermined hope and happiness, wove its threads of doubt through heart and mind, sombre, dark threads. Would its evil take Anthony and Luciano as it had taken Edmund, were they to become a family of four widows. Basil had been spared so much, his man's world was no more, replaced by a changing world, one in which lonely women must shoulder the load. Florence again cast her eyes to the clock on the bedside cabinet, it was ten past three.

Annie Eddowes had suggested Andrew Smithfield might be the best one to advise Florence. A thoroughly decent man with experience of planning policy at the council, he would know when the time was right for her to seek development status for the land at the old Colver site. It was all she had to offer Julia and Caroline, apart from the small house on Denman Street. In the morning she would go to Castle Road, face her dread. She prayed it would not create more bitterness between her daughters. Caroline had become resigned and yet Florence had noticed the way she looked at Patricia. Not with resentment but with a pitying stare. Caroline had her sons, the company of her mother, purpose to her days, while Patricia appeared to flounder through the murky affairs of their father, too proud to cry for help even though it was at hand.

Florence's eyelids at long last began to droop, feeling her drowsiness she spoke to The Almighty, at this quiet hour he would be all ears. "Please God, grant us the strength to deal with a changing world." Finally she succumbed to the weight of the early hours and sleep rendered faint her weary, "Amen."

So many years had gone by since she had last gone to bed in this house, she felt strange, as though she'd died and been reborn, ordered to start again from the beginning. Julia had lain the clock face down to stifle the sound of its ticking, surely it must be morning soon, she watched for a sign of first light through a chink in the curtains.

All explanation would be sought in the morning, her mother would want to know everything that had happened in Italy. To tell her that whether Luciano proved to be alive or dead she would not go back there would be hard to do. To declare the marriage over, to admit it had not worked when at its beginning Julia had spoken to her mother with such certainty, love, she had found love. This house had seemed always to be intent on banning love from its doors, Julia had grown up watching her mother fade away under the domination of their father. It had sapped her own confidence making her convinced that true love was an idealistic dream, in reality it did not exist. Then she had met Luciano and he had done things to her heart, wonderful, impossible things that had blanked out all previous pessimisms and doubts, lifting her above, way above her father's reach, no longer could he strike her with his harsh authority or confine her spirit.

This house, it rejected happiness, slammed the door on contentment, even now misery dwelt within. Julia had always imagined that when the time came Basil Stanford would want his favourite daughter to wear the 'Stanford crown'. What had happened following his death would no doubt be explained to her, but in truth, she didn't much care. Despite being the 'chosen one', Patricia lived under this roof in misery, Julia actually found herself feeling sorry for her, they were sisters after all, the same flesh and blood.

Anthony had stood little chance of having a wife in any real sense of the word while ever Basil lived. It wasn't Patricia's fault, just as their mother, Caroline and herself had been manipulated by him, so to had she been under his control. The only difference was Patricia refused to admit it for fear of appearing weak. It was time for change, a new order, one they could all subscribe to with hope and conviction.

Julia picked up the clock, it was a quarter past three. No sound came from the next room and yet she sensed Patricia also lay wakeful.

A job of work, a room to rent, that all vital ration book! Julia's eyelids were heavy as she made a mental list of priorities. Too drowsy to manage a prayer she trusted The Almighty would accept this account of her needs and in his merciful goodness, grant them.

In her bedroom Patricia at last cried herself to sleep, the tear soaked pillow she had used to hide the sound, the only witness to her unhappiness. The clock on her bedside cabinet had stopped months ago, it only needed to be rewound, her life needed to be rewound. In the darkness a tentative peace descended on Castle Road, defences breached and adversaries scattered, only that final push remained.

CHAPTER SEVENTEEN

Late November.

"You're quiet tonight Edgar, you're not sickenin' for somethin' I hope, Mrs.Evershed's lad's got the mumps, they say one side of his face is up like a beachball an' Shirley Shoesmith's got it an'all. It's not so bad for a girl but it can leave a lad short o' tadpoles later on." Joyce had noticed his unusual quietness over their meal, he'd seemed preoccupied, going through the motions but with mind somewhere else.

"I've been a daft bugger Joyce," he said, "let meself down."

She put aside her knitting, progress on William's jumper was slow but at least she'd managed to buy wool in her chosen colour, like the crysanths' on Annie Eddowes' shop counter. Edgar had been lodging with her for eleven months, he'd caused little bother, in fact it seemed easier to cook a meal for two than for one and washing and ironing was second nature to any woman. He was polite, hard working and popular with folk. When he'd celebrated his 21st birthday on September 3rd, Joyce had felt proud that this decent young man had come of age under her roof, a credit to his mam and dad had they been alive to witness it. Edgar Perry had been without parents since he was eleven. First losing his mother to meningitis when he was an infant and then through cruel fate, his dad eight years later in a tragic accident on a building site. A deep foundation trench collapsed while Jimmy Perry was working in it, burying him alive. Frantic efforts to dig him free were too late, a case of negligence was brought against the builder who in the event was so deeply in debt that he was declared bankrupt. Jimmy Perry was duly reburied with rightful dignity, a very sombre affair, due more to the strained relations between the family and Muriel Podmore, than to the manner of his demise. Edgar's dad had taken up with 'a woman' three years after losing his wife, during that time the young Edgar had lived with various aunts in turn but when Muriel Podmore arrived on the scene, Jimmy naturally wanted his son to return home. She'd fed him with scarcely more care than most folk would grant a cat and laundered his clothes, ever reminding him of her hours of drudgery on his behalf.

Following his dad's funeral there had been 'tea' laid on at aunt Margaret's house, where Edgar's belongings had magically appeared in the small bedroom he'd occupied for a year after his mam's funeral, everything he owned, down to the cardboard aeroplane he'd made at school when he was nine.

Edgar had found security with Joyce, a place in which to be content and gradually, through their easy conversations he'd revealed the nature of his past. He'd let down his guard, become confident enough to socialise, even to smile at the opposite sex.

"Yer best tell me what's botherin' yer," said Joyce, "a problem shared is a problem halved 'cause two heads are better than one even if they're only sheep's heads, mam could allus tell when we 'ad summat on our minds, she couldn't hear but mam knew us inside out, so come on then, cough it up, it can't be that bad."

"I've put Valerie Oates in family way, she's missed three of her monthlies."

Joyce had expected Edgar to declare some minor financial crisis or to describe a dispute at the pit at which he'd been tempted to join in the shouting. But this, not for a second had she anticipated this.

"Is it definitely yours?" Asked Joyce, finding his revelation difficult to believe.

"Well how would I know if it weren't? Besides we did, yer know, do it. The night o' me birthday, folk in the pub were feelin' relieved, Paris had been liberated, the war seemed at last to be goin' in the Allies' favour. Jerry hadn't launched his bloody V2's then, if we'd have known what wer' about to land on London we wouldn't have felt so cheerful. Bob Budgeon wer' in there with his squeeze box, everythin' 'e played sounded the same but we all sang anyway, whatever tune came into our heads. I only drank a couple o' pints an' Valerie had a shandy, we weren't drunk, just happy an' we got carried away with the atmosphere. She dragged me outside an' into the phone box, all giggles she wer', playful, like a pup. 'Just connecting you now sir', she said, 'when you hear the tone put it in the slot and carry on up to the pips'. How we managed it I don't know, there's not much room in them telephone boxes. To be honest, I wer' glad to get out for air, if anybody'd told me it wer' possible to make a baby as quick an' uncomfortable as that I'd have thought they were barmy." Edgar sighed. "I had mumps when I wer' a kid, at aunt Dolly's so it sends that tadpole theory out the window."

"Has Valerie told her mam an' dad?"

Joyce could foresee trouble, Tom Oates had the reputation of his father before him. Erasmus Oates had ruled his family with a rod of iron, poor Phyllis, his wife, spent most of her life covering up Tom's misdemeanours to save his skin, quite literally! Instead of turning him away from such harsh discipline, sadly it served as an example and Tom Oates perpetuated the trait, known for his fiery temper he had been the instigator of many a heated exchange with his fists at the ready and he worked at the same pit as Edgar.

"She's not said owt to 'em yet, I've told her I'll do the right thing an' marry her but she don't want to get wed, not to me anyroad, she made that clear enough."

"Oh Edgar, we need to consider the situation carefully, perhaps Valerie should tell her mam first, Mrs.Oates would likely think more of you if when Valerie does, you stand there with her, facing up to it, she'd know then that you'd offered to marry her daughter, otherwise Valerie might not make that understood. How well have you got to know Tom Oates from workin' at Birchdale?"

"He's at a different seam, hardly ever meet up with him. I see him at the pit gates now an' then, I've heard he can be a bit hot headed but first time somebody pointed him out I wer' surprised at how small he looked, must be the wiry sort I reckon, tougher than his size suggests."

Joyce rolled the half finished sleeve around the knitting needles and put it away in the bag, she couldn't concentrate any more tonight. If only William could come home, never one to lose his temper he would give young Edgar a good telling off, yet apply calm, sensible thought to the problem. Neither was William judgemental, Joyce could remember Annie Eddowes telling her about Victor, how William's youngest brother had a way of putting everything into perspective, it was true, Victor had inspired those around him to take a broad minded view, to reject pettiness for the corrosive influence that it was.

“Do yer want me to go Joyce, I’d understand if yer did, my troubles shouldn’t come to your door an’ I reckon Mr.Haynes would find me other lodgin’s, I could still come to see you.”

Joyce was alarmed. “No, don’t you go askin’ Jack that, we’ll be alright an’ so will Valerie, it’s a baby for heaven’s sake, when I think about the folk in London, killed, homeless, frightened to death. Gertie Wainwright’s sister Jean lost all her belongin’s when a bomb fell in the street where she had her flat, razed to the ground. It’s as well she were still at Gertie’s but can you imagine the terror of it all. What harm can a baby do? A baby’s a blessin’ an’ Valerie’s mam an’ dad’ll come to realize that, summat to look forward to.

Put kettle on Edgar, we’ll ‘ave a cup o’ Bovril before we go to bed. Don’t go botherin’ Jack, ‘e’s enough on his plate wi’ the pit. The ministry keep puttin’ pressure on management to up the yield, they must think that coal’s just sittin’ there waitin’ to be gathered up, like windfall apples, an’ Mrs.Bradshaw’s sunk into some sort o’ depression. She hardly ever comes out o’ that big house, the sister that come home from abroad seems to do everythin’. Hugh Porter’s got a peptic ulcer, some days I reckon it’s down to Eddie Wills an’ Jack to run the place, the other foremen don’t want any more responsibility than they’ve already got unless more pay goes with it.

Edgar busied himself with the making of the Bovril and Joyce allowed her thoughts to race ahead. A baby, it should come early summer if Valerie had missed three months. Edgar must surely have the right to be a part of its life, he’s the father, or so she claims. If only Tom Oates was a more reasonable man, the hot Bovril didn’t arrive in time to prevent a shiver travelling down Joyce’s spine.

“Have you been looking through the palings again, I’ve told you to keep away from there, you’re late for your tea. I shall ask granddad to speak to you, I’ve more than enough bother without you spending your time peeping at prisoners.”

Celia was stressed, she’d been delayed at Anthony Hemsley’s when a faulty can of apples on the pantry shelf had blown and ruptured, sending sticky pulp over the ceiling and walls. Trusting Mathew to be at home with Emily she had been dismayed and vexed to find her alone.

"It's not much to ask is it? I have to work and you should be here with your sister until I get home."

Celia was under even more strain than before as Sybil Brewer had announced that she could no longer cope with Gwendolyn's erratic behaviour. War or no war, Christmas aside, she would leave on December 15th and it was for Celia to find a replacement or seek other arrangements.

"Do you think uncle Freddy will have some POW's working on the farm at Bonthorpe? There are two at Halam, Liza Ollerton wrote about them in a letter to Edna, do you know they don't wear socks inside their boots? Liza said they wrap their feet in strips of cloth, a bit like bandages and wash the cloths each night, don't you think that's unusual. Liza says one of the prisoners who speaks a little English explained that it keeps their feet from getting sore, they prefer the bandages to socks."

Celia was in no mood for Mathew's fascination with the habits of German prisoners.

"Eat your meal and after it's gone down you're to have a bath, Emily's already had hers, you can top up the water with some hot from the kettle, I've not long lit the fire, poor Emily had to make do with a couple of inches. When your dad comes home I shall tell him that you insisted on wandering the streets in the blackout instead of looking after your sister, I'll tell him, I will." Celia's voice trailed to a woeful whisper and she began to cry.

"What's the matter Mam, I'm here now, is it because there's been no letter? One'll come soon, perhaps tomorrow, I bet there'll be two or three arrive at once, grandma had two letters from uncle George on the same day didn't she? Don't cry Mam, it'll be over soon, they say the people in Germany are virtually starving, they don't even have bread, it can't go on much longer can it?

"Your grandma Tozer is getting worse, that's why I've not taken you or Emily to see her for a while. Mrs.Brewer can't manage any more, it's time grandma went to stay somewhere safe, a place where specially trained nurses can look after her. No one, not Mrs.Brewer, not me or any other person on their own could watch over grandma both by day and night."

Mathew was quiet for a moment, then with wisdom beyond his years said, "At least grandma isn't aware of war, the last time we went to see her she thought she was Queen Victoria and it was pointless trying to dissuade her so I pretended to be a courtier, I bowed and kissed her hand, she loved it, she looked really happy. She may be in a world of fantasy but it is a kind world, kindly toward grandma anyway. The real thing hasn't been nearly as kind to a lot of folk."

He stopped short of speaking his aunty Caroline's name although the memory of uncle Edmund was ever close by. Celia had calmed, she smiled.

"Mr. Hemsley's pantry was sticky as a fly paper." She explained what had happened with the can of apples, "He's very kind, his mother became confused too. Eat your tea, there's not much of it but we're not starving." 'Not yet', now she spoke quietly to herself as Mathew hurried to his meal, 'Queen Victoria'! Celia managed a chuckle. If her mother was going to become anyone other than Gwendolyn Tozer it would naturally be royalty. A world of fantasy, right now Celia could readily lose herself in such a paradise.

Mathew's voice called out from the living room. "Christopher Spooner's got mumps, Rosie told grandma Annie to let you know."

A sigh accompanied Celia as she climbed the stairs to Emily, what more awaited its time to afflict them?

When Celia had asked Annie if she would go with her to the mental hospital at Mapperley, on seeing the look of misery which lined her daughter in law's face, Annie had felt like telling Celia to stay and mind the shop, to let her go alone, but of course that would not be right. Annie's head was filled with memories of May Watkinson's cruel decline, her lonely confinement behind a locked mind that allowed her no recognition of friendly, familiar faces, no recollection of happy times and sternly forbade hope to put even a hint of light into her empty eyes, which stared out at same such souls sitting about a room as though frozen in time, the only indication of life being the restless fingers and a curious inclination in some to sing, just a line now and again from a song, long forgotten by those more in tune with the present.

Annie felt glad that her own aunt Bella had left this world for the next without enduring a failing of mind between the two.

Now they sat nervously awaiting their appointment with the administrator and Celia was barely able to breathe through the torment gripping her chest. Annie tried to distract her.

"Myra Dodds' skin graft was successful. When she finally left hospital the first time Mr.Shilling said that she would need further operations but this has been the only time since then that they've deemed it necessary to graft skin from her good leg onto the damaged one. For such a young woman the daily dressings and outpatient visits must be disheartening yet the hospital is delighted with her progress and she should be home by the end of the week. Now that Jean is back here permanently, Jack and Myra have ventured to make wedding plans. I think they are hoping it could all work out to be next May. Jack goes to the hospital every evening to see Myra, what Edna says is so true, there is something sad about a fate, which demands a young couple start their married life with such a wounding and yet their obvious happiness, their wonderful indifference to it proves sadness to be ill placed. When Edna told Jack we'd be starting a bottom drawer he gave her that roguish look of his, tapped his artificial leg and said, 'top o' the list, metal polish for Saturday nights', then gave Edna a big kiss. 'That lad melts my heart', says Edna, always with a tear."

Before Celia had a chance to respond a door opened further along the corridor and a smartly dressed woman appeared, she walked towards them, gave a pleasant smile and said.

"You must be Mrs.Eddowes."

"Yes I'm Celia Eddowes and this is my mother in law." Celia stood up and now glanced at Annie.

"Another Mrs.Eddowes then surely, my name is Joan Faulds."

The woman had an easy manner, it helped still their nerves. "Come into the office for a few moments, both of you if you wish, I dare say you would welcome your mother in law's company Celia." She talked as they walked along the corridor. "I understand that it is your own mother who needs our care, and we do care you know. Despite the dread most people attach to this place life does go on here. When the word 'asylum' is used, right away it creates an image of almost caged madness and yet asylum in its true meaning is a mercy afforded to a person in need of sanctuary, refuge from possible harm. When the busy, preoccupied world outside can no longer offer sufficient shelter, here the vulnerable and confused are granted asylum. When the word is properly understood we become much less of a dread. 'Institution', now that is another misconceived identity many folk apply to us but unfairly as we are no more of an institution than a school, the city hospital or even the church. We simply exist because of the need and the need comes from the fact that we are all human and equally disposed. Now do sit down and tell me as much as you can about Gwendolyn, I have here the letter from her doctor. Joan Faulds closed the door, picked up the sheet of writing paper from her desk, drew up a chair and sat immediately in front of them. Not having the desk positioned between them made the whole thing so much less clinical and Celia related events with a tone of relief. She explained Mrs.Brewer's exhaustion and her own situation of needing to work to support her mother, William's long absence and their children, Mathew, developing fast yet still a youth and young Emily. She told Mrs.Faulds of Caroline's sadness, the devastation Edmund's death had wrought on the entire family.

Annie sat quietly, feeling a goodly measure of regard for this woman's willingness to listen without once interrupting Celia's account of events and outpouring of concerns.

"It is time for you to take a look around, what you have told us will help us to understand your mother, I hope that what you see here will help you to understand us. First we shall meet matron, I can't guarantee your visit will be without incident. Our residents can be full of surprises." She chuckled. "Suddenly undressing is a habit Maud finds difficult to break but she does neither herself nor anyone else any harm in the process and we just help her to dress all over again. Agnes talks to her husband although he died more than twenty years ago, we have all got to know Henry very well! Muriel can suddenly call out loudly, with no warning whatsoever, it still makes us jump sometimes even though we know that in her mind she's nursing at the Front in 1917, who could possibly tell what scene is before her eyes, certainly one that I have been spared. Mr.Oakley, Bill, now he used to work at the chain makers, he's eighty seven, every now and then he'll relive his working day, not physically of course, but in his head. He'll suddenly pour with sweat and grip the handle of his walking stick, just as years ago he put his might behind the sledgehammer. They all had a life and they still have a life, confused it may be but they are entitled to it. Now are you ready?"

Celia and Annie got to their feet. "Yes, we are," they answered in unison, encouraged by Joan Faulds' thoughtful preparation.

The ensuing half hour or so was a mix of emotions, far from easy but neither was it dreadful. Matron walked her wards and day rooms with an easy tread, the residents were either curious or indifferent to their presence and Maud did indeed decide to undress but having already been advised that it was her habit and caused no distress, it seemed altogether less disturbing than the air-raid siren, or the warden, rapping at the front door, shouting urgently, 'you're showing a light'.

When they finally stepped outside again, having arranged for Celia's mother to be admitted on Sunday the 10th, to be afforded 'asylum', both Celia and Annie felt relieved. The actual plan for Gwendolyn's transport, what must now happen to the house, the financial implications, all would wait for another day, it was time to go home, to that place so often taken for granted but on this day truly valued. 'Home' with all its problems and vexations, its work and worry. They walked arm in arm with no need of conversation, it had all been said.

Celia had found her mind drifting back to yesterday's events on and off throughout the morning, so when the clock struck one it was a welcome sound. She tidied her desk, it had been busy, now familiar with the routine and efficient over the filing, her work at the council offices was not unpleasant. Today however, Celia was glad to have reached the end of her shift. It was not just her mother's affairs which dominated her thinking, when school closed for the Christmas break Mathew's time there ended. He was fifteen, his birthday last month was significant beyond the usual greetings and kindnesses of family, now he must seek employment. He was bright, he'd achieved well at his lessons, the war dictated to a great extent his immediate prospects. One of the factories, Raleigh, Briggs, Bonhams among the most likely, but after the war ended, Celia hoped he might take up a period of further study, one of the professions. A niggle of guilt troubled her, was she becoming an off shoot of her mother, seeking to be posh? No, she had no illusions of grandeur, if Mathew had simply plodded along at school she would be perfectly happy with whatever work presented itself provided it was honest labour. Her hopes were for Mathew entirely, for him to carve out a secure future for himself away from the hungry jaws of the colliery, the endless, monotonous shifts of day or night, performing the same task over and over in automated fashion on the production line at a factory. Celia wanted her son to have the opportunity to spread his wings, to fulfil dreams. Then another niggle of guilt undermined her, was she subconsciously wanting Mathew to emulate her dear brother Edmund, the brother she'd lost to war and missed so much. She was about to leave the building through the side door when a voice called out.

"Celia, I've not seen you in a while." He hurried over to catch up with her, a little breathless he asked after the family, always his polite first enquiry. Andrew Smithfield was the most kindly of men and Celia felt at once relaxed. When she spoke of her mother's deterioration and the sad but unavoidable need for her to be admitted to Mapperley, he was genuinely sympathetic. Their conversation led to him suggesting that an ambulance might alarm Gwendolyn. He would be happy to drive them in his car, thereby rendering the journey less traumatic. "Mrs.Tozer might imagine it to be an outing, a change of scene. The authority grants me a petrol allowance to enable deliveries from the factory, over the last few months it has not been necessary to fully utilise it and so transporting your mother on the 10th would be entirely sensible, it would save the fuel required by the ambulance and prove a more vital use of the factory's resource," said Andrew.

"If you truly wouldn't be inconvenienced, then it would be helpful, mother I'm sure, would look upon a car ride as most agreeable. It's what she will make of her surroundings when she arrives that concerns me," said Celia with a heaviness about her last words.

"Don't worry in advance my dear, I know we are all prone so to do, but in this instance perhaps you should await your mother's reaction with optimism, she may surprise you."

Celia laughed. "Mother has many times done that," she hesitated. "Love is a cruel master sometimes, don't you think Mr.Smithfield?"

He nodded his head and sighed. I shall come first to Wollaton to collect you then we shall go to fetch Mrs.Tozer."

Celia was so grateful it was quite spontaneous, she kissed his cheek and whispered. "Thank you, from all of us, thank you."

"Mam, this is Edgar."

Mrs.Oates ceased from peeling potatoes and turned around. Valerie stood in the doorway, a young man beside her. "If you've brought him for tea it'll not be enough to warrant soilin' a plate our Valerie, yer should tell me at least the day afore so's I could beg a bit o' liver or kidney off Cheetham's. Trouble wi' you young folk is yer don't think."

"Mam, we've summat to tell yer. Edgar 'asn't come expectin' to be fed, 'e's come because," poor Valerie felt sick, "I'm goin' to 'ave a baby Mam."

Peggy Oates dropped the potato she'd been holding and it fell to the floor at her feet, her face turned as white as the enamel on the sink.

Edgar remembered what Joyce had said. "I'd marry your daughter Mrs.Oates, honest I would but she won't have me."

Peggy swallowed hard, her eyes travelled to the clock. "God help us Valerie, 'e'll be back any minute, I can't stand it, I can't." Her voice became weak and pitiful through despair, but then, as if a harsher reality took over, she began to shriek. "Get out, get 'im out now," she stared at Valerie her eyes filled with fear, then at Edgar, "run afore Tom gets sight o' yer."

Valerie stepped back and was about to push Edgar into the yard and follow but Peggy called out.

"Not you young lady, I'll not suffer it on me own, I won't let 'im strike yer but you've got to face up to it, once 'e's had 'is bout out 'e'll likely take 'isself off somewhere but you'll stay here 'til then. Shame on you our Valerie, 'e'll 'ave that lad's skin an' all for the sake of a daft five minutes wi' your brain turned off. I never had arf the schoolin' you've had but I managed to keep me knickers up."

She clung to the edge of the sink, the grubby water from her fingers running down in streaks over the enamel, her heart pounding. Valerie closed the back door, crossed to where her mother stood, picked up the half peeled potato, let it fall back into the water with the rest and without raising her voice said.

"I shall be twenty one next May, nobody can make me do owt I don't want to. I'm not marryin' him, I'll not wed Edgar, I don't love him, not Edgar Perry."

Peggy looked intently at Valerie, she knew her daughter's ways.

"And who do you want to wed, 'cause whoever it is, do yer think 'e'll be interested in you when he sees your belly swell from carryin' another man's kid. But you'll not get rid of it, I don't care if yer give it away or keep it an' look after it on your own, I'll not let you kill it an' likely yourself an'all. I've heard about them terminations they do wi' a knittin' needle, then the poor woman bleeds out like a stuck pig 'til there's no life left in 'er. You've been a fool Valerie."

The sound of footsteps approaching from the back yard silenced Peggy's tongue, they both stood mute yet the sound of their own hearts beating near deafened them.

Nigel Caffin looked so much older, Celia sat opposite his desk feeling compassion for the man. He gathered himself before speaking.

"It's good to see you Mrs.Eddowes, although the fact that you are here would suggest that something concerns you."

Celia could not declare her latest problem before showing that she was mindful of his sadness.

"I am so sorry about your son, we all are, William's mother Annie asked me to extend her condolences. Oh dear, that isn't right, what she really said was, 'tell Mr.Caffin that he and his wife are ever in my thoughts'.

He smiled. "Your mother in law recognises human nature in a solicitor. Few people seem to have that ability, it is as though they imagine us to be in some curious way 'different'. You are very kind Celia, Mrs.Eddowes too I know would voice only genuine sentiment. Perhaps one day she might call on my wife Stella," he hesitated,

"I believe they could share friendship, Stella finds it difficult, she keeps everything within."

"Oh yes, I'm sure Annie would, she has the very best of hearts, gentle yet such reserves of strength. I watched how she coped when Alice died, I'd like to think that I might show similar fortitude if, God forbid, I was called upon, but I'm doubtful. Annie's strength has come from all her years of struggle." Celia paused, her mind hovering over her next words but an inner sense propelled them forward. "William's father can be difficult, he would never raise his hand in temper as some men do but he has a way of wounding with his tongue."

Celia lowered her eyes, troubled by her frankness, but it was true.

"You must give my kind regards to your mother in law." His smile held reassuring warmth. "People are afflicted by many problems for which no solicitor has the answer, it is the evidence of human nature, which Mrs.Eddowes is perceptive enough to recognise. But there must be a matter over which you seek advice today my dear, I imagine it is regarding your mother's affairs."

Celia explained, he listened, inwardly wondering what more could happen to test this young woman's resolve.

"I have discussed with Caroline what to do about mother's house and I think we have arrived at a very sensible decision. You see Mr.Caffin, Moreleigh is a smaller property and now that Mrs.Stanford lives with Caroline and the boys, it occurred to us both that if they were to move to mother's it would afford them more space, the extra bedroom would make all the difference. It was Edmund's home as a boy after all, it was where he grew up. Instead of selling mother's house, if the law permits, we would prefer to sell Moreleigh."

"The law presents no impediment Celia but there is a greater value attached to the larger property, you would be entitled to more than a half share of the proceeds from the sale of Moreleigh if you chose to pursue the deficit."

Celia's reply was emphatic. "I wouldn't consider doing so for a moment. As I sit here I pray that William is alive, I make myself believe that he is alive, to have still that hope is so much more than Caroline has had for over two years. I would take satisfaction from knowing that she dwelt in surroundings, which, albeit a long time ago, once kept Edmund safe and happy in a very different world to the one in which we tremble and weep now."

"Forgive me Celia, I didn't expect your response to be any other but while the law does not present any impediment, my position as an interpreter of the law does require me to make you aware. With William absent and your brother tragically gone, a great deal of responsibility has fallen to you my dear. When your husband returns, he should acknowledge your capabilities."

In truth, Nigel Caffin held real doubt over whether Celia's unselfish attitude would be permitted if William Eddowes were here to oppose it. While it was for Celia and Edmund's widow Caroline to decide, he could imagine a very fraught atmosphere if William was ever defied, another of the many sources of struggle bringing fortitude to Annie Eddowes no doubt.

He led Celia to the door. "Let me have your instructions in due course," he said, "meanwhile I shall arrange for Mrs.Brewer's final pay, plus the additional sum by way of a thank you, as you stipulate. You will mention to your mother in law how welcome she would be at our home if she had just a little time free to spend with Stella? I do try but I confess to falling short, those reserves of strength about which you spoke, I wish that like Mrs.Eddowes I had accumulated more." Celia sensed he could barely contain his emotion, in kindness she replied briefly.

"I shall tell her this very day, I promise." She turned away and the door closed behind her without delay. There was something altogether unthinkable about a figure of authority, a professional man now weeping behind it. She recalled the words spoken by Joan Faulds at Mapperley, 'We are all human and equally disposed'. Celia brushed away a tear from the corner of her eye and hurried home.

Since standing with Valerie whilst she declared herself to be pregnant and urgently assuring Mrs.Oates of his willingness to do the honourable thing, only to find himself fleeing under threat of being skinned alive if Tom Oates caught as much as a sniff of him, Edgar had nervously but resignedly anticipated the unavoidable encounter one evening after work. Darkness fell before the end of dayshift and each night, the expectation of Tom Oates, looming out of the gloom to confront him as men streamed out through the pit gates had come to naught. Walking along the shadowy streets when he got off the bus was made unnaturally sinister by this continuing threat of come uppance. Edgar almost hoped for it to happen, get it over with, the uncertainty, the need to be constantly looking over his shoulder so as to be facing his assailant's famous fists was wearing him down. He'd fully expected days ago to limp home to Joyce with a bloody nose, the onset of two black eyes and minus some front teeth, but Tom Oates' quietness was unsettling. He would certainly by now be aware of Valerie's condition and remembering her mother's immediate reaction, the desperate woman's prophecy of imminent wounding, Edgar was baffled and perplexed.

Tomorrow was Sunday, a day off, he looked forward to an extra hour in bed and with his pay packet deposited safely inside his jacket pocket, he felt a measure of satisfaction at being able to hand to Joyce his keep, his dues. He'd noticed how she favoured his plate with what little meat there was, the same with bacon and cheese. When he'd questioned her and told her that he wasn't happy, knowing she denied herself to feed him with such a helping, she'd sat down opposite him, pointed at his plate and said. 'It's what mams do, I may not be your mam Edgar and I never knew your real one but I'm doin' it for her anyroad, not for you, but for her, because I'm here and I can'.

He was two streets away from the house when a figure stepped out from an entry. Edgar stood still, he felt sure it was Tom Oates, yet whoever it was appeared taller, broader, a bigger frame altogether. At first no one spoke, then a voice said.

"Over 'ere Perry, a gent don't carry out 'is business on the street for all to see an' 'ear, it's nice an' private in this entry, more fittin'."

Edgar moved forward so as to see the man's face, by now he was sure someone other than Tom Oates stood in his way.

"You're a coal black Sammy aren't yer Perry, giv' us a smile, do a little jig like one o' them travellin' minstrels."

Edgar wasn't about to yield to silly provocation, if he'd been man enough to make a baby then he must be equally robust through the course of this encounter.

"I don't know who you are but I reckon I know who sent yer, if I've to take you on before I can continue me way home then so be it, do what yer 'ave to."

Edgar stood with his fists at the ready, not once had he been in a fight but at least he'd defend himself, covering the remaining distance on his own two feet rather than lay in the gutter for hours was favourable, Samaria was a long way from Sherwood.

The man laughed. "I don't know where you come from pal but round 'ere we don't use fisty cuffs, not unless we're sorely pressed wi' no other way o' settlin' things. Now you've put Valerie in the family way, naughty boy Perry, yer can look on me as a sort o' go between, a middle man. Now all I need from you is arf your pay packet, just arf, Mr.Oates's not greedy. Babies cost money, cot, nappies, pram all that sort o' stuff."

Edgar was angered by his tone of voice, there was an implied threat yet his manner was childish. "I offered to marry Valerie, to do right by her and the baby but she doesn't want to marry me an' there's nothing I can do about that but when the child comes I'll see to it. I'll provide the necessary items. The baby's not due for some time yet, the money's as well stayin' in my care as it would be in Tom Oates', my mind would likely keep it safe for its purpose, goodness knows how many different purposes he might find for it."

"Arf your pay packet." The man, probably in his mid twenties, held out his hand menacingly. "Tom Oates may not be greedy but he's no bloody patience neither, cough up or else."

Edgar determined himself to remain calm. "I suppose this will be a weekly occurrence," he said.

"Usual terms apply, yer should 'ave thought o' your pocket 'afore yer dipped your wick."

The man sniggered and Edgar flexed his knuckles but just at that moment the sound of a door in the yard at the other end of the entry and footsteps over the cobbles flustered Tom Oates' stooge. He was about to run off but Edgar caught hold of his sleeve.

“Tell Valerie’s father I’ll keep my word, do right by the child but I’ll not work down the pit all week like a navvy only to hand over me money to the likes o’ you.”

The footsteps were now only seconds away from bringing someone close enough to see their figures, Edgar let go the sleeve and the man stepped back sharply as though he’d anticipated a blow from Edgar’s fist, he turned and ran. Edgar had not intended striking him and this sudden retreat he found almost amusing, so much for the big talk. Now Edgar stood to one side to let by whoever it was about to emerge onto the street.

“Evenin’, not so bad for time o’ year is it?” they walked off in the direction Edgar needed to take.

“No, not so bad.” Edgar’s response was an automatic politeness as his thoughts were far removed from the elements of nature.

He made for home, still awaiting his time to be skinned but the small brown envelope containing his wages was safe in his pocket still, and his self respect with it.

Joyce reached for Edgar’s plate, put it on top of her own and stood up. Throughout their meal she’d sensed that he’d been about to say something. She walked across to the sink and just as she was about to run some water, finally he spoke.

“I’m goin’ out for a bit Joyce, I shouldn’t be long.”

She tried not to sound worried. “Anywhere nice? There’s a ‘whodunit’ showin’ at the Odeon, Sylvia who drives the number sixteen said she wer’ goin’.

“To see a man about a dog,” said Edgar, he laughed. “I won’t be gone long enough to watch a film Joyce, I’ve an errand to run, by the time you’ve cleared away I’ll be back to make you a nice cup o’ tea, perhaps there’ll be a play on the wireless, if there is, we’ll both listen to it.”

Joyce looked directly at Edgar. “Don’t be doin’ anythin’ daft, I don’t know what goes on in Tom Oates’ head but I do know what’s in yours, goodness an’ decency. Every night this week I’ve arf expected yer to stagger in through back door, your face stamped wi’ the pattern o’ Tom Oates’ knuckles. Your clothes near’ ripped of your back an’ wi’ barely enough breath left to see yer through to mornin’. I know summat's goin' to happen an' it frightens me Edgar, it scares me to death." Her voice trembled and she sniffled up the gathering tears.

Edgar crossed to where she stood. "One day, Mr.Haynes will come home to this house and when he does I want him to know that I did my best to look after you, like I would if you were me mam, because I'm here, and I can."

He smiled and kissed her cheek. Lost for any other words Joyce watched him take his jacket from the hook and leave.

Peggy Oates sat sewing, mending the frayed hem of a bed sheet. Valerie was upstairs in her bedroom, cautioned by her father that if she went out this Saturday night he'd come after her and put welts across her palms with the old riding crop. It had ever been a curiosity to Valerie, her family being the sort, which generation on generation had been perpetually shod in hob nailed boots and never astride a horse with the trappings of gentry. Yet the leather bound crop had hung behind the privy door for as long as she could remember. As a small child she'd taken simple amusement from counting the times it swung to and fro as she sat on the tub, having prompted its movement when she'd opened the door. The crop dramatically lost its charm the day she witnessed for the first time, their father use it to beat her brother. Thereafter she would cast her eyes to the cobbled floor beneath her feet, too afraid to glance at it, and often dampened her knickers in her rush to be gone from that place where it threatened the dreadful consequence of her father's temper.

Tom Oates sat nodding off in the chair by the hearth, emitting regular wheezing sounds from his choked lungs, like some distant, stringed instrument rendering a melancholy lament, and the onset of dust ridden snoring escaped his open mouth between lips that tremored ahead of ever tormented breath, while a lock of lank, grey hair fell awkwardly across his brow, untrained, feral.

A knock came at the back door, Peggy cast a glance the way of her husband, he didn't stir. She put down the needle and thread and gathered up the folds of sheet from her knees.

"Is your husband at home Mrs.Oates?" Edgar Perry stood at the threshold. She inhaled sharply and put her hand across her mouth as though stifling an advancing cry of alarm. "It's alright Mrs.Oates, I'm not here to cause any bother but I need to speak with him."

Edgar's eyes shed kindliness and the harassed woman stood aside for him to come in. Still Tom Oates slept, his breath lifting slightly the ends of his lock of hair, one hand tucked under his braces. Edgar now stood no more than a yard in front of him and in that moment Edgar saw, not an angry, violent man but a tired, hard pressed product of back street life who reflected what for years had surrounded him. Peggy gently nudged his shoulder.

"Tom, Tom, the lad's 'ere, come to talk to yer."

He opened his eyes, squinting into the light, sat forward and coughed with all the force of a brewery horse clearing its throat of city smog. When he raised his face again it was deep purple from the effort and now his eyes stared out from it with menace. He made to stand and Edgar spoke.

"You'll know what took place earlier and did it serve any useful purpose, no it didn't, but you an' me talkin' face to face, like men with intelligence, now that would surprise folk wouldn't it Mr.Oates and it'd save your wife an' daughter from the dread created by this mindless bravado. The bloody world's at war Tom, savage, brutal fightin' that leaves women desolate, families wrecked. I don't know who it was yer sent to take me wages but after the way we work at that pit, all the back breakin' hours o' sweat we spill in its name, did yer really suppose I'd hand me money over with not so much as a whimper."

Tom glowered at Peggy. "The bloody arf wit, your sister's gormless lad, Wallace." She stood at the table making no sound. "Why do yer think I sent 'im instead o' goin' meself, I'd likely as not 'ave beat the livin' daylights out o' lover boy ere." Now he turned his attention back to Edgar. "Yer come close Perry, I reckon even twelve months ago I'd 'ave thrashed yer. Wallace Trubshaw is all yap, if you'd thrown a punch e'd 'ave run like a rabbit. I'm gettin' too old for fightin'. But your hollo' promises ave' all been heard afore. So you'll do right by the kid yer say? Stump up for its keep? Well I'll wager that you'll do a bunk, be long gone afore our Valerie births that baby."

Edgar protested. "Then you'd be a fool Tom 'cause you'd lose that wager. I've offered to marry Valerie but she don't want that an' I can't make her but I'll not abandon any child o' mine."

"Oh aye, it's all big talk now. Well I wash me 'ands of it. I only wanted to get money out of yer for 'er." He raised his eyes to the ceiling, to the bedroom above. "But what does Tom Oates know? When I started at pit I remember me father sayin', 'It'll make a man of yer', an' it did, a man old afore 'is time. Keep your damn money then Edgar Perry, you've managed to keep your skin. But don't dare think that you're goin' to land 'er wi' the kid when our Valerie's 'ad enough of it."

He pointed a nicotine stained finger at his wife Peggy, as though she were no more than an item of furniture. Meanwhile Valerie had heard the raised voices and stood at the top of the stairs listening.

Edgar held out his hand. "It's the way gentlemen seal an agreement," he said.

Tom Oates scoffed. "Save your arm strength for the pick on Monday mornin', now sod off."

As Peggy opened the back door for Edgar she offered a nervous smile and inwardly agonised over why her daughter didn't seize at the chance to wed this decent young man. When she had asked her that very question Valerie had answered sincerely, but in poor, weary Peggy's mind, naively. 'I don't love Edgar Mam an' I want to marry a man I love an' one that loves me back. Edgar would only marry me out o' duty'. Peggy had rounded with, 'you've been to the flicks too often our Valerie an' watched them soppy endin's'.

She returned to her sewing, the sheet draped over the arm of the chair awaiting her able fingers. Tom looked at her, muttered something inaudible and crossed the room toward the stairs, apparently off to bed. Valerie hurried into her bedroom and closed the door, praying he wouldn't enter.

Pushing the needle through the hem of the sheet Peggy reflected on her life's purpose. Mending, that was her lot, the sheet was a simple task and she could darn socks and sew on buttons with her eyes closed. It was the mending of differences, years of repairing the rents and tears in the worn out, patched up fabric of so called love between father and sons that had demanded all of her strength. Soppy endings, they were the stuff of story books and make believe films.

Upstairs the bed creaked as Tom Oates lowered his weary frame onto its aged springs. Behind the door of her bedroom Valerie breathed relief and the leather bound riding crop hung mercifully redundant behind the lavatory door.

Celia answered the bell at the front door. "It is kind of you Mr.Smithfield. Annie said she would come with me, to help with mother, there's room for her to ride too isn't there? She's here, she didn't want to take you out of your way by having to collect her from Gregory Street. Mathew," Celia called out urgently, "Mr.Smithfield's here now."

A tall youth ran down the stairs and stood alongside his mother, smiling and extending his hand.

"It's good to see you Mathew, but I didn't imagine you a young man, the boy is no more, I should have expected no other." Andrew shook his hand firmly. Then Annie appeared from a doorway, with a shy Emily, his natural manner soon put the child at ease.

"Now you will promise me Mathew that until I get back you will stay here with your sister. If Christopher Spooner didn't have mumps you could have both gone to see Rosie but your aunt Hilda said she'd more than likely call in with David and Rosemary, so you'll have company anyway. I've put a jigsaw on the sideboard, H.M.S.Victory, I hope all the pieces are there, the lady at Moffats said it was complete."

Annie cast an amused smile at Andrew, it was ever a mother's way, the need to feel everyone was safe and accounted for, the 'home' secure. War denied that and so even more care was given to those still within the reach of her arms.

Celia donned her warm coat and took a bag from the hall table, she pulled the door closed and by the time she and Annie reached the car, Andrew stood with the passenger door open.

"You sit in the front Mam," said Celia, "I shall stay in the back, it will be best that way when mother joins us." She let out a very random sigh and now it was

Andrew's turn to cast an understanding smile at Annie. Poor Celia, this afternoon could be nothing less than a trial, she had no need of words to express her anxiety, even Andrew, an unmarried man with no family to speak of, could imagine the emotion and for Celia, her mother's dementia brought an additional strain. One could only hope that Gwendolyn Tozer's confused state of mind might cause her to be less aware and accepting of her changed surroundings without distress, might allow her to dwell at Mapperley in her world of adopted characters, just as easily as she had done in that other place she once recognised as home, but where latterly, her condition rendered her constantly travelling through the past. When Celia had told him of her mother's inclination to be Queen Victoria among other identities of merit, he'd warmed to Gwendolyn Tozer's inspired choice. How much better to go out with style rather than to end without a finale of some consequence.

He drove through the quiet streets, not unusual for a Sunday afternoon, folk not necessarily religious, nevertheless clutched at the Sabbath, it represented goodness. Hard sometimes to reconcile God and war, Sunday felt different, even non believers, in a curious contradiction, hallowed its mystery, the possibility that Heaven did exist and opened its gates to the ever growing numbers lost to this earth.

"How is Charles Annie?" Andrew had not expected to be sitting beside Annie Eddowes this afternoon, inside him, deep inside, he felt tense, yet his fingers wrapped the steering wheel with a confidence, which came from her presence and on the outside he felt happy, what foolishness, but it was innocently gained and would be fleeting, a crumb from Charles Eddowes' table.

"He's well thank you." Annie chuckled. "Laura has seconded him, I do admire her powers of persuasion, although she had a powerful lobby in Samuel, between the two of them they managed to win their man! He is to narrate the nativity play at Harrow Road School. I can only hope the story of Christ's birth is not told with too much gravity, it should be the most joyous account after all. I think Laura wanted first and foremost to be able to write a letter to John about a Christmas he would remember with happiness, even though he's not here. For Charles, I know it will be a task to be dispensed with as quickly as possible, but it will do him no harm. Samuel is probably testing him on his delivery this afternoon, poor Charles, I do believe he's nervous at the prospect."

Annie smiled vaguely at the road ahead and they travelled in a pleasant atmosphere of easy conversation. When they pulled up outside the house Celia hurried to assure Mr.Smithfield that Mrs.Brewer would have her mother packed and ready so as not to delay him.

"I have nothing demanding that I be elsewhere my dear, I shall sit in the car until you appear at the door with Mrs.Tozer, then I shall come to you and carry the bags. Your mother can imagine me to be her Gillie, the loyal Mr.Brown, but travelling by car rather than by royal mount, and in England, although at quite the right time of year for the Queen to be residing at Balmoral." He laughed. "Do you know Celia I could quite happily subscribe to your mother's world of make believe, perhaps it is we supposedly sensible souls who slowly stagnate, bound by protocol and misguided inhibitions."

Annie and Celia walked up the path as he looked on. Sybil Brewer opened the door, and they disappeared inside.

"Hello Mother, we've come to take you for a ride, a sort of holiday, Annie is here, you remember William's mother don't you?"

Gwendolyn looked at Annie for several seconds before saying. "Didn't I go to school with you, we played a duet on the piano to raise funds for new text books, we wore pink gingham pinafore frocks and everyone clapped. You wern't very good but I played well so it didn't matter."

Celia sighed, "That was me and Elizabeth Askew, she did play well."

"I catch my train on Thursday morning," said Mrs.Brewer, "if you're not here before I go I'll put the key under the toad stone. She's had some broth but she wouldn't eat the junket. I've managed to get all of her clothes clean apart from one vest and two pairs of drawers, I'll see to them tomorrow and leave them on the bed. She could do with some new slippers, the one's she's got are almost through on the soles. I shall be staying at my brother's for a week or two, you've got the address if you need it. I think the living room chimney ought to be swept, the fire's been smokey these past few days and the tap in the scullery needs a new washer, the drip's gettin' faster. She'll ask at the hospital for a glass of sherry, I used to give her a small measure late afternoons until I was convinced it was giving her a headache but she got so irate when I told her it wasn't good for her I had to improvise, so she's been drinking a tot of cold tea with a dash of raspberry vinegar and her head's been better. They best do the same or she'll create merry hell, and tell them she likes a plain biscuit with it."

Finally Sybil concluded her detailed report and with Gwendolyn wrapped up against the elements they took a deep breath and opened the front door.

Annie had been pondering Sybil's remark. "What is the toad stone?" She asked.

Celia pointed to one of the stones bordering the path. "There, see, we always referred to it as the 'toad stone' because of its shape. It was Edmund who first noticed it one day when he was playing 'Jacks' on the path."

Sure enough, two thirds of the way along the line of border stones sat one, which had been sculpted by nature, toad, frog, whichever the onlooker chose, it did indeed display an uncanny likeness to either.

Andrew hurried up the path, at once picking up the suitcase and a smaller holdall. Gwendolyn's eyes were on him immediately.

"You," she said in a tone of authority, "have you paid for those?" She turned to Celia, "did you see him pay? Jessie thinks I don't know that he lets them have their boots and pay later, too soft," she let out a huff of frustration, "never make a business man." Her attention returned to Andrew, "There're the finest boots you'll find outside the Capital and you'd be obliged to pay a great deal more for them there, with no credit. Make sure you settle your account before squandering you money on ale and tobacco."

"Oh dear," said Celia, feeling truly mortified, "I am sorry Mr.Smithfield."

Andrew simply winked, put down the smallest of the baggage, stood directly in front of Gwendolyn, facing her with a radiant smile, and said.

"My dear, would you do me the honour of taking my arm."

The response was quite touching. She gently tapped the back of his hand with her gloved fingers and threaded her arm through his. Then with a real lift in her speech she said.

"Mother is expecting us for afternoon tea, don't worry if father is a little brusque, he considers it his duty to challenge any would be consort but I shall win him round."

Installed in the back seat alongside Celia the conversation lacked only mention of the mad hatter yet it caused not despair or even embarrassment, but rather a light relief from reality, a reality that paraded war and hardship before the eyes with as yet no definite end in sight.

Andrew parked the car as close as he could to the entrance.

"Thank you so very much Mr.Smithfield," said Celia.

"I shall carry in the bags then wait for you here," he replied.

"Oh no, really you should go home now, I must stay a while and see mother settled. But Annie doesn't need to be that long, once we've found matron and the ward on which mother is to sleep I'm sure there would be no need for Annie to be delayed, so perhaps you might wait just a little while."

The corridor was quiet, it smelled of mothballs and a hint of lavender. As they made their way to the office door these smells faded away and were replaced by disinfectant.

"We shall be quite alright now Mr.Smithfield, I think you will be more comfortable outside in the car."

Celia took the case from his hand, Annie took the smaller bag. Gwendolyn was too quiet, Andrew wished she could call out, some altogether outrageous remark, proof of her ability to dominate her fears and keep Mapperley on the outside of her imagination. To his delight she obliged him.

"Where's my purse?" The outburst came so suddenly from Gwendolyn it made Celia jump. "I need my purse," she was agitated.

"It's alright Mother, I have it safely in your suitcase."

"Then give him something, a gratuity, it is expected and only proper."

Annie spoke quickly. “I have my purse right here,” she held it up for Gwendolyn to see. “I shall attend to it of course.” It seemed to satisfy her and calm was restored. Annie took Andrew to one side. “You go, please. When the time comes for Celia to leave I know it will be upsetting, it’s very hard for her. I shall stay, I won’t let her go home alone.”

Annie felt he should leave them with a little light heartedness, it was a sobering thought, Gwendolyn Tozer was but a few years their senior, especially Andrew who was a year or two older than herself.

“Your tip,” said Annie with a smile. She let a mint slip from her fingers into his hand. He clasped it tightly.

As he drove away from Mapperley towards Brassington he fought a sinking feeling at the pit of his stomach. Perhaps that was it, Mrs.Tozer’s protection from the pain of awareness, how much more tolerable was it too dwell within the imagined character of someone else. He could be Prince Albert, the Duke of Wellington, Lawrence of Arabia, Captain Cook, the choice was limitless, sufficient to live every day in another man’s realm, a flight of fancy. And yet the sinking feeling persisted to the point of pain.

The fantasy was his, it involved no other, his alone, he would live within the character of Charles Eddowes for just a little while, closer in time, not so far removed from the here and now. Andrew felt inside his pocket for the mint, popped it into his mouth and by the grace of dear, courageous Gwendolyn, made believe.

CHAPTER EIGHTEEN

Late January 1945

"It's brass monkeys this mornin' Charlie, I can't feel me little piggies."

Bob Budgeon stamped his feet, cupped his hands across his mouth and breathed over them, before rubbing them together like a miser.

"If you do that for much longer I reckon friction'll set 'em alight. Your trouble is you don't eat breakfast, porridge my son, that's what keeps a man from freezin', sticks to your innards like a poultice. A mug o' tea an' a fag does nowt for body an' soul on a mornin' like this."

The vapour from Charlie's airways as he spoke coated the windscreen of the truck in condensation.

"Put the old rag over the glass Bob will yer, I've a job to see where we're goin'?"

Bob had only just thrust his cold hands into his pockets.

"Why don't yer do it yourself seein' as how you're so stoked up wi' porridge." He pulled a piece of rag from underneath the dashboard and grudgingly wiped the windscreen clear.

No snow had fallen yet the air frost was sharp, the temperature well below zero. At the beginning of the round only early workers or those coming off nightshifts were about the streets. Bins stood like monuments to a long ago uprising, their dented, misshapen forms playing host to the rime, which made them an eerie presence on the as yet dark streets. On the very cold mornings, eyes intent on finding something edible appeared out of nowhere and loath to miss the chance of a morsel, the creature would often stay long enough to be recognised as a cat, fox, even a badger, before scuttling off down an entry or leaping a wall.

Charlie sometimes imagined he drove through a scene of more recent battle, a ground strewn with corpses and burned out artillery, rats, wolves, opportunist raiders, having scented death, now feeding on the kill.

"Look." Bob suddenly called out, "Bloody hell Charlie." A woman, clad only in a frock and cardigan, stumbled along the pavement. "Is she drunk do yer think? She must be bloody freezin'."

Charlie pulled up at the curb but left the engine running, it had been a bugger to start this morning.

"We'll 'ave to speak to 'er, find out where she lives," he said.

They jumped down from the cab and despite the sound of the truck doors and the engine throbbing, the woman seemed oblivious to their approach. She was barely moving, Charlie reached her side and still she didn't acknowledge his presence.

"Aren't yer very well missus, why didn't yer put on a coat?"

Slowly she turned her head to show her face. There was no smell of alcohol about her but Charlie had seen her before, he knew who she was. A month or so ago he'd been on the late morning round in Castle Road, he'd come across a woman rummaging through her dustbin like a famished cat and in a most agitated state, muttering to herself, Charlie had recognised only the odd word or two. 'Empty, no, one little finger'. She had given him a cold stare and again muttered 'not empty'. Well if the lady didn't want him to empty her bin then he wasn't about to argue, so he'd touched his cap and left her to it.

Here, now, on the street, was that same woman, Mrs.Bradshaw. Charlie knew the house, as a lad he'd unwillingly stood at its front door with Jack Wainwright singing carols. It was where Basil Stanford would open the door and order them off in language none too gentlemanly, as though they dared to trespass with villainous intent. They would run down the path but once outside the gate Jack would stop and call back in a loud, fearless voice, 'an goodwill to you an'all Ebenezer'. Charlie was quite convinced that Jack pursued the yearly ritual simply for the satisfaction of disturbing Stanford's peace, it certainly never delivered a single farthing to their collecting tin.

"Knock on a door, somebody'll take 'er in," said Bob, "she's been at the bottle."

Charlie was alarmed by how cold she felt, her eyes searched his face but still she made no attempt to speak.

"Don't be afraid missus," said Charlie, "we'll get you somewhere warm, no good you being on the street like this when light breaks." He turned to Bob. "Take 'er arm, hold 'er up for a minute, don't let 'er fall."

Bob did as Charlie said, the woman seemed so feeble his own confidence was fast slipping away, he'd follow Charlie's command.

Cold fingers hampered his speed but Charlie unfastened his jacket, pulled it off and wrapped it about Mrs.Bradshaw's shoulders.

"We need to get 'er to hospital, she's not right, a doctor should look at 'er. I think she's got that thing, what do they call it? Yer know, when the body gets too cold to function."

"Frost bite do yer mean?" Said Bob, relieved that Charlie had now taken the woman's other arm.

"No, no, bloody hell, it's on the tip o' me tongue."

"Rigor," said Bob, trying to be helpful.

"For God's sake Bob, she's not bloody dead, though I reckon your brain must be. Hypothermia, that's it. We'll lift 'er into the cab, it'll be a squeeze but sandwiched between us she'll benefit from our body heat, it's not far to the General Hospital from here.

Bob huffed and mumbled annoyance at the slight. It was difficult to negotiate the manoeuvre in any sort of dignified fashion but Charlie eventually achieved to position the woman onto the seat, Bob, by now cold and fed up, jumped up beside her and shut the cab door with a shiver, while Charlie ran round and climbed in the driver's side.

"Put your arm around 'er Bob, keep 'er steady as we go."

Charlie lowered the handbrake awkwardly, her legs resting on his arm when he was obliged to nudge them out of the way.

"I'm not sure we should be doin' this Charlie, it'll likely lead to trouble wi' management, I bet some nosey bugger's been peepin' from behind their curtains, watchin' us manhandlin' a woman into a council vehicle."

"If we were out wi' Captain Nias an' the guard do yer suppose we'd leave 'er on the street in this state. If we went to the phone box an' called the ambulance we'd ave' to stay with 'er 'til it come anyroad, so it makes best sense to take 'er to hospital ourselves, the poor woman's ill an' hypothermic."

"She could 'ave frostbite an'all," said Bob, "me granddad got frostbite, 'is toes went black an' rotted off."

"Your granddad 'ad gangrene, not frostbite," said a despairing Charlie.

Bob muttered under his breath, "Trouble, it'll lead to trouble."

The young woman at the reception desk looked up with concern, the sight of what appeared to be two workmen, one at either side of an older woman, supporting her by the arms, the jacket of one man wrapped about her shoulders, suggested an accident of some kind. At last they had reached a source of help and Charlie spoke out clearly.

"We come across 'er in Driscoll Street, she don't seem able to speak, just stumblin' along she wer', dressed like she might 'ave been goin' for a stroll in the park, no coat, no bag an' as vague as me aunty Olive's tortoise, but I do know who she is an' where she lives 'cause I empty 'er dustbin every week. It's Mrs.Bradshaw, used to be Stanford, from Castle Road."

The receptionist considered it more important to fetch a nurse than to seek further details, she pointed to a chair behind the desk.

"Sit her down there, I'll only be a minute."

"Phew, it's easier emptyin' the bins," said Bob looking down at Patricia Bradshaw, now seated on the receptionist's chair, Charlie's grubby jacket still affording her some warmth, its collar turned up around her neck. "It's a crime Charlie, that's what it is, a crime, for a woman to look like she does an' still be sober."

Charlie smiled, the lady did indeed look to be under the influence, yet his instinct told him that her trouble was too severe to have been induced by nothing more than a liberal measure of spirits, she was suffering from something and whatever it was caused considerable pain.

Then, for the briefest moment, she looked up. "Ravenna, at Ravenna."

"What did she say?"

Bob was confused and anxious to return to work. Charlie was about to answer when footsteps hurrying down the corridor confirmed help to be at hand. The nurse spoke first to Patricia.

"You are at the hospital now, the doctor is on his way, we need to make you warmer, can you tell me if you hurt anywhere?"

Patricia shook her head but said nothing.

"I'm Sister Richey," her attention had now passed to Charlie and Bob, "will you leave your names with Miss Bell, she has explained how you came across this woman, I can see that you were about your work, you did well to bring her here, if she had collapsed then almost certainly she would have slipped into unconsciousness and in cases of extreme cold that can be very dangerous. She owes you a debt of gratitude but there is nothing more you can do so return to your work, I'm sure that when she is recovered you will see her again."

Charlie had no option but to ask. "Do yer think I could 'ave me jacket back only it's right parky outside nurse?"

"Of course, I'm sorry I should have thought."

A porter arrived with a wheelchair.

"Come on Bob, let's get out the way o' these good people."

Charlie donned his jacket and ushered Bob towards the door. By now it was daylight. The rubbish truck parked right outside the entrance, albeit with very little refuse as yet tipped into its rear, nevertheless struck the onlooker as far from ideal. Hosed down periodically to dilute the smell from household discard, still the tell tale remnants clung stubbornly to the gloomy, cavernous rear of the truck, as far removed from clinical cleanliness as it could possibly be. Charlie and Bob climbed inside the cab, it had been a strange start to their day but now they were late and would somehow have to make up time, a short dinner break and a forced pace the only way of catching up. Charlie drove towards Driscoll Street, to take up where they'd left off.

"I felt sure it wer' frostbite me granddad 'ad," said Bob, before cupping his hands over his mouth and breathing into them, then rubbing them together briskly.

"Ravenna," said Charlie, "the Eighth took Ravenna, some place up top of Italy. Wipe the windscreen will yer Bob. I reckon I could tell doctor where Mrs.Bradshaw's hurtin'." He let out a long sigh and put the truck into second gear.

Julia sat on the bus that would take her to Beeston. Since returning to England the route she'd imagined her life would take had turned out to be a direction not approved by fate, instead a diversionary course, unexpected and previously untravelled had led her to a situation that only a few years ago would have been inconceivable.

Patricia's nerves, so patently raw that day Julia finally arrived back from Italy, had become more so as the weeks went by. Julia's intention of finding rented accommodation in the event proved unnecessary as her sister, without discussion, took for granted her readiness to take up residency at Castle Road and sensitive to Patricia's state of mind she had accepted the arrangement, if only to spare their mother the concerns Patricia's obvious loneliness presented.

Julia had however secured work at the Boots factory where production had been turned over to the war effort. Medical supplies were soaked up like ink on blotting paper. Dietary supplements for young children were being distributed through infant welfare clinics, in the heavily bombed cities these appeared as mobile units. With food so scarce, every effort was made to keep the very young from malnutrition and possible deficiencies of consequence. Saccharin was being produced to supplement the strict rationing of sugar and Chloramine, for water sterilization, so vital in the war ravaged areas of not only Europe but Africa and the Far East.

Julia applied herself to the work with grateful energy, so long confined in Italy, her will now was defiant and she worked to the fullness of every minute, tiredness she shunned as an aid to the enemy. But Patricia, self assured, unbending, single minded Patricia was now as needful of nurture as a child.

The telegram had arrived a few days before Christmas, Anthony had been killed during the battle to take Ravenna. Patricia's emotion went beyond grief, so entangled was it by guilt and regret, she had sought comfort, an attempt at deadening the pain, in gin. A previously unopened bottle she'd consumed within hours abandoning the approved measure of two fingers depth up the glass. When Julia had realised, she'd taken the bottle, empty except for a dreg, and buried it in the dustbin whilst Patricia made the most of her gin induced stupor.

Julia needed to work, with no money an income of some sort was crucial, she could not countenance being dependant on her elder sister.

Caroline had recognised the need for her mother to return to Castle Road, the boys were in school and so her voluntary work at the hospital could continue, Jonathon was almost twelve and a sensible boy, Gregory would be nine in the summer. It was only fair, through her time of greatest need Florence had been there, a constant strength, now Patricia's need of their mother could not be denied.

"Next stop Boots." The conductor called out, it brought Julia's thoughts back to the present. Fastening the top button of her coat she stood and made her way along the aisle of the bus. Alighting just a few yards from the gates, along with several others, she voiced numerous 'good mornings' as workers arriving from opposite directions, converged upon the entrance to the factory yard. Mostly women, the men among them of a certain age, she had noticed one in particular, he'd smiled once or twice, he had jet black hair even though she estimated his age to be mid fifties, some of the other men were quite grey, or bald. Most Italian men carried a tanned complexion and black hair, still there was no word of Luciano, she tried not to think about it, the subject held too many anxieties, instead she seized upon her work for the salvation that it was, while at the factory there was no time to dwell on personal problems, the wider world with its many needs took possession of the mind and Julia felt no urge to resist. This morning much of her time would be engaged with orange juice and cod liver oil, protecting the strength of a future generation, surely there could be few activities more worthy.

Florence sat at the kitchen table sipping a cup of tea. It was a little after half past eight, she'd leave it another ten minutes then take up a cup to Patricia.

The tragic news of Anthony had touched them all, especially Caroline, tears again shed. Trying to move forward for the sake of Jonathon and Gregory, Caroline honoured her husband by doing what she believed Edmund would want her to do.

The move to Mrs.Tozer's house was due to take place at the end of the month, now just days away. Florence hoped to persuade Patricia to help, her eldest daughter's misery was in many ways self inflicted, she had eventually written a letter to Anthony but in wavering for so long the letter arrived too late and was returned, the only personal effect, Anthony wore no ring and carried no photographs. When Patricia had opened the sombre, brown envelope, along with her own letter to Anthony she had found the official communication written to herself, it expressed sympathy and regret that he could not be repatriated but his remains had been interred, alongside many of his friends and comrades, at a cemetery within Ravenna.

Patricia's reaction had been even more alarming than on receiving the initial telegram. Florence had sent for the doctor, he prescribed a sedative, that had been almost two weeks ago. Since then Patricia had eaten like a sparrow spoken very little and existed through each day like one condemned and awaiting the hangman.

Florence glanced at the clock, it could not continue, she would take up the tea and somehow persuade Patricia that life must go on.

Several envelopes had gathered, business correspondence concerning the mine, official, carrying the ministry stamp. Hugh Porter had telephoned a number of times, Florence had asked him to grant her daughter more recovery time and he'd been kind and patient. But given Patricia's position as owner, even though for Florence, observing the situation at close quarters it seemed unlikely Patricia would, at any time soon appear able and in control, Florence had not the authority to act on her behalf, to as much as open an official envelope despite affairs of the mine requiring ongoing attention. The supply of coal had never before been so vital or so vigorously pursued. If circumstances did not change very soon then Florence would have no option but to confer with Basil's solicitors, Neilson and Bradbury. It was not something for which she had any appetite, a venture, however brief, into that world so elevated by her husband each time he declared her incapable and unfit, she shied away from.

Florence tapped at the bedroom door then entered, expecting to find Patricia awake but disinterested in her greeting, as was the case each morning. The bed was empty, her nightgown lay over it. Florence put the cup down on the dressing table and hurried to the bathroom but there had been no sound of running water, the house was still. She looked in Julia's room, nowhere was Patricia to be found. Florence felt alarmed, rational thought would have predicted Patricia to have gathered her senses and taken herself to Birchdale, it couldn't be so, the mail was untouched and outside the car was parked in the usual place.

Feeling panic, Florence took deep breaths, Julia would be at Beeston by now. 'Calm yourself Florence', she spoke aloud, her stress eased and she turned over in her mind the most sensible next step. She was about to don her coat and go off in search of her daughter, when the telephone rang.

It was the General Hospital, Patricia had been brought in by kind workmen when they came across her, tired and very cold, earlier this morning. Could Florence come as her daughter seemed vague and reluctant to speak, it would help the doctor in deciding what best treatment to give if he could establish the cause of her confusion. Florence was suddenly overwhelmed by a feeling of frailty, yet it was neither to Caroline nor Julia that her mind travelled, Annie, she would be much more confident if her good friend Annie Eddowes were to go with her to the hospital. Annie was all but family, the connection would be considered loose by some but since their very first meeting Florence had felt comfortable and stronger when in Annie's company. She would call for a taxi and go right away to Gregory Street. Charles Eddowes must surely be mellowing, he'd surprised everyone by agreeing to narrate Harrow Road School nativity play, it would only be for a little while this morning and she would think of a way to repay his kindness if he took over Annie's duties at the shop.

"Bright young fella I reckon Percy," said Joe Hadwin, the foreman, "couldn't help wonderin' if the lad'd favour his old man's ways, Eddowes courts money they say. Mind you Charles Eddowes, the lad's granddad, he can be a funny bugger an'all." Joe's speculation was understandable, any new recruit to the workforce brought a degree of curiosity and in young Mathew Eddowes case that curiosity was fuelled by the reputation acquired by both his father and grandfather.

Percy Pollard looked out across the factory to where Mathew was about his first task.

"Never had a moments bother with his uncles, George and John, good lads both of 'em, but that William, poor old Reg Yeats at Players had a right barney with him you know, he wern't much older than Mathew at the time, he though he wer' goin' to run the place afore ever 'e got key o' the door to home."

Joe sniffed. "Well, give him his due, he's out there fightin' wi' the rest of 'em, poor devils. The Ardenne must be a cold, bloody place to be dug in an' they've got to cross the Rhine somehow, makes the Trent look like a minnow stream but Monty don't let much stand in his way an' say what you will about the yanks, they're cussed."

Percy sighed, "When I look across factory floor I see their faces, there's not one of 'em I don't think about. It'll never be the same again Joe. We used to turn out bicycles week on week, go home to our wives an' families wi' a bit o' money in our pockets, moan at 'avin' to hand over rent to landlord or swear at council rate bill, give missus her housekeepin' an' get 'er dander up by askin' why she needed so much, then sit in the pub wi' a pint while her dander died down. Now look out there, women, God bless 'em, workin' like good ens, willin' their men to stay alive. Young lads just out o' school, wonderin' if this bloody war'll end afore they're sent off for cannon fodder, an' old men like you an' me Joe, all turnin' out cartridge cases for Spitfires instead o' bikes for men to ride to an honest day's work. It'll never be the same." Percy shook his head in a gesture of dismay.

Mathew Eddowes had started work at Raleigh four days ago, his cheerful, polite manner made him popular with the others, especially the women who took every young beginner under their wing, an instinctive reaction, to keep them close until they learned the necessary skills. The older men had observed Mathew's eagerness to grasp the work and warmed to his youthful chatter at break times, while Mathew himself had stepped into that adult realm of paid labour with none of the resentment or dissatisfaction that years ago had made his father so unpopular. William stirred and schemed and belittled others, in his time at Players his arrogance had prevented him from acquiring the most basic but vital skill of all, how to fit in. William had ever been on the outside, while his son slipped easily into place.

Inside Percy's office his telephone was ringing.

"Baby's cryin' Joe, I'll talk with yer later." He lifted the receiver to his ear. "Pollard," he said, anticipating a call from the ordnance factory at Ranskill.

'Mr.Pollard, I'm sorry to bother you, it's Mrs.Edkins, I'm Ivy Tucker's next door neighbour, she works at factory. Can you tell her that her mam got a telegram this mornin', I think Ivy should come home for a bit, it's her brother Kenny'.

The voice tailed off and Percy recognised the quietness, he'd heard it before, tears and gulps of air that made no audible sound yet came down the telephone line in deafening volume.

"Are you alright Mrs.Edkins?"

"Yes, I'll be alright Mr.Pollard," came the brave reply, "but you will let Ivy come won't you, just for a bit."

"Mr. Hadwin'll take Ivy home, we'll not let the lass go on her own. Tell Mrs.Tucker I'm real sorry, Kenny wer' one o' the best an' he's not forgotten here at Raleigh."

Percy took a deep breath. Kenny Tucker, no older than the Eddowes' lad when he started at the factory, always talkin' about motor cars, had a fascination for them. He'd once shown Percy a picture, from a magazine, of a shining Lagonda, 'One day Mr.Pollard I shall drive a fancy car like that, I'll take it along The Ropewalk an' wave to the toffs'. He'd laughed, folded the page and put it back in his pocket.

Ivy was busy at her post, only a yard or two from Mathew, watching over him like a clucky hen. Percy beckoned to Joe Hadwin. It was not very often that Percy 'pulled rank' but this morning he must delegate the duty to Joe. Three times since Christmas he had taken a distraught woman to the office and watched her crumple before his eyes, not today, he couldn't endure it today.

"What is it Percy?" Asked Joe.

"Ivy Tucker, her brother Kenny, I said you'd take her home."

Joe's spirits sank, there was no merciful way of dealing with it, Ivy would know as soon as he told her she was to fetch her coat, she'd seen it happen to the others and no one was immune. For the new lad, now was the moment Mathew Eddowes would age years in the space of a few desperate minutes. Seeing a woman cry from grief wearied a man more than any amount of labour. Joe sighed, gritted his teeth and crossed the factory floor.

"Are you sure Charles doesn't mind, the more I think about it the more guilty I feel at asking?" Said Florence. She and Annie were in a taxi, on the way to the hospital.

"The shop is quiet, there are flurries of trade in and out, newspapers are a constant but the availability of so many items being virtually spent, whether it was me or Charles behind the counter we would be far from rushed off our feet. The only difference is that I find myself listening to people's anxieties and thankfully, their brighter accounts too, though they do seem to be considerably fewer. If I can't serve them with a full list of goods to meet their needs, then at least I can offer them patience. Charles feels no obligation in that respect, they will be 'dealt with' I think is the best way of putting it. But you shouldn't feel guilty Florence, sometimes I wonder what he thinks about when he's down in the cellar with nothing but soulless boxes as company and the old mattress we keep there for Samuel to sleep on when there's a raid. How could he not be worrying about the boys, it's so much worse on your own with little to demand your thoughts be elsewhere. Listening to the customers, to all their concerns I find a kindness, not to them but to me."

Annie smiled reassuringly at Florence as the hospital gates came into view.

"I've brought Patricia's night clothes and toiletries, I'm not sure what she will need, I'm not really sure of anything."

The emotion in Florence's voice was very evident, Annie squeezed her hand, and even through her gloves it felt cold. It was a curious fact that tension within defied every attempt at warmth from without. Every funeral Annie had attended chilled her regardless of the season, no comfort came from a hat, gloves or coat however protective against the elements their label claimed them to be.

The driver dropped them off right outside the hospital, Florence handed him the fare plus the expected tip, it reminded Annie of Gwendolyn Tozer. They had gone together to visit Gwendolyn, one afternoon in the week following her admission to Mapperley. Dear, tender hearted Florence had sat in a corner of the room, struggling to contain herself but the minute they reached the end of the corridor she'd wept, and Annie understood why. Just as Joan Faulds had described, life went on within that sheltered place and people did care, but still the inevitability of 'nothing more', tugged at the heartstrings 'til they hurt.

An enquiry at reception led them to ward 5 on the lower ground floor, they peered through the small glass pane in the door.

"Come along," said Annie, "positive thoughts."

The ward sister saw them and immediately crossed to where they stood.

"I'm Patricia's mother, Patricia Bradshaw, they telephoned asking me to come, this is Mrs.Eddowes, a family friend," said Florence.

"Ah yes, Dr.Wellesby needs to speak with you, I'll send word that you are here. Meanwhile, sit with your daughter, we are trying to put through as much warm fluid as we can, she was extremely cold when they brought her here. So far she has said nothing, she murmurs sometimes, a name possibly but we've not been able to recognise it. One of the young men fortunately knew who she was and gave us her name and address, otherwise we wouldn't have been able to telephone you as quickly as we did, she had no identification on her person, no bag, nothing in her pockets."

"Please tell me, who were these young men?" Said Florence, feeling utterly confused.

The sister explained. "Apparently they'd not long started their round, the dustbins. It was in Driscoll Street that they came across her. You owe them considerable gratitude, your daughter was close to collapse, not from exertion but from chill. They wrapped her in a jacket and lifted her into the cab of their truck and were infinitely sensible in driving straight away to this hospital."

"Oh my goodness," said Florence, "was Patricia aware of all this?"

"No, she was barely conscious."

They reached the bedside. "Patricia your mother is here." Sister smiled, "I'll leave you with her, doctor will come just as soon as he can."

Annie felt her presence an intrusion, but Florence had been insistent when she'd suggested it might be best if she waited in reception, clutching Annie's arm with one hand and the bag of night clothes in the other as if both were necessary to enable her next step.

"Hello Patricia, Annie has come with me for company, you remember William? He drove your father for a while after Mr.Madden left, well Annie is William's mother."

Florence stood by the bed, the hem of her coat revealing the poor woman's nervousness as it trembled in unison with her shoulders.

"Where were you going dear? If you'd waited I'd have gone with you."

Patricia turned to face them. "I was going home, Anthony will need his things, his books, he'll need his books."

Florence was close to tears. Annie instinctively felt that seeing her mother cry would not help Patricia so she attempted a diversion.

"I'm sure you must remember William, he can perhaps be a little over confident, I dare say your father had to rein in his ambition from time to time. William always wanted to run before he could walk as the old saying goes."

Patricia stared at Annie for several seconds. "Father died you know." She said nothing more, then thankfully, a nurse came and in a quiet voice said. "Dr.Wellesby will see you now, if you'll come with me I'll take you to him."

Annie thought this situation even worse than the one she'd shared with Celia that day at Mapperley, when they'd had to kiss her mother's cheek and say goodbye. Gwendolyn's dementia, for all that it was regrettable, didn't feel in the least bit morbid, yet Patricia Bradshaw's mind was somewhere desolate and sad.

He stood as they entered and offered his hand, Florence, ever polite, thanked him for his time and awaited his invitation to sit down.

"This is Mrs.Eddowes, a very close friend, I would like her to stay if you permit."

“Of course Mrs.Stanford.” Dr. Wellesby smiled at Annie and cast his eyes to a chair at the side of the small room, Florence took the seat immediately in front of the desk at which he sat, she looked timid.

“I shall listen while you tell me about your daughter, before we can decide her treatment we must first learn the story, when incidents such as these occur there is always a significant story.”

He leaned back in his chair, the movement caused his trouser leg to rise and from where she sat, Annie could see that his socks were bright yellow. Why, she could not have sensibly explained but the yellow socks in some strange way rendered him less formal. Surely they must have been a gift at Christmas from a very elderly aunt or at the other extreme, borrowed from a flamboyant son, dwelling still under his father’s roof.

Florence told of Basil’s death and the responsibility which passed to Patricia, through her father’s instructions. She spoke briefly of the marital disharmony, which had afflicted Patricia and Anthony and of the recent telegram that notified her of the devastating news, Anthony’s death in Italy, killed in action at the battle for Ravenna.

He was silent for a moment before responding.

“We are monitoring her temperature, your daughter was hypothermic when she came in, dangerously chill. Pneumonia could develop, so far she shows no respiratory difficulty but of course it has been but a few hours. My main concern however is her state of mind, her depression, she is I’m afraid severely depressed. Now that I have some background, ‘the story’, I can more confidently assess her condition. We shall keep her here until we are satisfied that her lungs have not taken infection, if pneumonia should develop, then of course she will remain at this hospital until such time as the lungs and chest are clear.

You see Mrs.Stanford, depression is an illness which affects the most complex area of the human body, the brain, the nerve centre that controls the whole. The expertise needed to restore your daughter’s mental health we cannot provide here. When the time is right we must transfer Mrs.Bradshaw to Mapperley, I have a brilliant colleague there, Maurice Lavery, he achieves remarkable results.”

Annie saw Florence tense at the mention of Mapperley, so soon after seeing Gwendolyn there it was not surprising. Dr.Wellesby had observed her reaction too.

"Your daughter is depressed Mrs.Stanford, she is not suffering dementia, even though events you describe are harsh enough to turn the mind of a less robust individual. If she resists pneumonia, and I dare to believe that she will, then it indicates a constitution that wouldn't shame a horse.

It will be to St.Annes that we transfer Mrs.Bradshaw, it comes under the administration of Mapperley but is the unit which specialises in temporary confusion, similar such cases as your daughter. The mind sometimes needs soothing, just as other such pains and discomforts require a formula to bring relief. Give it some time and all will be well.

Now why don't you go back to the ward and spend a few more minutes with Patricia, talk to her about simple, everyday things, don't worry if she doesn't respond, that's not important today."

He rose to his feet and the yellow socks disappeared from view. "We shall of course advise you of our intention prior to moving Mrs.Bradshaw but it won't be for a day or two so visit her again when you can. Our official visiting times are displayed at reception."

"I shall ask before we leave for the names of the two young workmen," said Florence, as she and Annie walked away from ward 5, and I shall write to each of them. Oh dear Annie, things are happening so fast and so strangely. I'm sure Celia will have told you that Caroline is moving to Mrs.Tozer's house, next Wednesday is the plan."

"Yes Celia did say but will that still be possible given the difficulties surrounding Patricia?"

Florence paused at the foot of the stairs and clutched the rail tightly.

"Fortunately, at this stage, Caroline has no need to move furniture, I'm sure that a little later she will sit down with Celia and together they will decide which items to keep and then whatever they choose will be transported to their respective abodes, leaving the rest to be sold. As you know Gwendolyn's house is fully furnished so in the immediate Caroline will take clothes, the boys' toys, some personal papers and photographs, presumably any food items remaining in the pantry at Moreleigh but beyond that nothing more, until they have time to arrange it. I believe she intends taking the things on Wednesday by taxi, it might necessitate two trips but it isn't a great distance. I suppose that Moreleigh will be put up for sale at some point, I think Mr.Caffin has been very helpful in advising Celia."

"I called on his wife Stella," said Annie, "just before Christmas and I have promised to visit again. They lost their son you know, I found her to be genuinely pleasant but struggling with her grief. She made me think of Catherine Appleyard, when her son Philip was lost at Gallipoli she buried herself in work, 'to keep body and mind from defeat', those were her very words. Now Stella Caffin spends nearly all her waking hours with the WVS."

Florence and Annie reached the top of the stairs.

"Are you alright?" Asked Annie as her friend stood still for a moment, catching her breath.

"I'm quite alright dear, it's talking as I climb that does it, anyone would think I'd spent years at the pit face to see me huffing and puffing." She lowered her voice and whispered. "It's likely my girdle is too tight."

Annie smiled with amusement, dear Davina Wright was always blaming her corset for any shortage of breath.

"I shall obtain those important names from the receptionist, then Annie dear I shall send you back to Charles in a taxi before he becomes anxious. I won't come with you that wouldn't be fair, he's seen quite enough of me for today I'm sure. Will you be alright if I go home now?"

"Of course, but I shall catch the bus and you were at the shop no more than five minutes this morning, so you certainly didn't delay Charles in any way. But I can understand how determined you are to write to those workmen, I dare say the letters will be in the post by this evening!"

Florence squeezed Annie's arm, grateful for her friendship and accord.

"Julia of course is blissfully unaware, she leaves the house early, yet another trial for her. Still there has been no word of Luciano. It becomes ever more challenging Annie, but I do try each day to sing with Bill Stribley. Do you suppose he's alive?" Florence's voice rippled with emotion, while Annie could only nod her head, and fervently hope.

You're tired Mathew, I can tell, only tomorrow morning, then that's it 'til Monday."

Celia had been watching him as he sat stroking Tilly, content simply to be still, not the usual eager account of his newly learned skills, a marked lack of interest in the POW camp and a surprising tolerance of Emily's repeated chanting of her nine times table.

"I'm alright Mam," he said, "just thinking about things. They're a good bunch of people at the factory, some of the women are especially kind, I suppose they do what comes naturally, you would be just like them, motherly, instructive, encouraging of someone new to the workforce, and yet they must all have their own worries. Ivy has been helping me all week but she had to leave early today. I must remember what I have learned, it's up to me isn't it, a man should take care of a woman, not the other way round."

Celia felt amused, her son, her boy, after just five days at the factory, considering himself a man. She wouldn't tease him, in truth she was proud of Mathew, for him to be tired must prove that he'd applied himself thoroughly. If tomorrow he chose to spend his Saturday afternoon peering through the palings at prisoners, then for once she wouldn't make a fuss.

Apart from doing a couple of hours cleaning for Anthony Hemsley, Saturdays Celia put aside for her own housework and for spending time with Mathew and Emily. She'd gone to Mapperley to see her mother every Sunday, for brief moments Gwendolyn seemed to recognise her but for the most part she dwelt in another time and place. Not distressed or agitated, just absent.

The threat of mumps now passed, this Sunday Rosie was coming to be with Emily. Christopher and Beryl would come with her and bring the board game they had for Christmas. Mathew most weeks had offered to go with Celia to visit his grandma but until now she'd thought it might be upsetting for him. Seeing grandma confused at home was one thing, witnessing her confusion in the surroundings at Mapperley was quite another and perhaps not appropriate for a fifteen year old. Yet the fact that he'd worked a week at Raleigh must entitle him to see for himself a harsher reality than his sheltered years thus far had allowed him. Celia was tempted to take him with her this Sunday, she should show him that she acknowledged he was no longer a child even though in her mind he was 'her boy'. It was a difficult balance to achieve, the overwhelming sense was to protect, to keep him from all hurt, but it was a mother's duty to prepare her son for life in the adult world, perhaps to begin with his own grandma was as good a lesson as any.

"Come on now Emily, that's enough arithmetic for one night, bed time, I put the hot water bottle in your bed half an hour ago."

"I'll take Tilly round the block," said Mathew, "there's a moon tonight."

"Well don't be long, I'm not sure if Tilly isn't coming into season and if she is you'll have Ludo, Mr.Bagley's old terrier from four doors down following you. I can't bear it if I'm waiting for the bus when he comes along, his nose is so cold!" Celia shuddered at the thought.

"What does coming into season mean?" asked a puzzled Emily.

Celia sighed from frustration. "To bed now, I'll explain tomorrow."

Emily ran upstairs making a mental note, 'ask tomorrow about dog seasons'.

Celia glanced at Mathew as he reached for Tilly's lead from the hook behind the door, it's just tiredness she told herself, when he comes back we'll all have an early night.

"I'm in bed Mam." Emily called down from her room. It was so much less worrying when they were of an age to be tucked up with a 'night-night' God bless kiss. What Annie had once said was very true, 'When they're little they're backache, when they're big they're heartache'. As she climbed the stairs to Emily she wondered what William was doing, was he warm enough? Was he well? She fingered her wedding ring and swallowed a pain so big, it lodged in her chest, the heartache, so much heartache.

Forli, Italy.

"You lead a charmed life Private, tell me how long have you been in the front line?"

"With respect Sir, it doesn't feel charmed." William Eddowes grimaced as another spasm of pain struck at his side, deep in his side. "Eighteen months, on an' off, more on than off Sir."

"Well Eddowes, I can't diagnose your condition one hundred percent accurately because my facility here is limited but I am as sure as I can be that you have gallstones, which have advanced to the stage of needing to be surgically removed. In this field hospital we perform the not infrequent miracle, your condition however is not needful of a miracle but it does demand a procedure which would defy the equipment I have at my disposal. You are no use to your section as you are so you will be transported to the American hospital at Leghorn for immediate treatment. Once you've recovered sufficiently to travel they will arrange passage back to England. It's not for me to predict by what means you will be transported when the time comes but I imagine it will be by sea. Recuperation following this type of surgery is usually three months, provided the patient is in other ways fit. You Private have survived eighteen months, tired, weary you may well be but were you not indeed fit then I doubt we would today be dealing with your troubled gut or anything else. You have a family I presume?"

"Yes Sir, wife and two children." William raised himself in the bed. "Excuse me Sir," then retched violently into the spittoon. Beads of sweat clung to his forehead while his pallor was ashen.

"Your wife will be informed of course. Some are saying that the end is in sight. I refuse to speculate, while I can diagnose your gallstones with reasonable confidence, through your reactions and the site of your pain, I couldn't begin to nominate the cause of this world's writhing and vomiting, its spitting of blood and burning excreta, it would take a man far more qualified. For my part I prefer to wait until the day arrives when that man, be in uniform or civvies, stands before me declaring the world to be 'out of danger' and saying, 'Galbraith, you can go home'. But for you Eddowes, I have the greatest hope that before a distant colleague, somewhere in dear old England tells you that he has no need of seeing you again, that you will pass muster, the bloody war will be done, finished, filed away with all the other debacles of history and you may return to a family life of some sanity with a gallstone in a jam jar of Italian origin to place on your mantelpiece, a souvenir of dictator Mussolini's downfall."

"Amen to that Sir," said William as he reached for the spittoon.

"Well Eddowes has managed to get 'isself somewhere nice an' warm, a Yankee hospital at Leghorn, gallstones apparently."

The man's expression was cynical and the less than respectful sniff that followed his remark suggested his disbelief.

"Come on now Battie, it wer' genuine enough, the poor sod wer' doubled up wi' pain an' as sick as I've ever seen a man," said another.

"Aye, I suppose, but 'e's a rum en that Eddowes, strange sort an' there's no denyin', where 'e is will be a bloody sight warmer. If a man didn't wrap 'is hands around to melt it first thing of a mornin' 'e'd not pass a drop o' piss."

Laughter erupted around the group.

"Oh aye Battie, meltin' it are yer? I've never heard it called that before."

"Well 'e's from Pickering aren't yer Battie? Winter lasts nine months o' the year up there, Yorkshire men develop the habit. Yer know what they say Battie, everybody's queer except thee an' me an even thee's a bit queer," came the voice of another.

"Ah shut up all, all of yer," said poor Battie, too fed up to appreciate the banter.

"Me father had gallstones," said Simpson, one of the younger men, "I don't envy Eddowes, dad wer' in agonies o' pain, lost pounds o' tallow, frightened me mam arf to death."

The group fell silent at the sobering reminder of a woman's worry. Nerves could gather pace under cover of silence.

"My ol' man wer' in the army durin' the last lot." A determined voice halted any advancing anxiety. "E' wer' brought up on a charge. 'It wer' like this son', e' said to me. 'I had to stand before the Major, a real posh toff. He wer' sittin' behind the table lookin' at me. Now this Major toff couldn't pronounce his R's an' when it got to the bit where he needed to say, 'state your wank and number', I said four times a week an' twice on a Sunday Sir'."

Raucous laughter filled the air, vapour rose from their mouths in the chill and set upon those troublesome nerves, chasing them away. It was the waiting, the cruel, cold waiting for a lift in the weather and the order to move. Good luck to Eddowes was now the unanimous, unspoken sentiment, with the postscript. Give our love to Blighty.

CHAPTER NINETEEN

Late April.

They had moved through the days like shadows in a spirit world, remote, lifeless. By night, darkness liberated the senses and what was confined by the glare of daylight, then found release. They had wept together, cried alone, hurt as a family, ached by themselves, all under the compassion of nightfall, while by day observing the ritual of living, the shop, school for Samuel, teaching for Laura, because they didn't know what else to do.

The telegram had come twelve days ago. John had been killed during the airborne operation to assist the Allied crossing of The Rhine at Wesel.

In his letters he had never revealed the fact that he served as aircrew, but apparently his duties for some time had gone beyond repair work on the ground.

Annie had held Laura as the young woman's heart broke, she had heard it, the sound as it ruptured, felt the trembling as its content rushed through every vein. Annie had held Samuel while tears poured from his eyes, draining away what little was left of youth and lain with Charles, sharing a grief that tore loose every nerve end until so intense was the pain neither could utter a single word. Even Ted Furniss had wrapped Samuel and himself about in that compassionate cloak of darkness when he'd tried to comfort the boy sobbing into the pillow beside him.

So close to what the government predicted to be the end, the past few weeks had produced an irony of despair. Harry Ollerton was missing, feared dead, Liza had received the telegram at Halam last month.

A letter had come from Francis at Bonthorpe, sadness had come to Ivy and Reggie's door, Molly was staying with them while her husband Walter was away. The telegram revealed Walter Small had been killed at Hurtgen Forest. For Harold, Molly's brother, it was proving especially hard, four German prisoners of war were working on the farm at Huttoft. Hatred was a disabling emotion and while Harold in the bottom knew it was irrational to despise every German, the love he felt for Molly in her grief made his work at the farm, often alongside the POW's as much as he could bear.

Henry Wainwright had been wounded, surgery had saved his arm from amputation but internal damage resulted in extensive blood loss and emergency transfusion, with the necessary removal of ripped intestines. Now in hospital at Portsmouth he was out of danger, but never out of Gertie's mind.

Only one area of life seemed to be offering relief, William had finally come home at the middle of last month. When Celia had received word of his treatment at the American hospital and been advised that he would be returned to England by hospital ship, the one word, 'gallstones', had swept comfort over her like the touch of a hand from a kindly God. Yet at any other time outside of war, the condition would have alarmed her, but at this time, gallstones was simply a familiar inconvenience, non military, many folk experienced the affliction in peacetime quite naturally, treatment tried and tested. A kindly God, Celia thanked him for granting William the mercy of gallstones!

The last letter from George had been brief and Annie sensed he'd written it shortly before action. His every word, as always, designed to convey love and strengthen hope, yet as Annie held the paper she felt the tremble where his fingers had folded it to place it inside the envelope. She heard his release of breath just before he sealed it and saw him kiss his son's name at the spot where he'd written it, just after his dad's and her own above the address. How far off Gregory Street must feel to George, so long away from home. There were moments when Annie thought her own heart might stop, every clang of the shop doorbell caused it to jump a beat until the sight of a customer restored its rhythm, not a telegram but Bill Rashleigh for matches or Mrs.Glasson for oats.

John was everywhere, he stood with her behind the counter, and beside her each morning when she smiled into Samuel's eyes before watching him walk along the street to school. John spoke over her shoulder as she stirred the pan of soup and she felt his warm breath brush the side of her face, 'smells good Mam'. His chuckle danced inside her head, round and round like a rhyme, *'Ring a ring o' roses, a pocket full o' posies',* he held her hand as Danny would hold her hand, that infectious chuckle, *'atishoo, atishoo all fall down'*. Then he'd let go her hand to clap at the fun. Now, whichever face she pictured, Danny or John, she felt the tiny fingers slip from her own and she bled, somewhere deep inside, the wounding bled.

It was two in the afternoon and Annie had promised to call on Edna. Charles had taken Samuel to see his uncle William and of course Celia, Mathew and Emily, being Sunday the shop was closed. Were it not for Ted, Annie would have stayed home, leaving Laura alone she could not have countenanced. It was strange how problems found answers, in ways which no one could have anticipated and by means that warmed the soul, when circumstances exposed it to a degree of cold severe enough to petrify every thread of faith within.

Laura's grief was immense and touched everyone but it was Ted Furniss who selflessly revealed an embarrassment he'd kept hidden for years, purely to help Laura and Annie loved him for it.

One evening after their so called meal, for not one of them had even the slightest appetite, Ted had gone upstairs and come down again with the book that Laura had loaned him when he first arrived. 'Far from the madding crowd'. In those early weeks she would occasionally ask him if he was enjoying the story. Always a little evasive Laura imagined he preferred other activities than reading until eventually the book was forgotten. But that evening Ted had stood in front of Laura where she sat by the scullery table, the book in his hand and said. 'I was never much good at school an' sweepin' chimneys with me dad didn't require me to either read much or write much. I'd like to know how, so will you teach me Laura'? It was a moment to be ever etched onto Annie's heart and since then, borrowing Samuel's early reading books, Ted and Laura had studied not just the alphabet, the formation of words, the recognition and writing of them, but also the needs of each other, Ted's need of confidence in a demanding world and Laura's need of a cause on which to concentrate. This afternoon they were engaged with the stories of Christopher Robin. Samuel's reaction had been just as Annie would have expected, 'When you're a bit better at it Ted we'll play hangman, I learned lots of words through playing hangman with dad'. There had been no hint of amusement at discovering that a grown man, working down the pit could be illiterate. Instead Samuel had encouraged and Ted's generous act had achieved far more than a lesson in reading, it had soothed a soreness, which afflicted them all and in a way none of them could have explained. The time spent on making Ted able to read 'Far from the madding crowd', included John, his presence so strongly felt, prompting if Laura's mind became distracted by sadness, qualifying the teacher to take charge over each day as it came.

Annie looked forward to spending some time with Edna and Billy. Despite their own tribulations they offered so much sanctuary. On entering No.24 Winchester Street Annie ever felt firmly anchored and safe from whatever elements might rage outside. Whether the assurance came from her memories of Harold, those blissful early days together, or whether it was simply the depth of friendship between Edna, Billy and herself she couldn't know but this afternoon Annie sought the fortitude given her by No.24, it had kept her strong all those years ago and it inspired her still.

Billy had the kettle on the stove before Annie had chance to sit down. Edna appeared to be stuffing kapok into an old grey sock, intrigued, Annie pulled up a chair and sat alongside her, she gave Edna a quizzical look.

"Now don't interrupt me rare moment of ingenuity Annie Eddowes, 'e's already tried to put me of me stroke." Her gaze travelled swiftly to Billy before returning to the object of her enterprise. "If yer must know I'm tryin' to make a lucky shoe for the weddin'. I've cut the shape from this sock and sewn it together, now I'm fillin' it wi' kapok, then I shall cover it wi' silver sequins an' stitch a blue bow on the front, like laces. I borrowed the pattern from our Vera, somethin' old, the sock, somethin' new, the shoe, somethin' borrowed, the pattern, an' somethin' blue, the bow. It come out of The Woman's Weekly years ago. Vera kept it thinkin' she'd make it when their Brenda got wed, but Vera's allus full o' plans that never come to owt. The summer o' thirty six she started a tapestry, goin' to get it framed she wer' to hang over mantelpiece at Christmas, but she wer' that upset when King Eddie abdicated an' run off wi' Mrs.Simpson, she packed it away in the wardrobe wi' the lords a leapin' an' the pipers pipin' still to do an' nobody's seen sight nor sign of it since."

"Here you are Annie, a nice cuppa." Billy put the tea down on the table and wrapped his arm around her shoulders, she felt the squeeze of his hand, it spoke louder than words.

"Thank you Billy. I feel better already."

He winked and looking down at his wife's handiwork said. "This part o' the process isn't so bad but when she starts sewin' on them tiny silver things 'er patience'll run out after the first arf dozen, won't it my love?"

"Yer can shut your mouth Billy Dodds or when you're asleep I'll stitch that up instead," Edna thrust the next bit of kapok into the sock to pack out the shape and apparently felt guilty over her threat to Billy's well being so added, "but I love yer, so I'll use loose blanket stitch then yer can still play your mouth organ an' whistle, *When the lights go on again.* Do you know Annie I'd swear he wakes up whistlin' that tune."

Billy leaned over and kissed the top of Edna's head, Annie saw the grin spread across her face.

That was the nature of this house, Annie loved it and everyone in it, the togetherness, that constant, unquestioned devotion. Billy lived for Edna and she in turn cherished ever fibre of him.

They had been wrestling with their reservations over the timing of Myra's wedding to Jack on May 12th. It felt too soon, the telegram sent to the farm at Halam, delivering despair to Liza. Jack's brother Henry, wounded and weakened. It didn't seem right to continue with plans to have the marriage take place as early as next month, when so much hurt prevailed the families. Edna had confided in Annie her concern that Liza might be refusing to believe that Harry was dead, Liza had spoken as though he would be aware of Myra's wedding when she'd said, 'Harry would be dismayed if they postponed it'. Edna couldn't bring herself to caution Liza's conviction, her denial of the almost certain truth. 'Perhaps I'm misreading what she means', Edna had said to Annie when they'd last sat together, 'perhaps Liza believes Harry's looking down from Heaven'.

They all got through the days as best they could and no one challenged the means.

Gertie Wainwright, between sobbing, had declared Henry to be desperate for a sister in law to tame his brother Jack and if he couldn't be out of hospital in time to be best man, then he'd be home soon after to claim his kiss from the bride. So despite all of their misgivings and the mix of emotions it was love that overcame them and Myra and Jack would be married at St.Andrew's Church on Saturday May 12th at 2 o'clock, with Janet, Catherine and Gillian as bridesmaids. All sincerely hoped that Henry would be fully recovered in time, but if not then Charlie Jones was able and more than ready to perform the best man's duties. In fact the whole thing had set his own thoughts on tying the knot with Maureen. Jack had teased him, 'If yer get a suit for my do yer may as well make good use of it, I do believe you're showin' a bit o' nous at last Jones'. All the families had been saving clothing coupons, sadness entwined the excitement, it threaded through ever bit of lace and satin and rested in ever jacket pocket but this young couple deserved a day to remember for all the proper reasons and no one would consider otherwise.

"I can only work on the fiddly thing when Myra's not here," said Edna. "She's gone to see Susie and Joe, I've told our Susie to keep her there 'til 5 o'clock, the girls'll likely be practisin' their hairdos, Cathy's hair is long enough to pin up an' Gillian wants ringlets, they're so lookin' forward to gettin all dressed up, not really surprisin' is it? At their age these past five years must have felt like fifty five." Edna pointed to the pattern, the page of Woman's Weekly on the table by her sewing box. "They reckon it takes four hundred sequins, if Billy 'ad both arms I'd make him stitch some o' the soddin' things on." She sighed and pushed the last wad of kapok inside the obliging grey sock.

Following the wedding Mr. & Mrs. Jack Wainwright were to reside at No.19 Northolt Road, a modest two up, two down dwelling not too far away from a bus stop. The previous tenants had been clean and tidy so little needed to be done prior to them moving in. It was part furnished, nets remained at the downstairs windows but they needed to hang curtains and acquire one or two essential items, otherwise the rest could come along by degrees. As Jack said, it was the neighbour on the left,

No17 who quite unintentionally convinced him it was the ideal place. A very elderly woman with a name quite beguiling and the most irresistible smile. Miss Patience Pennifold. Her white hair so thin it wandered across her scalp like cobwebs, while once youthful freckles, peppered her face and now deep lines travelled between them as though a naughty child had taken a pencil and joined up the dots whilst she snoozed. Her dress was of an age long gone and yet it suited her in every way, she was everyone's unmarried aunty and in his mind Jack had already adopted her, like his aunty Nora, innocent, unassuming, even timid, Miss Patience Pennifold touched his heart, they both appeared fragile and the modern world took little account of fragility.

Edna put down her sewing to drink her tea. "Funny how things work out, Jack'll be leavin' home as Henry's likely to be comin' back. Do yer think Jean Tennyson will stay at Gertie's or go to live at Mitchell Street wi' Nora, I know she's close to Gertie but I thought she might feel like givin' 'er a bit o' time wi' just Henry in the house, the lad's been away for so long, yer know what I mean. I've often wondered why Nora didn't take a lodger, it'd be company as well as help wi' the rent, though I don't suppose she ever spent very much all the years she worked for the Hymers."

Edna's mind was on the situation at Gregory Street, when George, God willing, came home. With Laura and Ted Furniss there it was obvious someone would need to find other lodgings. In her way, Edna was gently nudging Annie's thoughts in that same direction.

"I dare say the notion of a man in the house at night 'ould frighten Nora but a Bevin Boy or even a young woman, they need lodgin's sometimes, like that Enid Cole, she lodged wi' Bertha Duffin didn't she afore she married Charles, an' several o' the girls at Brassington come there to work from a distance away an' 'ad to find somewhere to live." Edna was pensive. "Would yer suppose that Nora's ever been close enough to a fella to 'ave any idea o' what they've got down below?"

"Really Edna she was the eldest, then came Harold and Frank before the other four girls. She may not have married but in that small terraced house on Mitchell Street and with all that she did to help Sarah do you honestly imagine Nora could have avoided sight of her younger brothers' nether regions." Annie shook her head in disbelief.

Edna sniffed. "Well I 'ad two brothers an'all but it wer' still a shock first time I saw it fully grown. Sidney Butterworth 'e wer' called, I thought 'e must 'ave 'ad some sort o' deformity til I saw the next one an' that wer' Billy, well yer could talk to Billy so I asked him, 'Are they all like that?' Do yer know what the daft beggar said, 'Depends what you feed 'em on'."

"It's a good job your husband is outside in the yard and can't hear you Mrs.Dodds," said Annie, "but I wish you hadn't told me that, a Sidney Butterworth frequents the shop, I shall never be able to serve him again without thinking of your enquiring mind."

Edna grinned but if she was about to say something then she had second thoughts, again picking up her stitching as Billy came back indoors with the basket of laundry he'd taken down from the clothes line.

The following hour passed quickly, neither mentioned the other's heartache, it didn't need to be said, just a knowing look, a squeeze of the hand and the strength behind the hugs when Annie had to leave, delivered their comfort, it was ever that way.

When Annie got back to Gregory Street she found Laura and Ted listening to the wireless, the expression on Laura's face was agonised.

"Mussolini's dead Mrs.Eddowes," said Ted, "it has to be true, they couldn't report it otherwise, not over the wireless, could they?"

Annie was confused and speechless. "The partisans got him, executed him, he's dead, Mussolini's a goner, it must be nearly all over in Italy now."

Annie's stomach turned, George, dear God let him be alive. She sank onto a chair just as the back door opened and in came Charles and Samuel.

"What's the matter?"

Charles could tell from the look on their faces that something had happened. Samuel held his breath until Ted spoke to relate events, he listened intently, to a boy of Samuel's age, what he heard was enough to enable him belief, confidence in his dad's survival. There had been no more telegrams, surely now it would be alright.

Charles observed Annie's quietness and recognised exactly what she was thinking. It was only five weeks ago that John was killed, all this time, waiting and praying, trusting and hoping and then, so close to the end, it was not possible to put into words the despair. This news of Mussolini placed relief in one hand and fear in the other, had the final battles in Italy taken George?

He crossed the room to where she sat, laid his hand on her shoulder and said.

"He'll be back, just a week or two more but he will be back."

Charles spoke with such conviction, his tone was unusually manly, often he could mumble in such a droning fashion it was hardly worthy of attention, at other times he would shout his authority as though by bellowing he'd be better understood. But his quietly spoken words this evening carried genuine purpose and Annie clung to them. She stood up and smiled at them all.

"April has been a month like no other," she said. "Jack Wainwright and Myra Dodds will, after all, marry in two weeks time, at the insistence of Liza Ollerton and Jack's brother Henry, despite the extent of their own troubles. They are determined, clutching at the hope, which next month affords. We shall clutch at May too, all of us, the war will end, it will."

Laura came to Annie's rescue, creating a diversion, a tactic each of them had learned over recent months and applied when emotion was about to spill.

"How is William today? When I saw Celia one day in the week she seemed very preoccupied but I expect it was simply tiredness, I know she's always busy."

Charles sighed. "He sees the army medics next Thursday. To be honest I don't know how he is, he looks well enough. Celia is anxious I can tell but if Mussolini is dead and if word from the Fronts is reliable, then the Germans will be forced to surrender. Unless the Eighth Army is needed to assist with the movement of prisoners or in clearing the concentration camps then I imagine they will be stood down and William will, in due course be demobbed. The American and Russian troops may require reinforcements but in the north the Germans are said to be staring at defeat, there too surrender would appear imminent."

Samuel tugged at Ted's sleeve, ready or not he needed the activity, "Give us a game of hangman Ted, while mam gets tea."

Early May.
Udine, Italy.

The atmosphere was strange, even the air seemed tired, too weary to lift itself so it hung about everyone's shoulders making movement laborious. Over the last three weeks the Allies had advanced mile upon mile through northern Italy, finally linking up with Tito's forces coming from the East. The wounded, the dead and ever growing numbers of prisoners securing their place, along with all the others, in George's mind and memory.

The men had been jubilant when word had reached them of Hitler's death, and by his own hand, suicide. They had all cursed him to hell but this fate felt just and proper, no decent man should have had to risk one single drop of the vile dictator's blood to fall on him. By his own hand was entirely fitting, although in the opinion of some, too short on suffering and spared of agony, a combination witnessed time and again among their own number, even hell would be too good a place for Adolf Hitler.

Vietinghoff, Commander of Army Group C, had signed the instrument of surrender on behalf of German forces in Italy and Freideberg had surrendered to Montgomery at Luneburg. The war in Europe was virtually over yet a quietness gripped the men, emotions were fluid, tears erupted without warning, relief could melt into uncertainty when disbelief undermined, and happiness rose and ebbed in a constant tide. When Corporal Bayliss had put a mug of tea in George's hand and said. 'Are we done do yer think Sarge'? George had nodded and replied. 'All bar the shouting Bayliss but there may well be a lot of shouting'.

Now George sat quietly with pen and paper, he'd already written Dear Mam, Dad and Samuel. For at least five minutes he'd stared at their names and rubbed tears from his eyes as that relief began to melt. Could he really write that it was over? The thought of his mother reading such a line sent joy welling up inside him, then would come a niggle of doubt and that joy ebbed.

Three times he'd been wounded, treated at the field hospital and returned to the front line. The doctor had remarked on his luck as each time the bullet had missed any tissue of real consequence. 'Somebody up there loves you Boucher'. It had not once occurred to George to mention any of it in his letters home, it was trivial, he was aware of what the Captain had been called upon to write, and in his mind pictured the agony of the recipients. George's letters, while ever he addressed them himself, would be a gift to his mam, anything else he tried not to dwell on. Finally he put his pen to paper and wrote the contents of his soul.

Everything here is calm, I am alive and in the company of my greatest friends. We are told that the Axis forces have been defeated, that we have won, what it is that we have won I am not sure. We stand here on ground that is now freed, a land that we have traversed from one end to the other, yet it feels foreign to us and we find little satisfaction. The guns have fallen silent and all other sounds of battle are absent yet we cannot sleep. We are congratulated by our commanders yet our achievements have come at such cost, shall we ever repay the debt? The worry of that alone takes away our appetites 'til we cannot eat. A bond exists between the men, among comrades. For those who have not been here with us it will be impossible to understand and they will likely dismiss it as mere sentimentality but it is far more than that. It is a kind of love, deep in its measure. Not tender, it shows itself in ways not at all familiar and poets will not find words to describe it, as we ourselves, if asked, could not express it. I have survived. One officer said to me, 'someone up there loves you Boucher', meaning Heaven of course. But it is here, on earth, that I have seen such sacrifice as could only be borne of love. We torment each other with roguish banter, we swear at one another, argue, and we sulk like children. We all earnestly pray in simple verse to our God, but it is to the next man, the shoulder alongside our own that we give our trust. We have sent to Heaven only the finest, the very best among us. As the ranks of Heaven are strengthened by these elite I imagine I hear an officer at God's right hand say, 'someone down there loves you Lord'. I shall dare to believe that one day soon we will be together, how I long for that day. I don't know what is to happen next, whether we will be sent back to England or whether we will be deployed to another place where our help is needed. We are all exhausted, yet if the order came that we must march a hundred miles then we would march but if there, we should raise our rifles our aim would be gone, the purpose lost. Our feet move but our minds are set, all that we now see through our sights is home, glorious home. I picture it, spring blossom in the arboretum, flower beds planted out in asters and geraniums at the embankment and the grass, mown as smooth as green velvet at Trent Bridge. All things previously taken for granted, of little note in the everyday scheme of things. Now a daisy is a wonder of creation and the thought of men, dressed in white, of opposing sides in pureness of white! Such a notion feels like fantasy. I shall take you Samuel to watch the cricket. I can think of few activities more appealing than to observe a contest between men so placid of nature as to face one another without contrivance. Cards have been the innocent pastime here when an interlude allowed but no one kept score, I suppose because not one among us felt inclined to speak either word, winner or loser, so we have been perpetually tied, shoulder to shoulder, neck and neck, all the way to the finishing post. I don't believe I have a competitive bone left in my body so Samuel will likely beat me at draughts, whist, hangman, cribbage, even at, 'race you to the corner dad'. I dare say that by now his legs are longer than mine anyway. We haven't received any mail for some time, I think supply routes have proved complicated. Just so long as all is well, I am sure word from home will catch up with us any day.

My love to all, as ever and always.

George, Dad.

XXX XXX

CHAPTER TWENTY

Late May.

Hilda put down the plate of food on the table in front of Jack, casting her eyes at the clock, her manner revealing her vexation.

"For goodness sake, you get later every day, for the last four on the trot you've not been home in time to see Rosemary before she went to bed, I thought you would at least make the effort today, it's Friday, she's hardly seen her dad all week. Why Jack, why is that pit so important? The war in Europe is over, men will be returning soon, looking for change, something different to the old system they knew before. Those who have survived will expect work and a decent wage, the prospect of a better standard of living. The thirties offered little to the labourer, the working man, surely he's proved himself to be worthy of recognition. We had plans Jack, what's happened to them? You were to be your own boss and build something new and better. Still you 'cow tow' to the Stanfords, it's tragic that Anthony Bradshaw was killed of course it is, but she showed little tolerance of him when they were together and despite Florence Stanford being friendly with mam, there must be someone other than you who could help her. Hugh Porter's health has been poor for some time, if it isn't his stomach that's playing up then he has a cough or cold, the man is obviously unwell, surely they could have recognised the fact and found a replacement. But you, muggins, allow them to take advantage of good nature, Eddie Wills should have more sense. You owe them nothing, but we had plans Jack, when the war ended we were supposed to turn our backs on the pit and live a different kind of life, free of coal dust and dread, a future of our own making."

Outside David was playing, his young ears couldn't avoid the unpleasant tone even if the actual words failed to register. His mam had been touchy all week. He didn't understand what it meant but he'd heard one of the older boys at school telling another that women got irritable at the time of the month. Apparently Gilbert Streeter's mam had lit a bonfire in their back garden and thrown Mr.Streeter's dart board onto it, when he got home from work all that was left of it was a piece of charred cork and some distorted wire, all because of 'the time of the month'.

David had been puzzled yet he'd sensed it was not a puzzlement best taken to his mam so he'd decided to seek clarification of his grandma, she would know, because although he was a man granddad got irritable at least every month. Some adult things seemed too complicated to be sensible yet according to Mrs.Flowers, from next door, it was kids who created problems. David often heard her chuntering away to herself on the other side of the wall in the yard, 'kids, one damn problem after another'. Though when her son Brian came home last Tuesday from the hospital where he'd recovered from a war wound she'd declared him to be, 'too good even for the angels'! David sighed and rolled his blue marble at the hollow in the drain cover, the rattle it made when it fell in was a better sound than his mam's curious irritation.

"There's no need to raise your voice Hilda," said Jack, trying to face the plate of food. He felt caught between two loyalties and his determination to be decent, to keep that all vital self respect, day on day put him under greater pressure. "You'll wake Rosie, let the child sleep in peace, haven't we all waited long enough for peace. Be patient can't you, Mrs.Stanford is nothing like her husband, the woman is doing her best for all three of her daughters. Mrs.Bradshaw is recovering slowly but can't be worried over affairs o' the mine. The middle daughter now knows that her husband is dead too an' you should feel compassion for the youngest, she is after all as good as family, through Celia. Hugh Porter isn't unlike Henry Wicks, a good manager. I've wanted to believe that his gut trouble would ease an' that he'd be back in the office soon. The least me an' Eddie could do was keep the job there for him an' if you see that as helpin' Florence Stanford then maybe you're right, but it was still the proper thing to do."

He put a forkful of mashed potato into his mouth and willed Hilda to leave him be.

Troubles never come singly was a saying that often proved true. When Florence Stanford had come to the mine to speak with Hugh Porter it confirmed what had been rumoured, that Patricia Bradshaw had been admitted to Mapperley, although the homespun diagnosis, which in its least authoritative description declared her to be 'off 'er head', had thankfully been amended by Mrs.Stanford. Acute depression following the news of Mr.Bradshaw's death, was not beyond the average mortal's understanding and due sympathy was granted her despite any less kindly thoughts they'd held in the past.

Florence had approached Basil's solicitors with her proposed solution to the current problem. Whilst Patricia was temporarily incapacitated, with Hugh Porter's help she herself would undertake all necessary correspondence with the Ministry and sign on her daughter's behalf any documents pertaining to the mine, which under normal circumstances would carry Mrs.Bradshaw's signature. She had written a note, the content of which she must ask Mr.Bradbury to approve and on her next visit to St.Annes she would obtain Patricia's signature by way of endorsement.

It was entirely in order, as Basil's widow she was the obvious nominee and for Mrs.Bradshaw to appoint her mother as signatory made best sense. If however Mrs.Bradshaw was not in agreement with this arrangement and therefore would not put her name to it, then the firm would act as her agent until such time as she was recovered. 'For a not inconsiderable fee', had been Florence's immediate thought.

In the event, after she had carefully explained the situation to Patricia, emphasising the temporary element of it, and placed the note on the table beside her, for her to read, Patricia had taken up the pen and written her name at the bottom of the sheet of paper without even a glance at the wording, as though merely adding an item to the end of a shopping list.

Just one month later, early in March, Eddie Wills had found Hugh Porter in his office doubled up with pain and in urgent need of a doctor. He had called for an ambulance, Hugh's troublesome gut, this time was beyond Milk of Magnesia. A perforated ulcer was later diagnosed. An operation and after care had kept him in City Hospital for weeks, not until mid April had he been considered fit to return home to his wife, to recuperate. Jack and Eddie had felt sympathy for Florence Stanford, clouds of dismay hovered over the woman, Mrs.Bradshaw's condition had taken a stronghold and the specialist had told her mother that improvement would come, but slowly, it was an illness, which required patience and an unknown length of time.

Despite him being long gone, Neilson & Bradbury were still very much Basil's solicitors and persisted in nipping at the heels of Mrs.Stanford, as though anticipating any day her decision to submit, to instruct them to act for her daughter, Hugh Porter whom she relied on now being indisposed.

In fact the mine was running smoothly, targets were met and through Jack's determination to keep the men informed, they all felt significant. Then, this afternoon, Hugh Porter had come to Birchdale to see Jack and events now overwhelmed him.

"I saw Joyce today," said Hilda, "Valerie Oates has had her baby, two weeks early, a little girl. Poor Edgar, it all seems unfortunate somehow." Hilda had calmed and she talked while she folded clothes. David, relieved by the quietness, now sat on the floor with his Meccano.

"Edgar's a good lad," said Jack, "got more about him than most." He put down his knife and fork, he'd managed to clear his plate. Hilda produced fine meals considering how little was available but his appetite had left him, only his mother's belief, instilled in him from childhood, 'waste of food is sinful', had enabled him to force it down.

"Something happened today, not a bad thing, but it challenges me, us, our immediate future," he said. "Some in our position would seize upon it as a good thing, a really good thing. Hugh Porter has decided not to come back to his job. He explained it to me, his reasoning. He was very poorly, at one stage seriously ill. Mrs.Porter found it frightening, I suppose she was afraid that he might die. You see they've no family, I imagine she's made some friends here but apparently she's a very shy woman. She does have a sister living down south. Hugh's words to me today were, 'I've had enough Jack, Mrs.Porter wants us to move closer to her sister and I can't deny her'.

Hilda abandoned her folding and sat down beside Jack, she sensed his anxiety and made no attempt to interrupt.

“Hugh came to see me before speaking to Mrs.Stanford, he intends recommending me as his replacement.”

Jack pondered that conversation of earlier, Hugh Porter had obviously been thinking about it for weeks. His manner had been quite firm when he’d told Jack to resign from the Union, ‘You can’t be manager whilst you’re Union rep’. He’d explained why Jack and not Eddie. ‘He’s made of the right stuff too but he’s older and young blood is what the position needs, Eddie realises that. The men trust you Jack and you know what makes the cogs turn and keep on turning’.

It had knocked the wind out of Jack, stopped him in his tracks. Initially he’d responded by saying, ‘I’ve not had the schoolin’ for it Hugh’, but his remark was dismissed.

‘Nationalisation is coming, we both know it, the government has already taken over the coal stocks, it can only be a matter of time before they do likewise with the collieries themselves, the entire industry, they’ll need good managers Jack, men with experience, with insight, and a level head, that’s where a lot of managers go wrong, they lose the true meaning of the word level. Even, fair, are words, which could be substituted for ‘level’. Lose the meaning Jack and the cogs stop turning’.

Hilda had sat in silence, she too had been pondering, how could her own modest plans hope to compete with the offer of manager.

“That pit owns you Jack,” she said, “and it won’t relinquish its title will it? No matter what we might sit here and dream of, always the mine will prevail. I suppose I should be thankful, as manager you won’t be at the pit face, there’ll be less grime clinging to your collar, scoffing at my efforts with the Sunlight Soap and your lungs might carry you to a reasonable age before they start wheezing alongside me at night, you might achieve to satisfy yourself that because of Jack Haynes, those who sweat away their days at Birchdale nevertheless do so with a good heart as they bathe in self respect.” She picked up some socks and began to sort them into pairs. “You must do whatever you see fit Jack but one man can’t change attitudes and I fear you’ll destroy yourself trying.”

Jack, without really thinking, took a sock from the small pile and sought its mate.

"I can't believe, even if Mrs.Stanford is in agreement, that Mrs.Bradshaw will be," he said. "The woman might be suffering some kind of nervous breakdown but she's not mad. I'm tellin' you all this Hilda because it's only right that you should know, but the likelihood of Jack Haynes becomin' manager is too slight to spend a minute worryin' over."

Curiously his words stirred something in Hilda and she bewildered him with her response. "Don't sell yourself short Jack, you're every bit as capable as Mr.Porter and above all else, you're decent."

It was David who innocently dispelled doubt but at the same time postponed dreams. "Look Dad." He held up his creation in Meccano, a miniature pit head, his version of that familiar landmark, the steel housing for the winch. "It works, see." David turned the wheel to demonstrate.

Hilda sighed, picked up Jack's plate and walked across to the sink. What was the use of arguing, the pit was everywhere, in the mind of their child, in the dirty washer water, and seemingly in her husband's blood. One day, perhaps one day! She ran water over the dishes and drove it from her mind.

Jack took the model from David's hand and gazed at it.

"What do you think Dad, is it okay?"

Jack rubbed his fingers over the wheel. "It's good Son, I've never seen a better one, but next time try an' make somethin' your mam'd like, a house with a door an' four windows at the front, I reckon she'd love that, that's what we'll do David, a nice big house with four windows for your mam."

David smiled knowingly and lowered his voice. "Tell me when Dad, I best make it when it's time of the month!"

Celia was relieved to be out of the house, William was in a difficult mood, in fact the past few weeks had been trying. The army doctor had authorised two months of extended leave when William had gone for his medical assessment three weeks ago. 'There could be little purpose in sending you back to your unit now Eddowes', he'd said, 'you'll be demobbed within that time, or soon after'.

William was impatient, the war had been an obstacle to his progress, the fact that it still raged in Asia, where the Japanese continued to fight despite Allied gains, seemed to be outside William's concerns. Perhaps it was concentrating on the future that enabled him to blot out the recent past, whatever it was Celia struggled with the nature of the days. The happiness she and the children felt at his homecoming had been beyond measure and knowing he was recovering from surgery and in need of care and convalescence Celia had explained the situation and with regret, handed in her notice at the council offices. However, as her hours at The Park for Anthony Hemsley were flexible she had kept her work there and more often than not went on a Saturday afternoon when Mathew was home and for a couple of hours in the early afternoon on a weekday, while William was resting.

Her mother's mental state had not deteriorated further, most folk would consider it to be bad enough, yet when Celia visited she saw more pitiful confusion in some of the other patients. Gwendolyn was still briefly herself, the rest of the time she might be any number of identities but seldom did she become agitated and even then, was easily soothed by the mention of Queen Victoria. Her favourite character by far was the old Sovereign and a few minutes spent in conversation about her never failed to restore calm. It was a curiosity no one could explain, the doctor had told Celia that while he had no idea why Victoria had such an effect on her mother, he nevertheless believed that the association Gwendolyn made would extend her life. Those whose agitation could not be eased succumbed to stress placed on their hearts, while Gwendolyn was fortunate in having a release valve. So it was that Celia visited Mapperley when she could, always taking some small gift and supporting her mother financially as she felt obliged to do, only as much as she could afford, without her wage from the council it was a minimal amount but it allowed her the comfort of knowing that Gwendolyn Tozer was not entirely at the mercy of the state, how horrified her mother would be otherwise! No, Celia must continue her few hours at The Park despite William's objection. At first he'd seemed pleased that she'd finished at the council, now he told her repeatedly that she should have kept the decent job and left Hemsley's employ, who could find a woman to daily for him from anywhere. Celia disliked William's manner on the subject, Anthony paid her well, certainly as well as the council and was happy for her to organise the hours she worked to suit herself, he reimbursed her bus fares, always with an additional amount and showed his appreciation with a simple, 'thank you so much Celia', each time she left the house. The Bevin boys too were grateful of her efforts and now all felt like friends. Yet William, her husband whom she loved so much could reduce her to tears with his thoughtlessness. She had heard women speak of the inner torment, which plagued the lives of some men when they finally returned from the first war and Celia was sensible enough to realise that William's mind must at times struggle with images and memories too awful to confide to others, so she made allowance.

The surplus furniture from the two houses Celia and Caroline had put into auction and Morleigh had been put on the market early in March with an estate agent. That had proved another bone of contention. William on coming home soon turned his attention to the sale, expressing his dismay at the fact that Celia had not seen fit to await his advice, she pointed out that she had felt it her duty to support her mother's care at least to some degree but it seemed not to register and he'd gone on to announce that he was considering buying out Caroline's share, which he had already worked out to be less than Celia's due to the difference in value of the two properties and how much more sensible it would have been to conduct the sale without involving the agent and as a result avoid paying commission to a third party. Celia had made the observation that when she and Caroline first discussed the matter they had no way of knowing when William would be home but that met with short shrift. Initially it was his intention to rent it out and use the title deed as collateral to finance the acquisition of some land likely to be suitable for development. Celia had wanted to ask if she might have a say in any of this, half the property being her's after all, but he had been home for such a short time and away for so long, enduring unimaginable horrors, she felt not entitled to upset him by asserting any right of her own. She could only hope that his notion would pass, his thoughts change direction but he appeared delighted with the idea. So this afternoon Celia made her way to The Park far from confident yet looking forward to other company for an hour or two, or to be on her own as the case may be, if Anthony was out, the key would be beneath the boot scraper by the side door.

She tried the latch, it was unlocked so she stepped inside and called out.

"Only me, Celia."

There was no reply, perhaps Anthony was outside in the garden, he'd mentioned that he needed to cut back the hedge and today's weather was ideal for the task. She hung her jacket on the hallstand and went straight away to the scullery where in the under sink cupboard she kept her utensils and pinafore. Today she would do upstairs, again Celia called out but still the house was silent. She picked up the bucket of cleaning stuff, put on the pinafore and climbed the stairs, if she did Anthony's bedroom first she could look out over the back garden. He preferred to sleep at the back, less sound from passing traffic, the Bevin boys were just glad to have such pleasant accommodation, after a shift at the pit it would take more than the sound of a motor car to keep them from sleep.

She tapped at the bedroom door, in case Anthony was resting, though it wasn't his habit to take an afternoon nap, not expecting a response she'd turned the door knob and it was just open when a voice said.

"Yes." He sat by the window. "Celia, I forgot you came today," he at once stood, "I shall go downstairs out of your way."

"Is everything alright Anthony?"

His behaviour was unusual, normally he would be eager to chat for a few minutes, he'd once said, 'You bring a welcome element of regular life Celia, a much needed addition to a house filled only by single men'.

"I'm quite well my dear, a little pensive today perhaps, family matters, but nothing to bother you with Celia, you have quite enough to think about as it is. Please, don't let me delay you, I know how anxious you are these days not to be away from home for too long, I can understand how much William would want your company after so long denied it, it does seem unfair that you should be here, occupied with our dust." He gave a vague smile and walked away. Celia felt like telling Anthony that actually she was in no hurry to return to William's moodiness but instead she called out.

"I shall make you a nice cup of tea when I'm done up here, it won't take me long."

Celia had come to the conclusion that it was the way of houses, they stayed cleaner longer when the fine weather arrived, the bleak winter months, which demanded fire in the grates subjected a house to draughts that drove the dust into every nook and cranny, demanding far more time and scrutiny. She listened at the doorway, he'd gone into the drawing room, she could tell by the slight squeak, many times she'd rubbed her polish cloth over the hinges and Anthony had applied oil yet still the door to that room determined itself to squeak. Davina had always referred to, 'the drawing room', while Anthony called it the sitting room, perhaps that was why it had developed a squeak, a token gesture of annoyance at its change of title.

Celia worked with a will and by half past three she had done the bedrooms and the bathroom. The stairs didn't look too bad they could wait until in the week, he was so quiet down there she felt the tea to be more important. Celia had heard Annie speak of Anthony's sister, Margaret, who lived in Manchester, presumably the family matter he'd mentioned was concerning her or a member of her family.

"Here you are." Celia placed the tray on the occasional table beside where he sat, she was about to add that the sugar jar was empty when he spoke.

"You must have spent time here with Davina Wright on numerous occasions I imagine, through William and the rest of the family. Did Charles visit here too, he seems less attached somehow?"

It was an odd question Celia thought but she answered honestly.

"Charles at times can be unsociable, I don't mean him any disrespect but Mrs.Wright's hospitable nature and wonderful generosity seemed not to render him in any way obliged to return it. For Annie, whose character is so similar to Davina's, it must have been embarrassing, but Davina paid it no heed, I suppose tolerance and wisdom come with age."

"They were very close friends you know, Davina and my mother," he said, "I sometimes wonder what they would make of this place now. It's curious don't you think that the house has never been a family home, no children tucked up in their beds, no young imagination creating bits and bobs with card and glue to adorn the shelves like a really lived in house. Without a young generation the future of this place could only be as it has ever been, staid and mirthless."

"Frank and Ivy, with their two children lived here for a while," said Celia, "surely Annie would have told you about them. Frank was Harold's brother, Frank Boucher and he married Ivy who was Davina's housemaid, although I don't believe that title was ever correct. Davina was very fond of Ivy, so fond that she asked them to live here, to make their home here when they married. Young Harold and Molly came along in due course, Davina was in her element, this big old house had a family, children were tucked up in their beds, the rooms were lived in." Celia hesitated for a moment. "Then came the war, the Great War as they dared to call it. Frank was killed. I'm not sure for how long after that Ivy and the children remained here, I believe she went to her mother's for a while. Eventually she remarried, a lovely man named Reggie, they all live at Skendleby now, quite close to William's brother Freddy. I only know all this because over the years Annie has tried to explain family history to me, I'm sure she would be able to tell you lots about that time, anyway, have your tea while it's hot. If you're alright I shall be off now and I'll see you in the week. If you need help with the garden Mathew would be more than happy to lend a hand, he could come of an evening now it's light or next Saturday afternoon."

"That would be kind, thank you Celia, thank you so much."

Before going home Celia wanted to call at Gregory Street, to see if there had been any further news of George, the letter that arrived last week had caused such joy, relief in measure that pained. Yet along with the joy was the grief, John was not coming home and George had no awareness of his younger brother's death. Annie couldn't bring herself to write a letter to him that delivered misery, just as his words were carefully chosen for their kindness, so too must her's be.

Celia peered through the shop door, one customer who appeared to be paying Annie for her purchases but no one else. It was easier to pop into the shop, she couldn't stay for very long and entering through the back door would suggest she had more time to spend there. The customer left and Celia went in, finding Annie alone made things easier, she would have to mention her concerns over Anthony, his behaviour had been very different today, it troubled her.

Annie was pleased to see Celia, she planned to visit them at Wollaton tomorrow, to see William, his health was more or less back to normal but having not seen him for a fortnight she felt she should. Knowing that Celia tried to find a chance of going to Mapperley on a Sunday she intended asking her if it would be helpful if this weekend, she went instead, to give Celia a break, spending just a little time with William either before or afterwards.

"Have you heard anything more from Italy?" Celia asked as she sat down on the chair by the counter, to take the weight off her feet for a minute.

Annie reached for a small bar of chocolate from the shelf behind her, leaned across the counter and dropped it into Celia's bag, putting a finger to her lips. It still seemed strange, something so small and innocent as a couple of ounces of kiddies chocolate, needing to be handled like contraband.

"We've heard nothing since, but that letter was more than I dared to hope for so I shall be gratefully patient."

When Annie then asked about plans for the following day Celia's reply surprised her and though she wouldn't voice her thoughts to Celia, Annie felt anxious.

"I don't know what it could be, he said a family matter but he wasn't at all himself, it's probably nothing, my silly imagination but I left The Park today feeling uneasy." Celia sighed. "William is being tiresome at present, full of schemes and plans you know what he can be like. I honestly think Mam that your time would be better spent calling on Anthony Hemsley tomorrow, he might confide in you, if he really is troubled. But don't let on I said anything, pretend you just happened to be in the vicinity. I shall go to see mother and Caroline is going with me. Julia is calling for the boys, the colliery band, with what members it has, is going to play at the arboretum, afterwards she'll take them to Castle Road to see their grandma. Although Caroline hasn't actually said, I think she will probably spend a few minutes with Patricia, if she would like me to I'll go with her for a bit of support, it would seem odd if being so close by we didn't visit. I'm not sure if it would be better to see Patricia after we've hob-nobbed with Queen Victoria or before. It's ironic don't you think, dear mother and Patricia Bradshaw both in that place and in many ways alike. 'Run of the mill, ordinary', neither accepting of such simplicity as others do, I don't believe either one of them could bear to be ordinary or run of the mill. Perhaps William should take note of what can be the result when constantly seeking a larger grander, more auspicious life." Celia let out a long despairing breath. "Anyway I'm to meet Caroline at the bus stop at ten past two."

"Enid occupies so much of William," said Annie. "I suppose that's natural enough. His mother couldn't help herself, she seemed never to be truly content, yet I sensed sometimes that a part of her wanted so much to be ordinary, run of the mill, but something inside of her denied it. It's difficult to explain, especially after so long but when she died it felt to me as though fate had cheated her, she was beautiful to look at, why be so blessed, she was intelligent with a husband who loved her and two young sons so why, why was she granted all that only to have it taken away? As William's grown older I'm sure he's asked in his mind that same question. Perhaps he's driven to achieve for his mother's sake, it is an explanation and possibly easier for us to accept than to challenge his unrest.

I shall call at The Park tomorrow, Margaret may be unwell, Anthony and his sister do correspond more often these days I believe and he's mentioned speaking to her over the telephone sometimes. I had noticed that he didn't collect his newspaper yesterday, if he doesn't call this evening then that gives me reason to go there and see if all is well, so he won't suspect you of sending me Celia. Give my love to Caroline and to Gwendolyn of course."

Mrs.Glasson arrived at that moment in need of her rations so Celia gave Annie a grateful smile and hurried off, she should get home, William could be less than tolerant of Emily's liveliness. Mathew would probably have recognised the fact and taken her with him to walk Tilly, even the dog's last tiddles took longer most nights and Celia sensed that it was because Mathew found his dad difficult to talk to so avoided awkward conversation. She would ask Mathew to help Mr.Hemsley with the garden at The Park. It could prove beneficial to them both, young company for

Anthony and a place where Mathew could be occupied for a little while outside of home when his work at the factory was done for the day. Celia felt a rush of tiredness, life seemed to be a continual juggling act and her arms ached from the effort, while her head throbbed from want of respite.

It was the end of shift and Edgar walked from the pit gates feeling so much more of a man. While the circumstances were far from ideal if was a fact nevertheless, Edgar Perry was a father. He had been as good as his word when last month he'd gone to see Valerie with an envelope holding forty pounds to enable her to buy a crib and a pram, nappies too. This evening, after tea, he would scrub up and call on the Oates with the layette, compiled proudly by Joyce.

Tom had been quiet, now and again he would purposefully linger at the pit gates until Edgar appeared, then catch his eye and throw him a hard look. Such behaviour Edgar had no time for and so he'd merely wave his hand and call out 'alright Tom'. The almighty bust up, as Edgar had heard it described, which at the beginning most men had anticipated witnessing, not without a little relish by some, in the event never took place and now, months further along, it was stale news, replaced by other more recent issues and Edgar sensed that Tom Oates, of weariness, had taken the opportunity to bow out of the ring and surrender his title to a younger contender.

Everyday Joyce waited and hoped to see her William. The Stalags were being cleared and the men taken to medical facilities where army doctors were to give them a thorough check. If deemed to be well enough, those long incarcerated individuals would then be put on board ships back to England. According to Bevin's statement, the active troops would be demobbed over a period of time, the actual date depending on a man's age and length of service. For women back home it was almost cruel, they existed in a constant state of nervous tension. Even for Joyce who could believe that William was likely to return at any time soon it was that element of fear, for she did indeed feel afraid, the dread of seeing her husband weakened and frail, thin from years of deprivation. Each day she tried to prepare herself mentally, and then waited, waited, and waited some more.

Joyce was stirring a pan on the stove when Edgar walked in.

"It'll be ready by the time you've washed," she said, understanding of Edgar's eagerness to see the baby, a little girl, his daughter. She wouldn't voice it but Joyce too held a genuine longing to see the infant and hoped that one day before too long , she would be allowed a visit, that Valerie would put the baby in her arms for a moment. "I heard some good news on the way home from the depot." She chatted to Edgar as he poured hot water into the sink and stripped to the waist to wash. "Mr.Mazarelli and his family came home this afternoon, goodness knows how they'll sort out the mess. You won't 'ave heard o' them, they were taken away before you came. Italians yer see, interned some place in London even though they'd lived on Garland Street for donkey's years. It was two daft youths, clever dicks, yer know the sort, they set fire to the Mazarellis' house. The firemen managed to stop the blaze from spreading to the bedrooms but they said the downstairs wer' damaged summat dreadful. They've allus been a real hard workin' family so I reckon they won't rest until they've got their home back to what it was. But it makes me feel ashamed when I think that two little toe rags could consider themselves entitled to destroy the Mazarellis' home because o' some crackpot dictator. What's the sense in our soldiers fightin' to keep these shores from invasion if the likes o' them two hotheads, born an' bred here, God help us, don't think twice about tryin' to burn down a house on Garland Street."

Through the sound of his soapy hands slapping the back of his neck Edgar said. "Perhaps some o' the lads from pit could get together to help, I'll see what I can do."

Edgar stood with the parcel of baby clothes under his arm and knocked at the back door. Peggy appeared to be pleased to see him, a smile spread across her face and this time she opened the door without evidence of alarm. Tom sat in his usual place by the hearth, there was no fire of course, the temperature required none but it was his habit to stare into the grate. Most men chose that same spot at which to cogitate, be it work and money, especially the lack of it, or the political scene and the ways in which they would alter it. Edgar wondered if they ever realised that whatever the subject of their contemplation, however many radical changes they arrived at, all went straight up the chimney without effect. Many were vociferous in calling for change at the top but were themselves too routined to alter the habits of a lifetime. Edgar tried to steer clear of political wrangles, he'd once overheard Hugh Porter say, 'Whoever you vote for, the government always gets in'. It was true of any parliamentary election, once the euphoria of victory died down and human nature imposed its sanction, the working man was again obliged to look up at his superiors, until the crick in his neck induced the weariness that once more drove the hours spent by the hearth, staring into the grate, cogitating on a way of achieving change.

"So you've come to see your kid then Perry," said Tom, "happen I wer' wrong about you. They're upstairs, Valerie's feedin' it, she'll call 'er down in a bit."

His last words were directed at Peggy and Edgar felt an overwhelming urge to respond with, who's she the cat's mother? But Tom was at least peaceable and Peggy's expectation was of nothing other.

When Valerie came down the stairs with the baby in her arms Edgar's heart skipped a beat, he didn't notice the look of resentment on Valerie's face, her moodiness as she passed the small bundle to him, his eyes were solely for the child. He felt strangely tearful and quickly spoke, to hide the closeness of tears.

"Joyce has sent a parcel, she kept it to white apart from a cot blanket an' that's lemon, she said to tell you that now she knows it's a girl she'll try to get some pink wool."

"It cries, it just cries all the time," said Valerie ungraciously.

"All babies cry," said Edgar, "what else can they do, they can't talk can they? Anyway, she's not cryin' now. Have you given her a name yet?"

He found the little face looking up at him, nothing but charming, he blew her a kiss and the baby acknowledged it with a change of expression, the lips seemed almost to mimic his own.

"Mam wants to call her Elizabeth," said Valerie, "it'll be Lizzie Oates, what sort of a name is that?"

"It doesn't have to be Lizzie, she can keep Elizabeth, or Beth if she wanted to shorten it and why do you say Lizzie Oates, if I'm her dad then it should be Perry,

Elizabeth Perry." Edgar was confused, he'd always imagined any child of his to carry his name.

"What difference does it make," said Valerie tetchily, "yer best sort it out wi' mam, I'm not bothered one way or the other."

Valerie's indifference towards the baby Edgar found hard to tolerate and after half an hour or so his better judgment told him he should leave before he spoke out of turn.

"Are yer off then lad?" Said Tom. "Easy when yer can walk away from it isn't it Perry?"

"I know my way back here Tom, if Valerie doesn't want to abide under the same roof as me then I can't alter that but I'm surely entitled to visit my daughter, I won't cause any bother an' when Elizabeth needs somethin' I'll pay for it."

Edgar turned to Peggy. "I'll be off now Mrs.Oates, Elizabeth is a nice name for your granddaughter."

Peggy followed him across the scullery to the back door, opened it and as he passed her to walk through to the yard she whispered. "Thank Joyce for the layette." Her face looked flushed, what mother could not be embarrassed by such pathetic behaviour from a daughter.

He whispered in return. "Early days yet Mrs.Oates, I reckon what comes naturally to most women your Valerie has to learn, but it'll be alright, you'll see." Edgar couldn't help himself, it was entirely without aforethought, he kissed Peggy's cheek.

She closed the door, turned around and for a moment just stood looking at them, Tom, Valerie and the Moses basket on the table. Elizabeth Perry, the child must be registered as Elizabeth Perry, for its own sake.

Annie could not fathom Charles at times, when a customer had come into the shop this morning excitedly telling her that the Mazarellis had come home, right away she thought of the satisfaction Charles would derive from going to Garland Street, to hand to the Mazarellis the money donated by the kindness of folk who wanted to make a gesture of help. People had been appalled by the wicked act of arson directed at a family innocent of all wrongdoing, their only crime, if indeed such a word could be correctly applied, a birthplace somewhere in Italy. To anyone with knowledge of the Mazarellis, the way in which they had been removed from their home of years, to be interned miles away in the blitz ravaged capital, this was the crime.

When Annie had told Charles that she intended calling on Anthony Hemsley, explaining the concern that Celia had expressed and added that she wouldn't stay long as she wanted to go to Wollaton afterwards, to see William, he'd been snide. So often in the past she'd reminded him of the friendship between Anthony's parents and aunt Bella, they had been good and kind, she didn't expect Charles to feel any loyalty but he should at least acknowledge her own need to be mindful of past kindnesses. Out of respect for Alice and Walter Hemsley and fondness for aunt Bella's memory she felt unable to distance herself from Anthony, he was an extension of that friendship and nothing more.

Instead of being glad to call briefly at Garland Street, where he could deliver encouragement to the Mazarellis, Charles rounded on her with. 'Why don't you take the damn money, it was your idea'?

Annie had been dismayed to think that it was necessary to explain to him the fact that Mr.Mazarelli, like any other man, had his pride. Coming from a woman, even though the money represented not charity but the good wishes of friends and neighbours, it would be harder for Mr.Mazarelli to accept, but when handed the envelope by Charles, a fellow man, it would come across as a good turn, simply a, 'welcome home you were missed'. Grudgingly Charles had left the shop just before Annie, taking Samuel with him and casting one last sarcasm her way. 'Don't forget his newspapers, although I don't suppose they'll be the first requirement in his hour of need'.

Annie paused outside the front gates, those familiar railings, the many mature shrubs and the way the old house seemed to hide behind them, like a shy child peeping over the back of an arm chair, just the eyes showing and a mop of hair. The roof held a coating of moss at which the rooks and crows tugged industriously to obtain lining material for their nests.

Annie remembered vividly the first time she'd come here with Saul, how curiously fate had bound her to this place but there was no time for reminiscing. Opening the gate and walking up the path to the side door she felt anxious, instinctively she sensed sadness within. If it was as she feared then what help she could offer was limited but she could spend a little time with him, no one would be able to cure Anthony's pain but if only for a few minutes, she could share it. Charles, if aware would likely feel some understanding but Donald was Anthony's secret. At least going to see William should go some way towards placating Charles, an atmosphere around the tea table was the last thing Laura needed and even Ted was sensitive to stress since news of John. In fact Ted had matured noticeably, along with his literacy skills. It was a source of pleasure for Annie, seeing him advance and Laura took pride in this young man's progress.

Annie hesitated before ringing the bell. When Celia had described Anthony's manner and voiced her concern, it had been Donald who first entered Annie's mind. She had not told Anthony about John, it hurt so much to speak of the telegram and she supposed that subconsciously she'd been reluctant to show the reality of loss to Anthony whilst he had a son serving abroad still.

She was about to try the latch when she heard sounds coming from the back garden. She walked quickly to the corner, Anthony appeared to be cutting back the laurel hedge with not the best of care, rather he attacked it, the section he'd done looked forlorn. Annie called out, at first he didn't hear, the second time caused him to stop and turn around. His face said it all, looking as he did on the outside could only come from intense pain on the inside. She recognised it, felt it herself again, that cramp somewhere in the heart, it knotted every artery and vein, twisting, contorting until no part of the body functioned as it should, especially the mind. She took his arm and led him to the old bench.

"Sit a moment or two Anthony," she said.

He raised no objection and sank onto it almost gratefully.

"Celia sent you didn't she?"

Annie smiled, dear Celia's attempt at being discreetly concerned hadn't a hope of success.

"I am supposed to tell you that I just happened to be in the area. Celia was worried about you. When did you hear?"

"For months Annie I have thanked God that Donald lived, telegrams bringing grief, week on week to so many, and still I heard nothing untoward, my thanks to The Almighty were regular and constant. I trusted his mother to tell me if Donald's wife received the very worst news. Why did she wait for so long to let me know? Donald was killed six months ago, I've been believing and giving thanks when all that time he was already dead. He's gone Annie and I never knew him, my son, and he didn't know I existed, his father. This house was for him, so one day he would know that he mattered to me, what use any of it now?"

Annie swallowed hard. "I am so sorry Anthony, words don't comfort, in fact they can do the very opposite. When Donald's mother learned of his death she would have become inert, unable to move or speak and as the hours and days went on she would have wrapped herself about in a silence, which to others might seem cold and unnatural but to talk of his death, to physically tell anyone that he'd been killed drove the hurt and intensified the pain until the heart near stopped. I think that is why she has only now found the strength to either write about it or speak of it. You must understand, all her energies would be exhausted through thinking about it, day and night without interlude."

Annie hesitated for a moment, then continued, Anthony made no interruption.

"I didn't tell you either, six weeks ago the telegram came, John had been killed. It happened towards the end of March. Customers to the shop are unaware, you see neither Charles nor myself could bear the well meaning but unending condolences, each one driving the hurt. Of course, in time they will come to know, but not yet, we've not sufficient strength as yet."

Anthony rested his hand on her arm, tears, trying not to be seen, nevertheless slipped down his cheek. He uttered not a word. They sat quietly for several minutes, not an awkward silence but a necessary one, a moment in time free of challenge, each other's emotion entirely understood. Annie was the first to speak.

“You told me that Donald had a daughter, his mother didn’t wish for you to make yourself known to Donald and you agreed to that but she cannot keep you from Donald’s child, you are at liberty to recognise your own granddaughter. This house is a kindly place, it has doubtless witnessed all manner of tribulation, like all others, but still it has granted comfort. What you were to do for your son you may instead do for your grandchild but without waiting for your own death before allowing the young girl to be aware. That is a small mercy denied to Charles and me, John was lost before fathering a child. Donald lives on within his daughter, seize upon that blessing Anthony.”

The sound of voices approaching the side door confirmed the Bevin boys to be home.

“They’ve been to The Meadows, cricket I believe,” said Anthony.

Annie recalled the passage from George’s letter and she thought aloud.

“Men in opposition, facing one another in pureness of white.”

“Yes,” said Anthony, “such a happening would seem impossible now. What do you suppose a little girl would think of this latent granddad?”

“A child’s mind is ever receptive Anthony and their hope knows no bounds, all you require is courage and possibly a little more tolerance of the laurel, allow it to keep a bit more of its foliage if you will, from where we are sitting it appears to have laid bare its soul.”

Celia stepped outside the hospital door and took a deep breath.

“It always feels airless in there,” she said, “perhaps that’s why Maud takes off her clothes. I wonder who took the tulips to mother, it might have been Mrs.Cheetham, cousin Robert’s wife or even Mrs.Brewer. She’s back in Nottingham, I had a letter from her, she’s renting rooms at Arnold. It was never her intention to stay at her brother’s for too long but I thought she would seek another housekeeping position and live in, like she did with mother. Anyway, she’s obviously had enough of that sort of thing as in her letter she says she’s stringing pearls for Packhams, the jewellers and minding a four year old boy while his mother does jury service. It sounds to me like a very fraught situation, I can only assume that the two activities don't overlap."

They began to walk to the bus stop. "William came to see me yesterday afternoon," said Caroline.

Celia stopped walking and stood quite still in the middle of the pavement, she looked dismayed and from her expression Caroline knew that he'd not told Celia of his visit.

"William didn't mention to you that he'd called to see me?"

"No, he's not said a word, it must have been while I was at Anthony Hemsley's, I can't imagine it was merely to pass the time of day, what did he want?"

Caroline chuckled, "You know him well. He told me that he wants to buy my share of Moreleigh."

Celia interrupted. "Oh no, I am so sorry Caroline, I honestly thought it was just another of his silly notions that would fade and be replaced with yet another scheme he deemed more lucrative. He presumes far too much, I swallow his thoughtlessness for the sake of Mathew and Emily but I won't allow you to be presumed upon. If I'd known it was William's intention to call on you I'd have apologised to Mr.Hemsley and gone with him so I could correct him if he persisted in suggesting a difference in the value of our interests in Moreleigh. I won't have it, I told Nigel Caffin that I wouldn't hear of such a thing."

Caroline thread her arm through Celia's and they began to walk along again.

"Please let him be," she said, "he's correct in maintaining that there should be a greater value attached to your share, Gwendolyn's house is a much larger property. Promise me you'll not argue with William over this. When father died his instructions created so much stress for mother and put distance between us as a family. 'Money and property', if I wrote it as a mathematical question the word avarice would follow the equals sign.

Edmund lost his life through the battle to restore peace to the world. What would that salutary fact now make us if we allowed our families to be denied peace of mind through petty differences, selfish pursuit of money and material goods. I don't want that, not just for our sakes but for my boys, for Mathew and Emily too, because believe me it touches everyone, young and old alike. We are happy living where we do and fortunate to have still a share in Moreleigh, it is more than enough. No amount of wealth could bring back Edmund. Please you will promise me, let William be."

Celia was close to tears, how could William be so selfish, not to mention devious, going to Caroline's while she was working at The Park and then not telling her that he'd voiced his miserable intention to Caroline, but she gave her word, nodded her head and whispered.

"I promise."

They walked on for several minutes before Celia said. "I know William inherited a sum of money from Davina Wright but I didn't imagine it to be anywhere near enough to buy your share of the house. I never ask him about finances, I'd be afraid to. William has always been of the old school that considers a woman to be too frivolous to be trusted with even a hint of what might be deposited with the bank. Annie would know, she was an executor of the will but it wouldn't be fair of me to ask her. William can be so sullen and if he thought she'd been talking to me about his affairs then I'm sure he would make a scene. God knows, Annie has enough upset as it is.

Everyone else grieves for John, yet William ploughs on, nothing must get in his way, no one is allowed to hinder his progress. I'm surprised he doesn't claim to have personally despatched Hitler!"

"Now that is a little harsh," said Caroline, squeezing Celia's arm. "The war is almost over, even in Asia the Allies are winning. Mother told me about George's letter, Annie let her read it, she cried of course, mother has had so much to make her cry over the years, this time however they were happy tears.

Look, the bus is coming. Hurry up, we'll try to get a seat upstairs, I like to look at the pigeons on their nests, there are four on the roof of the post office."

They ran the next ten yards or so, Celia's feet empowered by a thought both amusing and satisfying. How disgruntled William would be if he knew that Caroline found pigeons far more interesting, more worthy of her attention, than his own grandiose schemes.

CHAPTER TWENTY ONE

Late June.

"Well ladies, if this don't turn a few a few heads on the bus then I'll be a monkey's uncle."

Henry appeared at the bottom of the stairs dressed in his demob suit.

"The full Monty this is aunty Jean, I've even got a spare pair o' trousers for when these wear through on the arse from my sittin' down so long."

Gertie looked at Jean and sighed. The doctor had declared Henry fit to perform light tasks, office work possibly. Only until his wounds, which were now healed, had taken time to regain strength, especially those having undergone the procedure carried out by the surgeon to remove a section of intestine. Patience would be rewarded if Henry accepted that for a while he needed an occupation not physically taxing.

So today he was off to an interview for the job of 'teller' at Barclays Bank. His numeracy skills had always been good, he'd never been in trouble with the law and even though it wouldn't have been his choice of employment under normal circumstances, if offered the job Henry Wainwright would commit himself to the post with all integrity.

He'd bemoaned to Gertie, 'if I don't find something to do Mam I shall go mad'. At no time before had he possessed a suit, matching jacket, waistcoat and trousers. As yet few men appeared on the streets in their demob attire, most were still abroad, apart from those like Henry, recovering from their wounding, and others who before hostilities worked in construction and civil engineering. With the urgent need of rebuilding blitzed areas, the repair of roads, sewers, water mains, all the devastated utilities, any men previously engaged in this type of work were being brought back to England ahead of Mr.Bevin's demob scheme and sent immediately to a job.

The contract to produce all the demob suits had gone to Montague Burton. It hadn't taken very long for the recipients of these brand new three piece suits to come up with an affectionate acronym. While appreciative of the gesture, it remained a fact that all the suits were identical, when wearing them all men would look the same. 'The full Monty', was fast becoming a reference to their tailored image, as common and familiar to those men now in possession of it as the traditional 'three piece suit' they'd been awarded at birth!

"What do yer think Mam, good enough for the bank?" Henry stood erect and winked roguishly at his aunty Jean.

"You'll do," said Gertie. "If yer call in to see Myra after, then tell her if they're goin' to Edna's for their dinner on Sunday, to come here for tea."

Henry laughed, "Our Jack never 'ad it so good, women fussin' over him, a wife, two mams an' even Miss Pennifold. 'E told me that Myra waves him off to work of a mornin' from the back door an' Miss Pennifold watches from her front room window to wave to 'im as he goes by an' Jack the soft beggar, blows them both a kiss."

"Good luck Henry, I think you look very smart."

"Thank you Aunty Jean." He planted a kiss on her cheek, hugged his mam, held up his thumb to reassure them of his intent and went out through the door whistling a tune.

"Are you sure he doesn't mind my staying here?" Asked Jean.

"For the umpteenth time, Henry is glad to be alive," said Gertie with a hint of exasperation. It was awful hard for him, comin' home to this house an' his dad gone. With Jack married, an' livin' somewhere else, just him an' me'd feel lost, so stop your frettin' afore I lose patience. Nora's agreed to take Annie's Bevin boy so she'll have company. George should be home next month, Samuel bless his heart, can barely wait. I wonder if that young school teacher might take a shine to George, the poor lass lost John an' I've heard Annie say what good pals Samuel an' Laura have become. Stranger things have happened, look at you, all them years ago when you thought Randall would be a good match for Nora, low an' behold it wer' you he fell for."

A smile spread slowly across Jean's face. "I don't rightly know which of us fell first," she said, "I do know I should be grateful to Nora, she allowed fate to favour me didn't she? Who could tell, we can only hope that Laura finds happiness with someone and George too but whether it will be with each other I certainly wouldn't want to predict. So much has happened, nothing's the same anymore." Jean's voice tailed off to a whisper and sensing sadness Gertie intervened.

"Now don't you go all maudlin on me Jean or you'll set me off an'all. Fetch your jacket, we'll go to see Mavis, I said we'd help her pull their dresser away from the wall to clean behind it, she didn't want to ask Eddie, by the time he gets home of an evening he's too tired to be bothered. Him an' Jack Haynes are determined to keep that pit runnin' smooth. Mrs.Stanford took Hugh Porter's advice an' now Jack's the manager officially he's not goin' to allow any part o' that place to fail Mrs.Bradshaw's inspection when she comes back on the scene. Apparently she's been allowed home for a couple o' weekends, to see how her nerves cope an' they're goin' to extend the periods through the course o' next month, if all goes well she'll be discharged. I suppose you've got to hope so for her mother's sake. I only know all this because Hilda told me, I bumped into her an' Rosemary at the arboretum the other day. I thought she seemed a bit down, worryin' about all the responsibility Jack's taken on I shouldn't wonder. I know what it's like, all the years Steve worked at pit he couldn't just do his shift an' forget about it 'til next day. There were three parties in our marriage, him, me an' the pit, an' lookin' back, it wer' pit that 'ad the most of him. I can't help feelin' sorry for Hilda, Jack is a good husband, so was Steve, that's the trouble, decent at home an' at work an'all. We women, the wives, love 'em for it, while the pit takes 'em for granted. But if we as much as called that place black they'd swear it wer' white. Loyalty, I'm beggared if I ever understood a loyalty that binds a man to a filthy hole in the ground an' I'd bet poor Hilda don't neither."

Henry stepped off the bus feeling confident, he was dressed the part and in his mind he'd gone through the likely questions and prepared considered answers.

He'd walked several yards along Parliament Street when an elderly woman, coming towards him from the opposite direction, raised her walking stick and called out like she hailed an approaching coal barge.

"Hey, you."

For her years she possessed still a voice capable of travelling a distance and commanding attention. Henry turned his head to look back, surely there must be someone else in the woman's sights, but apart from two other women, walking together, ten or twelve yards behind him, there was no one.

"You, I'm talkin' to you," she said, with enough authority to drill an entire regiment. By now they stood at the same spot. "It's all fine an' dandy you walkin' about askin' folk who they're goin' to vote for, you'll likely want my opinion today, makin' out it matters to yer but if it wer' that important why did I have to wait just short o' me three score year an' ten afore they'd condescend to give me the vote, I'll be eighty seven come September, if I live that long. Well yer can tell your man, whichever one 'e is, that Evelyn Scrimshaw's lived long an' seen a lot. For the last six years we've had war an' hunger, for twenty years afore that we struggled to recover from the first lot o' war an' hunger an' though we wern't at war through them twenty years, we knew nowt but strife an' hunger for all o' them an'all. If they can't see that bringin' men back to nothin' better than they knew afore they left won't do, then it's for the likes o' me to say it. Them as aren't dead need work an' a decent life, a medal to pin on their chest they can neither eat nor drink.

Years o' struggle an' war, if they think ten minutes o' glory is all our lads deserve then we shot the wrong devils. So you in your fancy suit can report back to your fella that Evelyn Scrimshaw won't be swayed by fancy words that amount to no more than a dab o' rouge on a pale face, the country's ashen an' it's their job to bring the colour back but coverin' up the pallor wi' make up's no good, it needs nourishment, recovery from the belly out, an' I'm not talkin' about rationin', I'm talkin' about work, a man's right to it, honest labour wi' honest pay, his bread an' butter. Not queuing half way down the street from labour exchange door while his soul sits on a shelf in the pawn shop. I'm surprised you haven't shoved a leaflet in me face, perhaps you've run out of 'em, but when they print the next one it should say in big letters, 'this time we'll make a damn sight better job of it'. Uhm."

She walked off leaving Henry full of admiration. At first he'd though the old woman tuppence short of a shilling but soon realised that his attire suggested he was one of the many enthusiastic folk making the most of the next few days to canvas hard before election day on July 5th. What spirit! Eighty seven years of age and he'd wager, afraid of nothing. Rather than correct her mistake and tell her that in fact he was wearing his demob suit to attend a job interview, he'd watched her progress along the pavement and said quietly 'God bless you Evelyn Scrimshaw'.

As he walked towards the bank Henry determined himself to take a leaf out of Evelyn's book, to be direct, to take no nonsense, swallow no whitewash. She was right and he would vote only for the man who vowed to do a damn sight better.

Henry waited until the young woman was free then walked up to the counter.

"I've an interview here at half past ten with Mr.Drummond, Henry Wainwright's my name."

Standing where he was the need of a teller became obvious, the second woman was heavily pregnant.

"I'll show you to his office Mr.Wainwright." She turned to her colleague, "won't be a minute Shirley."

She led him through a side door and up a flight of stairs, stopped by a heavily panelled door with a small brass plate marked 'manager' and knocked twice with her knuckles.

"Come in."

"Mr.Wainwright is here Sir." She beckoned Henry forward with her eyes and closed the door quietly the second he'd passed through. He could hear her hurried tread as she returned to the pregnant Shirley.

Alec Drummond was on his feet the other side of an impressive desk extending his arm. They shook hands.

"T-t-take a seat Mr.Wainwright."

"Thank you Sir," said Henry, settling himself on the chair at his side of the desk.

The questions in themselves were more or less as Henry had anticipated but he'd not been prepared for the poor man's unfortunate stammer, at times so severe Henry found himself offering up the words, which Mr.Drummond so painfully sought, until the process struck Henry as a formality too far. So when Mr.Drummond said.

"T-tell me w-what w-was your p-previous experience?"

Henry decided that his new suit and gentlemanly manner was all well and good but this situation needed common sense and a bit of Evelyn Scrimshaw.

Mr.Drummond Sir, I can count, add, subtract an' multiply, I've never been dishonest an' I'm a good timekeeper. When I left school I went to work at the scrapyard because that's all there was, now that might sound to you like a far cry from the job as teller at this bank. But you'll have heard the old adage, 'where there's muck there's money'. Well I can assure you Mr.Drummond that at Abel's yard there's always been plenty o' muck an' it's turned into money by the same principle this bank an' every other business employs, interest, commission, call it what you will but the result is profit. Honestly gained, fair dues. Now between the scrapyard an' my current attempt at becoming a teller there were experiences........." Henry paused and took deep breaths. "Experiences Sir, which I sincerely hope this bank never needs the like of."

Henry's hands trembled in his lap as his eyes fixed on the cold grey pewter ink well on the desk in front of him, reminding him of steely gun metal trained across a divide. Neither spoke for several seconds, then Alec Drummond said.

"I recognise the d-demob suit Henry, y-your exp-perience at the scrapyard will b-be more than s-sufficent. I b-believe this b-bank needs your exp-pertise." He smiled, stood and again extended his arm, the two men clasped hands firmly.

"Thank you Mr.Drummond Sir. At my last place of work we had an expression that got used a lot. 'Give me tomorrow's hellfire, I'm done with today's'. You see if we could say that word 'tomorrow', then we still had a chance."

"Tomorrow's hellfire." He uttered only those two words but Alec Drummond delivered them with not a hint of impediment.

Henry found his own way downstairs to the floor of the bank, he waved politely at the young woman teller as he crossed to the front door, she responded with a warm smile, having already made a mental note of his name. Henry Wainwright, he would make an acceptable replacement for Shirley, was the thought widening her smile as she watched the young man disappear into the street, not bad, not bad at all!

Joyce could not still the butterflies inside her, the letter had said that William's ship would dock at Southampton around mid morning. She'd travelled down by train overnight and found a cafe close to the port for a cup of tea, where she'd sat for as long as she'd felt it proper given that she'd not ordered toast, she couldn't eat anything, nerves had taken over her stomach completely.

The very first thing she did when the letter arrived was to find Tommy. The envelope had been waiting for her, on the mat just inside the front door, when she'd got in from work five days ago.

Excitement, panic, fear, elation all consumed Joyce when she'd read its content, but with no mam or dad to run and tell, it was to her eldest brother Tommy that Joyce hurried.

Rosie had been giving Beryl a bath, the child sat in the water along with her dolly, which had been thoroughly washed in readiness for bed. The sight drove an ache in Joyce, it was just a little girl in a bath tub but emotion ran high and Joyce had felt deprived. For so long separated from her husband, rendered barren by a spiteful fate that wanted her waywardness punished and denied any means of making amends, she'd gazed at Rosie's domestic scene and wanted the same. Tommy's sensitivity had enabled him to recognise his sister's anxiety, he'd read the letter, hugged her and said, 'I'll go with you to the station and see you off, don't worry Joyce, William's coming home and there's nowhere else on earth he'd rather be or anyone else he'd want to be with except you'.

Now Joyce made her way to the dock, a few dabs of powder over her nose and cheeks and a light touch of lipstick, which she'd ordered her shaky fingers to apply before the mirror in the public conveniences, had been her attempt at bolstering confidence. The brooch William had given her on their first wedding anniversary she'd pinned to her jacket. Was she the only trembling wreck of a woman or did others feel that same way?

People were assembled, three, four deep right along the dock side, all ages, small children on the shoulders of men, teenage girls, youths, and the women whose faces held a look of disbelief at the grey hulk of ship, growing ever larger as its Captain brought her into the approaches. Officials walked the throng, keeping folk a safe distance from the edge and out of the way.

Joyce hung back, her sense told her it would be a little while yet before the vessel was alongside and the men disembarked in some kind of orderly fashion. It was warm, the sun had risen sufficiently to send its rays over the top of the lower buildings, picking out the floral patterned frocks, that had been carefully stored in drawers between tissue paper and a fiercely guarded bar of scented soap, to await this day.

A girl of about twelve stood a yard or so in front of Joyce, a silvery alice band holding back from her eyes her pretty brunette hair, each time she turned her head to say something to her mother, who stood beside her, the sun caught it and a bright light flashed on, and then off when her eyes returned to the front, as though it sent a coded message along the dock and out over the water. 'I'm here dad and so is mam'.

Last night, when Tommy saw her onto the train, he'd kissed her forehead and under the lights of the station platform she'd noticed for the first time how much he resembled their father. Now Joyce could understand why their mother aged so, not granted to Edith Spooner was a moment like this, not even a quiet place in the cemetery to visit with flowers. William was almost home and though her stomach ached from emptiness and her head from tiredness, Joyce's heart made ready, as best it could, for more relief and happiness than she deserved. She whispered into the air, "I'm sorry Mam, I love you."

At that very instant the ship sounded its hooter. Joyce sniffled up a trace of wateriness and laughed. It was as if her mother's hearing had been restored and she'd acknowledged her daughter's words from on high.

The next few minutes seemed to pass in a daze, activity, noise, a lot of noise yet Joyce felt strangely apart from it. People had begun to call out names, to wave. She moved forward, the mother and daughter had now disappeared into the crowd. Men, soldiers, stood about the deck, at the rail, all gazing down at the scene below them, some jubilant, animated, waving and shouting, others like Joyce, living these moments through a haze of emotion, nervous, yet overcome with relief, impatient, yet unsure of how they would express themselves when hearts finally united.

Joyce now trained her eyes on the faces of the men, a line of khaki moving slowly along the deck, undulating as tall, short, tall, short made for the gangplank, caterpillar like, the lower legs visible through the rails, synchronised, propelling all forward. Now some were on the ground where they became instantly fused with a loved one, arms locked, hundreds of people around about them but oblivious to everything but each other. Some of the younger children were overawed and cried. Even Joyce struggled to remain calm as the faces kept moving along and still no William.

At last, it was him, he was talking with another man, then he looked out over the side, Joyce waved her hanky, it caught his eye and his face broke to a smile, within seconds the man beside him must have spotted someone too as his arm went up to wave and Joyce could read his lips when he called out 'Mam', over and over.

Finally William stood before her, his kitbag slipped from his shoulder to the ground at their feet. All sound was gone, silenced, in one another's embrace the world stood still, nothing but their muffled heartbeats, which with just one skip, found identical rhythm, marching together in perfect step to that place called home.

The train was packed even though they'd put on extra carriages. Joyce and William had found seats in a compartment, which was immediately filled by two families, a boy of no more than nine years squeezed into the seat between Joyce and his mam while the dad sat opposite with a little girl of about four on his knee. The other couple sat to his side, the mother trying to reassure a confused young boy who seemed worried by the close company of the man, his father, whom he barely knew. Heads peered in through the sliding door continually as other folk made their way along the train in search of a seat, the sound of booted feet drumming on the floorboards, women's voices expressing annoyance and dismay at the crowding. While the soldiers preferred seemingly to remain mute, too weary to enter the fray and far too grateful to be fighting over a seat, when that seat was on a British train over an English track under a free man's sky. The guard checked his watch and blew his whistle, the last two or three carriage doors slammed shut and the engine rolled forward. For men inside it was a motion that stirred the senses, moving, advancing, gathering pace, out from the tunnel like gloom of the station and into the open, smoke from the engine's stack passing by the windows, purpose, intent, fixing the mind, faster, faster, forward ever forward to the other side, but this time it led them to home. Trying to make themselves believe its truth demanded all of their hope, every ounce of their strength and what faith they had left in their reserves, for the latter had been sourced almost to exhaustion. Their quietness sat alongside the women's tiredness and the children either engaged with the passing landscape or succumbed to the need of sleep.

The ticket collector did his round but with a feeling of guilt at intruding on the stillness within the compartments, the invasion of privacy and he moved reverently from one to the next as though he received the offering at a church service.

The sun too seemed wearied by the morning's events and now disappeared into clouds that hastened to catch it before it fell to earth, the sun firmly in their grasp the clouds whisked it away leaving behind an empty grey expanse.

Lulled by the constant motion of the train Joyce's eyelids could resist no longer, her head fell onto William's shoulder and she slept. Staring into the glass of the window at his other shoulder, William briefly caught the reflection of his own face between roofs and chimneys, open land and fleeting glimpses here and there of bomb damage, as the train careered past to meet its scheduled stops on time.

It was when they reached Devizes that Joyce awoke, she'd been vaguely aware when some passengers got off at Salisbury but with one ear cushioned by William's collar she'd not roused herself but slipped back into cat nap semi consciousness.

It was the change of occupants to the compartment in which they sat that brought Joyce back out of her sleepiness to observe their new travelling companions, two men, probably in their late fifties, smartly dressed, one had charge of a shoulder satchel. They sat opposite William and Joyce, offered a polite smile and settled themselves comfortably, unfastening the buttons on their jackets and loosening just a little their ties.

Again the guard blew his whistle and the doors slammed shut. The train gathered speed and after about ten minutes one man looked across at William and spoke.

"Only six days to go, I'm sure a man like you, coming back from the war will be eager to cast his vote. Would you mind telling us which party you'll likely be supporting and the policies that have persuaded your thinking?"

The billboards in the towns and cities for weeks had displayed posters representing the three main parties and although Joyce couldn't fail to be aware of the impending general election, as more than one enthusiastic candidate had knocked on her door promising wonders he would perform in her name, she'd nevertheless felt little interest. These two besuited men were apparently engaged in the parliamentary process of canvassing votes, seeking opinions to gratefully embrace or endeavour to convert as the case might be.

William felt little patience for the situation but responded courteously.

"Sir, I imagine it's the uniform that suggests to you that I might be harbouring an opinion on a future government and who should best lead it. Where I've been until recently, to have any opinion was frowned upon, perhaps that's why I'm reluctant still to voice the views of 'a man like me' as you put it. For men waiting to be demobbed it will prove difficult to empty their minds of what has gone before and holding an election now will feel to them premature and insensitive when so many are forever denied a voice, an opinion. While others will determine themselves to speak in volume for those dead, because they're no longer here to speak for themselves, listening is the key, men have always been more ready to shout than to listen. For my part gentlemen, your approach and your question, albeit polite, would have counted for so much more had you been able to ask it in Stalag 12. Here now on this train I am indifferent."

The two men fell silent and Joyce breathed a sigh of relief when they got off at Swindon. Less tired and now more at ease she chatted to William about family, her work, Edgar and the baby. In her letters she'd tried to keep him up to date with events back home but to be in his company enabled her to fill in the gaps, simple things relating to his nephews and nieces, the fact that Raleigh, Bonhams, many of the factories had returned to peacetime production. William listened and responded easily. She asked if the man from Ilkeston who'd been at the camp with him was on his way home as well. William's reply was brief but charged with deep feeling.

"Yes, Roley made it, he bloody well made it."

When the train pulled in at Derby where they must change William was in haste to get out and onto the platform, he scanned it with his eyes, up and down, then spotted him.

"Come on Joyce, hurry up before he goes."

William ran to where a man stood with two women, having just alighted from a carriage to the rear of the train. Joyce hurried to catch up.

"Meet my mate William," said Roley Cheeseman enthusiastically. "This is Evie Will' an' me Mam."

William took their hands in turn.

"Pleased, so very pleased to meet you both," he said, then turning to Joyce, "this is my dear wife Joyce."

The introductions were warm and happy but the train to Nottingham would be soon and they couldn't delay.

William and Roley embraced with a passion that brought tears to the eyes of the women, it was a passion that bore pain, one another's pain, suffered selflessly for so long. Neither spoke, not even to say goodbye, for each would abide in the other's heart forever.

It began to rain and darkness advanced quickly, it was almost a quarter to nine. Platform 5, Joyce and William needed to catch the Nottingham train at platform 5. Now the sound of heavy rain clattered above their heads on the canopy and where a gutter was blocked by some debris the water started to cascade to the ground, splattering about the base of a lamp post, tormenting a spent matchstick which could do no other than dance to the rain god's order. Pigeons took shelter in the rafters, lowering their heads as the drumming sound of the cloudburst intensified.

It lasted for six or seven minutes then stopped abruptly. Only four other people boarded the Nottingham train, the rain had released different smells and damp smokiness clung to clothing. Even the train, having pulled into the station through the deluge seemed to protest the assault, as the pistons drove the wheels slowly forward it began to shudder along its length, like a dog shaking itself free of the wet.

Joyce could feel dampness at her feet, splashes of rainwater had found a way inside her shoes but this was the last bit of the journey.

"I'm glad Mr.Cheeseman is back with his family," she said, "he was beside you on the boat when you waved and I could tell that 'e'd spotted someone in the crowd. They'll soon be home at Ilkeston."

William sighed. "Terrible things have happened Joyce and most of the world is ignorant of them. Those who canvas for votes as though we can all move along, assured of greater things, would choke on their promises if they knew the arf of it. I've done me years an' I shan't sign up for more, happen our Jack or Raymond can find me a job. I've only ever known the army, apart from odd jobbin' when I left school 'til I wer' old enough to apply. What do yer reckon civvie street might find for 'a man like me'. Again he made reference to the remark made by the pollster who had boarded the train at Devises.

Joyce squeezed his arm. "We don't need to think about any of that yet, I've got a week off work, so we can please ourselves."

It was after 10o/clock when they reached the back door of home, Joyce was about to lift the latch when she hesitated and took a step back.

"No, you open it Will', open your own back door and reclaim within."

By now he was almost too tired to bother but he did as Joyce bid him. It was so quiet inside the house, he'd expected the young Edgar Perry to rush forward and from a misguided sense of obligation, shake his hand until fragile bones gave way under youthful patriotism. Joyce too was surprised by the stillness, but a note lay on the table, the salt pot placed at one corner.

'I'm having an early night Joyce, I shall sleep soundly knowing that tomorrow I shall meet Mr.Haynes at last. Goodnight to both, Edgar'.

She handed the note to William. "Bless him," was all that she said.

William read the words and recognised the thoughtfulness behind them, perhaps Edgar Perry possessed greater insight than he'd given him credit for.

William would have preferred to come home to just his wife but he was sensible enough to appreciate the fact that war invaded more than just territories, back doors, front doors, could do nothing to halt its advance. Edgar was also a tool of government, used more than employed, dispensable, replaceable, valued most when his vote counted and at twenty one, ripe for the gathering. Yes, thought William, I look forward to meeting you too Edgar lad.

"I've a pan o' stew, it won't take me long to hot it up, I managed to get an oxtail from Cheetham's an' when I told 'em you were comin' home they threw in a bit of ox cheek an' sent their best, said I must feel proud."

Joyce lit the gas as she chatted. So, Cheetham's was the handshake to crush fragile bones. William kissed his wife's cheek.

"Not much for me love I need me bed more than I need food. I'm poppin' out to the privy for a minute, won't be long."

William sat in the lavatory listening to the distant sounds of the city, old familiar sounds. He scuffed his boots over the cobbles, pictured his mam, his dad, Victor, images to ease the hurt inside him, and he shed tears. While Cheetham's ox cheek yielded to the gas flame, Sergeant Haynes, or 'a man like him', cried for the last time. It was over, tomorrow would begin anew, without a uniform to define him.

Even though faith was worn thin he sent a thank you to the Almighty from that most humble spot at which he sat, it was for Roley, not for himself, he knew that at Ilkeston, before this night was out, Roley would do the same, each would thank God for sparing the other.

No besuited official, canvassing for votes, could ever understand how insignificant was their pursuit. Too much had happened of which they were ignorant and six days gave nowhere near enough time to adequately listen, or to comprehend. William rubbed the palms of his hands over his knees and forced himself to stand up. Outside in the yard, noise from squabbling cats and the sound of a neighbour, intent on getting rid of them. The splash as the contents of a bucket of water more than likely missing the animals, struck the dividing wall. William smiled, at least some things never changed!

CHAPTER TWENTY TWO

Late July.

"Right then Mrs.Dodds, I don't need to drill today, I'll explain but let's have you sitting upright."

Mr.Fordyce adjusted the chair while the dental nurse smiled at Edna and offered a tissue. It struck Edna as unusual, it had never happened before but she wiped her lips.

"Ta," she said, feeling slightly unsettled by the nurse's expression, for a moment unsure whether she'd been expected to use it on her mouth or to wipe her eyes. If they were about to tell her that all her teeth needed to come out and she must wear dentures then one flimsy bit of tissue would be of no use, Edna would want a proper hanky to weep into and a large gents' at that.

She'd always dreaded false teeth. Spectacles, hearing aid, walking stick, any of these she could accept graciously but the thought of lying in bed beside her Billy with shrinking gums, while in a pot on the bedside cabinet a set of dentures lurked in a bit o' bicarb' was the stuff of nightmares.

Her mouth had been getting progressively more uncomfortable, she had looked into the mirror for ulcers but couldn't identify any one spot that might account for the soreness and it felt different somehow to the ache when a tooth needed to be drilled and filled. Billy had told her to go to the dentist and get whatever it was sorted out.

'It could be an abscess developin' or your tongue might 'ave rattled somethin' loose', was how he put it.

"I think the problem is not one that a dentist could relieve Mrs.Dodds," said Fordyce. "I am going to write a letter to the hospital requesting an appointment with Mr.Ansell, the consultant. Your soreness could be caused by the inflammation at one side of your tongue, don't be alarmed, I simply want them to check your mouth at the hospital. I am confident that none of your teeth have decay, so no dentures for you

Mrs.Dodds. At your last visit you told me that you would rather scrub the council house steps from top to bottom every day 'til the cows came home than have to wear false teeth. It stuck in my mind and since that day I've not walked across slab square and the council house without thinking about it. The hospital will send you an appointment, which you must attend."

His smile appeared more generous than usual and the nurse opened the door for Edna with the most cheery, "Take care Mrs.Dodds."

Glad to be outside in the fresh air Edna circled the inside of her mouth with her tongue, inflammation! She could just imagine what Billy would have to say if she told him that her tongue had inflammation. Ah well, Mr.Ansell would likely deliberate on the matter, Edna took some satisfaction from the thought of sticking her tongue out and all entirely polite.

She made her way back to the bus stop, convincing herself as she walked along that by the time a hospital appointment came in the post the soreness in her mouth would be gone and Mr.Ansell's time could be saved for someone more needful of it.

The usual mix of people were about the city centre, women on errands, a few older men, a group of four nuns, hurrying towards the convent building, their black frocks following them on, rippling in the draught their fleet steps created, as though sweeping from the ground all trace of man's iniquity and taking it away with them to that place where it might seek grace.

Edna paid little attention, all were sights familiar to her but the sound of a newspaper vendor, at this hour, it was only four o'clock? The man was shouting out with more animation in his voice than was normal, she drew closer.

"Read all about it, special issue, Atlee takes it, Churchill defeated, read all about it."

The election had taken place three weeks ago but because so many men were still abroad no result could be declared until all the votes had been gathered and counted.

A man had stopped to buy a paper, Edna thought she was seeing things, could it be? Then he turned around, it was, it really was George Boucher. His eyes were glancing the headlines of the newspaper, Edna ran, calling out his name, he looked up, immediately tucked the newspaper into his pocket and hurried towards her.

"Hello Edna, I've missed you, Billy, everyone, now here you are, first to welcome me back."

Edna sniffled, half laughing, half crying. "You're the special issue George, does your mam know you're 'ere, she didn't say owt when I saw 'er the other day?"

"I didn't write to tell her when the boat would be due, she'd have made the journey somehow, between doing everything else. I took a room at Southampton last night and caught the first train this morning. I dare say there'll be tears, this way we won't have to share them with so many other folk, within minutes of the steps being brought alongside the dock was awash yesterday, I looked on the scene but briefly, emotion as raw as that calls for privacy.

How is Billy? I've thought about him a lot, I'm sure some days I tethered myself to Billy, in my mind he was a constant, steadfast, I stood a chance if I stayed with Billy Dodds, I don't mean any disrespect of Charles but he didn't speak to me in the still moments like Billy did."

Edna swallowed hard. "Billy's just the same, daft as ever."

"Thank God," said George, "you must tell him that I shall come to see him as soon as I can, shake that big hand of his and claim all the yarns I've missed while I've been away."

Edna's heart began to ache, she knew that Annie had not told George about John and although Edna had never held Charles in much regard, his grief over John had touched her, Billy too had felt for him, Charles was a difficult man to like, seldom did he show any proof of having a heart but losing John opened up cracks in his crusty old shell, briefly his heart was glimpsed and sympathy made every effort to reach it. The opportunity was fleeting, it was soon concealed, locked away again. Now George was too late to see the proof for himself and it felt truly sad.

"Now look 'ere George Boucher, 'tis not wi' me yer should be wastin' time chattin', get home to your mam, give Annie 'er life back, she's existed while you've been gone but she's not lived since the day you walked away up Gregory Street. 'E might be a funny ossity some times but I reckon Charles'll be more relieved to see you than yer think."

George was quiet for a moment. "I heard about John, only recently but I do know and yes, he is a 'funny ossity' as you put it Edna but I've called him dad for a lot of years and we all loved John. We'll face it together, I think I understand Charles more than I used to. After Alice died he dropped a little of his guard and we met somewhere along a past road. Anyway, you're right, I must be on my way."

He kissed Edna's cheek, picked up his bag, which had slipped from his shoulder and was about to speak again but Edna was insistent.

"Home, an' make haste."

He gave her a roguish look. "That's what I've missed Edna, a dominant woman, nothing gets a man's pulse racing like a woman with real prowess."

"Don't come your fancy words wi' me George Boucher," she called after him as he hurried away, then chuckled at a thought, speaking to herself, 'my Billy, God bless 'im, 'as been lookin' for my prowess for years an' every now and then I let 'im find it an'all'.

"Read all about it, Labour take power, Tories out, read all about it." The vendor held out a paper to Edna as she passed by.

"So what? An' if yer carry on shoutin' like that your tongue'll likely get inflammation, it happens yer know, to the best of us."

Prowess, what was the point of having it if you didn't use it!

Samuel sat in the yard whittling a piece of stick, they looked simple enough, the gypsies made them in quantity, he'd found some twine on the shelf in the coal shed to bind around the top of his peg, if his first attempt went well he'd make some more.

He missed Laura and Ted, everyday he held out hope of his dad's return and when bedtime came without event Samuel's spirits sank a little more. Laura had gone back to her parents in Birmingham at the end of the last school term. She'd explained to Annie that while ever she was surrounded by reminders of John she couldn't concentrate on her work and propel herself forward of misery. She found herself absent in thought from the children, if it continued then as a teacher she would be failing them, so she'd handed in her notice to Harrow Road School with much regret. 'I shall always keep in touch, I promise', had been the last thing she'd said to Samuel before going and he could never doubt Laura's word but it didn't comfort, it created yet another ache deep inside him.

He was thirteen, that awkward age when a youth was perched like a peg on a clothesline, one leg clinging to innocence, the other straining to find maturity and only flimsy thread between the two, which would hold or snap as fate decided. Granddad had been irritable of late, more than usual, Samuel was convinced Charles' moodiness had been a part of the reason for Laura leaving. They all grieved for John, but the tense atmosphere Charles' manner created could only be borne by those with no option, Laura had her own mam and dad, who could feel truly surprised at her wish to return to them rather than abide at Gregory Street with an abrasive Charles?

Samuel did at least see Ted sometimes, after all, aunty Nora was family and now that school was finished for the summer he could call round of an evening and play draughts or dominoes with Ted, even hangman. Ted's reading and writing had so improved they used long words and varied the game by nominating various categories, such as place names and famous people.

Aunty Nora was a dear with only the very best of intentions, but would whisper in their ear when either one came close to being hanged and Samuel had concluded that Nora was an undiscovered genius, capable of recognising words simply by looking at the dashes! Footsteps on the side path caused him to look up, knife and peg fell to the ground.

"Dad, Dad." At this plain backyard on Gregory Street Samuel's war was won and George surrendered willingly to his son's arms. After a time not measured George spoke, his voice unsteady at first.

"Come on now, let's find your grandma." Samuel picked up his dad's bag from the cobbles.

"It's just us now, Laura and Ted have gone, Laura to her family in Birmingham and Ted to aunty Nora's. Granddad's at home."

The kitchen was quiet but for a pan which simmered over the stove emitting smells of onions and lentils. Faint voices drifted back from the shop, then the clang of the doorbell and silence. Samuel could wait no longer, he ran through to Annie and grabbed her arm, pulling her to the kitchen. The cellar door was ajar, Charles was down in the store, it felt correct, his dad and his grandma should have this moment to themselves. Charles' voice rose up from the cellar.

"This old mattress can go now surely, mice have chewed a corner, rag n' bone man should come along tomorrow, take the other end when I pass it up."

Samuel stood at the top of the cellar steps and clutched at the old striped mattress when it began to emerge, Charles followed it with a grunt of impatience. Samuel said nothing but stood to one side, now Charles could hear Annie sobbing. He went to the kitchen, a weakness took all strength from his legs and he sank onto a chair. The shop doorbell announced the untimely arrival of a customer. Samuel touched Charles' shoulder.

"I'll go Granddad."

Andrew Smithfield stood at the counter, he smiled, genuinely pleased to see Samuel.

"Could I have a loaf please, brown or white, either will do. It's good to find you helping with the shop, your grandparents are well I hope?"

Samuel took the bread from the shelf and wrapped it in tissue paper.

"Dad has just come home, they're in the back, I don't think they're up to serving anyone for a minute or two."

Andrew held out his arm to shake Samuel's hand and shook it like a man who'd just been granted a fortune. He put a half crown on the counter and said.

"This is the day we shall never forget for all the 'right' reasons. Please tell them I am more relieved than I can properly say." He glanced down at the coin, his voice emotional. "No change Samuel, I don't expect any change."

He gathered up the loaf and hurried off. Samuel had never really thought about it before but how strange it was that such a pleasant man should be without a family, it seemed a shame and a bit sad. He put the half crown in the till and was about to step around the mattress that had been abandoned on the floor, when a tiny mouse ran out from one corner of it and down the side of the cellar steps. Samuel smiled to himself, he wouldn't tell granddad, this was the day when even a mouse was entitled to share in the happiness, a day never to be forgotten, and for all the right reasons.

Joyce cleared away the dishes, they had settled to an easy routine, at first it had seemed strange, Edgar had been a little unsure of what to do, should he chat to William, tell him about things at the pit or would Mr.Haynes consider him an intrusion and prefer him to keep himself to himself.

William was not naturally a difficult man and Edgar was young, young enough to be his son, the lad had no option but to work at the pit where the powers that be had sent him, he was deserving of some kind of home life and over the course of the past month William had found himself warming to Edgar's character. The evenings passed pleasantly, the two men had gone out for a pint together once or twice and Joyce felt able to dismiss her anxieties, it was going to be alright.

William sat reading The Evening Post while Edgar perused a special issue he'd bought from a vendor on his way home, with only a limited interest in politics much of its content he skipped over, but a picture of Churchill, the man who'd taken more weight on his shoulders than could be carried without lasting effect, now rejected as folk clamoured for change, this image Edgar looked at and felt dismayed.

Party politics were brutal, as rough as that street game that used rules like weapons, British Bulldog, getting hurt was all part of it, there might only be one man left standing but casualties went home to lick their wounds and next day the contest would start all over again, winners and losers, taking their turn as a matter of course.

To Edgar it had always appeared futile but he looked on the picture of Churchill and felt gratitude, to the inevitable inquest into his downfall which the paper had undertaken to hold, Edgar gave scant attention. The wound must be sore enough, publicly rubbing in salt to worsen the hurt brought a dishonourable element to the game, leave the British Bulldog alone, that was Edgar's political belief.

A sound outside in the yard alerted Joyce to someone's arrival, she stopped what she was doing and wiped her hands. Valerie had parked the pram and was lifting the baby from it, her movements hampered by a large box, perched in front of the child, while a bag hung from the handle, tied on by a piece of string. The young woman pushed past Joyce and with no attempt at politeness said.

“Where is ‘e?” Given chance, Joyce would have answered but Valerie was across the scullery and into the living room before Joyce could utter a word. “She’s been registered a Perry, like you wanted, I’ve had enough. If you’ve got somethin’ to say then say it to me mam ‘cause it wer’ ‘er as made me have it.” Valerie thrust the infant at Edgar like the child was burning her fingers. “I’ve brought the pram an’ most of ‘er stuff, you’ll have to collect the crib tomorrow, she can sleep in the pram ‘til then. I tittied ‘er right up to last Sunday so you can’t say I didn’t do me best, she’s on bottle now, there’s baby milk in the bag. She won’t sleep she never does.”

Turning her attention away from Edgar, she passed a quick glance at William, said “Hello,” then returned to the scullery where Joyce had stood wringing the towel between her hands as she’d listened to Valerie’s outburst.

“It’s no use Mrs.Haynes, me mind is made up, I won’t keep ‘er, she’s as much his as mine an’ ‘e can ‘ave my arf. I’ve brought back the things you sent round an’ bits that me mam got an’all.” She took a deep breath. “I want me life back, God knows I’ve tried but I can’t be doin’ with it anymore.” She sniffled as though dismissing a trifling nuisance, when Joyce made no reply, being quite literally lost for words, Valerie left.

Elizabeth Perry began to whimper but it was Edgar who looked most likely to cry out loud. How could Valerie Oates abandon her baby, their baby, any baby?

William got to his feet, he was calm, not raising his voice but his words were forceful.

“Leave it tonight lad, she’ll not bend while that mood persists, in the mornin’ you’ll take the child back, if Valerie gets a night’s sleep she’ll see sense then.”

Joyce was trembling, Valerie’s unleashed frustration had felt far from a moment of tiredness. William now stood at the back door.

“I’m goin’ to see our Jack for an hour, I’ll tell ‘im that Edgar’s got somethin’ important to do first thing so he’ll be late for work in the mornin’.” He pulled the pram in through the doorway, “Not a baby Joyce, the lad’s one thing, I can accept that but if the Oates won’t keep the child then it’s for Edgar to deal with the problem." He walked across the yard to the entry leaving Joyce staring at the pram, in their home, a pram, baby things.

"Joyce I think she's hungry." Edgar carried the little girl into the scullery, "She keeps puttin' her fist into her mouth like she's wantin' milk."

Joyce put the kettle on to boil, found the tin of formula and a feeding bottle, while the water heated she sorted through the box and found nappies and Vaseline. Elizabeth was quiet in Edgar's arms as he walked about the room gently singing to her, she appeared content but it was sensible to have a bottle ready anyway so Joyce mixed a feed and stood the bottle in a jug of cold water.

"It's too hot yet, I expect she needs changin'."

Joyce spread a towel over the table top and lifted the baby from Edgar's arms. She'd changed babies before, when helping her sister Kathleen but here, now, Elizabeth Perry took anchor in Joyce's heart, the soft skin, the searching fingers, those little legs, stretching free of the nappy. Her face, two eyes, a nose and a mouth, that's all it was, a sequence of innocent features, yet it wiped away six years of war at a stroke.

"Sit down Edgar." Joyce put the child back in his arms while she tested the temperature of the milk and wiped the bottle dry. "Put it to her lips, if she sucks hold it at an angle that keeps the milk over the end of the teat or she'll suck air an' get wind, but take the bottle away if she's not bothered about havin' it. I'm goin' up to empty a drawer in the chest, the pram's too awkward to get up the stairs, a drawer will serve as a crib tonight. I won't be long sortin' it out, you're alright for a bit aren't you Edgar?"

She smiled encouragement, he looked nervous but Elizabeth took the milk readily so Joyce carried the bag of baby things up to the bedroom. She sat for a moment on the side of their bed. William had not once judged her, all that time ago when she'd told him of the trouble in Loughborough he'd treated it as past and gone. But Joyce had judged herself, taken punishment and so many times been consumed by regret. Now she wasn't sure if she could take anymore.

She pulled out the bottom drawer of the chest, it held winter clothing, the jumper she'd knitted for William lay on the top, it could stay at the bottom of the wardrobe for tonight. She carried the empty drawer into Edgar's room and lined it with a flannelette sheet, tucking the surplus material underneath. Valerie had brought a cot sheet and blanket, it was warm, the sheet would likely be enough to lay over a baby this time of year. When she woke in the night Joyce would tiptoe downstairs to help Edgar, William would understand that, he wasn't unkind, not unkind just shocked at Valerie's behaviour and like he'd said, in the morning she'd see sense. Joyce did her best to convince herself that all would be well, yet inwardly she was as fearful as Edgar, he'd become like a son to her and she knew him well enough to be sure in her mind that he'd never give up the child to the authorities. If Valerie didn't relent and William refused to let the baby stay then Edgar would leave, take Elizabeth and do whatever he must, the nature of his own childhood wouldn't allow him to part with his daughter.

Those old torments returned, her past failings, she'd confessed them, taken her punishment and begged forgiveness, now she felt responsible for passing trouble to Edgar, perhaps she tainted others.

He appeared at the doorway, a big smile on his face. "Elizabeth's asleep, she took her feed an' fell asleep Joyce, good as gold."

Annie lay wide awake, Charles was sleeping, she envied his ability to nod off so quickly. When she got up yesterday morning little did she know that before the day ended, George would hold her in his arms and say, 'It's over Mam, it's over'.

Samuel had hung on his dad's every word all through the evening, happiness seeping through his pores, 'til he glowed with contentment, not until he had gone up to bed had Annie felt it possible to tell George about John, she couldn't have spoiled Samuel's joy, he'd waited so long and endured his dad's absence without once causing bother, the separation was hard enough for a child waiting with its mother, but for Samuel it must have been doubly hard.

It had struck Annie as odd that George didn't ask about John, she knew that Charles couldn't face it, his expression confirmed it and after talking with George, mostly about William and Freddy and the situation at the factories, Raleigh in particular as Mathew was working there, and the gradual return to peacetime production, Charles declared himself, 'off to bed' leaving Annie and George sitting quietly together. Despite the conversation over Raleigh, George had not spoken of John. Charles seemed to have overlooked the fact that as well as being George's old workplace it had been John's too.

George had listened to the sound of the bedroom door closing, then alone with his mam the stillness released his thoughts ahead of Annie's.

'It's alright Mam', he'd said, 'I already know. When your recent letters came with no mention of John, even up to the last one you wrote, I sensed there was a reason why. While we were fighting, when everything was turmoil, we were aware of nothing more than could be seen in front of us and what little we were able to glimpse over our shoulders. Some of the officers it was possible to get close to as men, others not so much. But one Captain Dreyfus I got to know quite well, especially in the last few weeks. I asked him if he could find out if a John, Mark Eddowes, RAF, had been listed dead since January. I gave him John's date of birth, I didn't have his service number. It was about ten days ago that Dreyfus sent me word, John had been killed, his details were on a list of casualties, men lost, following the raid to help Montgomery get his troops across The Rhine'.

Annie had listened while despair tightened her chest, while George's words were recorded in her head, for they did indeed record and now they persisted in speaking to her, over and over without interval. In the morning she would explain to Charles, and to Samuel she would simply say, 'It's alright your dad knows'. Perhaps now they could begin to speak easily of John, all the wonderful memories they had of him. Annie would often whisper his name to herself, feeling his presence in everything she did, yet until George was home and he too held John safe within his heart it hadn't felt right to move forward in that way.

Anthony Hemsley occupied her thoughts as she stood behind the shop counter, he would call for his newspaper and everyday Annie hoped he would have news to lift his spirits but still his misery could see no end. He'd written to Donald's mother asking her to let him have their granddaughter's name, he'd explained in the letter his reason for asking but as yet there'd been no reply and his despair seemed ever deeper with each day that passed.

Annie looked at the clock on the bedside cabinet, just after two, she slipped her feet from under the covers, pulled on her cardigan over her nightie and crept downstairs, a cup of hot milk might help.

The old mattress was propped up by the back door, threat of a shower prevented it from being put in the yard and the coal shed would transfer too much blackness, despite its age the rag n'bone man would likely find another home for it. It had originally been part of a first size bed Charles had bought for William, it had travelled with the family along with all the other familiar items until eventually the bed frame was too weak to be trusted but the small mattress had been kept, one of those things that one day there might be a call for. In the cellar during the air raids it had cushioned Samuel and sheltered with them, sharing their fear like an old friend.

The warm milk comforted, it began to still her mind, it was already Friday morning, William, Freddy and Hilda were as yet unaware of George's return, the thought of delivering happiness replaced the anxiety and she at long last found some ease. She should creep back to bed until the papers arrived, had the mattress been a bit bigger Annie would have laid it on the scullery floor and slept with an old friend. Not a sound came from Samuel's or George's room, Charles' steady breathing confirmed he'd not roused. She lay still, her eyelids heavy, her brief commune with Heaven not seeking to disturb The Almighty at such an hour but intended for Harold, who would surely be watchful this night, a thank you for keeping safe their son.

William picked up his dinner bag from the table. "I'll be off then," he turned to Edgar, "chin up lad, the lass'll be waitin' for yer, she'll be out on the street watchin' for yer comin', you mark my words."

He rubbed his hand across Edgar's shoulder and crossed the room to where Joyce stood, tell tale bags under her eyes, evidence that she'd not slept, though her wakefulness could not fairly be attributed to the baby, Valerie's prediction that Elizabeth wouldn't sleep had proved wildly exaggerated.

"See you later then love," said William and gave her a kiss, he couldn't look into her eyes this morning but it had to be said, they were too old to cope with a baby. Home, his wife, they had kept him strong and these he already shared with

Edgar. But a baby, which was nothing to do with Joyce and himself, William couldn't accept, it wasn't fair. He rambled through the injustice as he made his way to work. He'd started at the pit last week, curiously there was something about the prospect of working underground that now appealed to him. War messed with a man's head, it sent him snarling and growling into the kill, wound up, frenzied, one day at Armageddon, the next incarcerated, held in a state of ignorance, waiting, everyday waiting fate and all above ground, in sight of man and God. As William neared the pit gates a voice behind him interrupted his thoughts.

"I warned 'im, right at the start I told the lad to think long an' hard, but no, 'e wer' sure of isself, 'e'd be there for 'is kid an' whatever it took in money 'e'd provide an'all." Tom Oates now stood alongside William. "It's no use in thinkin' yer can land Valerie's mam wi' it when the lass gets fed up, them was me very words to Perry. Our Valerie's not daft, she knows her three R's well enough, 'er trouble is she thinks life's a bloody fairy tale, wi' a pretty young maiden, a bogey man, a bloke in shinin' armour an' a happy soddin' endin'. She wer' up wi' the lark this mornin', all dolled up, when 'er mam asked where she wer' off to lookin' so smart, Valerie answered like she'd just read the last page o' the story book, 'To work Mam, I'm off to work', an' that wer' it, the end. I don't know what the lad'll do but I give 'im fair warnin' so I did."

He walked away leaving William standing at the spot, a wretchedness taking hold in his stomach, men streaming past him to begin the shift, beleaguered yet in full view of them all, and in sight of God. Didn't anyone care, couldn't God be bothered? He carried on through the gates, a few hours of relief underground before facing what he knew the evening must bring. He could not countenance the baby in his house, it was too much to ask.

Edgar pushed the pram and baby things along the street, rising above the judging looks and muttered asides cast his way by those of such nature but relieved nonetheless at reaching the Oates' back yard. Before knocking on the door he looked over the box and into the pram at Elizabeth. Joyce had bathed her before he left, the large bowl on the washstand had served the purpose well enough, now she was sleeping, he would speak out in his baby's defence, tell Valerie that her description of a child who never stopped crying was false and unkind, she was the one bleating like a kid. Peggy opened the door, he could see at once that she had been upset, her face was blotchy and her expression full of misery, heavy with it, weighting all her features so none could lift on seeing him standing there, expecting what she couldn't give.

When she'd poured out her torment Edgar could feel only compassion for the poor woman but as he retraced his steps, still with Elizabeth and the pram and baby things, a feeling of dread took over. Mr.Haynes had shown no interest in her, she'd stirred only once in the night yet William made no reply when Joyce remarked on the child's contentedness. Where would he go with a baby, how could he work and look after Elizabeth?

He was surprised to find Joyce still at home, she should have left for the depot before now.

"I went to the phone box, called in to tell 'em there'd been an emergency, a family crisis, that I couldn't make it today. I had a feelin' that you'd not get to the pit, that you'd be back, an' not by yourself neither."

Edgar related events while Joyce sat with Elizabeth on her knee, the child was awake, clutching the bib of Joyce's pinafore, making no disturbance.

"Where's Valerie workin'?"

"Don't know," said Edgar, "Peggy didn't know but she told me that Valerie went out for a couple of hours the other day, left Elizabeth with her, apparently she's done that a few times. Tom doesn't know, she's always been back before he gets in from work. What shall I do Joyce? I don't think Mr.Haynes is goin' to let us stay here, I can't blame him, really I can't, it's not his problem."

"You'll 'ave to miss a day at the pit it's too late to go now anyway. Fetch the crib, she can't sleep in a drawer til she's big enough for a bed. William'll soften, it wer' a shock last night, Valerie bargin' in like that an' flouncin' off again but e'll realize that she's no good to Elizabeth, any mother who can just turn 'er back on 'er baby's not fit. William's brother Victor wer' born not right, a bit simple, but their mam kept him, loved him, they all did, woe betide anybody as tried to hurt him, it'll be alright Edgar. Tommy's wife Rosie'll let us have Beryl's things, they'll 'ave been the rounds, but kiddies grow so quick it takes several of them to wear 'em out. Me sister Kathleen's first was a girl, they called her Elizabeth an'all but it soon got shortened to Beth. She 'ad two boys after that but me brother Joe's wife Susie 'ad two girls so what Beth grew out of got passed down to them an' when Rosie 'ad Beryl, Susie handed 'em on to 'er. It's what families do, I wer' the lucky one in our house I suppose bein' the eldest girl I 'ad new bits an' pieces but mam 'ad a picture o' me wearin' Tommy's dungarees and I can remember goin' to bed wintertime in his old striped nightshirts. Even King's an' Queens 'ave to make do wi' the same hand me down crown don't they?"

Edgar found reassurance in Joyce's positive approach.

"It's a good job we stuck to Elizabeth then," he said, "it would be a bit confusin' havin' two Beths in one family."

When Edgar used the word 'family' Joyce's heart leapt but she dare not dwell on it.

"You run along now, I'll mix a bottle. Collect the crib an' give the poor woman my best, I don't want Peggy to think I blame 'er, it's a wonder she's not gone mad, livin' with 'er Tom, an' a daughter like Valerie."

As Joyce put the baby back in the pram a rush of guilt came over her. As a daughter she herself had been the wayward one, that cause of distress to her own mam. She could never have done what Valerie did, leave a baby, but she shouldn't be so ready to judge when life had a way of punishing unworthiness. Doubt cast its shadow over Joyce and she busied herself, she'd told Edgar it would be alright, 'Please God I didn't mean Valerie any slight', she whispered the words as she ran water into the kettle and took down the iron from the shelf, 'Busy, keep busy Joyce', she cautioned herself, yet still she felt the eyes of judgment upon her.

Their meal was almost ready, she'd looked at the clock every minute of the past fifteen. William would be home any time now. Neither Joyce nor Edgar knew that Tom had furnished William with an account of Valerie's early departure to a place of work. Joyce was so nervous she could barely function and Edgar tried desperately to believe that what Joyce had said would be the case, that William would relent.

The sound of work boots crossing the yard caused them to exchange worried looks, he stepped inside, hung his dinner bag on the hook and crossed to the sink.

"I've got hot water ready," said Joyce, "an' it's bacon puddin' for tea, I managed to get some suet from Cheetham's."

The waiting was unbearable but still William said nothing. Elizabeth slept in the pram by the dresser, a bottle of milk made ready to heat for her next feed sat on the table.

"Edgar went with her, first thing, but Valerie had gone out, to work, there's nothin' poor Peggy can do. Tom rules Peggy, she'd be too afraid to cross him, so Edgar could do no other than bring Elizabeth back here. She's not been a spot o' bother all day. Edgar would 'ave gone to the pit but by the time 'e'd fetched the crib it wer' too late."

William washed at the sink. Joyce laid the table, her fingers awkward from nervousness. Finally he sat down at his place, his gaze set at the bottle of milk. Edgar stood in silence by the stove, Joyce handed a plate of food to him.

"That's William's," she said.

He carried it across to the table, as he put it down in front of William he spoke softly.

"I've already put her things back in the box, I'll leave as soon as she's had her milk in the mornin'. I do understand, I know folk find it hard to care for a child that's not their own, it don't always work out an' yer can't make it happen, if the feelin's not there I reckon it's kinder not to try."

Joyce came across with Edgar's plate and her own. "Eat up or it'll go cold, mustn't waste food."

They laboured through the next ten minutes, the sound of knives and forks the only interruption to the strained silence, a brief snuffle from the baby as she turned her face to slowly wake made Edgar sick with worry.

At that moment a 'tap tap' came at the back door, it was already ajar and Tommy Spooner appeared.

"Sorry to come at tea time, don't mind me, I shan't stop long, Rosie'll have mine ready when I get back, but I've just come from Kathleen's. Ernie's been pickin' gooseberries, a big basketful. Like Kathleen says, there's not enough sugar for them to use up the lot on their own, so she's sharin' 'em round, I said I'd drop some in to you on me way home. We've got a basinful an'all, that'll be a job for Rosie tonight, top an' tailin' gooseberries, the lads won't want to know about that part but they'll eat the stewed fruit fast enough, the young buggers."

He chuckled as he put a bag of fruit on the draining board. When he walked across to where they sat he saw the pram by the dresser. "Hello, who's this then?" Tommy looked down at Elizabeth. "You're a little sweetheart aren't yer?" He guessed it was Edgar's little girl, Joyce had told Tommy all about her weeks ago, it didn't occur at all unusual the child being there, he presumed Valerie must need Edgar to baby sit for a while.

Children and Tommy were a natural combination, no more of a challenge to him than shaving of a morning. He sensed an awkward quietness and it puzzled him. Then William got up from the table and walked away, out into the yard. Joyce burst into tears and ran upstairs, while Edgar gathered up the three plates, sighed and said.

"Mr.Haynes is right, it's not for him to provide a place for me an' Elizabeth, we'll be goin' in the mornin', first thing. Valerie's give' up, can't cope, doesn't want the baby, I'm her dad so it's my problem to sort out. I can understand why Mr.Haynes isn't happy, away all that time, then finally gettin' home to find it full o' strangers. It's alright Mr.Spooner, honest, I don't want to cause any trouble."

Tommy couldn't believe what he was hearing, to him it made no sense. There must be more to it than just a baby. He went outside to find William, he sat on a makeshift bench, his head in his hands. Tommy sat down beside him.

"What's wrong Will', it's not like you to get upset, is it a money problem, is somebody chasin' yer for money?"

"It don't feel like I've come back to me own home Tommy. All that time away I longed for Joyce, our home, each other. Edgar's a good lad, I can't fault him, but he makes things different. Now I know he needs somewhere to stop while he's at pit so I told meself, can't be helped Haynes, get used to it. When the lass burst in an' pushed that baby at Edgar I felt angry, she had no right, it might be Edgar's child but it's not his house, he don't hold the rent book, but I saw Joyce's face, she weren't worried for me, she wer' frettin' for Edgar. An' who's supposed to look after this baby? Joyce isn't a young woman, what about her work?"

Tommy chuckled. "Yer daft beggar William Haynes, yer can't see the wood for the trees. Joyce worships the ground you tread on, why do you think she took in a Bevin boy? The war effort, doin' her bit, it mattered 'cause every single thing folk did to help, includin' fuel production, would bring an end to it, bring you home. I can only imagine what you've witnessed and endured Will', but while you were away fightin' an' then stuck in that Stalag, we struggled an'all. I've buried more folk than it wer' their time to be buried, young people, gone long afore they should, even babies. Sometimes a baby dies an' that gets to yer like nothin' else. You were seven in family, same as us, I wer' the eldest I know, but I can hardly remember a time when there wasn't a baby in our house." Tommy sighed long. "When mam died Joyce took it really bad, we all did but Joyce, well you know what happened in Loughborough, she convinced herself that it wer' all 'er fault, that her waywardness aged mam. But it wer' life that aged me mam, she wore herself out through lovin' us so much. Then Joyce got took bad an' they told her that she'd never have children, it felt like a punishment to Joyce. She'd tend this baby an' love it but that's not what makes her cry. It's Edgar, she knows he won't abandon his child, that's the sort o' man he is, decent, self respect's important to him. If the baby goes, so will Edgar an' he's the son Joyce though she'd never have. He's got no parents, they died years ago, no siblings, he's taken to Joyce like the mother he's been missin' for most of his life. You're loved no less Will', don't yer suppose that her heart's big enough for a family same as her mam's was, same as your mam's was. You're a lucky man Will', you came back, an' able bodied at that, our dad didn't, an' yours made it home but the war 'ad done for him, it just prolonged the agony for your mam.

In my job I spend a lot o' time listenin', I listen more than I speak. Sometimes when folk are grievin', they feel the need to tell somebody things they'd normally keep tucked away, like trinkets in a jar, an' I'd be that somebody. I might 'ave known 'em for years but they'd sit down with me an' between the tears they'd take the lid off the jar an' let me see what they'd kept to themselves. I often wondered if the Vicar was so privileged, not all the trinkets were shiny, some 'ad lost a bit o' glitter here an' there, but I soon realised that I hadn't really known them at all but by listenin' I learned a lot. Now it's all in my trinket jar, borrowed, to remind me.

It's only a baby Will', a lovely little baby, I reckon the Gods favoured you, you've been spared to come home to a wife that's devoted to yer, a would be son that most folk'd feel proud to have an' now maybe a granddaughter, so why you're out here sittin' on this old bench considerin' yourself hard done by is beyond me.

She's my sister an' I love 'er, so I'm askin' yer Will' not to punish 'er, she don't deserve it. You'll manage if she finishes on the buses, you've work at pit, so has Edgar, besides a family don't cost as much as you'd think. Look at me, I've never been a big earner, I'm lucky to 'ave me job but I only work at Handley's, I don't own the place but me an' Rosie manage okay, an' we've got four, God love 'em.

Go back inside Will', sit Joyce down wi' a nice cup o' tea, to top an' tail them gooseberries, while Edgar sees to little 'en. He's already done the washin' up, while we've been sat out here the dishes have been rattlin' in the scullery."

At that moment Elizabeth began to cry. Tommy stood up. "Tell Joyce I'll see her soon an' if she wants to come round wi' the baby then Rosie'll be in 'er element." He squeezed William's shoulder and walked away to the entry, whistling cheerily, as though nothing at all out of the ordinary had occurred.

'Decent, self respect's important to him'. Those words took hold in William's head, the principles his mam and dad had all their lives abided by. A weariness came over him, conflict demanded too much of a man, just a baby, that's all it was, he'd grown up with them, like Tommy. Granddad eh! The hurt was there still, but fading. William Haynes, a family man. 'A family man'. He said it to himself twice and smiled as he thought of Victor, the last baby in Florrie and Albert Haynes' house, the last but never the least, who said everything twice. Inside Elizabeth's crying had ceased, he would go to Joyce, his wife's tears could dry now too, it was alright, he needed only to listen, to listen and understand.

Florence felt grateful that Patricia's homecoming was to be today, Sunday, that quieter day of the week. At St.Annes the doctor was satisfied that she had recovered, like every other mortal she would have bad days and good days, governed by events about her but the deep depression that Patricia had experienced could be attributed to the loss of her husband at a time when her emotions were already at the brink, pushing her over the edge.

Her present mental state was sound, she had negotiated her way through the therapy sessions, acknowledging her own shortcomings and recognising Anthony's difficulties, displaying regret and remorse but most importantly, accepting that the past was beyond changing and it was the life ahead that mattered now, only by living it to the best, could Patricia Bradshaw find peace of mind and lay old torments to rest.

Julia decided not to accompany their mother when she went to meet Patricia but instead to make the house look cheerful, with flowers in the hall and the living room, she'd bake a cake, they'd saved their butter and egg ration for the purpose.

What was left of Anthony's things, together Julia and Florence had dealt with. His clothes and shoes to the Salvation Army, his books to the book shelf from whence they came, the binoculars to Jonathon and Gregory, so that they might remember their uncle Anthony, but keeping his walking cane and umbrella, which would remain placed inconspicuously just inside the front door, Julia had persuaded her mother that some physical evidence of Anthony would prove a comfort to Patricia, despite the doctor's instructions. The framed picture of Lionel Bradshaw was an awkward item, Cynthia Woolascroft would seem the most obvious caretaker of it yet neither Julia nor Florence felt inclined to approach her so it now reposed between the wall and the wardrobe in the spare bedroom. The items of furniture had been put back in their rightful places and the hallway restored to normality.

It had been a task for which they'd felt great anxiety but Dr.Lavery had insisted it was necessary, as much a requirement as the tablets prescribed to calm Patricia. The dose of tranquilisers had been reduced gradually and now just one a day was deemed sufficient.

The house meeting her satisfaction and a cake sitting on the cooling rack, Julia made the most of a few quiet moments and sank into an armchair, which like herself, felt the worse for wear. Hope was a contrary companion, abandon it and what was then left? Endure with it and be forever chasing rainbows. Luciano had died at the hands of the partisans around the time of Mussolini's capture and execution so when Julia had been imagining him already dead and beyond helping her, in fact he'd been alive and concerning himself with the furtherance of his leader, 'hail to the homeland', but his wife was not of the homeland and so was best left behind. It hurt, in spite of knowing in her heart that be Luciano alive or dead, their marriage was over, her dismissal, with seemingly such ease, no backward glance as he marched fascist style into Hitler's new world, pained the senses. Patricia should be thankful that Anthony died honourably, leaving her with the opportunity to make good the memories. Luciano's legacy granted Julia nothing she could respectably record. She was now at her middle age with a confused childhood, an unsettled youth and a meaningless marriage as the background to her widowhood.

Her mother had sought advice of Andrew Smithfield over the land at Colver, to keep it as an investment had been the outcome, he held the opinion that land would be a valuable asset, bearing greater interest than a sum deposited at the bank. Rebuilding the destroyed areas and new development on fresh sites would be a crucial factor of any government plan, of necessity they must grow the economy. War costs in both warm blood and cold, what was borrowed must ultimately be repaid and cold blood always commanded the highest priority. Solution was found first at the pay packets with taxation. No work meant no pay packet so construction would be the prime mover, the kick start to the country's climb out of the trough the past six years had gouged across society, Colver would play its part, 'sit tight and be patient', had been Mr.Smithfield's verdict.

Caroline had agreed the sale of her share in Moreleigh to William Eddowes, Celia had been distressed over it all and Julia had been tempted to call on William, to ask if he'd studied from the same text book as her father, that notorious title, 'How to wear two faces with impunity'. William might not have been in Basil Stanford's employ over long but he'd learned his trade from a master.

What would now happen at Birchdale troubled Julia as well. Patricia had seemed detached from the mine while at St.Annes, seldom mentioning the place and Florence had been happier keeping her free of possible concerns over the workforce and production. Hugh Porter's departure had created a moment of anxiety but in the event affairs of the pit had been without difficulty beyond the usual day to day complexities likely to challenge any operation heavy on manpower.

Patricia had given no hint of her intentions, while colourful flowers and a cake were meant sincerely as a comforting, welcome home, realistically they stood little chance of softening Patricia's attitude if it was to be as before. A sound in the hall alerted Julia to their arrival.

"We're here and ready for a cup of tea, rationing aside, we shall take it a bit stronger than they do at St.Annes."

Their mother's voice was bright, it afforded Julia confidence and she ventured out from the refuge of the living room and into the hall where her sister would surely note the changes. If she did then she chose to make no remark other than to declare the flowers pretty and to comment on the inviting smell of baking. So far, so good, thought Julia, then at once felt guilty, it was insensitive to be already judging Patricia, unkind even.

"Come through I've the kettle filled ready and a tray laid. The cake is a celebratory confection, generous in sentiment if frugal in content." She embraced Patricia warmly and although she could not have defined it in any way that would make sense to another, it felt easy, no need of prior approval.

"Before we left we went briefly to see Celia's mother," said Florence. "Dear Gwendolyn is rather like your cake Julia, missing some ingredients but impressive nonetheless, Queen of her very own realm and I shall remain loyal to her, visit as often as I can."

Patricia smiled at her mother, it had been some time since she'd felt at liberty to do that most natural of gestures, if it caused her father to frown, wherever he might be observing her, then she no longer cared.

The war was almost over, everyone was saying so and at last it felt believable. When the tea was poured it was Patricia who raised her cup.

“To better things.”

Their three cups chinked together in a chord of hope. Julia cut the cake, passing the first slice to Patricia.

“I found some food colouring, pink and green, so I used it in the mix and made us a rainbow cake.”

CHAPTER TWENTY THREE

August.

"I'll get you another one Dad, same again?"

William picked up their glasses from the table, The Standard was busy, the number inside making the most of the last ten minutes of drinking time.

"No, not for me," said Charles, "I'm off home now, I told George I might go with them to watch the cricket for an hour, he's taking Samuel to Trent Bridge."

"Well I won't bother either then. Celia's going to see her mother and I've a few things I need to do, I should be off as well. So you think you might set the ball rolling Dad, make an appointment to see the solicitor? It would be too upsetting for mam, I know she sorted out Davina's affairs at the time but this is different, we shouldn't expect it of her." William put down the glasses. "See you soon then Dad."

Charles raised his hand in a half hearted wave and William left. 'Shouldn't expect it of her'. Those words galled Charles, Hemsley was expecting of too much, 'depressed', was he really supposed to swallow such rubbish. It was the fourth time Annie had gone to The Park to see Anthony Hemsley out of concern for his melancholy, why was the man so depressed anyway? If it happened again then he, Charles, Annie's husband, would go there and give Hemsley something to be depressed about, bloody man.

Charles festered within, yet unless Celia was a conspirator in it all then Hemsley was far from being himself. Celia had spoken of her own concerns several times when at the shop collecting his paper on the days she went there to work and often the previous two or three issues if he'd not ventured out himself. On the odd occasion Charles had served him little conversation took place, there was no love lost between them, only a slender tolerance. Celia's continued anxiety would seem to prove Annie's concern genuine and her visits to The Park entirely innocent, Charles' good sense told him this was so but a bad sense, a troublesome sense tormented his mind.

Now William had brought up the subject of John's affairs. Charles had been putting it off and Annie's thoughts he was convinced had not once been with the matter of their son's 'estate', as William referred to it, since the dreadful day when the telegram arrived. Now Charles must speak with Julian Russe, seek advice. John was a young man, it was unlikely that he would have made a Will, his bank account could not have been that significant prior to him enlisting and Davina's money was paid into his account later. Nigel Caffin and Annie dealt with that. If John had made a Will then it would likely have been done through Chaucer, Caffin and Holt, because of the connection that firm had with Celia's brother, Edmund Tozer. Charles favoured speaking first with his own solicitor, to establish correct procedure given the vague situation. Nigel Caffin would almost certainly consider Annie to be his client and on this occasion Charles wished to have his authority acknowledged. While Annie attended the suffering Hemsley, he must deal with the miserable matter of John's affairs.

Besides, William now had a bee in his bonnet, there'd be no peace until Charles was able to declare the outcome of his enquiries, no reprieve until William's thirsty curiosity was satisfied, until he was rid of the bee!

As William walked along a growing frustration nipped at his mood, irritating, annoying him. He'd heard that Jack Haynes had been looking at a house on Chalfont Drive, three bedrooms, gardens front and back, spending Hilda's money no doubt, the affluent pit manager. William kicked a pebble into the side of the road and cursed, "Damn him."

Moreleigh was now officially William's, he had seemingly dismissed Celia's title as readily as he'd judged Jack for acquiring Hilda's and recognised no hypocrisy on his part. Tenants were due to move in at the end of the month, once in regular receipt of rent he could turn his mind to securing a parcel of land. He'd studied a map and the old Colver mine appeared the prime example of a future development site and now Stanford's daughter Patricia was back at the helm William was itching to make approach of her, one in the eye for Basil if he could persuade the flaky

Patricia to let go that piece of spent industrial land for a price, as yet not reflecting a value attributed to the city's expansion.

He was curious as to what might happen with John's money, he would have received the same amount from Davina as did himself and tragic though his brother's death was, presumably a considerable sum sat in the bank doing nothing but earn a modest interest. He'd waited a respectable length of time before broaching the subject but his dad should seek to begin the process of proving John's estate and closing his bank account.

The women seemed preoccupied with Anthony Hemsley's health, fortunate William perceived that to be, while Celia was concerning herself with events at The Park she was not making enquiry of William as to his intentions. Celia expected him to find a job of some sort, well he'd been that route before the war and now had no desire to travel it again.

Mathew seemed settled at Raleigh despite his mother suggesting that if he wished, now men were returning he could undertake a further period of study, to enable him to enter one of the professions. 'I don't think I'm cut out for an office job Mam', had been his response, 'I'm not sorry to see an end to shell cases but bikes interest me and uncle George will be back at the factory soon'. William had bitten his tongue for once, with George only recently home he'd let it pass, but his unspoken thought had been, how uninspired, what could possibly be interesting about a bike unless you were entirely without ambition. Freddy somehow saw the future in his beloved land, but not as William imagined it, ploughed and furrowed it was still just land, either too wet or too dry, and even at its best, little more impressive than a row of allotments from which sprouted up a few creosoted sheds and water butts. While George saw the future through people, his was a simple socialistic belief, in man was untapped potential, creativity and invention. Well, they were entitled to their day dreams but William's expectation for the future couldn't be met with an abundance of wheat and potatoes, or a new bicycle that would take a man to his work faster than did his old one. Housing, the spread of building work generally was the accepted way forward and first benefit would be gained by those holding land suitable for development. Any money to come his way from John's estate William would invest in property or land. He'd wait until next week before calling on Mrs.Bradshaw, then if his approach was successful he'd make an appointment with the bank manager at Braithwaite's, Birkett was gone and good riddance. With the residue from Davina's legacy and the income from rent of Moreleigh he could put a feasible proposition before the new man. Feeling almost smug William made mental preparations for his meeting with Patricia, assessing what should be just the right degree of flannel, her late father's influence on him, how much he'd learned from Basil, his admiration of her own business acumen. She was after all a woman and unlikely to be concentrating her mind solely on matters of commerce, especially as she'd only recently been discharged from Mapperley. Negotiating a good price for Colver shouldn't really challenge him too much, he'd survived the war for goodness sake.

He felt in his pocket, there was enough change for the bus. He'd banked on his dad declining the offer of another drink but it served a purpose to offer it, grease the wheels as it were, in case Charles proved to be the one who must deliberate over John's money. William held out his arm at the sight of the No.46, there was no one else waiting at the stop, no one in his way, just as he liked it. He stepped onto the boarding plate feeling confident, next week he would go to Castle Road, but for now, "Middleton Boulevard", he said in response to the conductors usual 'where to'?

"You could catch a bus on the ring road and be at Celia's in less than ten minutes. David would go to Harrow Road School if we lived there, it has a good reputation, an' bein' closer to Wollaton Park would be a bonus too, now the POWs have gone it's a fine place for David and Rosemary to run about, a lot more space than at the arboretum. If you want we could view it tomorrow afternoon."

Jack was trying his best to encourage Hilda, he genuinely believed that if she were to see No.17 Chalfont Drive, then she'd find fresh enthusiasm. Not so very long ago, to move to a larger house was what she'd wanted and Jack's reluctance had frustrated her. Now it was as though the notion of moving simply for moving's sake irritated her, as if in so doing the pit still won and Hilda seemed determined to stand her ground against the pit.

She stopped what she was doing and came to sit down with Jack, the children were upstairs asleep.

"I look around sometimes at other women, the war has done a strange thing, it achieved to confine some, they were locked away in a realm of their own and even now it's over, they move about quietly, remote from the rest. But conversely, the others it liberated, they have more confidence, a measure of self esteem, and a desire to look good. There's a hairdressing salon on Alfreton Road, it's for sale, as a going concern, I'd like to buy it."

Jack was quite taken aback, he had no idea. "But you don't know anything about hairdressing," he said.

"When I was younger I would spend time with a friend from Clarendon, Laura, she's married now, lives at Ratcliffe so we don't really see each other anymore, moved on like folk do. We spent hours on a Saturday doing each other's hair, I always enjoyed it and I wasn't that bad at it either, I could pick it up easily from an experienced woman."

"What about David and Rosemary?" Jack was struggling to make sense of it.

"Rosemary could go there with me, I used to go with mam to the workshop when I was little older than Rosemary. I would leave in time to be home for David coming out of school. Two stylists work there now, I'd keep them on, learn from them, but on the plus side I could keep the accounts myself, that would save an expense. It's a good business, the agent tells me it makes a healthy profit."

"So you've already spoken to the agent before sayin' anythin' to me."

Jack felt slighted, it wasn't right, he was her husband, she should have told him of her interest first.

"Well you've already spoken to an agent about the house on Chalfont Drive so what's the difference?"

What she said was true, in fact he'd actually looked over the property, albeit very briefly, one evening after work, he couldn't deny her logic.

"It's your money Hilda," he said, "I didn't realise you were keen on that sort o' thing, it would seem very different to workin' in the library."

"It's 'our' money Jack, it's always been our money. You work at the pit to earn for us all. If we acquired any sort of business then I would do the same, it would be for you, me and our family. I was hoping that you'd go with me to look at the place, speak with the agent, do the deal." Hilda looked at him like a duck looks up at thunderclouds.

"It doesn't sound as though you need me." Jack stared into the hearth.

"Then you couldn't have been listening properly," said Hilda.

Jack raised his face. "Who are the agents?"

Hilda smiled. "Marshalls."

"If it's really what you want then make an appointment to view, one evenin', not before half past five, the vendors will appreciate that, it's unlikely that they'd welcome prospective purchasers when they're open for business. If we ask Mrs.Flowers nicely she'll keep an eye on Rosie an' David for an hour, I don't think you should involve your mam until you're quite sure, we don't need to tell Mrs.Flowers where we're goin', only that we have an appointment, but you could do no other than tell mam if you asked her to come and stop wi' the kids. If it don't work out then Annie won't have been worried."

"Why do you suppose she'd be worried?" Asked a puzzled Hilda.

"Because she's your mam an' that's what mams do."

Hilda got to her feet, leaned over to kiss his forehead and whispered, "Thank you. I'll finish making up your dinner box for the morning, it's pilchards again." She sighed, "We shall all look like a pilchard soon."

He didn't voice it but Jack nevertheless thought it might explain the curiosity of it all, it was a saying he'd heard his own mam use, 'fish is good for the brains'. Perhaps Hilda had eaten so many pilchards that she now felt compelled to use her new found abilities, hairdressing! Mrs.Bradshaw could become a customer, he smiled to himself at the image, which came into his head, Patricia Bradshaw, sitting in the hairdressing salon with an apron round her neck and shoulders while Hilda snipped away with the general purpose scissors and Rosie sat on the floor gathering the clippings to put outside so the birds might line their nests with something soft.

Liberated women, with self esteem and wanting to look good. Whatever would his dear old mam have made of that?

Annie settled in the chair opposite Charles, a pair of Samuel's trousers in her lap and her sewing box by her feet. She'd tried all day to avert her eyes from the front pages of the newspapers, now there they were again. Charles following his usual practice sat hidden behind The Telegraph having already perused The Evening Post. She threaded her needle, there was a hole in both pockets and Samuel was lamenting the loss of a penknife, which must have fallen through.

"I have to go out on Monday morning," said Charles, "I shall leave in time to get into town by half past ten, I won't be long."

No further information was forthcoming and Annie knew better than to ask but looking up when he spoke had compelled her to observe the images on the front pages of The Telegraph, scenes of destruction in black and white, yet in Annie's mind, blood red, flesh coloured, laid waste Hiroshima. When two days ago news broke of a second atomic bomb, dropped on Nagasaki most folk had felt disbelief, the end of the world, of mankind must surely be nigh. But the city traffic hadn't halted in its tracks, children still skipped with ropes and rolled marbles, and men and women, having awoke two mornings since, ventured to look once again into the sky for sunshine and not for a terror that was thrust through the cloud as a single finger but opened to a mighty palm that smothered everything beneath it with ferocious intent, before retracting amid a plume of fire so immense, it surely scorched the gates of Heaven. Yet not the end of the world but the end of the war, at least that's what the headlines declared.

George and Samuel had gone to The Odeon to see Captain Kidd, with Randolph Scott and Charles Lawson. Since his dad returned Samuel had spent almost every waking moment with him, even going with George to see Percy Pollard. With school starting again early next month George had asked if there was any hope of a job at Raleigh in September. Percy liked George Boucher and he'd shut himself in his office and wept when he'd heard about John, but with so many of the women enjoying that degree of independence their work at the factory gave them and demand for bicycles not yet fully recovered, vacancies were limited. However Percy had a notion that like George and Samuel, dads would come home to their children and find renewed happiness, an end to all the bad, and the resumption of everything good. He'd asked George to come up with a design for a child's bicycle, something just a little different, to reflect a new beginning, they'd run through its production costs and provided they allowed for a reasonable retail price after profit and the design met with all safety aspects, then when George came back to work in September it would go into production with the rest.

It was an opportunity seized upon with relish by George and he'd begun the first drawings of his 'Raleigh Rascal'.

"We're getting too old for this shop." Charles spoke from somewhere beyond Hiroshima! "With men beginning to return through demob families will again increase, it's bound to happen, doesn't take an expert to work that out. Rationing will eventually come to an end and it will take younger bones than ours to do justice to double fronted premises like these."

He didn't go on to say that according to an article, which he'd read in The Evening Post, the Co-op was grasping the nettle by looking to expand in the belief that the future would be brighter, trade would recover, all it required of those in commerce was confidence and investment. Charles had attached his own observation to that, 'and more heart for the challenge than Charles Eddowes could muster'. Annie wondered if it was a veiled intimation, if in fact Charles thought George should be considering his future as a shopkeeper rather than returning to Raleigh. Although George had said nothing to suggest it, Annie imagined that in due course he would want to find a small house suitable for Samuel and himself. He had the money from Davina, it was only natural for him to look beyond the back rooms of the shop for their future abode. The prospect of life at Gregory Street, sharing the space with Charles and her must prove daunting, especially now Samuel was showing maturity. Alice died thirteen years ago, hopefully George would find love again, if Annie was sure of anything then it was the selfless devotion of her late daughter in law, Alice wouldn't wish him to exist in loneliness, he had family but they couldn't fill the void, it was a kind of loneliness, which could only be banished by a constant, a wife to make comfort, make warmth, to make love.

"I'd not thought about anything other than the shop," she said, "we manage, customers are loyal, we're not that old after all."

"You look tired these days, you'd have time to spend with your grandchildren if it weren't for the shop. You let Hemsley drain you, it's about time he bucked himself up, for the life of me I can't think of any reason why that man should be depressed, unless he's grieving for something or someone he can't have."

For a moment Annie thought Charles had somehow discovered that Anthony had fathered a child, a son whom he had now lost to war. But Charles lowered the newspaper and the look on his face made her realise that it was a slight, a suggestion of impropriety. It annoyed her, added to which his absence from the shop for so much of each day was the real impediment to her spending time with their grandchildren, not to mention his irrational resentment of Jack Haynes, which rendered her visits to Hilda almost clandestine.

She was saved from having to respond to his caustic remark when the back door opened and William walked in.

"Any chance of a cuppa Mam? I've been doing a few jobs at Moreleigh so I thought I'd drop by on my way home, are you two on your own?"

"George has taken Samuel to the pictures," said Annie putting down her stitching, "I'll get the kettle on." As she walked across to the scullery she overheard William say.

"Have you been yet?"

So for whatever reason Charles was required to be in town by 10-30 on Monday, it concerned William. It was best to divert her thoughts and as she made the tea it was Anthony Hemsley who occupied them. When she'd called at The Park last Sunday afternoon he'd shown her a letter that he'd received from Donald's mother. In it she wrote that she needed time to consider his request and given the nature of same, she felt it would not be fair to deny the child, but the decision must ultimately rest with Donald's widow. She would do her very best to explain the past, with all its complications, to her daughter in law but in the meantime Anthony should be patient and not predict the outcome, only time would tell.

Annie could sympathise with the woman's dilemma but it was the little girl's future that now mattered the most. Each passing week, for Anthony proved more anxious than the one before, but a letter, worded as it was, must surely grant hope. She carried the tea through to Charles and William.

"I thought I might send Emily to piano lessons, poor Mathew is tone deaf but that's probably helpful when working in a noisy factory like Raleigh. It can be evidence of refinement in a young woman, the ability to play the piano, might help her get on in life, what do you think Mam?" Asked William, looking up at Annie as though confident of her endorsement. Her opinion was sought over piano lessons it seemed though Annie suspected that actually it counted for little.

'Remember what you are my girl'. A lifetime ago aunt Bella had been wise enough to recognise what that life might be.

"If Emily would like to learn piano then I think it would be a nice idea William."

"Celia used to play a bit," he said, between gulps of tea, Annie sensed he'd achieved what he came for and was now in a hurry to be gone, "when she was a girl, the piano is still at her mother's house."

Annie could read William's mind and she felt dismayed, it compelled her to point out. "Edmund played the piano too, rather well as I understand from my conversations with Caroline."

"Yes but neither Jonathon nor Gregory show any aptitude so I thought Emily may as well have the piano, the hardest part will be transporting it to Wollaton, they're heavy aren't they?"

Not as heavy as Annie's spirits, she walked back to the scullery thinking to herself that George and Samuel needn't have gone to The Odeon to see a pirate, they had only to wait for William to come to Gregory Street.

“I am truly sorry for your loss Charles, I wondered what brought you to my office, it’s been some time since we last met. I wish it could be for some other purpose than to discuss your son’s affairs.”

Julian Russe sat in the very same room in which Gerald Meakin sat the day Charles came to declare Saul dead and to register his own impatient interest in his father’s estate. The decor was different, the space appeared lighter but today Charles felt no urgency, as much as he’d wanted back then to discover the sum of his inheritance, if only to satisfy Enid’s demands, today he wished to hold it at bay, to keep the memory of John intact, not invaded by officialdom despite that impatience now manifest in William.

“Although you think it unlikely that John would have made a Will I shall nevertheless have to establish that as being the case, if as you mention, he may have done so through Chaucer, Caffin and Holt, they would have furnished him with a copy whilst they retained the original. Yet you say no such document has come to light among his things. I shall speak with Nigel Caffin over the telephone, to request they look through their files, in these circumstances, if no Will is found, I am obliged by law to place a notice in the newspapers of John’s death and invite any person with a bona fide claim against his estate to register it with this firm within two weeks of the date the notice appears.”

Charles smiled. “John wouldn’t owe anyone as much as a halfpenny, but I understand.”

“You say John, along with his brothers and sister inherited a considerable sum of money through Davina Wright, also that he was not married and therefore leaves no children. Unless there is in fact a Will, which states otherwise, the sum of John’s estate, when proved will pass to you Charles, his next of kin.

Had he died prior to Mrs.Wright’s estate being administered, then your other children would automatically have received a greater sum, the money, which would have been due to John, his brothers and his sister would have inherited, apportioned equally of course.

I can’t imagine it being of any comfort to you whatsoever right now, but John has likely secured you some measure of ease as you grow older Charles, you and your wife both. It may prove a painful help to you but we can only trust it grants satisfaction to John."

Charles had not really thought of how John's money might be dealt with until last Sunday when William had said he should pursue the matter of John's estate. Only then did it occur to him that William anticipated being a beneficiary, the bee in the bonnet.

Charles needed air, the office in which he and Russe sat stifled him with memories and threat of William's frustrated discontent gripped his throat like a warning.

"I shall leave it with you Mr.Russe," he said getting to his feet. "Write to me when you know more." They shook hands briefly and Charles walked to the door. He paused and without turning said. "Thirty four, John was thirty four, the prime of life, he had no debts, none, John like his mother, only ever gives."

Jack was to meet Hilda and the agent at the hairdressers on Alfreton Road at twenty past five, the bus had been a few minutes late, a quick glance at his watch told him he'd need to hurry when he got off at his stop. It felt so unlikely, the thought of viewing the interior of a women's hairdressing salon having just left a coal mine, a stark contrast in every way. At the pit was little to please the eye, never 'dressed' it stood under the elements, windswept, sun baked, frost bitten, drenched, taken for granted by all who passed by every day of its life. Yet Jack had seen it at daybreak, at sunrise when the deep black silhouette of the pithead stood proud against a sky of gold, asking some small recognition for that of itself, it surrendered in good faith, to man. Never 'dressed' nor wanting to look good, for the most part ignored as an 'eyesore' but Jack had come to know its soul and cared for it, for its plain honesty, Jack cared.

On the bus he imagined the women to be observing him as though aware of his destination. Whispering to each other, 'his wife's going into business, she was a Clarendon girl you know, he's older than her, strange match'.

When Patricia Bradshaw had come to the mine office last Monday, Jack had felt threatened, he shouldn't be manager, he'd no schooling worth mentioning, he lived still at the same address, the same small rented house that had been his mam and dad's home, he didn't speak with cut glass refinement, he couldn't think in shades of elitist blue or shed the skin he grew up in and parade a shiny new one. She had introduced herself to Jack, 'Mr.Haynes, we've not actually met before, although we knew of each other and I suspect, had our own impressions, do you think we might erase those with this handshake and free ourselves of hindrance'?

Her approach should have allowed Jack to dismiss any self doubt, but just the evening before Hilda had told him that she wanted to buy a business and to run it herself, a ladies' hairdressers, a complete unknown for Jack. Now he was about to alight the bus and that same sense of inadequacy brought a pain to his gut. A few yards ahead he could see Hilda standing with the agent, he quickened his step.

Mr.Haynes, good to meet you," said the smartly dressed gent extending his hand, "I'm Bernard Priestly." He reached inside his jacket pocket and produced a key. "The business is current, the vendor employs two young women, I imagine they hope to be retained by the new owner. I understand the salon trades from 9am until 4-30pm five days of the week but closes for a half day every Wednesday. I have seen some figures and they read very well, and from my own viewing as I went room to room taking the details, I consider the premises to have been maintained in good order, the interior decoration is as you would expect, given that business is ongoing here and the facade, as you can see, has been painted this summer." He turned the key and opened the door. "After you my dear."

Hilda cast an excited look at Jack and entered. Inside it was as far removed from the pit as it was possible to be. Of most interest to Jack was the actual extent of the property, as if reading his thoughts Priestly said.

"I'll show you the facility at the back, it's small but useful."

He led them through to a sort of kitchenette containing a couple of stools, a sink and a two ring stove. The back door opened to a concrete yard with a lavatory and space for a dustbin. The yard exited into an alleyway, clearly the favoured haunt of tom cats, the smell of their urine was intense.

"It's a rare opportunity, few business premises become available freehold but the real plus to this one is the space above, currently it's used for storage but quite frankly it could be utilised much more. I'd go as far as to say that someone with enterprise could incorporate the upper floor and extend the business, I understand some ladies will pay for a manicure and various treatments to enhance their skin," he hesitated and with a hint of embarrassment added, "even procedures to remove unwanted hair. If you'll follow me I'll show you the space above."

Jack began to wonder if they were viewing the right business, it sounded more like the nature of an abattoir than somewhere a woman might go to have her hair shampooed. But he kept his eyes peeled as Priestly led them from one area to the next, making mental note of any points of concern.

Upstairs there were two rooms, a door from one to the other. Jack could see what Priestly meant, a few boxes at one end of the first room, the second stood empty but for an old coat stand and a shabby mirror on the wall. Jack took a close look at the floorboards, he couldn't see any sign of woodworm, nor did he detect any smell of damp, the windows were sash and appeared reasonably sound.

"I suppose the ground floor has electricity but none up here," said Jack, "what about the roof space, I'd want to check the rafters, do you have a torch?"

Priestly seemed surprised. "Not with me today I'm afraid, I could meet you again and bring one then."

Hilda was growing anxious, if Jack didn't approve of the place then that would be that, why was the loft so important, the salon looked good enough and that was the priority. Jack was pensive.

"I would want to make a thorough inspection of the roof timbers an' nails, to eliminate any likelihood of costly repair work an' I'd need to see if there's a firebreak between these premises an' the roof space of the shop next door. It's on for enough money, given the few problems I've noted. One of the wash basins downstairs has a crack an' although the big window at the front has been recently painted, I could tell that a lot of filler had been used where the wood has some rot. The alley out the back causes me some concern, it presents a possible security risk, where does it lead, I saw the dustbin so I imagine there's public access. Nothing disastrous but all points to be borne in mind. I'm no hairdresser but like any other business it must keep books, we'd need to see the last two years figures and the appointment books, they would reveal a lot about the business. Where I work the custom is pre determined, it's meeting the demand that causes our biggest headache but in this sort of trade I can see it has to be the regularity of the Mrs.Browns and Mrs.Whites that's crucial. There's competition out there in town an' women aren't as predictable as we men folk, I'd wager the faces at The Standard don't vary one night from another, but ladies like variety, they can look at a shop window an' find pleasure in the activity of seein' what's different from the last time they looked, while a fella is happy with the same, he knows where he is with the same."

Hilda could see why Hugh Porter had such faith in Jack and felt confident in recommending him to Mrs.Stanford. Jack's questions and observations rather than suggest his disapproval of the property, in fact implied his interest. He wasn't one to waste time, either his own or that of someone else.

"Shall we meet here again tomorrow Mr.Haynes?" Asked Priestly.

"Aye, alright, make it half past five if yer will but let my wife take another look around downstairs now, it might be difficult for her to come again tomorrow, we've young children, a neighbour is minding them for us."

Jack glanced at Hilda and smiled, if her heart was set on it then he'd do his best to get her a good deal as money would need to be spent on the place. Either the vendor was sufficiently wealthy as to not need to utilise the rooms above or it was the other extreme, they were too hard up to stand the cost of maintenance and improvement, the latter was the most likely thought Jack. He watched Hilda as she studied the layout of the salon, she looked happy. Love was a curious thing and Jack knew that above all else, he loved Hilda. It was just this liberated woman malarkey that puzzled him, a man's job was to provide for his family, take care of them, so what was it that women were so desperate to be liberated from? Even here there was a stove and a sink.

Finally they were ready to leave. Bernard Priestly shook Jack's hand as they were about to go their separate ways, but then Jack made one last enquiry.

"We are genuinely interested, so it would seem only proper that we should know who we are dealin' with, you must have the vendor's name."

"Of course," said Priestly, "I believe that the only reason she's decided to sell is her age, they're a very successful couple and while this business has proved profitable through an established clientele, I imagine the good lady is ready to shed a small part of their endeavour, I think it has only ever been an investment, as I understand it, Mrs.Woolascroft bought the premises in her own right after her father died. Do you know Cynthia Woolascroft at all?" Priestly directed the question at Hilda.

"Not personally but I do know of her," she replied.

"Nice lady, pleasure to do business with." Priestly hurried away.

Jack sighed, if his instinct was correct there'd be little movement on the asking price. Sufficiently wealthy! His first assessment had been the accurate one.

Some time had passed since he last had occasion to open the gates and walk to the door of the Stanford's house, all that he'd witnessed, all that he'd survived apparently made no impression on the place. It stood just as ever, no evidence of skirmish, no trace of any hostile encounter, somehow it had escaped any attempt at defeat despite all the years of harbouring a General, intent on domination.

William looked towards the side path, for a second undecided, but no, today the nature of his business entitled him to knock at the front door. At first there was no reply, he knocked again and the sound of the latch being lifted on the inside confirmed someone was at home.

"Yes." Patricia Bradshaw stood in the open doorway, her expression told William that she couldn't bring his name to mind, although his face was familiar.

"William Eddowes, I was your father's driver for a while, some years ago, I've been at the front with the army but I'm back now and I wondered if I might speak with you, it is a business matter."

"Oh yes, of course, now I remember. I've got to know your mother over the past few months, she's often mentioned you, and your brothers, George and John. I was so very sorry to learn that John had been killed. I lost my husband, Italy, he was killed in Italy. Come in William, mother would normally be here but she needed to go into town. How is Celia? She was kind enough to visit me, with Caroline, when I was unwell. I believe your mother in law was being looked after in another part of the hospital. Mrs.Tozer would appear to have a strong constitution, the doctor told me that I had a robust constitution but it can't compare with the fortitude of my mother, it's found in so many of that generation don't you think? I see it in Annie also, they are all so much stronger than their looks suggest. The war was a hideous, monstrous thing yet I cannot deny it brought out the true character of women, which I am quite convinced will forever now remain. The so called fairer sex is perhaps less obliging, not afraid to flex her muscles, ready to stand up for herself. Come into the living room William, I'm afraid if it's work that you seek then I could only direct you to Mr.Haynes or Mr.Wills at Birchdale, unlike my father, if I need to go somewhere I either take a bus or drive myself."

William's hackles rose at the mention of 'Mr.Haynes', well, what he was about to put to Patricia Bradshaw would send Jack Haynes to the back row, the jumped up nobody. This was a business deal and if it went through then William wouldn't care if Mrs.Bradshaw travelled in style or in a donkey cart and Jack Haynes could cough and spit through his days at the pit if that's what satisfied him. Land, getting that land at Colver was all that mattered but he must stick to his plan, a few gracious words about Basil, lay on the charm. Flexing muscles indeed!

Patricia sat down by the window. "Please do sit William." She felt intrigued, his manner suggested more than merely a request for work.

"It feels strange to me, coming here and knowing that Mr.Stanford isn't going to appear at his brisk pace, instructing me to drive him to some important meeting or other. I'm sure my own ambition was instilled in me by your father. While my dad has worked his way and done enough, for whatever reason he shied away from any speculative venture, the safe route, he's only ever chosen the safe route. Mr.Stanford taught me a wider vision, to open my eyes and look beyond, not to be afraid of taking a risk, it was an element of business, which rewarded the brave. I'm sure you must miss him a great deal."

Patricia felt tension inside herself, but she had vowed not ever again to be governed by her father's authority, not even through memory, or his influence lingering still in misguided individuals like William Eddowes.

“Life is certainly very different now that he is no longer here but we have our own strengths, my mother, Julia and Caroline. It was a harsh fate that made us all widows but life goes on. All that aside, you obviously wish to ask something William, there is no need of preamble, business should be direct, it is only hindered when unnecessary niceties cause confusion.”

William shuffled his feet and cleared his throat, as though about to address a gathering.

“I did my bit, more than, but the war is over, now I can turn my thoughts to the future, for my family. I am looking to buy some land, as a simple investment. The old industrial site at Colver, it serves no useful purpose to you and with all the other responsibilities you have on your shoulders I wondered if you might consider selling it to me, I’m prepared to pay a fair price of course.”

“I’m afraid William that you are speaking to the wrong person. Colver is not mine to sell. It is owned jointly by my sisters, you would need to approach them. Julia works at Beeston but is here in the evenings. Caroline is at home more because of the boys so it is probably most sensible that you first speak with her, they would both need to agree a decision obviously. I really couldn’t tell you what their response might be.”

Patricia offered a smile and William, now thrown completely, mumbled a vague, “I see”. He got to his feet. “I’m sorry to have troubled you, I didn’t realise.”

“It’s no trouble, it’s good to see you again. I feel quite a connection with your family these days, not least through Jack Haynes, I understand he’s married to your sister Hilda.

Hugh Porter was entirely correct in recommending Mr.Haynes, I do believe the mine is in good hands. I find myself looking forward to calling there and spending time with him and Eddie Wills. They are totally opposite to Mr.Stanford and I don’t think he would understand them at all, but thankfully, I do.

Be careful William, on the back of war the nature of business is likely to be quite ruthless, risk and reward may prove to be an unfortunate dogma to embrace now.”

As he walked away from the house William tasted bile, a bitterness on his tongue that prompted him to spit into the gutter. The rumours had all been of Basil's heartless favouritism, his selection of the fittest, as one sharp tongued individual had put it, adding that in Stanford language 'fit' meant suitably unscrupulous. William could hear the voice of irony mocking him, 'checkmate Eddowes'. If only he'd known, then his attitude towards the proceeds of Moreleigh he would have modified somewhat, and Emily could have found accomplishment without the need of a piano. Yet Caroline had been compliant, what was to say she would not be so again over the land at Colver. As for Julia, he didn't know her at all but she'd been hapless enough to marry a fascist, it wouldn't suggest brilliance of mind. It was a complication but the offer of money in exchange for a piece of derelict land must surely tempt them. Women liked to shop and now the war was over, gradually would return to the high street their reward for having 'made do' for so long. In fact, on reflection the two younger daughters, considered less astute by Basil, could well prove weaker in negotiation. He would call on Caroline this evening, the sooner the better, before Patricia had chance to point out the possible benefits to them keeping Colver, she would no doubt sit and cogitate the matter and her father's influence could persuade her. William had been surprised to find Patricia so alert, he'd imagined her illness would have left her passive.

He'd seen among the legal notices in the newspaper, one entered by Meakin and Kirk, referring to John's Estate, he'd not mentioned it to anyone, not even Celia, but it had encouraged him to believe that progress was being made and he had no doubt whatsoever that John would be entirely free of debt. John wasn't a business man, he never strayed from the old recognised way, had he survived, then like George he'd have been content to return to Raleigh, to do Percy Pollard's will.

"Cooee, wait up."

An urgent shout caused him to turn around, Maggie Hillier hurried to catch up. In typical Maggie fashion she planted a kiss on his cheek and thread her arm through his, just as she would have done years ago. Time and events seemed to bounce off Maggie, impervious, nothing dampened her spirits or subdued her enthusiasm.

"Tell me William Eddowes what you've been up to, you always have a scheme, a plan, they go around in your head like a novelist's plot. Tell your Maggie."

That sparkle, which had ever shone from her eyes and softened William's heart, even now could drive away his torments.

"My plan is to buy you a cup of tea at that cafe on Clumber Street and a toasted teacake, if the fairies have produced one."

She laughed, why couldn't Celia laugh that way? Why was the delight granted to Toby Hillier? All those years ago when William had walked Maggie down the aisle and given her away to Hillier he'd asked the Gods that same question, there'd been no answer then and there was no answer now.

The house was quiet, Jonathon and Gregory had gone up to bed an hour ago. Caroline knew that sleep wouldn't come yet, so much kept her mind from rest. She stared at the corner of the room where the piano used to stand, now a different colour to the rest, protected from the light of the window the wallpaper behind the piano had retained its original pattern and shade, while around the room it had faded to a tired trace of what it once had been.

Had she spoken too sternly to William? The last thing she sought to do was cause upset to Celia but he antagonised, his manner was quite without consideration for others, William thought only of himself. When he'd finally got around to revealing the real purpose of his visit, after at least twenty minutes of contrived pleasantry, Caroline had instantly determined herself not to concede to his wishes this time. The way he'd approached her over the sale of Moreleigh had been so calculated. He'd made no mention of Edmund, it was insensitive, William was capable of putting aside all sentiment, of taking the inconvenience, which was family, and shutting it away in some remote compartment of his carefully constructed scheme.

When she'd responded to his request of the piano by saying how well Edmund had been able to play his reaction had been dismissive and hurtful, 'but your boys aren't the musical type are they'? That was his ignorant remark. It was an audacity given that he hardly ever spent time with them and made no effort to be any kind of uncle, even before he went away. But if Emily was to learn the instrument then her uncle Edmund, if he'd been alive to say it, would have told her that he was delighted for her to find pleasure in music and gratified that it would be on the very piano her mother and he had played. So this evening when William had come to the house and implied that he was trying to help Julia and herself by taking Colver off their hands at a fair price, her tolerance finally ran out. To describe his departure as being like a dog with its tail between its legs wouldn't be too far removed from reality, he was annoyed and frustrated by his lack of success and sulking over Caroline's reprimand. He reminded her so much of her father, not in looks, although they could both express their disgruntled mood quite clearly through a sourness of features, those accusing eyes, that nose raised in disdain and the pouting lips, but in their malicious design, whether consciously or unaware, they bore such similar characteristics they could be taken for kin.

Caroline stirred herself, not prepared to look on the piano's unfortunate legacy any longer she took the small occasional table and placed it in the middle of the vacated space. The fern, which over the years had grown to impressive height and breadth, she fetched from the hall and positioned on the table. It wasn't ideal but it would do for the time. Caroline had stood up for herself and a sense of wellbeing began to replace her stress, she was strong, capable and unafraid, she smiled to herself and spoke out loud.

"Edmund, dear Edmund, we shall be alright. I don't know what became of your friend Bill Stribley but if he is with you then tell him I have heard his Hallelujahs and been grateful for them."

On Monday she was to begin paid work as a nursing auxiliary at the hospital, the prospect pleased her. Casting her eyes to the corner of the room a thought occurred to her, she could not now play the piano but then, neither could she play it before! From now on Caroline Tozer would make music with the spoons, God bless Bill Stribley.

When Edna first opened the envelope two weeks ago she'd noted the date and time of the appointment with Richard Ansell and quickly put it underneath the tea towels and aprons in the kitchen drawer, no need to say anything to Billy or the girls, it would likely be something and nothing. But the closer each day came to that date, 30th August, a Thursday at 2-40 in the afternoon, the more nervous Edna became.

Billy had gone to the ironmongers, the back door needed a new shoot bolt. 'Go to Moffat's while you're about it, see if they've got a wringer, ours won't last much longer, it's been threatening a 'walkout' for weeks'. Edna had given him another errand to keep him out of the way while she got ready, he'd presume she'd decided to go to Myra's for an hour if he got home to find her missing.

Now she sat in the waiting area outside Mr.Ansell's clinic, looking across to the opposite wall where a clock displayed the time as being five past three. She sighed, the new shoes she'd put on pinched, only the left one. She eased out her foot just slightly, at home she would have kicked the damn thing off and rubbed her tortured little toe before packing the shoe tightly with screwed up newspaper to stretch the leather, then putting the pair out of sight at the bottom of the wardrobe, to forget about the miserable things until the offending left shoe had yielded to the Evening Post. Here, with other people sharing the waiting area she could only ease her toes free of the offending leather and suffer the throbbing in the name of dignity.

The magazines on the small table paraded images of pretty young women wearing fashions the like of which it was impossible to obtain and stories intended to transport the reader to happy ever after land, not to mention remedies for every conceivable ailment except inflammation of the tongue.

At last, "Edna Dodds."

A nurse had appeared at a side door, looking around the room for a likely Edna. Pushing her foot back into the shoe, Edna stood up, stiffened her back like a trooper and followed stoically.

Mr.Ansell was not at all as she'd imagined him, a younger man, fair haired, relaxed in his manner, even his style of dress was less formal than any doctor Edna had seen before, certainly very different to Mr.Bob Bob.

"Hello Mrs.Dodds, take a seat." He glanced at a sheet of paper on the desk in front of him. "Mr.Fordyce writes that you are experiencing soreness in your mouth, which he cannot attribute to any problem arising from tooth decay or abscess. He also informs me that you are a no nonsense woman who calls a spade a spade." He began to chuckle. "That makes my job very much easier Edna, may I call you Edna?"

"Well that's me name, mam didn't go in for anythin' too fancy when it came to us girls, me sisters are Ada an' Vera."

"My mother's name is Vera," he said, "a popular name now of course, there'll be more than a few girl babies born in the near future who'll become Veras I shouldn't wonder. Now, I need to take a look inside your mouth, don't worry."

The nurse came forward and encouraged Edna onto the couch. "Slip your shoes off dear," she said.

Edna was more than happy to oblige. He shone a light into her mouth.

"Wide as you can please Edna, now raise your tongue so that I can look beneath it, very good." He used some kind of instrument to gently prod her tongue, it didn't increase the soreness too much but it made Edna want to swallow. As if understanding that was the case he withdrew the small device and said.

"Do you smoke Edna?"

"A bit, I started after the accident four years ago, our youngest Myra, a lorry ran over her, she wer' in 'ere for twelve months, Mr.Shillin', 'e wer' 'er doctor. Me nerves wer' all over the place, I asked Archie, Myra's young man if 'e'd bring me a packet o' cigarettes, 'e worked at Players so 'e could get 'em a bit cheaper, just one or two a day, that's all. Myra's married now, got wed last May. She still has to attend the skin clinic at General an' nurse comes to change 'er bandages at home, 'er leg, the lorry went over 'er leg. But it's good, she manages well, it's ulcers she's got to be careful of, mustn't stand on it too long." Edna's voice became progressively more emotional as she explained.

"I remember that accident," said Ansell, "so it was your daughter. She is in the very best of hands, they come no finer than Robert Shilling. It must have been a most traumatic experience for Archie too but a happy ending at least, sometimes I think it is especially hard for loved ones who must look on and feel helpless."

Edna sniffed into her hanky. "Archie wer' killed in Italy, poor lad. Myra an' Jack Wainwright got together again, when 'e come home injured. They'd fitted him wi' an artificial leg, you'd 'ardly tell to look at him. Jack wer' sweet on Myra years ago, I think about Archie a lot, 'e wer' a good lad, but Jack's a good en an'all an' 'e loves the bones of our Myra, 'e's like my husband Billy in lots o' ways, don't complain, just gets on wi' it, Billy wer' injured in the last lot, lost an arm but still tough as hemp on the outside, soft as butter inside."

Richard Ansell found it difficult to find the right words to say, so much sadness had prevailed the last six years but this moment touched him and tugged at his heart strings.

"Sit up for a moment Edna while I explain to you what I need to do next. I'm going to take a small sample of tissue from the side of your tongue, you'll barely feel it and it's very quick, hopefully it won't make your soreness any more troublesome but I'll give you some medication that should ease it, just in case."

"Why do you need to take the sample?" Asked Edna, genuinely puzzled. "What's wrong wi' me tongue?"

"Well until I've run some tests I can't say with certainty but as soon as I have the results I will see you again and then I can be more informative."

Edna gave him a knowing look. "Tell me what might be the worst an' what might be the best, yer may as well, 'cause I shall only imagine everythin' from leprosy to the plague if yer don't give me some idea."

"There is evidence of abnormality at one side of your tongue," he hesitated and Edna interrupted the silence.

"Well doctor, if you were to look, you'd find evidence of abnormality on both sides o' the family so it's not surprisin'."

Ansell admired Edna's spirit. "We may need to remove the affected area, fortunately it doesn't look to have spread too far."

"Is that the worst or the best?" Edna moved her tongue around in her mouth, as though testing its reaction to his prognosis.

"Let's wait until we have something positive to tell you Edna. I shall write to you as soon as I know more, it takes a little while for the tests to be proved, try not to feel too anxious. Did you come on your own today?"

"I've not said owt to Billy or the girls, I'm sixty six, by the time yer reach my age there's not much yer 'aven't come across, no point in worryin' them. It's what folk say isn't it, when someone asks their age, 'as old as me tongue an' a bit older than me teeth'. So there you are Mr.Ansell, it's a sixty six year old tongue, happen it's just worn out."

The procedure finished, the nurse helped Edna from the couch.

"Sit on the chair dear while you put on your shoes."

Mr.Ansell rubbed his chin, like he pondered a particular piece of knowledge.

"I believe 1879 was a very good year for tongues, one of the best." He smiled and held open the door for Edna to be on her way. "You have the tablets, only take them if the discomfort around the area from where I took the sample distresses you, it should pass within forty eight hours anyway."

"Thank you doctor," said Edna, "your very kind but I've allus known my tongue wer' the common variety, it don't improve wi' age, it's the same now as it ever was, apart from a bit of inflammation."

He closed the door and turned to the nurse with a long breath of frustration. "Who's next nurse?"

She consulted her list. "Margaret Hopwell, six monthly check, breast cancer, in remission."

"Ah yes, call Mrs.Hopwell then nurse. How many more today?"

"Two."

He looked at his watch. "As soon as clinic is over take Mrs.Dodds' sample to the lab and tell them it's urgent I want them to begin the process right away."

"It's good of yer to come to see me Joe, they reckon I should be alright once I'm fully recovered from the op'. It's sore but nothin' compared to what it's been.

Monica wer' gettin' fed up o' me moanin' an' groanin', especially as it wern't on 'er account, if yer know what I mean."

Ray chuckled and actually blushed. It was a relief to see him in a hospital bed after having had surgery on his bad back.

Not until the war ended and he could step down from his work as an auxiliary fireman had Ray countenanced seeking medical help for the tremendous pain he'd been suffering. He tried to explain what it was the surgeon had done, but for Joe it was all too complex and outside his limited knowledge, something to do with discs and vertebrae, Joe was more than content simply to see his old mate looking happier.

"I best be goin' Ray, I've to collect one from the mortuary. Do you know it looks exactly the same in there now as it did when I worked there all them years ago? Smells the same an'all. I've got the van parked around the back, take care of yourself Ray, yer know what they say, 'good people are scarce so we must look after the bad'." Joe laughed. "I'll be seein' yer." He paused at the door of the ward and waved back.

He made his way along the corridor and down the stairs, several yards ahead of him, a familiar figure stepped out of a side door, from one of the clinics. Surely it was Susie's mam, anywhere else Joe would have automatically called out, 'Edna' but it didn't seem proper to make such sudden noise inside a hospital, to appear careless of sick folk's need of peace. She appeared to be walking slightly lame, it felt odd, Susie hadn't mentioned anything. If Edna had come through a ward door he'd have assumed she'd been visiting someone but the door of a clinic? Joe reached the corridor that would lead to the mortuary. After he'd collected Stanley Roper from the fridge and done the necessary back at Handley's, he'd go home and ask Susie about it. Edna was stoic, never one to complain but this afternoon, seeing her walking awkwardly along the hospital corridor, albeit several yards away, she'd looked old and Joe had never before thought of Edna as old, Susie's mam was timeless and often priceless! He quickened his pace. 'I'm on me way Stanley'. Suddenly the corridor, a moment earlier so familiar, now seemed miles long.

“Me soddin’ shoe were pinchin’ me foot that’s all, yer can tell Joe that ‘e’s not about to get rid o’ the mother in law just yet.”

Edna was perplexed, she’d not intended saying anything to them until Mr.Ansell gave her the results of his tests. Now here was Susie holding the inquisition and Billy stood with a look of terror all over his face. Why did Joe Spooner have to be at the hospital the very moment she was coming out of Ansell’s clinic? Now they’d all be worried up and fussing over her, because Susie would run off to tell her sisters despite anything Edna said to dissuade her, it was the last thing she’d wanted. Determined not to cause Billy undue stress she carefully explained what had happened at the dentist, the meeting with Ansell and the precautionary tests, making light of it.

“But why on earth didn’t you tell us Mam?” Said Susie. “You shouldn’t have gone on your own.”

“Well you wouldn’t expect me to drag yer along for me dentist’s appointment so why would I take yer wi’ me to the hospital, ‘e only ‘ad a poke about in me mouth, it wer’ no different to what Fordyce done. It’ll all turn out alright, you see if it don’t, I’m already feelin’ better, the inflammation must be easin’, them tests’ll show there’s nowt wrong wi’ me. I’m goin’ to put the kettle on.”

Edna walked across the scullery to the sink, it was a fib but she couldn’t bear to think of her Billy fretting day and night ‘til they knew, and besides, if they were going to cut off half her tongue, then surely she was permitted to tell the odd fib or two, while she still could.

CHAPTER TWENTY FOUR

Late September.

"She's so content Joyce," said Annie.

Elizabeth lay in her pram fingering her rattle, her full pink cheeks proclaiming her good health. Annie put her own hand where the infant could reach it, Elizabeth took hold of Annie's finger and smiled up at her.

It was impossible to comprehend, what must go through Valerie Oates' mind as she sits in Woolascroft's office having surrendered her baby and rejected motherhood in favour of becoming a wages clerk. But Annie passed no remark to Joyce, she could imagine how much had already been said on the subject. Elizabeth Perry was loved and cherished by a family, now her family and that was all anyone needed to care about.

Annie wondered if Hilda had said anything to Joyce about the salon yet but as Joyce made no mention, it would suggest not. Hilda and Jack had decided that until the conveyance was more advanced it was wise not to declare their intentions. Jack had been apprehensive from the start. Annie could sympathise, he must feel anxious, it was a big step to take and while Annie didn't doubt her daughter's ability and resolve she could understand why Jack would be struggling to accept the logic of it. Two young children and he committed, at least for the immediate future, to the running of the mine. Charles' reaction had been predictable. When Hilda had implied that it would be best not to tell him until they actually owned the salon, Annie had persuaded her of the likely resentment her dad would feel, knowing that he'd been kept in the dark quite purposefully. Better to let him get used to the idea. But determined to ignore the fact that it was Hilda's own wish and intent, he insisted that Jack had put her up to it. 'Haynes knows how to spend someone else's money', had been Charles' unworthy aside.

"I bumped into your George the other day," said Joyce, "he was chattin' with Mr.Mazarelli. They've managed to put the house back in order but Mrs.Mazarelli is still so nervous she won't go upstairs to sleep at night, she can't drive it from 'er mind, it's as if the poor woman doesn't know where she belongs anymore. I told him I'd take Elizabeth to see 'er an' that made Mr.Mazarelli cry. 'She'd like that very much, il bambino', 'e said an' kissed his fingers then touched Elizabeth's forehead with the kiss. I think they're lovely people."

The shop door opened and in shuffled Bill Rashleigh. Annie had been feeling concerned about him for a while, he'd aged dramatically since his wife died, there'd been a button missing from his waistcoat all week, Annie wanted to stitch one on for him, she'd even brought her sewing box through to the shop and placed it under the counter to await an opportune moment. Joyce put her few bits of shopping on the end of the pram.

"We'll see you again soon." She smiled warmly at Mr.Rashleigh and left.

He flopped down onto the chair by the counter, looked at Annie with searching eyes and said. "What is it I've come for lass?"

Annie seized her chance. "You've come so I can sew a button onto your waistcoat Bill."

"Oh aye," he said, "so I 'ave."

Julian Russe apparently suffered from hay fever, his eyes were red and watering, he'd sneezed several times in the space of just ten minutes, his explanation, while perfectly feasible, nevertheless did little to ease Charles' impatience. If the man couldn't tolerate pollen then why didn't he think to inform his new secretary of the fact? Surely a man in his position, supposedly bright, could have foreseen the problem. It was a woman thing, flowers indoors, they all did it, he should have advised the young woman of his malaise if exposed to blooms. The offending vase of Michaelmas Daisies had now been removed but their effects were still present and causing delay to Charles' consultation.

They had got as far as finalising John's estate. It had proved comparatively straight forward, the war office had provided formal confirmation of John's death, a duty no doubt all too frequent, the probate office was satisfied that all was in order and Russe had advised Charles that the balance, after fees, was now deposited in his account at Braithwaite's Bank. After yet another sneeze and urgent activity with his handkerchief, Russe spoke again.

"Mr.Cartwright is progressing well with the conveyance Charles, solicitors for the Cooperative Society have nothing to gain from dragging their heels, I'm sure a company like the Co-op is up to telling their legal representatives that they expect the matter dealt with at a certain cost and within a stated time. The contracts should be ready for exchange any day now with completion by the middle of next month. You've not yet decided on any particular property I understand."

"No, I shall rent for a few weeks, give my wife a chance to look as well. The shop is a tie, we can't both be absent from it at the same time. When we moved from Hood Street it was with very little pre-knowledge of the shop on Annie's part, circumstances at the time dictated it must be that way. This time I think I owe her some measure of choice. George and Samuel live with us still but I can't imagine George won't already be considering a place of his own, like the others he inherited when Davina Wright died, it's only natural that he should want to buy a property, he'd be foolish not to and I sometimes think more wisdom dwells quietly within George than in any other of his siblings. What he actually thinks of me God knows, but there is a great deal to commend in George Boucher, my stepson."

Charles' words struck Julian Russe as sincere, a certain opinion of Charles Eddowes was held, perhaps not altogether justifiably, by some folk. Russe himself had been taken aback more than once by Charles' indifference to the accepted courtesies. Today his manner was pleasant enough, apart from his impatience over Russe's hay fever symptoms, which Charles had failed to conceal. He seemed more at ease, with himself and with those around him.

The sale of the shop and the prospect of finding a house for their retirement, which his wife was to help choose, must surely have brought a long awaited relief to him. Perhaps it was all due to their late son, John, a way of honouring his memory.

"I'll be in touch very soon I'm sure," said Russe. "Good luck Charles and my regards to Mrs.Eddowes."

Charles walked along thinking of William. Since that Sunday in The Standard William had called at Gregory Street regularly, always asking the same question when Annie was out of earshot. 'Anything settled yet'? The bee in the bonnet! Charles went from one moment thinking he should give the money to William so he might be once and for all content, to letting himself believe the words used by Julian Russe when he'd said that John had granted his father and mother some ease. It was all wrong, all of it. John should be alive, he should be walking through the back door at Gregory Street after his day's work, whistling a tune. John would often whistle and sing, William never did, William whined and droned, yet just as Enid had done before him, he'd made first claim on Charles' affections, kept his brothers and sister a distance back. He had only to say that word 'Dad', and Charles weakened. Enid had only to look into his eyes and blow him a kiss and Charles had been putty in her hands. The only time he'd denied William was when he'd come to Gregory Street and declared his financial plight as Birkett put pressure on him over his mortgage. Charles had resented Stanford's hold on William, the way he'd wheedled his way into William's head, coloured his thinking. As a youth William had often been discontent and the first war took Charles away from him, not just physically but emotionally too. If Basil Stanford hadn't manipulated the situation in the way that he did, then despite that long period of separation, Charles could have found his own way back to William. Although he tried, Stanford always managed to put himself in just the right spot to create an obstacle. 'Yet still William had only to say, 'Dad'.

Annie cleared away the dishes from their meal, George and Samuel had gone to see Caroline and the boys. They had promised to help her redecorate the living room, strip the faded wallpaper and put up new. On their visit a couple of weeks ago George had been dismayed by the way William had arranged collection of the piano and simply left Caroline to make good the decoration.

Samuel enjoyed the company of Jonathon and Gregory so while the three boys made their own amusement George was to begin the process of restoring Caroline's living room.

Annie left the pots to drain and sat down opposite Charles. Only two days left of the month, it was difficult to believe that so much time had already passed since George's homecoming. Today was his birthday, she'd given him a card and with coupons she'd saved, managed to buy him a smart shirt at Burton's but they'd not had any sort of celebration since he'd returned from the war. No one could have been reasonably expected to cope with one given their grief over John. Now Annie felt she should do something to mark his birthday at least. On a shop day it was difficult but a Sunday did afford an opportunity to prepare a slightly more significant meal, albeit within the tiresome bounds of rationing. It was Saturday tomorrow so the gesture would only be two days late.

"I thought on Sunday I might make a surprise for George, a belated birthday tea, it can only be simple, there's so little to work with, but if for no other reason, I think Samuel deserves it, don't you?" Annie could but direct her voice at the usual screen of newspaper.

His reply came like a bolt out of the blue, though he uttered it in such a casual fashion he might have been remarking on the weather.

"I've sold the shop, or as good as, we've possibly two more weeks here but then we'll have to vacate the place."

He'd done it again, pulled the rug from under her feet.

"I don't understand, why, to whom and where are we supposed to live?"

He folded the newspaper onto his lap. "I've sold it to the Co-op, they agreed a fair price, it was an opportunity too good to let pass. They were looking for suitable premises with an eye to the future. We shall rent for a few weeks, while we look at likely houses. Don't worry we can rent somewhere big enough for us all until George buys his own place. I know he must be thinking of doing so and we shouldn't stand in his way. He's sure to feel disinclined to leave you, but we won't be around forever, he needs to find security for himself and Samuel, besides, while ever he lives with us what could be his chances of marrying again? On his own with a young son it wouldn't be long before a soft hearted woman came along and took them under her wing."

Annie prickled. "Is that what happened Charles, was I the soft hearted woman that just gathered you into the warmth?" His expression showed his awkwardness, he hadn't meant that, he'd not even thought it.

"John's estate has been proved, he left no Will so the law requires the money be paid to me, his father, his next of kin. I didn't make the law, I didn't seek it to be that way, but it is. I didn't want to upset you by speaking of it before, it was only finalised a day or so ago. I'm doing this for us, for John. And yes, I think it would be a nice idea to mark George's birthday on Sunday but just the four of us, no one else, a meal for four is enough for you to create from what little is available."

If it was to be a surprise for George then Charles didn't want William to spoil the occasion, for at some point he would pursue the subject of the money, William couldn't help himself.

Annie knew the discussion was over as Charles picked up the paper and resumed his concentration on 'births, marriages and deaths', or whatever else seized his attention from within those folds of newsprint. Two weeks, two years, two decades what difference would it make? They'd been married for thirty eight years and still she had no idea what went on in Charles' head, or for that matter, in his heart.

Billy had turned over and over in his mind what Richard Ansell had said. 'The tests have confirmed the presence of cancerous tissue, we need to remove that part of your tongue to prevent further spread'.

Edna had been so calm, she'd spoken quietly to tell him that she needed to think about it. Her words pained Ansell, Billy recognised the anxiety in his voice when he explained to them that it was important he perform the operation as soon as possible.

On their way home from the hospital Edna had made Billy promise not to tell the girls what it was. 'Not 'til I'm ready Billy, yer can tell 'em when I'm ready'. That had been nine days ago and Billy felt frantic with worry. He'd been thankful of his night shifts, by day it was all he could think about and each time he'd tried to persuade Edna to tell Mr.Ansell she was ready it had resulted in tears and upset. 'It's my soddin' tongue, nobody else's, I'll make up me own mind in me own good time'. Then she'd cry, they'd both cry and Billy would hold her in his arm and through his tears comfort her as best he could, 'It'll be alright love, it's alright', words, which drove the most dreadful hurt in Billy.

But it couldn't go on, and now as he walked along Sherwood Road he prayed that before this weekend was ended Edna would say, 'I'm ready'.

He'd met Jack Haynes on Forest Road, it happened that way sometimes, Jack would be going to his work as Billy was coming home from the Exchange. For a moment Billy had been on the verge of pouring it all out to Jack, vent the pressure that built up inside him but this morning Jack was in haste, he and Eddie Wills were to be visited upon by Mrs.Bradshaw, so Billy had wished Jack the best of luck and the moment had passed. Billy was frightened, it sounded serious, he'd heard of cancer, he didn't understand the condition but he was aware that it could take life. The thought of losing Edna denied him breath.

It was strange how an incident from an age ago could suddenly come to mind. He remembered little Danny Eddowes' funeral, the absence of Charles from the graveside, coming across him at the arboretum, that blow from Billy's fist that sent Charles to the ground. It was something that Charles had said that now took hold of Billy's emotions. Charles' description of his torment at the funeral of his first wife, Enid.

'The pain of a thousand wars ripped at my soul'. Billy had never felt regard for Eddowes, he couldn't like the man but today, as dread followed Billy around the corner into Winchester Street he acknowledged Charles' pain and felt pity of it.

"Well we've passed inspection I reckon Jack," said Eddie.

Patricia Bradshaw had just left. Eddie had put Jack's quietness down to his concern that all Ministry paperwork, pay books and ledgers should be accurate and up to date.

"What would yer say Eddie if I wer' to tell yer that we'd bought a ladies hairdressin' salon on Alfreton Road, or Hilda has, she insists on sayin' 'we' but it's her money an' her idea. We decided not to say anythin' to folk until things were settled, her mam knows, but nobody else yet. I shall go mad if I don't tell somebody, I just can't make it sit right in my head. I thought she wanted a bigger house, that was what she said she wanted a while back, but when I suggested we look at a place on Chalfont Drive, out came the revelation, 'I want to buy a hairdressers'.

"Phew, somethin' like that comes with a lot o' pepper Jack," said Eddie, trying not to sound overly shocked but he could understand why Jack had been so quiet earlier and it hadn't been the scrutiny of Mrs.Bradshaw occupying his thoughts. "Does Hilda know about hairdressin' then?"

"She reckons she can pick it up from the stylists who work there an' meanwhile she'll shampoo, do the books, that sort o' thing. She even plans to take Rosie with her, there is room for a kiddie to play. Before all that there'd have to be money spent on the place, it's not bad, but a bit jaded lookin' inside, an' upstairs hasn't seen much attention in years."

"Who's sellin' it?" Asked a curious Eddie.

"Fred Woolascroft's missus, got too old to be bothered with it, accordin' to the agent. She's never worked it herself, only ever employed 'stylists' as he referred to 'em. She acquired it years ago, as an investment, she won't drop the price an' Hilda's set on it, so we agreed, the deal should be done an' dusted soon.

Perhaps I can persuade the boss to become a 'client'. That's another one o' them fancy words, I've allus considered meself to be a customer at the places I spend money so I'm not sure what it is you have to do to become a client, happen it's in the breedin'."

Poor Jack, his analysis was amusing in many ways but Eddie detected evidence of that familiar demon, which nibbled away at Jack's confidence, it had been there when he first took over the running of the pit.

"I've heard it rumoured that Dick Woolascroft's in trouble again," said Eddie. "Debts, he's never been any good that one, his old man told him years ago that if he got himself into debt again then it was for Dick to get himself out but I suppose his mother can't bear it. She's done it before, sold a place, it was rumoured back then that Dick was the reason. She had money in her own right, left to her when her father died. She had brothers, you know that Cynthia Woolascroft is Mrs.Bradshaw's sister in law don't you?"

Jack had no idea. "You know a lot more than me Eddie," he said.

"Well it was Mavis told me that, an' she learned it through Hilda's mam, I think Mrs.Stanford had been chattin' to Mrs.Eddowes about family and mentioned the fact that Anthony Bradshaw was Cynthia's younger brother. I don't suppose there's much love lost, not since that scandal over his secretary anyway. She'll likely be approvin' of Hilda takin' a business out o' Cynthia Woolascroft's hands, so she might well become a client. They reckon that Dick dodged conscription by claimin' that his wife couldn't manage without him, she suffers from Crohn's disease but the truth is, Dick Woolascroft's no more of a home lover than a stray dog. It's usually gullible, younger women that fall for his line in charm, he flashes a bit o' money in front of 'em and they feel flattered I suppose, poor sods. You have to feel a measure of sympathy for his mother, I don't think Fred's the easiest to live with but Dick, she must rue the day she conceived of him. I tell yer what Jack, when we knock off at dinner time I'll buy us a pint an' we'll drink to the success of your wife's venture. The war thrust women into work they'd never done before an' put money into their pockets, they're entitled to spend some on themselves an' why not a nice hairdo, just the ticket?

Things are changin' Jack, a man might walk back but he marches forward, it's the way of the world, an' nowadays I reckon the women are marchin' as well!"

Charles stood behind the counter, looking from side to side of the shop, the shelves of monotony, his surroundings for too many years, soon he would be rid of this tiresome ritual, freed of obligation to serve a thankless public their papers and odds an' sods of everyday 'wants'. It grated on his tolerance, a few would express their 'need' but most, without even thinking would say, 'I want so an' so', want, always in want. It was just after six o'clock, Annie was getting their meal ready, she'd said little since he'd told her about the sale to the Co-op other than asking him to speak with George, to enable him time to begin the process of looking for a house he could favour for Samuel and himself. He would do it this evening, tell George of his decision to sell and his reason for doing so, he'd understand, surely he'd be approving of his mother's release from this miserable place that served as a convenient 'whining stop' for all and sundry. A figure walked past the right hand window and the door opened with an urgent clang of the bell. It was Hemsley, why was he here, Celia called for his paper earlier in the afternoon.

"Good evening Charles," said Anthony, "I shall settle my paper bill, I mustn't start a new month in debt." His manner was polite, there was nothing about his approach that warranted Charles' rudeness but without any word of courtesy, Charles tore the receipt from the newspaper accounts book, pointedly held it up between the fingers of one hand whilst with the other he counted the coins Anthony had placed on the counter. It was antagonistic but Anthony said nothing to cause ill will. The transaction complete he enquired after the family's health and asked.

"Is Annie about? Just a quick word I won't keep her."

Until that moment Charles' resentment had simmered slowly, silently it had simmered. Now Anthony's presence, his request of Annie, though, 'he wouldn't keep her', turned up the flame and Charles' temper reached the point of boiling.

"What is it you want Hemsley, 'want', that bloody word. Do you think I'm a fool, all these weeks of preying on her, turning out all that sentimental drivel about old friendships, she's my wife, mine, and you're right, you won't keep her. I've stood for enough, I've held my tongue but it's time I said it Hemsley, go find yourself another woman to comfort you in your mysterious state of depression. If you can't find one soft enough, then put your hand in your wallet and buy one, there are places you know, very accommodating, you won't even need to work your charm, they'll open their legs for no more than the cost of a haircut and shave at the barbers."

Anthony would listen to no more of this. "You are out of your mind Charles, you rant and rave like a madman. I'll not stay here to be the subject of your twisted imagination, you have the mentality of a man possessed. A devil abides within you Charles."

Anthony walked towards the door but Charles ran across the shop floor and dropped the catch to lock it, he stood with his back to it, barring Anthony's way.

"Leave us alone can't you, I lost a son to the war, I'll be damned if I'll lose my wife to you."

"Don't push me Charles, let me by."

George and Annie appeared at the doorway behind the counter.

"Whatever is all the shouting about?" Said Annie.

George didn't speak but the anguished, fiery look on Charles' face was enough to make him anxious for Samuel, whom he'd told to stay where he was, sitting at the table, doing his maths homework.

"Don't be alarmed Annie," said Anthony, "I shall leave by the back door." He walked towards her but Charles cried out.

"So respectable aren't you Hemsley, that big house in The Park, late father who worked in one of the professions. While Charles Eddowes lives over his mediocre shop, son of a man 'in trade', isn't that what you think?"

Anthony paused briefly by Annie and George, cast a despairing look and hurried through to the kitchen.

"Nice to see you Samuel," he said to the bewildered boy.

But Charles was on his heels. "My father at least taught me decency, he chose not to hob nob with the influential, he preferred to make his own success and I might only be the keeper of a back street shop but I have something you'll never achieve Hemsley, I have a family, we're both old, you're too old, but I do have my family, mine, Hemsley, mine."

Anthony could not contain his anger any longer, the need to fight back, to defend himself from the frenzied attack Charles had launched upon him finally released his arm and he fired the volley.

"You're a bastard Charles," he spat the words with contempt, "you never knew your father but I can tell you who he was, you're the illegitimate son of Nathan Wright, his bastard."

The back door was open, William stood in the threshold. George went to Samuel.

"Go upstairs it will be alright, I'll come up in just a little while." He spoke calmly, gathering the boy's homework from the table and handing it to him. Then he took his mother's arm and led her to a chair. "Sit down Mam." He smiled into her face and let his fingers tenderly brush hers.

Now a silence had descended upon the scene. Anthony felt wretched. Charles was stunned and William, who had called hoping to learn from his dad that John's affairs were finally settled, following what he'd just heard stood rooted to the spot, dumbfounded.

Charles was first to speak. "Close the door William and sit down. You can't expect me to believe such a slanderous thing Hemsley, why say it, why would you think it?"

"You pushed and pushed at me Charles. A man can only take so much, you drove me into a corner 'til there was nowhere for me to go, corner any man and he'll lash out in desperation.

There were letters, I'm sure if mother hadn't developed dementia she would have destroyed them, removed any possibility of their content being read by anybody other than herself. After she died father was too distraught to sort any of her things, he lived for only a short time without her. I found the letters when I was clearing the house with Margaret. She doesn't know about them, it didn't feel right to tell her but they struck a chord with me. Suddenly I wasn't the only man to have committed that most cowardly act of fathering a child and walking away from it. I had an illegitimate son Charles, Donald, the war took him too.

Nathan Wright put Hilda Braithwaite in the family way, she was carrying you when Saul Eddowes married her. There was some kind of arrangement, the letters weren't specific. He wasn't your natural father Charles but I agree with you when you describe him as a decent man, Saul Eddowes reared you and remained ever loyal to his family.

Donald's mother told him that his father had been killed in the war, her husband had been killed, that much was true. It was what she wanted, and I agreed her terms, I was a married man you see. That was 'our' arrangement." He let out a long sigh.

"Davina and mother were the very best of friends, Davina confided in her, and in her loneliness as she grew older, Davina's letters became quite touching." He looked across the room at Annie. "I'm sorry, so very sorry Annie, I only wanted to speak with you briefly, to tell you that Donald's mother has let me have the name of my granddaughter, also the name and address of Donald's widow, who has agreed to see me. So I am going away for a while. The Bevin boys will keep the house safe and provided Celia is able, they will appreciate very much her continued help, I shall of course leave an envelope of money for her and the young men will do their very best to be clean and tidy about the place."

He walked slowly to the back door. "I won't ever bother you again Charles. Goodbye Annie." With a slight creak of the door hinge, he was gone.

Charles turned to Annie. "All this time I've believed it was you, something about you that kept Davina close but it always puzzled me. Why? A woman of means, with some standing, befriending a seamstress from Eddowes' Workshop on Winchester Street. Now I fathom it, Davina was able to stay close to me, her husband's flesh and blood through you, her young 'friend'. It was me, all along it was me, I was the prize, you were the way of winning it. And the money, I asked myself so many times. Why? She had a cousin, you told me she was fond of Hardwick, yet all she owned she left to our children, my children, Nathan Wright's flesh and blood. Now it all fits, it's little wonder I could never understand father, he wasn't my father, I was merely 'an arrangement'.

William had stood in silence, his mind working apace. He looked directly at George as he spoke.

"Well would you know it, some folk have all the luck, inherit by default, all they need to do is hover around the fringes."

"I don't want your money William, you can have it all, I lay no claim, I've spent not a penny of it." George's response was stern.

"No, no George." Annie cried out, she stood up. "I gave Davina my word. I couldn't understand why it was so important, why she became so agitated until I gave her my word. 'Promise me Annie, promise you will see that my wishes are upheld'. She referred to her Will and showed to me a large sealed envelope, made me take note of where she put it, in a side drawer of her writing bureau. When she died and I learned the contents of her Will I remembered her words and thought she must have anticipated a reaction from Lawrence Hardwick. I felt anxious, it would have been entirely understandable if he'd questioned the bequests and I expected some contact from him, some intervention, but there was none. Now it's clear to me, I know why Davina was so intent on securing my word, it was you William, you lived with her for a comparatively short period but how well she came to know you, your ways, you were her anxiety. 'Promise me Annie you will see that my wishes are upheld'. Please George, don't make me break that promise. It's what she left to me, more valuable than any amount of money, she left me her trust."

Annie began to cry. George took her in his arms. "It's alright Mam, don't cry."

William was defensive, resentful of the slight.

"But it's true, I am her step grandson, the law would recognise me as such and Freddy also, even John and Hilda, step grandchildren, what other could they be? But George, what ties does he have, none. So what I said is correct, like it or not it is correct, 'by default', George can do as he pleases."

"That's enough William, aren't you ever satisfied, on and on, that bloody bee drones on and on." Charles was despairing more with every minute that passed.

"Oh, you think I've said enough do you Dad, William needs to shut his tiresome mouth, is that it?" William's frustration commandeered his tongue and ordered it to do its bidding. His father was standing up for George, after all that had just been revealed it was George that Charles sided with.

"Well, as this is the hour of truths why don't we cast another into the ring? This family is a sham, we've lived on lies for years. 'Your mother died in childbirth, the baby too'. That's what you made me believe, I grew into a man believing it, but mother had an abortion and it killed her didn't it, it killed her, isn't that the truth Dad?"

Charles' eyes flared, he took George by the sleeves of his shirt, shaking him with rage. "You told him, why did you have to tell him, in God's name why?"

Now William unleashed a desperate rancour. "He knew?" You told him the truth but lied to your own son, you let me go on believing that my mother died in childbirth when the truth was that something awful drove her to her death through a back street abortion and you told him." William pointed a finger at George like he thrust a viper full of venom.

"I didn't, I didn't tell him or anyone, I swear I said nothing." George stared into Charles' eyes, he felt for his pain but never would he have divulged their conversation of that night.

Now Charles rounded on Annie. "Then it was you, it must have been you, there is no one else." He was frantic in his accusation.

"How could you think I would tell William such a thing Charles, I told no one but Harold and he took that secret to the grave."

Charles wrung his hands and cried out in despair. "He knows, one of you must have told him, it had to be one or other of you."

"It wasn't them." Now William cried out, emotion so raw his shoulders shook and his voice cracked from the weight of heartache as he delivered the final assault to Charles' crumbling frame. "It was neither of them, Stanford told me, it was Basil Stanford!"

Charles swayed like a drunkard, breath knocked from him, he made no sound but sank onto a chair. Annie and George looked at one another with confusion and disbelief. After several seconds that felt like an age, Charles raised his fallen face to William.

"Was the child his, was it Stanford's?"

"I asked him that," said William, his voice now lowered by weariness, "it wasn't his, I could tell from his reaction that he spoke the truth."

A sudden sound claimed their attention, through all the agonised exchange they had forgotten Samuel, now he stood in the doorway, looking so young, too young for any of this.

"I've finished my homework except one equation, I couldn't work it out."

Annie got to her feet, smiled at the boy and said. "Your dad will help you with that but you must be hungry Samuel, we are going to eat now. Mr.Hemsley has gone home, I don't know if uncle William will stay for some tea?" Her gaze passed to William.

"No, it's alright, Celia will be keeping mine, she'll wonder where I am, I best be off."

Charles was about to say something but Annie gave him a forbidding look and under her breath cautioned him. "He's a boy, he's just a boy." Even Charles recognised the truth of that, for Samuel looked so innocent, unscarred, clean of cuts and bruising, until now.

William left and Annie went to the stove. "Lay the table George, you can put out the bread if you will please Samuel."

Charles forced himself to move from the chair that had mercifully caught his downfall. "I'm going to cash up, I'll only be a few minutes." As he walked by Samuel he rubbed his hand across the boy's shoulder, and fought the tears.

The shop had been abandoned, the door was still locked so Charles opened the till to count the day's takings, as was his routine each evening. Bang, bang! An urgent rap came at the door and a shrill voice accompanied a set of eyes, peeping in above the Oxo sign.

"I come nearly an hour ago but you wer' shut." Mrs.Glasson gestured towards the sign on the shop door which still displayed 'open'. "I want a box o' sulphurs to light the gas."

Charles took a box of matches from the shelf, crossed the shop floor, opened the door, thrust the matches into her hand, and said only. "And we're still shut." He closed the door again, turned the sign and returned to his cashing up. "Want, bloody want," he muttered to himself.

While a bewildered Mrs.Glasson hurried along repeating. "Glory be, glory be."

George had gone with Samuel to aunty Nora's, to see Ted, Annie could appreciate their need of Nora's simple household this evening. She dare not think beyond the moment, the old expression, 'things will look different in the morning when you've slept on it', did little to soothe her. Things were already very different and Annie could think of no way to make them look better. She cleaned the stove, scouring every little spot and blemish to keep busy. Charles sat staring at the floor, not even the newspaper could keep him from his misery. She gathered up the bucket of dirty water and was about to go outside to tip it down the drain in the yard when he spoke. "Come and sit down, please."

Annie seldom heard Charles use the word 'please'. There was no harshness in his voice, more a subdued tone of regret, that tremor to his words, like a child feeling sorry for its misdemeanour and needing to hear that it was forgiven.

She sat down with him, he raised his face to look at her and that need spilled. He began to cry, to sob, to rock backward and forward, the sound of his utter despair rose to the ceiling above them and hung there, on the air, trapped, intense misery that could see no light, no way out. Eventually Charles sniffed, wiped his cheeks with his hands and in turn, rubbed them over his knees.

"Was Stanford William's father, he could have been. Stanford pursued him, whenever I met the man he wanted to speak of William. 'Fine boy you have Eddowes, I've often wondered what it must be to have a son', that's what he'd say."

"Whatever nonsense are you imagining Charles? William is your son." Annie's response was so certain, so sure.

"How can you know, if I'm no longer sure then how could you be?" He stared at Annie willing her to give him a reason not to doubt.

"It was when Davina sat upstairs in bed, recovering from bronchitis, Sarah was staying at the house to care for her. We were in the bedroom, the three of us, I remember Danny was asleep downstairs, Davina had forbidden me any visit until she believed there was no longer any possibility of passing on the infection to Danny." Annie caught her breath, a tear had found its way to the corner of her eye.

"She asked me to reach into a drawer, something she needed, a hanky, or mints possibly, I can't exactly remember. When I moved the hankies and stockings there it was, looking up at me, a small framed photograph of William. Yet how could it be, I'd never ever given her such a thing, I'd never seen the photo before. Then I realised it couldn't be William, the photograph was too old, even the style of the young man's dress was dated. But there wasn't merely a similarity, it was a striking likeness. I didn't say anything then, Sarah was present and Davina was anxious that I find the mints. Yes it was mints, she'd been chuckling and it brought on a fit of coughing, she wanted something to suck. It wasn't until sometime after that an occasion arose at which I felt it appropriate to ask her about the photograph."

'Ah yes', she said, 'that photograph'.

I remember thinking my question seemed to cause her a moment of unease but then she answered confidently enough.

'Nathan was very young when the picture was taken', she said, 'his features had not then matured to the look he carried as a man and of course he grew a moustache, which greatly changed his appearance'.

"I had no reason to doubt her word or to further question it. I found it the most curious coincidence that Davina's late husband had looked so much like William but it went from my mind, replaced by all the many distractions a growing family presented.

The likeness in William, to Nathan Wright, could only come through you Charles, he is your son just as Freddy is yours, and I have always believed that the baby Enid was too frightened to bear, that too was your child. She was terrified of childbirth, not simply nervous, as many women can be, but truly terrified. So many times I've regretted going to your house, to see Enid, to tell her my news. I was pregnant, each month I'd hoped, and when I'd missed twice and recognised something within me was different, I knew, I was going to have Harold's child. If only I hadn't told her, she must have known that day that she'd conceived again, how could she confide her fear in me after I'd just poured out, in excitement, my delight at being pregnant? Neither could she have declared her torment to Bertha. Enid sought help from someone, the very worst kind of help, but that baby was yours Charles, I know it."

He'd listened in silence while she explained. "Then how could Stanford have known, how?"

Annie took his hand and smoothed it with her own. "I can't answer that Charles because I don't know, he's dead, we shall never know but what I am sure of is sufficient knowledge for me. I was fond of Saul, to me he was always kind, he made me feel safe, I was very young when I began at the workshop but his gentle manner gave me confidence. Despite our changed understanding of the past I shall ever think of Saul as your father, in life indeed he was your father, he deserves to be remembered as nothing less."

"I'm sorry for what I said, I didn't mean it and it isn't true." Charles wrapped his fingers about Annie's as he spoke. "Davina tolerated me but she truly loved you and George. I shall see to it that he keeps all his money. William will have more than enough.

It happened when I took some stout to George, a few days after Alice's funeral. I found him fingering her locket. When he likened Alice to Enid, because they'd both died through their desire to be a mother, I was sickened. He knew that Alice's condition was accelerated by bearing Samuel and of course he believed that Enid died in childbirth. I couldn't stand it, not that, it was a slight on Alice's name, on her memory, she was nothing like Enid, nothing. It all came out, I couldn't help myself. I told George everything." Charles sighed and continued. "I was going to speak to George this evening, about the sale of the shop but we've all learned enough for one day. I shall tell him tomorrow. I can't imagine a belated birthday celebration will be what George wants, can you?"

Charles looked into Annie's eyes, his face was drained of colour. They sat quietly, too tired to think anymore, either of the past or of the future, sharing with no demand of rhyme or reason, the frail present.

Charles had clung to the shop all morning, he'd broken the news of its sale to George over their breakfast. George had shown little reaction, after the previous day's revelations Annie imagined the news that in the next two or three weeks the Co-op would take over the premises felt scarcely significant. Charles clearly couldn't bear inactivity today, he needed distraction, hence his uncustomary willingness to suffer the 'whining public' until it was time to turn the sign to closed at midday.

Annie wanted to call on Edna and Billy. It was Edna's routine to come to the shop on a Saturday morning but yesterday she'd not arrived. Annie was concerned, Edna had not seemed herself when she'd called the week before, now Annie felt the need of Edna's company, for the selfish reason of seeking comfort and to make sure that all was well at No.24.

When Annie asked Charles, 'what will you do, we all need a diversion'? He'd replied with a logical suggestion, stocktaking. He would record the stock in both the shop and the cellar, make adjustment for the predicted sales over the next fortnight and arrive at a valuation. It was the request of the solicitor.

It did seem strange, almost all the family were considering the sale or purchase of a property, Hilda with the salon, William with Moreleigh, Charles the shop and presumably George would very soon seek to buy a house for himself and Samuel. Where Charles and herself would find their future abode Annie couldn't begin to speculate and this afternoon, couldn't trouble her head over it anyway.

Winchester Street was quiet, she walked along with an easy peace as companion. This old street made no demands on her, it expected little and claimed even less. Annie had paid her dues to this cobbled back street long, long ago and now it caused her no bother. The back door was on the latch, she stepped inside and called out.

"It's only me."

Edna appeared to be writing a letter and Billy stood over her, looking intent on his purpose. It struck Annie as unusual, Billy wouldn't normally impose his authority, he'd learned it best not to if he valued the quiet life.

Edna looked up. "I'm signin' the prison warrant, agreein' to me sentence, they want to put me away."

"You put some sense into 'er will yer Annie?" Billy let out such a hefty sigh Annie felt alarmed.

"What are you talking about Edna? They wouldn't dare put you inside the prison, you'd be too disruptive an influence." Annie chuckled but no mirth came from Billy and Edna's face was set firm.

"Sit down Annie, yer may as well know, I've to go into City Hospital to 'ave an operation, there's summat wrong wi' me tongue." Edna explained, purposefully omitting the more disturbing details. "I've written the letter to Mr.Ansell, I wer' goin' to post it but Billy insists 'e's takin' it to the hospital 'isself in the mornin'. I could be in there as long as a month they said. This family'll 'ave its own ward wi' its own beds in that place, the way we're carryin' on, like normal folk 'ave their own pews in chapel, what wi' Janet, an' then our Myra, now I'm to be stuck in there an'all."

"Oh Edna, why didn't you tell me before now, I knew there was something troubling you last week, I could tell."

Billy's expression suggested that it was more serious than Edna was letting on. Annie prompted her.

"What exactly is wrong with your tongue, we've been friends for almost all our lives Edna, surely you can confide in me?"

"It's inflammation, a disease, cancer, that's what they call it. Mr.Ansell says they must cut off the bad part to stop it spreadin'. I keep tellin' meself they're wrong, it'll turn out to be ringworm, I've heard it said that you've only to touch a bit o' wood that an affected cow's rubbed 'erself on an' you'll catch it an'all. But for the life o' me I can't remember lickin' the inside of a cowshed, so happen Ansell's right, me tongue's got human disease."

Annie's heart sank. Poor Billy, and the girls would be beside themselves with worry.

"You'll tell me when you've to be admitted, as soon as you get word, you will won't you Billy?"

He nodded. "I'll make sure you know Annie." He gave her a brave smile. "So that's the best we can do today, we're a couple o' miseries. Cheer us up Annie love, tell us summat happy."

Annie swallowed hard and thought even harder.

"Mrs.Glasson got her first great grandchild last Thursday, almost ten pounds, a boy, glory be."

CHAPTER TWENTY FIVE

October.

George lay in the darkness pondering, it felt safer here in his bedroom, no one to observe him, to question his quietness. He'd now completed the redecoration of Caroline's living room. Since that dreadful day when so many anguished words were exchanged and tears shed George had tried to remain calm, for Samuel's sake.

Caroline was kind she was not responsible for 'the sins of the father', but when Charles became aware of George's desire to help her restore the unfortunate situation left behind by William, he'd become so agitated that for the good of his mam George had gone to the house straight from work three evenings in a row and ended the task. However in the process of so doing Caroline, quite naturally, had prepared a meal for him and he'd sat at the table with Jonathon, Gregory and their mother each teatime and found himself enjoying the simplicity of those few minutes. They were uncluttered by doubts and misgivings, the boys would laugh, Caroline would smile at their fun, no one challenged, it was that pleasure of sitting briefly with contentedness that caused George now to lie in the darkness pondering.

When Charles had explained to him the sale of the shop to the Co-op George couldn't deny the easement it would grant his mother, it was true, she did look tired, in fact lately it was beyond tired, she was haggard. But Charles had spoken this evening with George, outside in the yard where no one could overhear and let loose his feelings. 'You sit with the devil's kind, she's a Stanford, think of this family, your family, leave her alone'.

It was unjust, Caroline was undeserving of his condemnation but George knew that Charles' ill temper would persist if he defied him. There was a house vacant to rent on Ainsley Road, Percy Pollard had mentioned it in passing, when reminiscing about his old mam, the duchess. Eventually George would buy a property, some security for Samuel in the future, but for now he felt an overwhelming need of returning to that familiar street, like Percy reminiscing, remembering, living again, if only in his mind, the time of love and happiness with his Alice.

The war had revealed to George such an intensity of suffering that before putting on his khaki and swearing his allegiance, he'd never have believed it possible to prepare a man for the sight, the sound, the smell and worse of all the feel of death, rent flesh, blood spilling onto Godless ground, cries of agony, faint murmurs of final breath, yet worst by far, the feel. Limp, wrought remains that hung from a man's arms as he carried death, each one a sacrifice, a life given and yet taken. The feel, deep inside of anger, of grief, bewilderment and hopelessness. 'My God, why hast thou forsaken me'? Men mouthed the words in their sleep and on their waking, they'd glimpsed Calvary and knew that 'feel' of utter despair. It was home, the thought of home, be it earthly or heavenly that enabled a man to raise his head and believe there was something beyond. It was his own back door, his mam, his wife, they awaited him, he'd see them again, beyond the sacrifice he would see them again. It wasn't religion or even strong faith, it was love at its most pure and that was the unfathomable mystery, through all the carnage, the rampant evil, thread love at its most pure. He couldn't halt them and no one was there to see them, in the darkness tears fell from George's face to the pillow, he whispered her name, Alice, he was tired of conflict, the atmosphere at Gregory Street was strained, Charles' mood unpredictable. 'Birthright', what a source of torment it could be, was there ever a 'right' actually attached to birth? Neither William nor Charles seemed able to move on and George knew he must take Samuel to somewhere he could breathe a lighter air. If only he was able to take his mam from the troubles but even now, after all the hurt, she carried on as always. George finally fell asleep questioning.

When Annie told Charles that the hairdressing salon was now Hilda's he replied with his usual spite.

"You'll be even more useful to Haynes soon, someone to look after his kids while his wife earns."

She would not demean herself by acknowledging his remark, instead she said. "Edna goes into hospital on Monday, Billy has leave from his work at the Exchange for a week but she's likely to be in hospital for three or four. The girls are all very good, Liza is back from Halam so Billy will have company at No.24, but it's distressing for them all and I shall want to visit Edna, so please understand that. Visiting is limited to one hour each evening and afternoon."

Charles felt quite shocked, Edna was of those indestructible people who had only to gaze sternly on any would be affliction to send it hastily on its way.

"What's wrong with Edna?" He asked, sensing from Annie's tone that it was serious.

"She has cancer, in her mouth, they need to remove a part of her tongue. Alice had leukaemia, that too is a type of cancer, I don't fully understand, it's all to do with blood cells."

Charles was pensive for a moment, then he said something quite unexpected. "Poor Billy, tell him I'm sorry." He looked at Annie as though it pained him, as though Billy's anxiety actually caused Charles pain! He stood up. "I've to see Russe in the morning, he should have the completion date. Normally the Co-op would close the premises for a few days then open under their appointed manager, after checking stock and making alterations to suit themselves presumably. As this shop incorporates a news agency that's not really possible, I believe they want me to remain here until closing time on the day they take over, to go through the paper orders with the new man, introduce the paper boys who do the rounds, that sort of thing. Russe will hand them a set of keys at noon on the given day, the money must be in my account before that can happen of course. It means that you'll be on your own with the removal men, so I had thought that Edna could help you, obviously that can't now be the case but you could ask Celia, I'm sure she won't mind. I'm going up to bed." He sighed, "Don't you need your tongue to be able to speak?"

"Yes," said Annie, "we'd by mute without one, the world might be a better place if mankind was mute."

London Road was a hive of activity and it soon became apparent why, a burst water main, it added to the already soggy day. The sky had darkened rather than grown lighter since daybreak and rain had been falling steadily. Charles picked his way through the confusion and now stood in the doorway of Meakin and Kirk, shaking the wetness from his hat and wiping his shoes vigorously on the mat. The receptionist in the inner office was apologetic, as if in some way responsible.

"I'm sorry you've had to negotiate your way through the water problem Mr.Eddowes, shall I take your hat and coat?" She hung them on the stand. "Mr.Russe is ready for you."

The young woman had a pleasant smile but Charles found himself studying the movement of her mouth, the brief glimpse of her tongue as she spoke. Removing a part of Edna's tongue? The thought of it was really quite upsetting and difficult to imagine.

"Ah Charles, take a seat."

Russe appeared to shuffle various documents, Charles hoped they were pertaining to his own affairs. He'd not yet mentioned anything to Annie about the house, he must declare his intentions soon. It was strange how things could sometimes work out, when he'd discovered No.1 Winchester Street was available to rent it felt almost destined and curiously significant, of all places, just a few doors up from Bella Pownall's old house. Being a corner property it was slightly larger, both bedrooms were double and the living room was a decent size. It hadn't been his original plan, his intent of allowing Annie some choice had been genuine enough but all that was changed last Saturday by Hemsley and William. Now with the situation surrounding Edna and Billy, surely a dwelling so close could only prove a comfort to Annie.

"Well Charles I have a date, Monday 15th, the Co-op will expect all outstanding accounts to have been settled prior to completion, I trust you'll not have difficulty persuading customers to oblige."

"It's really only newspaper bills," said Charles, "I've never offered credit on other items, it shouldn't be too difficult, not if I tell them they'll be customers of The Cooperative Society in future and therefore entitled to divvy."

Russe smiled detecting the note of sarcasm in Charles' remark. "Mr.Talbot has accepted your offer for No.1, however he insists there must be a rental agreement until the conveyance is completed. In other words he's willing for you to move in on the 15th but wants rent over and above your offer. He's protecting his interests

Charles and equally you should protect yours. He could instruct his solicitor to drag it out a bit, get an extra month's rent, the conveyance should be reasonably straight forward but he might consider it an opportunity to squeeze two month's rent out of you instead of one, he is a landlord after all. I advise you to cap the agreement. The Deed to be in your name at the end of the month or you pull out."

Charles thought for a second. "But what if he calls my bluff?"

"I think that highly unlikely, Talbot knows you've made him a good offer and he won't be keen to waste money on a solicitor's bill which results in no gain for him."

"Alright," said Charles, "set it up. Have you prepared the documents for the bank? I shan't tell William until it's done. He's sure to question why I made arrangements for a joint account, but he needs to be reined in, Celia is bright, she shouldn't be working as a cleaner in The Park, she's deserving of better, the money should enable her to cease all that nonsense.

You must think my actions odd given that William has two brothers and a sister?" Charles looked at Russe as though anticipating the man's curiosity at least.

"It is not for me to reason why Charles, only to guide you within the law. Whatever your purpose, I hope it will not deny your family peace. It would seem an even greater tragedy if John lost his life to war only to have unrest brought in his name."

Charles gave Russe a resigned reply. "I believe the others will, in time understand, that I did it for peace, to silence the droning bee once and for all, and for 'all' of us."

Charles waited until Annie climbed into bed beside him to tell her of the outcome of his meeting with Russe, he acknowledged to himself that it was cowardly, Annie wouldn't raise her voice while Samuel lay in the next room.

"The completion will be Monday 15th, we have to leave the shop free of outstanding accounts, apart from paper bills there's only a couple of weeks owing from Edna. It's not important I'll write it off, they've enough to think about without that."

Annie grew a little suspicious, perhaps it would prove unworthy but such generosity of spirit towards Billy was completely out of character, did it pave the way for an awkward announcement?

"I want you to believe that it wasn't my original intent but circumstances have changed. I know that Edna will ask you to be there for Billy, should anything bad happen. As it turns out, with her being so poorly and all the troubles arising from that for Billy and the girls, I can't think of a better place, especially for you, than Winchester Street. No.1, it's right on the corner so it's a little larger than most, both bedrooms are double so there's room for George and Samuel. It was for rent but I put in an offer to buy and the landlord has accepted. We can move in on the 15th but it will be a rental arrangement for the first month until the Deed is conveyed."

He paused waiting for some response from Annie but she didn't speak. He continued.

"William will give us no peace until I satisfy his agitation, I did let him down. He went to war knowing what happened to his mother and he'd learned the awful truth from that vile, bully of a man, Stanford. I should have told William myself years ago, I could have eased the hurt somehow, smoothed the jagged edges of it so's not to rip and tear. What I've done will likely offend you, it will seem grossly unfair, you will have been expecting much more but I did it for all of us, to grant us some relief from William's endless want, always that relentless, demanding 'want'. I've made over all of John's money to both William and Celia. Russe has deposited it in a joint account at Barclays, I know you consider Braithwaite's to be set in their attitude, even though Birkett's gone. Celia is deserving of better than William gives, you are deserving of better too and I'm sorry, but you were happy at Winchester Street with Harold so perhaps you can be happy there again with me."

He willed her to speak through the darkness of the room, to get it over with now, before daylight broke on another Saturday. At last Annie said something and Charles' fingers tightened beneath the sheets, she would be dismayed.

"For myself, I have no expectation Charles but it's hard on Freddy and Hilda, we both know that George wouldn't agree to accept another penny after William's outburst but why not a share for the other two?"

"Freddy did well when the Cropleys died, he's established, he doesn't need more. As for Hilda, she married Haynes, it's for him to provide for his family."

Annie was tired, too weary to start an argument, too bewildered to properly understand.

"The Delaneys used to live at No.1," she said, "they had a greyhound, I even remember its name, Godfrey! How many people call their dog Godfrey? Mr.Delaney would walk it every night before bed, always at ten o'clock, not a quarter past or a quarter to, but exactly on the hour he'd set off to walk Godfrey round the block. Mrs.Delaney was very proud of her Irish potato cake recipe. They were a big Catholic family and all went to Mass at St.Joseph's every Sunday. I must try to make Bill Rashleigh understand what's happening at the shop, he's already confused, at least I was able to sew the button back on."

Charles had no idea what Annie was rambling on about, Delaneys, potato cake, buttons, but just as he'd thought, she'd not raised her voice and now he'd declared his plan he could sleep. There was one strange coincidence, though Charles, like Annie was weary and it registered but briefly in his mind. The landlord selling No.1 was called Godfrey Talbot. Godfrey the Catholic greyhound was a predecessor, so 'God' seemed to feature in a vague sort of way, perhaps not entirely God forsaken then.

Annie had gone to see Edna, tomorrow would be the day of her admission to City Hospital and no one was sure when the operation would take place, they assumed either Tuesday or Wednesday.

Charles sat at the kitchen table preparing a notice to go in the shop window, advising customers of a change in ownership, thanking them for their patronage and requesting payment of all newspaper bills by the end of the week. In fact it was worded so politely that George, looking over Charles' shoulder, automatically cast his eyes across the table to see if Annie had left a note for Charles to copy.

Samuel had taken himself off to Caroline's, to organise Jonathon and Gregory in the production of clothes pegs, he'd actually completed some respectable samples and gathered orders from neighbours. George had not been untruthful when he said he had one or two important things to attend so give his regards to Caroline and explain. But if he'd been completely honest he would have told Samuel that a conversation he needed to have with granddad wouldn't take long and he looked forward to seeing Caroline later. Living with Charles was like walking a tightrope, the effort to maintain balance used up so much concentration, by bedtime everyone was spent.

"I've arranged to take next Friday off work," said George. "We don't have that much to move really, a bit of bedroom furniture, our clothing, Samuel's few bits and pieces. One of the men at Raleigh has a van, he says I can have the use of it to take our stuff from here to the house on Ainsley Road."

Charles looked surprised and George read his thoughts.

"Not the same house I rented with Alice," he said, "same road but several doors further along. I'm only renting for the time, it's convenient for Samuel's school and my work. In a couple of years or so Samuel will be at the threshold of work himself and who knows where we might decide to settle more permanently. I understand you're buying a house on Winchester Street. I was too young when we left there to remember aunt Bella's house and I only ever think of No.24 as being Edna and Billy's, although I was born in the front bedroom of that house.

Mam has never asked you for anything of consequence, ever working hard and completely loyal, in the bottom I believe you've always known that. We are all feeling the frailty of this family, it's been rubbed bare at the seams and only conscious effort will save it from falling apart. Where ever I live I shall always keep a spare room." George looked into Charles' face as he spoke those last few words.

"For your mother?" Said Charles.

"Yes, for my mam."

It was good to see Liza again, so much seemed to have happened since Myra's wedding when she was last back home and aside from her obvious worry over her mam, she looked well. The outdoor life suited her, Annie wondered if she would return to the farm or seek work in town in due course, but there'd be plenty of time later to talk of such things.

Harry Ollerton, like so many, was lost forever, Liza now seemed to have accepted the reality of it but Annie was wise enough to recognise Edna as being Liza's anchor and the situation was especially hard for the young woman. Her eldest sister Annie had Alec and Janet, Susie had Joe and the girls, Myra had Jack but Liza, dear little Liza who pulled her sheep on wheels over the flags at Edna's feet before protesting her banishment to the cobbled yard where 'it won't go' became the cry. Liza who displayed so much patience of Miss Turpin's woeful condition, now needed her mam as much as she did when just a child.

Edna was cheerful, though Annie sensed something was on her mind, something urgent. A couple of times she'd tried to persuade Billy to go with Liza to the arboretum, 'the lass 'as been cooped up indoors ever since she got home an' she's used to bein' out in the fresh air, walk around the arboretum, shuffle through the leaves, take a dry crust for the pigeons'. In the end only bluntness would serve the purpose and Edna said.

"For God's sake give me an' Annie arf hour on our own, there's stuff I need to talk to 'er about an' I don't want you two stickin' your noses in."

Billy looked at Annie with an expression that said, 'does she really think I can't guess what she's going to ask you'?

Annie gave Billy a wink and whispered into Liza's ear as she saw them off at the back door. "It's alright, you haven't got your sheep on wheels anymore but you've been banished anyway, just until your mam's got everything tidied up in her mind." Liza smiled and understood.

"The girls are as good as gold, all of 'em, they'd never see their dad want for owt but sometimes we need to talk about stuff that our kids shouldn't 'ave to listen to, yer know what I mean. If anythin' happened an' I wer' gone, you'd allus be there for Billy wouldn't yer?"

Annie took Edna's hand in her own and nodded. "Billy is the easiest of men to love, I don't know anyone who doesn't love your Billy, I've loved him since he gave me Harold, I shall always love him, I'm surprised you feel it necessary to ask. Anyway, I've news, you'll be really surprised, and pleased I hope."

Annie began to explain the sale of the shop, their move on the 15th to No.1, George's decision to rent close to where he was so content with Alice, she made no mention of the dark side of the past eight days, trying to sound positive and approving. Edna made no interruption, patiently waiting for Annie to finish speaking. Then came her response!

"After all these years you've worked your fingers to the bone for 'im an' asked for nowt, 'e's got the nerve to bring yer back to where yer started. There's nothin' different about the corner house, the lavatory's outside like all the rest, the bedrooms might be a bit bigger but that only makes 'em all the more perishin' cold in winter."

Edna's temper was roused, she looked at Annie with increasing concern, and real intent in her expression. "Sod it, I don't care, I give him me word an' now I'm goin' back on it but it needs to be said an' you Annie Eddowes, need to hear it. Andrew Smithfield loves you, 'e's been in love wi' yer for years. Oh I know it won't make any damn difference, you'll never leave that misery, but I want yer to promise me summat." Now Edna's voice began to break and tears welled. Annie was shocked and confused, whatever was Edna saying?

" 'E told me years ago, I don't reckon 'e meant to but 'e wer' all upset, missin' the old aunt an' full o' regret over 'is life. I told him you'd never leave Charles an' 'e knew that wer' true 'cause you're too decent, but I also told him to be your friend, an 'e allus 'as. 'E's a good man, promise me Annie that you'll never turn your back on Smithfield's friendship, promise me."

Tears streamed down Edna's cheeks and she shook like a leaf. Annie wrapped her arms about her.

"I promise Edna, please, please don't cry. I give you my word, I shall always be there for Billy, no matter what, and I'll never turn away from Andrew Smithfield's friendship. There now, please stop crying, Billy and Liza will be back soon."

Annie's own emotions tightened her chest as she clung to Edna. Eventually the tears subsided and Edna took a hanky from her pocket, wiped her eyes and blew her nose.

“Stick kettle on,” she said. “The farm sent six eggs home in Liza’s case so we made a sponge, it’s in the tin on scullery shelf, we’ll ‘ave a piece, there’ll be none ‘o that in City Hospital.”

Annie had carefully packed up all the china apart from the everyday bits they’d need until Monday, wrapped the few ornaments in towels and placed them between spare blankets in a box and begun sorting their clothes.

Charles was tetchy, the sign in the window sent everyone into the shop with the question, ‘who’s taking over’? By now his necessary request of a handful of customers that they settle their newspaper bills, had become something akin to the highwayman’s, ‘Stand and deliver’!

It was difficult to find chance to call on Florence yet Annie felt it would be quite unkind to leave Gregory Street before letting her know to where they were going, so she asked George if he’d tell Caroline so word could reach Florence through her daughter. Annie had called at Hilda’s after leaving Edna last Sunday. While Jack had detected an anxiety in Annie, Hilda had been full of enthusiastic plans for the salon and the move from the shop to No.1 seemed not to cause her concern, for which Annie was thankful. It was as Jack had walked with Annie across the back yard that he’d said, ‘If you need any help, I know you’ve George and William on hand but I’m here an’all’. Then he’d stood at the entry, turned to her and with gentleness said, ‘Billy’s told me, I haven’t said anythin’ to Hilda, she knows Edna’s goin’ into hospital, but she doesn’t realise how serious it is’. Jack’s voice held compassion and it was his description of Billy that would stay with Annie forever. ‘Everybody’s shoulder but his own’.

Today, Wednesday, was to be the operation, it could be over by now, close to noon. Someone would call to tell Annie the latest news, they’d promised. As she organised the various packed boxes Annie’s thoughts went from Edna to George and back again, like a pendulum swinging from one source of sadness to another. She would miss George and Samuel very much. She could and would see them often but no longer at the table each mealtime or in and out of the back door with, ‘I won’t be long Grandma’ or ‘see you in a bit Mam’. She scolded herself for being so selfish,

George had come back from the war and had his life still, but it did little to ease the heartache and her worry over Edna weakened her fingers until packing became hindered and slow. It was almost half past three when a tap came at the back door and Susie appeared.

"It's only me Annie," she said, "dads still at the hospital, he'll stay until four but they've told him he may as well go home and get some rest. The operation went well enough but Mr.Ansell was disappointed that he'd had to take away more than he'd hoped would be necessary. Mam's still asleep, they will keep her sedated for a while because she needs to be calm, I don't think they want her to move too much. Until after the weekend Sister said they'd allow only dad and one of us girls to be by her bed at the same time. Her face is very swollen but that will soon go down, Sister said it's what they would expect." Susie sniffled. "I daren't let myself cry Annie, if I did then I don't think I'd ever stop."

Annie held Susie in her arms and whispered. "It will be alright, we must all stay strong for your dad's sake. I just know that Edna will be back at No.24 before too long and we shall all be told off for being so feeble."

Susie chuckled. "You'd never guess the last thing she said to me yesterday as I was leaving the hospital, knowing that I wouldn't see her again until after the operation. 'Your nets want washin' our Susie'.

The removal van was due at 9 o'clock and Celia was coming to help. Annie had not seen William since that evening and although she recognised that Charles had arranged the joint account with the best of intentions, it troubled her. Celia's entitlement to some authority over the money Annie couldn't help believing would irk William, there would be heat in the situation, which could ignite if Celia, albeit innocently, stirred the air.

George and Samuel had loaded the borrowed van with a few pieces of furniture, not all could be accommodated at Winchester Street so for George to take them made only sense and their other belongings, clothes and general items travelled with them in one trip. Annie had been itching to follow them last Friday but Charles had frowned when she'd suggested it so rather than cross him she'd carried on with her packing and cleaning, she wouldn't have the Co-op thinking she was a poor housekeeper, or shopkeeper.

Yesterday afternoon Charles had declared himself 'worn out' and going to bed for an hours sleep. Annie thanked The Almighty for sending her the blessing, donned her coat and went straight away to see George at Ainsley Road. It was as if they'd been expecting her, there was a simple ration of food in the cupboard, the beds were made, even a vase of flowers on the table, everywhere looked clean and homely. They'd both looked at her and burst into laughter. George had glanced at the clock, it showed ten past two, and said, 'ten minutes late Mam, I bet Samuel you'd be here by two, now I owe him a florin'.

It was a fact, both of them, George and Samuel were perfectly capable, they must have observed Annie as she cooked and cleaned but even so, simply being in that house with them for a couple of hours had satisfied an urgent need within Annie and she felt better for it.

Charles' voice called out from the shop. "The van's just gone by."

They could only carry out and load from the back door. Annie had assembled in readiness as many bags and boxes as she could in the kitchen and scullery. One small box she had fastened down securely with string and tape and labelled it, 'precious'. Not because of its delicacy as such, but because it contained John's simple treasures, gathered since childhood. His clothes, the ones he'd not taken with him to Birmingham mostly had fitted Samuel. George was not as tall as John had been, but broader across the shoulders, while Samuel for his age was a good height but with a leaner frame.

"Are yer there missus?"

The voice of one of the removal men drifted in from the yard but just then Annie heard Celia say. "I'm here to help, I'll find mam."

Annie was surprised by how relieved she felt to hear Celia and to know she had company. Charles was tied to the shop all day, he didn't expect to get away until he'd been through the routine of the evening papers with the new man.

Gradually the back rooms began to look bare and the van to look full. Annie had bundled their bedding from last night into a laundry bag. She'd been up since five and even Charles was dressed by six. The men were efficient, accepting the offer of a mug of tea halfway through their task. By a quarter to twelve everything was in the van and they were ready to leave. Charles gave Annie the keys, he'd paid the month's rent in advance so had them already.

"I'll be there as soon as I can," he said, "don't struggle to do everything today, you won't have the shop to bother with so there'll be plenty of time."

Annie and Celia sat on two kitchen chairs, wedged between the table and a single wardrobe.

"Hold on tight when we go round a corner, it's not that we'll be travellin' at any great speed but things can shift in the back o' the van so keep your eyes open."

It was a strange feeling, being so enclosed, no way of seeing where they were going and something underneath the van floor rattled each time a wheel found a dip in the road's surface. At last they began to slow down and stop. The back doors creaked as the men opened them and from somewhere, a hornet, disturbed from its autumn sleepiness , now circled Annie's head in agitation, Celia waved at it with the bellows that had sat in the coal scuttle at her feet and obligingly it flew over the top of one man's head and disappeared.

"We're 'ere missus, I couldn't park right outside the door, too near to the corner, if a copper were to come along 'e'd 'ave summat to say, but we're close enough, me an' Alf won't take long to get your stuff inside, just tell us where you want it put."

Annie turned the key and at once smelled dampness, inside was drab and chill and as she walked from the front room to the back, her eyes fell to the floors, they needed scrubbing. The lampshade in the back room was shedding its fringe and it hung below the bottom rim in several places, like a grubby petticoat too long for the faded skirt above. The knob on the scullery door was cracked across the middle and pinched the skin on Annie's fingers when she turned it and a 'long dead' beetle lay in the middle of the flagstone floor.

"Oh Mam," said Celia with a heartfelt sigh.

"We'll 'ave to bring in first what we loaded last if yer understand missus," said the bigger of the two men.

Annie nodded and walked back to the street, she stood briefly on the pavement and looked towards the other end, it was quiet outside No.24, she could just see the gates of the old workshop in the distance.

They all busied themselves carrying in whatever they could. The men took the bedroom furniture up the stairs but Annie asked them to leave it positioned a little distance from the walls, she would need to wash the skirting boards and clean off some mould spots. Now too involved in their work to notice, a car pulled up outside Billy's and a man got out, knocked at the door and disappeared inside. After twenty minutes or so Andrew Smithfield stood at the step, shook Billy's hand and said.

"Let me know if there is anything at all that you need and do please give my fond regards to Edna."

Feeling concerned and saddened he got back into his car, sat for a moment to gather his thoughts, it had been last Saturday morning when he'd learned from one of the women at the factory of Edna's need to go into hospital. So today he'd come to see Billy, to enquire after the family, especially Edna. What Billy told him caused him anxiety, Edna in a strange way had been a source of strength to Andrew over the years, he couldn't imagine a world without Edna in it. His thoughts were vague, disturbed as he drove along, but a removal van and the figure of a young woman caught his eye and brought him back to alertness. Surely it was Celia. He stopped and looked more intently. It was definitely Celia Eddowes. He wound down the window and called out.

"Mr.Smithfield, what a surprise," she said, a smile of pleasure lighting her face. "Annie is inside, won't you stop for a moment?"

He was puzzled but no doubt all would become clear in due course. Celia led him through to the scullery where Annie was boiling water to clean the shelves before she could stack the pots and pans.

"Look who's here Mam," said Celia, sounding genuinely delighted.

Annie felt the heat rush to her cheeks, of all the people! She'd never once imagined Andrew Smithfield would be in Winchester Street today, of all days.

He'd explained his visit to Billy and that immediately calmed the ridiculous panic she'd felt at seeing him standing there with Celia, and his kindness, his consideration, which typically he had shown for Edna's family eased Annie's awkwardness. He was a friend, a true friend to them all, and that was 'just' what he was, a reliable, constant friend, yet Annie had thought of Edna's revelation, it embarrassed her, how foolish.

Celia seemed willing to explain the nature of things, the sale of the shop to the Co-op, George moving to Ainsley Road, Annie was more than happy for her to do so. If he felt at all bewildered then he was too polite to show it. Realising the men were anxious to finish their job and he was causing a delay, Andrew smiled warmly, allowing his eyes to stay a little longer on Annie's face than was necessary but his words on leaving were.

"My regards to Charles, I hope you will both have a happy retirement from your years of service to we fickle public, I shall miss seeing you when I call for my bread."

Celia watched him walk away and though she couldn't define it she sensed an air of defeat about him, it was as if he carried a regret of some kind. Perhaps the factory was causing him to worry, it was a trade badly affected by the war, only those contracted to make uniforms had been kept busy. She hoped not, Celia liked Mr.Smithfield, of all people he deserved happiness and comfort in his old age.

It was evening, growing dark, Charles had still not arrived. Celia had left in tears at around 4 o'clock, yielding to the dismay she'd tried bravely to conceal all afternoon. Annie felt sure that William had said nothing to his wife of the money, it was a trouble waiting in the wings. Billy would be at the Exchange now, he'd resumed his night shifts, visiting Edna in the afternoons. Tomorrow Annie would go with him to see her dearest friend. The house with all its demands could wait, she'd not seen Edna since the Sunday of last week, she missed her. Although a Saturday morning was usually the only time they'd see each other apart from some Sunday afternoons when Annie wasn't required to be elsewhere, the fact that Edna was absent from No.24, curiously created her absence from everywhere, it was unnatural and alarming.

It was almost half past nine when Charles finally arrived. 'It was a long day so I stopped at The Standard for a pint', he'd said, between eating two slices of bread and dripping. 'I'll make a start in the morning'. With that he'd presumed there was a bed made ready for him to sleep in and after a quick visit to the privy, he'd gone upstairs.

Now Annie stood at the open back door, listening to the distant sound of the city, looking out across those same roofs and chimney pots she'd looked on as a girl. St.Andrew's church clock struck ten but no sign of Mr.Delaney or Godfrey, only Annie Eddowes.

She stepped back inside, bolted the door and put out the light.

CHAPTER TWENTY SIX

"I'm grateful for your company Annie," said Billy, as they made their way along the corridor to ward 8. Mr.Ansell says that Edna's speech will be affected, quite possibly severely. She's forbidden to even try for at least another week, so she's got a notepad an' pencil an' she tells us off wi' them."

"Hello Mr.Dodds," said a cheerful nurse, as Billy opened the heavily sprung door and stepped into the ward. "Your wife has been very busy with her writing today, I think she must be feeling considerably better." The nurse chuckled.

Edna sat back against the pillows, bruising still evident around her mouth and some kind of tube draining fluid, hung from one side of her lips. Yet her eyes smiled and Annie went forward to kiss her forehead. She caught hold of Annie's hand, then wrote something on the pad.

'You're cold.'

"No," said Annie, "only my fingers, the rest of me is warm."

Billy leant over his wife and kissed her with such tenderness. Annie had resolved to be strong, not to cry but she couldn't help it, tears welled and spilled over.

Billy went to fetch another chair. Edna couldn't bear to see Annie upset on her account, she waved one finger from side to side like a stern teacher reprimanding a naughty child. Then she wrote again on the note pad and held it out for Annie to read.

'No need to get all upset, me mam were forever telling me I had tongue enough for two'.

It was the most needed half hour of Annie's past week, to see Edna, to squeeze her hand, and yet it was the most hard to bear. They sat with a simple understanding between them, with love Annie recognised it to be. One hour of visiting only was precious, Annie looked over at Billy and said.

"I shall leave you two to enjoy each other, I know Liza and Susie are coming tonight but I shall come again on Thursday."

Edna caught hold of Annie's sleeve and pointed to a lovely vase of flowers on the cabinet by her bedside, Annie could tell she wanted her to read the card attached to a stem of carnations.

'From Andrew Smithfield, with every good wish for your speedy recovery'.

The old fashioned and knowing look that came to Edna's tired face warmed Annie's heart. She waved back to them from the door and did her best to steel herself before facing the street. People passed along the pavement, no more than a blur as she walked to the bus stop. Then she heard a familiar voice calling her name.

"Annie," Myra was coming towards her, hurrying awkwardly on her damaged leg. "Oh Annie." She threw her arms around her, clinging like a limpet. "I'm pregnant Annie, I'm going to have a baby. I'm going to the hospital to tell mam, she'll be pleased won't she, it will make her happy Annie won't it?"

Annie held her tight. "It will make her very, very happy Myra."

Forming words to answer the young woman was hard as Annie stared over Myra's shoulder at the faded remains of a wartime poster, forgotten, overlooked, left on the old brick wall behind where they stood, for the elements of nature to erase it from man's sight. Only those who had lived with its presence for the past six years could recognise its purpose, but Annie had read it many times and now the irony of its message made saltier the tears stinging her cheeks as they fell down her face in a flood.

'Careless talk costs lives'.